Connor didn't know whether to smile or scowl.

Satan's balls, how did she manage to look even more bonnie than she had last evening?

"Mairi, ye look..." he paused, as if the words were stuck somewhere between his heart and his lips. "...beautiful." When would the sight of her quit stalling his breath? Hell, he needed a bucket of cold water to pour on himself before he hauled her in his arms and promised her the world.

"Yer new interest could not keep her hands off ye."

Ah, there it was again. That delightful spark of jealousy. But did it mean that she still cared for him?

"She wants me to take her riding in St. James's Park after tea."

"And are ye taking her?"

"I haven't yet decided."

"I agree that decisions involving our suitors should be made with care," she said. "Fer I have one to make, as well."

"Do ye?" He wanted to take her in his arms and kiss the fire from her lips.

She nodded. "The queen has chosen two possible husbands fer me. Lord Oxford or yer friend, Captain Sedley."

Something in her expression stilled his heart. She was speaking the truth. No! No way in hell!

Praise for
Seduced by a Highlander

Ravished by a Highlander

"Deftly combines historical fact and powerful romance...There's much more than just sizzling sensuality: history buffs will love the attention to periodic detail and cameos by real-life figures, and the protagonists embody compassion, responsibility, and unrelenting, almost self-sacrificial honor. Quinn's seamless prose and passionate storytelling will leave readers hungry for future installments."   —*Publishers Weekly* (starred review)

"4½ Stars! TOP PICK! Quinn once again captures the aura of the Highlands. Here is an amazing love story where characters' deep emotions and sense of honor for their countrymen will enchant readers."   —*RT Book Reviews*

"Incomparable...Paula Quinn expertly interweaves fact and fiction so well that you will come to truly believe every one of her characters can be found in the pages of history...Ms. Quinn has a gift for creating characters for whom you genuinely feel affection and even come to adore, and this couple are two of the most memorable I have had the pleasure of reading lately...a romantic adventure of the heart, where emotional confrontations leave an unforgettable impact."   —SingleTitles.com

"5 Stars! I found myself amazed...The writing style is so vivid, I could almost see the scenery and hear the battles within the halls of Camlochlin Castle. This author is one to watch!"   —HuntressReviews.com

"I absolutely enjoyed this book. It's full of action, adventure, and more than a little bit of passion...This was my first venture into Paula Quinn's writing, but it will not be my last."   —NightOwlReviews.com

A Highlander Never Surrenders

"4½ Stars! TOP PICK! Quinn uses her wit and whimsy to develop memorable characters who steal your heart...a romance that brings passion and history to life."

—RT Book Reviews

"5 stars! Paula Quinn is a master storyteller and her gifted skill stands out in each enchanting scene of this breathtaking story...As for the suspenseful action and secretive mysteries in the story, Ms. Quinn is unparalleled when it comes to keeping the reader riveted...an innovative and unforgettable love story."   *—SingleTitles.com*

"5 Stars! [A] gripping tale of seventeenth-century romance. Quinn has done awesome research...With this story's strong plot, wonderful repartee, and well-developed characters, this is truly a book that will captivate you and one you won't want to put down! Definitely a top pick and I look forward to more great reads from this very talented writer!"   *—FreshFiction.com*

Laird of the Mist

"4½ Stars! TOP PICK! Quinn captures the aura of the Highlands brilliantly, delivering a tale rife with Scottish lore and infamous feuds. She combines passion, history, danger, and intrigue to perfection."   *—RT Book Reviews*

"The Highlands of Scotland come alive in *Laird of the Mist*...Paula Quinn knows exactly how to capture the imagination of her readers by giving them memorable characters and enthralling plots."   *—SingleTitles.com*

Lord of Seduction

"Quinn is an author to watch."
—Publishers Weekly (starred review)

"4 Stars! Readers will fly through the pages and wiggle in their seats...Feast on this medieval banquet!"
—RT Book Reviews

"Passion, peril, and plenty of medieval political intrigue...expertly crafted historical romance."
—Booklist

Lord of Temptation

"Features a sinfully sexy hero who meets his match in a strong-willed heroine...An excellent choice for readers who like powerful, passion-rich medieval romances."
—Booklist

"Quinn's lively romance...offers two spirited protagonists as well as engaging minor characters...The sharp repartee and dramatic finale make this a pleasant read."
—Publishers Weekly

Lord of Desire

"4 Stars!...fast-paced and brimming with biting, sexy repartee, and a sensual cat-and-mouse game."
—RT Book Reviews

"Gloriously passionate...boldly sensual...Quinn deftly enhances her debut with just enough historical details to give a vivid sense of time and place."   *—Booklist*

Also by Paula Quinn

Lord of Desire
Lord of Temptation
Lord of Seduction
Laird of the Mist
A Highlander Never Surrenders
Ravished by a Highlander
Seduced by a Highlander

Tamed
by a
Highlander

PAULA QUINN

FOREVER

NEW YORK   BOSTON

Forever
Hachette Book Group
237 Park Avenue
New York, NY 10017

ISBN-13: 978-1-61129-773-7

Forever is an imprint of Grand Central Publishing.
The Forever name and logo are trademarks of Hachette Book Group, Inc.

Printed in the United States of America

*To Vincent, John, and Lori. It's all about family,
and you're the very best.*

Cast of Characters

Captain Connor Grant
Graham Grant, Lord Huntley ~ *his father*
Claire Stuart, Lady Huntley ~ *his mother*
High Admiral Connor Stuart ~ *his uncle*
Finlay Grant ~ *his brother*
Mairi MacGregor
Callum MacGregor ~ *her father*
Kate Campbell ~ *her mother*
Rob ~ *her eldest brother*
Tristan ~ *her brother*
Colin ~ *her brother*
Lord Henry de Vere~ *Earl of Oxford's son*
Lady Elizabeth de Vere~ *Earl of Oxford's daughter*
King James II
Mary of Modena ~ *his wife*
Davina Montgomery ~ *King James's daughter and Rob's wife*
William of Orange ~ *King James's nephew and son-in-law*
Nicholas Sedley ~ *Captain in Prince William's Royal Navy*
Richard Drummond ~ *Connor's Lieutenant*
Edward Willingham ~ *Cornet*

A Lass, the Third

Chapter One

*Y*e're a lass; my daughter, and I'll no' have ye fightin' in a battle."

Mairi MacGregor stood with her father in the Banqueting Hall at Whitehall Palace, staring up at him in mute fury and disbelief. She was a lass. What the hell kind of reason was that to refuse to let her return home in the morning with the rest of her kin?

So what if the lass her brother Rob had rescued from the hands of the Dutch admiral Peter Gilles at St. Christopher's Abbey was King James's daughter, and was now on her way to Camlochlin? If the princess royal's enemies did, in fact, follow them and attack Mairi's home, she wanted to be there to help stop them.

But there was a bigger reason she didn't want to stay in England. It had little to do with it's being hotter than hell on Judgment Day, or that the nobles sitting around her beneath grand murals painted by a Protestant king's favored artist looked down their noses at her Highland dress and barbaric customs.

"Faither, if this Dutch admiral attacks Camlochlin, I would like to fight."

He gave her a horrified look that changed with her next heartbeat to one rife with warning. "Never suggest such a thing to me again."

"But ye know I can wield a sword!" she argued, blocking his path when he moved to pass her.

Aye, she knew how to wield a blade, and she was not afraid to face one. There were many times when she had, and they were not on her father's practice field. But she could never tell him that she and her brother Colin were part of the Highland rebel militia who cut down Covenanters and Cameronians, those Scottish Presbyterians who had bound themselves to maintain their doctrine as the sole religion of Scotland. Protestants, many of whom sat in Parliament, believing the Highland ways, with a chief ruling over his clan, barbaric.

"Ye refuse me because I am a woman!"

"Ye're damned right!" he said louder than he intended. He cut his molten gaze to Lord Oddington passing them and looking over his shoulder. "Ye will remain here," he told her, lowering his voice. "Colin will remain, as well. I dinna' know where ye both sneak off to at home, but ye willna' be doin' it this time."

Her eyes opened wide with alarm at what he suspected, but she couldn't give up her pleading. "But..."

"I willna' be persuaded, Mairi." His gaze on her softened. "Ye are my daughter and ye will obey me in this. Ye will remain here until 'tis safe to come home. I love ye and I will do whatever I need to do in order to keep ye safe."

He walked off to join her mother at the far end of the hall, leaving Mairi alone with a dozen curses spilling from her lips.

Damn it all to hell, but she wasn't about to sit on her arse while her life was taken away from her. She was Callum MacGregor's only daughter and as such she had been denied the rigorous training her three brothers had enjoyed growing up. But that hadn't stopped her from learning how to wield a blade or fire an arrow. She could fight. She *wanted* to fight.

But it had not always been this way. Once, long ago, she had been content to think of a life like her mother's, protected and adored in the arms of a warrior. She had wanted a quiet life, one with a man who vowed to tell her how bonnie she was to him every day, until the end of their lives. One with bairns of her own, in a home he'd promised to build for her, where tenderness and love meant more to her than religious or political wars.

Connor Grant had birthed those dreams, and then shattered them all when he left her to serve England's Protestant King Charles.

She hadn't seen him in seven years. She had put him out of her thoughts, out of her life for good. But tonight, he returned.

Mairi had not been in her father's chambers when Captain Grant arrived at Whitehall and had given her kin the news that the Dutch were responsible for the attack on the abbey. She had stayed away, hoping to avoid him until she returned home. But she wasn't going home.

All the years she had spent learning to protect herself from every kind of weapon, even deceit, could not prepare her for this day. She wished she were blind so she could not see the love of her youth, deaf so she could not hear him. But what would it matter if she was so afflicted? She knew his face better than she knew her own. She'd grown up looking at it, falling in love with it. She knew every one of the thousands of emotions that played so openly across his features. The way his eyes spoke for him, as clear as any words falling from his lips. She still heard his slow, thick drawl in her dreams, more like the purr of a lion than the voice of a lad. He had haunted her for the last seven years and she hated him for it. She hated him for making her lose her heart to him when she was too young to stop herself. For sweeping that heart away on dreams of their future, and then taking them from her without looking back.

Connor Grant was a part of her life she preferred to forget. But she could never forget the way he looked the day he left Camlochlin—resolved, despite the tears she foolishly shed for him.

She did not want to see or speak to him now. She was not certain she could contain the bitter betrayal he had left her with when he abandoned her...when he abandoned Scotland, and, mayhap, even his faith.

Her eyes shifted toward the entrance. He was coming. He'd gone to have a meeting with the king and was likely finished and on his way to the Banqueting Hall right now. Her fingers twisted a loose thread in her kirtle, over and over, until the coarse wool made her flesh raw. But that was the only outward sign of the turmoil within her. She breathed steadily, even offering a temperate smile to the woman approaching her.

"If Lady Oddington continues to ogle my husband," Connor's mother, Lady Claire Stuart, said, coming to stand beside her, "I will have no choice but to relieve her of her eyes."

Casting Lady Oddington a pitiful look, Mairi sighed. "Ye would think she would exercise more caution around him after ye *accidentally* stepped on Lady Channing's gown and nearly tore it from her body."

"Sweeting, that was Lady Somerset. Lady Channing lost her wig when my ring caught into it as I was passing her."

Mairi laughed for the first time that evening, but her mirth faded when her gaze drifted back to the entrance.

"You mustn't be angry with him," Claire said softly. Of course, she was speaking of Mairi's father. She had quit trying to help Mairi see her son's side of things long ago.

"Ye know I can fight, Claire."

"Still, you must obey him. He loves you."

Och, how many times had she heard those words throughout her life? She knew her father loved her, but he loved his sons as well, and he had no trouble letting *them* fight.

"I will be here with you if it is any comfort."

"'Tis," Mairi told her honestly. If she had to remain here, she was happy that her friend was staying behind, as well. After losing four daughters at birth, Claire had taken her under her wing as if Mairi were one of her own. 'Twas Claire's life Mairi wanted to emulate after Connor left. Before ever gracing Whitehall Palace's grand halls, or being titled Lady Huntley of Aberdeen, Claire had been a rebel outlaw, fighting against the usurpers of her cousin Charles's crown. She taught Mairi everything she knew about combat. As she looked now though, adorned in a gown of dark claret, her flaxen tresses swept unfashionably away from her face into a crown of curls above her head, it was difficult to imagine her wielding a spoon, let alone a sword.

"I know you don't like to speak of him…"

Mairi wound her thread tighter. Hell, mayhap 'twas not a good thing that his mother was staying.

"…but I was hoping the two of you might—"

She heard nothing after that but the hum of viols coming from the balcony above and the peal of thunder that shook the walls. She saw no one but the man framing the entrance. Dear God, how was it possible that he had grown even more handsome?

Unlike most of the lesser mortals at court, dressed up like colorful peacocks in their elaborate silk costumes and high heels adorned with wide-ribbon bows, Connor wore high, military-style boots over buff-colored breeches that clung to his long, muscular legs. A sheathed claymore hung from one hip and a holstered pistol from the other, lending to the air of danger and authority that surrounded him. He stood apart from the rest like a leopard, lithe and confident. A blend of his two heritages, he stood tall and elegant like his royal English side, but thicker boned and more imposing than any Englishman, thanks to the Highland blood that coursed through his veins. He wore his ostrich-feathered military hat under his arm, leaving his hair to fall to his chiseled jaw in streaks of warm amber and pale flaxen. His red-and-white short coat boasted shoulders broadened by strength and brawn rather than yards of ruffle.

Helpless to do anything else, Mairi watched him stop to share a greeting with Lord Hollingsworth and his wife. He looked older, more experienced in things she might never understand. But his smile hadn't changed. It was charming, sensual, and playful all at once. To make it even more heartrending to any lass with a set of working eyes in her head, it was adorned by a dimple on either side; the right, deeper than the left and needing only the slightest encouragement to appear.

That is, until his eyes, eclipsed behind silken strands of gilded gold, found her and cut through her flesh like hot iron.

The thread in her fingers popped.

"Will you try, Mairi?"

She blinked and looked at Claire. Try what? Rather than admit that she hadn't heard a word Claire said because Connor had stepped into the hall, Mairi nodded. "Aye, of course."

"Thank you, sweeting. That means much to me." Claire leaned in to kiss her cheek, then took her by the hand and pulled her forward.

Hell. Mairi tried to dig her heels into the floor when she saw where her friend was leading her, but Claire tugged her onward.

The hall grew smaller. Her feet felt like they were carrying her through cooled molasses. Each step that brought her closer to Connor twisted her stomach tighter and made her want to run the other way. Ridiculous! She feared nothing. Had she not, on three separate occasions, charged headlong into the fray when the militia kicked down the doors of her enemies? Why did she allow Connor Grant to make her palms moist, her breath shallow, her heart pound madly in her chest?

Because once, he had been the reason she smiled, the reason she dreamed and hoped. She had breathed him for so long that when he left, she could not breathe anymore. But finally, she had. And she would continue.

She despised the royal uniform that stretched across his wide shoulders like a clingy mistress, but she could not deny that he looked even more imposing in it than in the Highland plaid he used to wear.

The ladies of the court certainly seemed to like how he looked if the number of them hovering around him was any indication.

Glaring at them, Mairi wondered how many of these

seemingly proper English trollops Connor had bedded since he had left Camlochlin. Quite a few if the gossip that traveled from England to Scotland counted for anything. How could he have traded her heart in for theirs? Was it their close-fitting gowns or their ghostly, painted faces with heart-shaped patches on their cheeks that he preferred? Bastard.

"There you are!" Claire exchanged Mairi's hand for her son's when he bent to kiss her.

Mairi's cursed knees went a wee bit weak at the sight of him so close now she could smell the wind on his clothes.

"Miss MacGregor," he offered briefly, straightening from his greeting and offering her neither smile nor scowl.

"Captain."

His jaw, shadowed with several days' worth of golden whiskers, had grown harder with the years. Or had it only gone harder on her?

"Be wary of Lady Hollingsworth." Claire leaned in closer to her son. Her eyes, following the harlot as she traipsed across the hall to her husband, were the same stormy blue as Connor's when they flicked back to Mairi. "She has claws, that one."

"Rest assured." Connor's voice stole across Mairi's cheek like a balmy breeze on the moors. "I am indifferent to claws."

Mairi crooked her mouth at him and stifled a snort an instant before it left her lips. His words proved him the rogue he was rumored to be. Just as she had meant nothing to him, neither did the other women who shared his bed and his laughter. She was proud of herself for not flinching when his cool gaze settled upon her, this time, for longer than a moment.

"Do ye wish to say something, Miss MacGregor?"

"Nae, Captain, not to ye."

Amusement sparked his gaze, but there was no warmth in it. "Ah, Mairi, ye remain consistent, at least."

"*At least* one of us does," she parried, her composure as coolly detached as his.

His grin went hard in an instant. "I see ye have kept yer tongue as sharp as yer blades."

His leisurely perusal of her skirts, or more likely the split in them, made her belly flip. Damnation, she did not want to be here, conversing with him. She had finally put him out of her mind. Finally moved on with her life without him in it. Seeing him again tempted her to remember. Once, she had wanted nothing more than to be his wife, but she fought those memories as passionately as she fought against the extinction of the Highland way of life. Because of him, she had become a warrior.

When he met her gaze again, accompanied by a crack of thunder that shook the palace walls, she expelled a breath she didn't know she'd been holding and did the only thing she knew to protect herself. She attacked.

"Tell me, Captain Grant, do ye always precede the gloom of a storm?"

He gave her a very English bow, adding to her insult. "Only when ye are waiting at my destination."

Mairi thought of the dagger tied to her thigh, but realized regrettably that she could not kill him right here in front of his mother.

She turned her most practiced smile on Claire instead. "I should go find Colin—"

"Pardon me, Miss MacGregor."

The proper English voice coming up beside her drew a silent sigh from Mairi. The night just kept getting worse.

She offered her smile to Henry de Vere, the Earl of Oxford's son, as he spared a brief greeting to Lady Huntley. Mairi had met him the day after her kin had arrived at Whitehall. His profuse knowledge about everything and everyone at the palace had enticed her into spending time with him. If there were any Presbyterians roaming Whitehall, he would know of them. Unfortunately, she was beginning to fear she'd spent too much time with him. For he followed her about like an eager pup and made it quite difficult to steal into any of the guest's rooms for any valuable information she could bring home to the militia.

"I was hoping to have a word with you before the tables were cleared and to ask you for the first dance this evening."

"Why, of course, Lord Oxford." Seeing a way to use him to her advantage by getting her away from present company, she looped her arm through his and gave him a slight tug. "But remember, I only know the one courtly dance ye were kind enough to teach me."

"Then allow me to teach you a dozen more." Lord Oxford looked up at Connor as his hand stole over Mairi's knuckles. "Unless, of course, you made a prior promise to someone else?"

Connor offered him a stiff smile and stepped out of their path. "She is yers fer the evening."

Mairi wanted to slap him good and hard, and then do the same to herself. Why did his casual dismissal feel like a blow to her chest? She knew he no longer loved her— no man could be apart from the lass he loved for seven damn years! But had he truly grown so callous?

"If I had made such a promise"—despite her roiling insides, she spoke with all the sickeningly sweet civility she could muster—"Captain Grant of all people would understand if I broke it."

She wanted evidence that her barb had pricked him. She wanted to hurt him, to repay him for every moment she had spent weeping over him in her bed. But his smile returned, as if he knew the secrets of mere mortals and found them amusing.

"Aye, not only would I understand," he said, "but I would expect it, as well."

A dozen curses battered against her teeth, but she contained them all and let Lord Oxford lead her away. She would show Connor no interest. Pretend he was not even here. An easy endeavor she mastered against those she hated.

And she certainly hated him.

Chapter Two

*C*onnor watched Mairi leave with her frilly admirer and clenched his jaw to keep from cursing aloud. He'd like to give her a swift kick in the arse to hurry her departure. If she wanted to revile him for the next fifty years, let her. If she chose to dance with every man at court, let her do that as well. He'd wasted enough years pining over her. She was no longer his and was free to do as she damn well pleased.

But hell, he thought, watching her take the floor with Oxford, she was still the bonniest woman he'd ever laid eyes on. More beautiful than he remembered. She stood apart from every other woman in the palace, donning her out-of-place Highland earasaid with the supreme confidence of a queen, her chin tilted with the defiance she'd inherited from her father. The years had had little effect on her. Her long, coal curls still captured the light as they fell over the swell of her breast. Her skin was as flawless as it was when she was a lass of five and ten summers. Only her eyes, still as blue as the heavens above Camlochlin, were colder.

The music from the balcony drifted downward, filling him with memories of his long days here before he and his men had been sent to Glencoe to keep peace between the MacDonalds and the Campbells. He hadn't wanted to return, mostly because he knew Mairi would be here for the coronation, but also because he never truly fit in with all the posh and luxury of the king's courts. He was a Highlander, and he couldn't stomach being surrounded by false pleasantries and overindulged peers.

He missed Scotland already and he'd only been away for a se'nnight. He wished he were lying in his tent, upon the cold, hard ground, rather than here, with them... with her... mostly with her, even for a day. He was grateful that the MacGregors were returning home in the morning.

He hadn't wanted to leave his home in the Highlands... or her, for he'd loved them both. He'd had no choice. As fourth cousin to the king, it was his duty to serve his family name. A duty he had not renounced but accepted with pride. The blood of warriors flowed through his veins, after all; his father, commander of the MacGregors' brutal garrison, along with his mother, had risked his life to help restore Charles to the throne. His uncle and namesake, High Admiral Connor Stuart, once, long ago, defied generals and endured the pain of torture in the Tower.

It had been his turn to defend the throne and Connor had gone without quarrel. But Mairi had never forgiven him for leaving her to serve under a Protestant king. He'd written her, asking her to join him in England. She refused every request. She'd left him with no other choice but to let her go. It was what she had wanted. What she told him would make her happy. So he made himself forget her, and stayed away from Camlochlin, remaining in the army even after his required service to Charles had been fulfilled.

"I had hoped your reunion would go better than that."

Connor looked down at his mother and shrugged the encounter off his shoulders with a glib quirk of his lips. "A hope that will only continue to disappoint ye if ye hold on to it."

His mother offered him a tender look before she drew in a steadying breath and looked toward the dance floor. "She is staying here."

"What?" Connor didn't realize he'd spoken until his mother startled at his tone and lowered her own voice so that only he could hear.

"Callum doesn't want her at Camlochlin in the event that the Dutch come looking for the king's daughter. Colin is staying, as well, for the same reason."

"What reason is that?"

"Their passion for the blade."

Connor's expression darkened. "Hell, ye continued her lessons in battle even after I...and her *father*, asked ye not to."

"There is nothing wrong with her knowing how to wield a sword." His mother glared back at him.

"Save that wielding a sword in practice is quite different from wielding one in true battle. She doesn't know that or she would not even consider fighting men who recently murdered a convent full of nuns."

His mother sighed and gave him a rather pitying look just before she smiled at her husband cutting through the crowd to reach them. "Connor, dear, there is much you don't know since you left." She gave him no time to ponder her oddly disturbing statement, but bestowed her most radiant smile on his father.

"How went yer meeting with the king?" Graham Grant asked him after tipping back his cap and kissing his wife. "Will we be fighting the Dutch then?"

Aye, here was what he should be concerning himself with. England's new Catholic king had dangerous enemies who were very likely planning an imminent revolt. "Not before James knows fer certain who ordered the attack on the abbey." They already knew about the exiled Earl of Argyll's alleged return to England's shores to gather forces against the king. The Duke of Monmouth could not be far behind. But, it was Prince William of Orange who had the most to gain should James be usurped. Connor let his gaze settle briefly on the king's nephew and son-in-law sitting at the dais on the other side of the hall. As the king's alleged firstborn, William's wife, Mary, was next in line for the throne.

Their quiet conversation came to a halt when Lord Hartley and his daughter Eleanor stopped to give them greeting.

Connor smiled as decorum dictated, but all too soon his thoughts and his gaze returned to Mairi. She was staying, and he had no doubts that she was going to make his life a living hell. Just looking at her made his guts ache. He'd sworn to himself never to risk his integrity on her constant rejections again, but seeing her again tempted him. She was his past. She'd spent every day in it—fearless, reckless, passionate about everything she believed in, including them. He used to think of her on the blackest of nights, when he and his men had gone without food and had had to fall asleep in the snow, looking up at the stars. Loving her had kept him going when he had to fight another day. He thought she would eventually forgive him for leaving. It nearly broke him when she never did.

He'd told himself for more years than he cared to admit, that he could and would resist her if he ever saw her again. He was a captain of the Royal Army, esteemed for his skill on the battlefield, his supreme control over conditions that would have made other men crumble. But he'd forgotten the fire that pulsed through Mairi's veins. It charged the night with bolts of energy that shot through him like lust-tipped arrows when she set her disdainful gaze on his. He almost smiled at the memory of her eyes tearing through his as she'd gone head-to-head with him a few moments ago. She was still the spirited mare he'd always wanted to tame. The thought of doing so made his cock feel heavy strapped within the tight confines of his breeches.

He clasped his hands in front of him and narrowed his gaze on Lord Oxford. What did he know about the son of Charles de Vere, other than that Connor didn't like him? His family were professed Protestants, the popular religion to be in England at present. It made Mairi's interest in him peculiar, since she was as zealous in her hatred of Protestants and Presbyterian Covenanters as she was toward him.

"Why do ye stand here in silence instead of going after her?" his father said after the Hartleys moved on. "Ye're a Highlander fer hell's sake, son. Take what ye want."

Connor accepted a drink from a passing server and, bringing the cup to his lips, smiled at his father. "This isn't the Highlands. Men are expected to behave more civilly here. More importantly"—he downed the cup's contents—"I don't want her."

"Yer eyes say something different."

"Ye misread then," he replied in a rather sluggish tone to prove the topic bored him. "Have ye seen my men?"

He looked around, putting an end to the conversation he did not want to have.

"Aye, they headed off to The Troubadour and asked me to tell ye to meet them there."

Ah, thank the saints for his men and for the tavern. He sure as hell didn't want to be here while Mairi danced the night away with a dozen different suitors. "I'll see to them then and return later." He left with a wink to his mother that brought a smile to her lips despite the knowing look in her eyes.

He cut across the floor, eyeing Oxford as he led Mairi back to the table. When she took her seat, Connor's gaze swept over the fine contours of her profile. Her face was ingrained on his heart. Every part of her was. He dipped his gaze to that alluring tear in her skirts, where twice now he'd caught sight of the curve of her knee, then back up, to the creamy roundness of her cleavage.

She'd grown into a woman without him.

His breath stalled at the sensual sweep of her lashes as she raised her gaze to his and then looked away, denying him what she offered Oxford. Another smile.

She still heated his blood, even after she had cut out his heart.

Nae. He was no longer that pitiful sot who wanted what was no longer his, despite the number of women who had sought to win his heart over the past seven years and failed. Fool. How many had he rejected because their hair was not as black as Mairi's, their eyes nowhere as blue?

He cursed her, and his own feeble resolve and left the Banqueting Hall without another look back.

He stepped outside and looked up at the charcoal clouds passing without rain. Hell, it was going to be another balmy night. He left the gate toward Parliament

Street, his boots clicking hard against the stone. She was staying. How the hell was he supposed to avoid her when they were living in the same place? He wanted to be as far away from her as possible. Away from the temptation of smiling at her, staring at her, strangling her.

His heavy breath echoed through the narrow, empty streets as he drove on toward The Troubadour. What he needed was a handful of drinks and a wench in his lap. He reached the small tavern and stepped gingerly out of the way of a body being tossed out onto its arse. He felt better already. Here was what he needed…to be in the company of unrefined, uncivil men who would rather a kick to the face than a wig on their heads.

"Connor!"

Connor's dark scowl softened into a grin as wide as his shoulders as he strode forward and hauled his dearest friend into a crushing embrace. "'Tis good to see ye, Tristan."

"And ye, old friend." Mairi's brother pounded him on the back. "Though I must tell ye," he said, stepping away, "ye look a wee bit pasty. Ye have seen my sister then."

Connor's smirk went dry as he tossed his arm around Tristan's neck and led him toward the table where his men sat. "Aye, but let us speak of more pleasant things. I see ye've already met some of my men."

Their reunion was cut short when they reached the table and a lad with dark curls and hardly a hair on his face rose to his feet. "Captain," Connor's cornet, Edward Willingham, said, offering him his cup before Connor motioned for him to sit. "We were hoping you would join us."

"Aye," Richard Drummond, Connor's lieutenant, raised his cup to him before guzzling its contents. He swiped his sleeve across his mouth, then motioned to a serving wench to bring more. "Yer friend MacGregor here told us ye'd likely be miserable upon yer return to the hall."

Connor cut Tristan a foul look before slipping into his chair. The last thing he wanted his men to know was that he had once loved a lass more than waking up victorious the morn after a battle. "Aye, being holed up with all those English milksops has a way of wearing on my pleasant nature."

"I'm English."

Connor looked up as another man he hadn't seen in a pair of years clapped him on the back before taking a seat with the rest of them.

Beside him, Drummond scowled into his cup. "Is that something ye truly feel is worth boasting about, Captain Sedley?"

"Indeed I do, Scot." Nicholas Sedley, captain in Prince William's navy, turned from his leisurely appraisal of a serving wench's full, swaying hips and flashed him a grin that Connor had seen him wear before he took Drummond down on the training field when the three had first arrived at Whitehall for duty. "While you were chopping wood behind your hut, I was being meticulously groomed in arts you cannot even pronounce."

Drummond, despite being below him in rank, merely slid his pitying gaze to Connor and nodded. "Milksop."

It felt good to laugh—even at his friend's expense. Not that Nick took offense to being called a coward. He was one of those men who knew perfectly well how capable he was in everything from the battlefield to the bedroom.

"I heard you've been keeping peace between some clans in Glencoe." Sedley turned to Connor with a doleful look. "Is there nothing more worthy of your sword than stopping Highlanders from killing each other?"

"There could be." Connor reclined in his seat, his smile slow and curious. If William of Orange were planning a deposition, Sedley would likely know of it. But would he tell Connor anything? "I have reason to believe that Admiral Gilles has returned to England."

"Oh?" Sedley arched his raven brow. "Isn't Gilles the Duke of Monmouth's right-hand man?"

"So I've been told." Connor glanced at Richard and Edward, silently warning them to say nothing of the attack on St. Christopher's Abbey while another serving wench set down a fresh round of drinks before them. "If Gilles does serve Monmouth, then I have reason to concern myself with his arrival. Unless of course, the admiral traveled here with the prince."

Sedley shook his head. "I've heard nothing of him, or of Monmouth for that matter."

How the hell did a captain in William's navy know nothing about a small naval fleet secretly landing on England's shores? Sedley wasn't going to tell him what he knew. He'd grown loyal to his liege, and why not? They were both Protestants.

Connor was thinking of the next question to put to him when a pretty blonde serving wench fell into his lap.

"Why, Captain Grant," she pouted, looping her arms around his neck, "you returned to England and didn't come see me?"

Connor smiled at her lush pink lips, then closed his eyes and almost shook his head to chase another set of more venomous lips from it. "I just returned this day, Vicky."

"You could have called me to serve you."

Aye, why the hell hadn't he? Vicky's tender fingers had helped drive Mairi away in the past. Why was he wasting time thinking of Mairi now? It had taken him four years to admit he'd lost her, three to heal from it. He'd be damned if he considered allowing her in his life again—or anywhere near his heart. He could find ways to avoid her. It would be easy in a palace with fifteen hundred rooms and hundreds of acres of land.

"Will you be coming to call on me later then?"

He blinked, remembering Vicky on his lap. "Mayhap another time," he said, giving her a tender push off.

Sedley was the only one who watched her go, his pale gray eyes darkening with desire. "Mind if I seek her company?"

"Go right ahead." It was the second time tonight that he'd given his consent to losing a woman. This time though, he meant it. He would figure out tomorrow if and what Sedley knew about Gilles. Now, he simply wanted to enjoy the company of his men, and of his closest friend. They had much to catch up on, many stories to share—his far less frolicsome than Tristan's, he was sure.

"Ye haven't penned me a letter in over a year. How are things with ye, ye bastard?"

"Looking up." Tristan smiled while Connor raised his cup to his lips. "I wish I could say the same fer ye."

After a hearty swig of his drink, Connor nodded, thinking of the days ahead with Mairi MacGregor in them. Satan's balls, he wished it too.

Chapter Three

I didn't know you were acquainted with Captain Grant."

Mairi looked up at Lord Oxford's profile while they stepped out into the warm, moist night air. Dear Lord, did it never rain here? It was England for hell's sake!

"Ye have sat with me and Lord and Lady Huntley. Ye know we are friends."

He laughed shortly, visibly at himself. "Indeed, that is true. I fear I chose to forget their son and the remarkable effect he has on women."

Damnation, she was tired. Her feet were sore from dancing and her nerves were ready to snap from seeing Connor, and then not seeing him again for the remainder of the night. She'd imagined their reunion thousands of times. She, strong and unfazed by his charms. But he had not been charming at all. He'd been cold and detached. He had even insulted her. She didn't want to speak of him. She wanted to go to bed and forget this day and the ones ahead. She should not have agreed to let Lord Oxford escort her to her chambers, but, hell, the man would not take nae for an answer. "What do ye mean, his remarkable effect?" Och, what in blazes did she care? She hadn't meant to ask. She didn't want to know.

"The flush across a woman's cheeks. The shortness of her breath. The flame sparking her eyes." Oxford turned to look at her. "The same effect he has on you."

Mairi would have laughed right in his face if her denial of his charge wasnn't already battering against her lips. "Captain Grant has no such effect on me. I dinna' even like him!"

"He's quite handsome." He looked away now, hiding the scar extending from his eye to his jaw on the opposite side of his face.

Poor man. Mairi suffered a pang of sympathy for him. No lady at court had ever lost her breath from looking at *him*. He wasn't unattractive. In fact, he was quite comely if not for the ridiculous wig atop his head. His eyes were wide and deep brown, ringed by lush dark lashes and his nose was rather small for an Englishman. It was true, he was as dull as a rusty blade, assaulting her with end- less compliments and his vast, yet useless knowledge of everything English since the first day she showed him any kindness. She had only done it to gain information on his family. So far though, he'd given her no reason to suspect he was anything worse than a Protestant. In fact, she had discovered that the Earl of Oxford's brother had raised an army called the Horse Guard Blue to fight on the king's side back when Charles had been restored to the throne. Lord Oxford and his father were too busy kissing the new Catholic king's arse to scheme against him. The de Veres loved the courtier life more than their religion. Zealots, they were not.

So what if he had a tendency toward making her sleepy?

He was kind to her, and that was more than she could say
of any of the king's other noble guests. "Lord Oxford, I
prefer a man who keeps his word over one who polishes
his smile before slaying lasses with it."

When his gaze on her went soft, she cursed inwardly.
Mayhap that was not the wisest thing to say to him. He
clearly fancied her. How could she tell him she didn't
share his sentiments without crushing what remained of
his self-worth?

"Please, call me Henry as I've requested of you these
many days." He took her hand and brought it to his lips.
After a lingering kiss, he looked up at her. "Then I need
not worry about him snatching you from me?"

"Of course not. I mean, I am not yers to lose." She
softened her smile in an effort to cushion the blow. "I
will think fondly of ye after I return home, as I do all my
friends."

He looked like she'd just told him his father was found
dead in the courtyard.

Hell.

"I am not returning home as soon as I had planned and
I had hoped ye might teach me more dances."

"Of course." He brightened, his hope restored. "And
perhaps, if you will continue to grant me your favor, I can
win something more."

Mairi smiled as they reached her room. Hell, it was
going to be a very long stay.

"We shall see, my lord." She gave him a slight pat on
the arm, opened her door, and slipped inside before he
could say another word. She shut the door and bolted it,
not really trusting that he wouldn't plunge inside after her
while she slept.

"What shall ye be seeing?"

Mairi startled and spun around at the sound of her brother's voice. "Colin, must ye always come up on a person as silently as the wind?"

He held open his arms from where he reclined in a chair by the window. "I was already here. Should I breathe more loudly next time to announce my presence?"

"Aye, ye might." She sighed and pushed her back off the door. In truth, she was happy to see him. He had taken the detour with Rob and a few others just before her kin's troupe had reached the English border on their way to James of York's coronation. She had not seen him in over a pair of weeks and she had missed him. Of her three brothers, she was closest with Colin. They shared much in common, including their loyalty to Scotland, their love of the sword, and secrets too perilous to tell their father.

"What are ye doing in here?"

"I thought ye might like to know how Connor's meeting went with the king."

"Thoughtful of ye, since ye have waited three hours to tell me." She cut across the room and poured them both a cup of water.

He accepted the offering and waited for her to sit down on the bed. "Ye appeared distracted by the same man I assume was just at yer door."

"The meeting, Colin," she reminded him, careful not to let him sway the topic toward a more personal direction. Colin possessed an uncanny skill at discerning meanings and expressions without having to hear a confession. If she began speaking of Oxford and his interest in her, her brother would somehow connect her indifference to the English lord to a certain Scottish captain. Colin was the only one who knew the full effect Connor's betrayal had had on her. He had followed at her side, offering his comfort in silence while she wept. She would not have him think, even for an instant, that Captain Grant still held any influence over her.

"The king requested that I remain with him after Connor gave him the news about the Dutch attack and left his solar."

Mairi's brows arched with interest. "James does not trust Connor then?"

Colin narrowed his eyes on her over the rim of his cup. "Why would ye think that?"

"Because Connor served a Protestant king for seven years," Mairi reminded him, unable to keep the sting from her voice.

Colin smiled, coming to some conclusion Mairi was certain was the incorrect one. "He asked me to remain because he wanted to question me about any survivors at the abbey."

"Did ye tell him about Miss Montgomery?"

"Nae." Colin lowered his hazel eyes behind a spray of dark lashes. "But I know now fer certain that she is his daughter. He believes her dead and Rob wants it to remain that way. Our brother suspects her enemies reside here and Connor agrees. We must say nothing. If they know Lady Montgomery didna' perish in the fire, they will continue to look fer her."

"Ye told faither Gilles's men followed yer group to Ayr. So they already know she is alive."

Colin shook his head. "They dinna' know fer certain."

"Och, why did Rob have to bring her home to Camlochlin?"

"Because 'tis the only place she will be safe, Mairi."

"And if faither is correct and the Dutch attack our home... Colin, we should insist that he allow us to return home with him and the others. I dinna' want to be here, where 'tis 'safe.' I want to fight these enemies—"

"That is precisely why he leaves us here," her brother told her succinctly. "He suspects our involvement with the rebel militia. He knows we will not cower and hide if the Dutch attack. I know ye hate hearing this, Mairi, but ye are a lass and he—"

"Och, do not say it. Ye know I can fight as well as ye."

When he tossed her a skeptical glance, she conceded. "Well, better than most then. Ye must tell the king that Davina Montgomery lives. Let him go to Camlochlin to fetch her and hide her away somewhere else. I want to go home."

"I may tell him," he confessed, "but not fer that reason. I believe she is safest with our kin and I willna' jeopardize that. If I tell him, 'twill be because he thinks his daughter is dead and he grieves the same way our own faither would. He has the right to know the truth."

Mairi smiled at him. "Ye speak as if ye care fer her."

"Everyone who will ever meet Lady Montgomery will care fer her."

A cryptic answer. So like Colin to obscure his passion behind ambiguity. No enemy would ever know what he was thinking—another trait she shared in common with him.

"Ye do not mind being here rather than at her side to protect her then?"

"Rob can protect her," Colin told her quietly. "Besides, I think her faither needs my protection more at present. He is a staunch Catholic, and even though none have voiced their displeasure over that fact as of yet, someone has already attempted to do away with his true firstborn *Catholic* heir."

He made a valid point. A rebellion seemed likely. She might not have concerned herself over it if Charles were still king, since he was a Protestant, but, och, to have a Catholic on the throne again.... "What can we do?"

"All we can do at present is keep our eyes and ears alert. Prince William of Orange was most likely behind the attack on the abbey, but the king will not move without proof since guilt could also lie with the Duke of Monmouth or the Earl of Argyll."

"What does Connor think of all this? He is one of the king's captains, after all."

"I am not sure Connor has thought of anything but ye since our journey back to Whitehall together." When Mairi laughed, Colin silenced her with a serious look. "Sister, I had a chance to speak with him while we traveled here and I think—"

"Please, Colin." She held up her hand to stop him. "I do not wish to speak of him."

"Ye didna' tell me he asked ye to come to England with him."

"Because I had no intentions on coming here. I didna' want to live in England. He knew that well enough. What would I ever do here, besides perspire my bloody arse off?" She ignored the slight quirk of his mouth. "Nae, my home is in the Highlands. He made his choice to leave. 'Twas arrogant and heartless of him to ask me to give up the place of my birth, knowing how I love it."

"He did not mean that the two of ye should remain here fer the remainder of yer lives."

"Nae?" She sprang from the bed, having heard enough. "Look how long he has remained, Colin. How is it ye could discover where Cameronians hold their secret meetings but ye dinna' see that his requests were but a way fer him to escape his guilt over leaving? He asked me to come here knowing I would refuse."

"Well." Her brother gave her hand a gentle squeeze as he too rose from his seat to leave. "Ye are stuck here with him until faither sends fer us. Try not to use one of those daggers ye have hidden so cleverly beneath yer skirts on his belly."

"I cannot promise that," she told him while he headed for the door. "He tempts me to use my dagger on him just by opening his mouth."

Colin tossed her one more infuriatingly skeptical glance over his shoulder before he left.

Instead of undressing and going directly to bed, she went to the window and looked out at the dark sky. She scowled at the full, milky moon lighting the courtyard below—the same light that shone on Connor's face the first time he kissed her beneath the braes of Bla Bheinn, the first time he told her he loved her.

Dear God, she wouldn't think about it. That period in her life was over. She had moved on.

Still, she couldn't help but wonder where Connor had gone off to tonight. Likely, he'd gone to meet one of his many lovers and was still with her now, kissing her the way he used to kiss... Nae, she did not care.

If she'd accepted Duncan MacKinnon's marriage proposal last winter, or even Hamish MacLeod's the year before, she'd likely be in Torrin or Portree instead of here. But she no longer wanted to be a wife, controlled by a man, especially one she did not love.

Her thoughts drifted back to Connor and the question she had asked herself since the day he left.

Would she ever love again?

Chapter Four

*C*onnor leaned against the outside wall and watched quietly while the MacGregors bid farewell to Mairi and Colin. They were truly leaving Mairi here. He should have stayed in Glencoe. He could have told the king that he'd been ambushed on the road, stabbed in the leg and couldn't make it back for the coronation. Hell, he would have inflicted the wound himself if he'd known she was staying.

He eyed the figure hanging back, just inside the entryway. Oxford. What was going on between them that the man would wait so eagerly for her to be away from her father? Thanks to Tristan, Connor knew that Callum MacGregor didn't like the Earl of Oxford's son. In truth, Callum didn't like most Englishmen. A sentiment Connor thought Mairi shared. He was wrong. When he'd returned to court last eve, she was already gone...and so was her dance partner.

Oxford's pacing back and forth, along with his peering outside every five breaths, agitated Connor. It was as if he had already laid claim to her.

Like hell he had. Another thought crossed Connor's mind that darkened the scowl already on his face. Had Oxford kissed her? Had Mairi allowed it? He turned his gaze to her while she embraced her mother. She could not truly care for Henry de Vere. Could she?

"Connor."

He blinked away from the women to find the Mac-Gregor chief striding toward him. Callum MacGregor hadn't changed in seven years. He was still big as a mountain and as powerful as a storm. From the corner of his eye, Connor saw Oxford disappear into the shadows. Wise...and rather telling. If there were nothing between him and Mairi, there would be no cause to hide from her disapproving father. Not that Mairi cared overmuch if the laird approved or not. She'd always had her own mind and did as she pleased, most times to prove that she was just as capable as her brothers were in any task they performed. How many trees had she followed him and Tristan up when she was a wee lass, or leaped on a horse that was too big for her, or been caught aiming a bow at the backside of some child who'd slighted her? He almost smiled remembering.

"I have a favor to ask of ye," her father said, reaching him.

"Ye have but to ask it, my laird."

"Keep yer eyes on my daughter."

Anything but that. Connor didn't want to keep his eyes on her. He wanted to keep them off. He wanted to disappear in the lists, the tavern, any place he wouldn't have to see her.

"Of course," he replied dully. "She will be safe here."

Callum nodded, gave him a hearty pat on the arm, and turned to move away. He paused as a thought occurred to him and came close once again. "She willna' appreciate my worryin' over her, so dinna' tell her of my request, aye?"

"Aye," Connor promised, albeit grudgingly. Brilliant. She would think he followed her about for some foolish purpose that had nothing to do with her father.

He thought about returning to Glencoe and his post. He could make it back in two days. What could possibly happen to Mairi with his own father here to keep eyes on her?

A movement at the entrance drew his eyes there. Oxford waited like a cat about to pounce. Connor couldn't really blame the man for wanting to win such a spirited lass. His own gaze returned to her. He understood why any man would want to clutch her to his chest, even while she resisted, and quiet her protests with his lips.

The thought of Oxford kissing her boiled Connor's blood and made him long to be away from the palace even more than usual.

A short while later, Mairi watched her kin mount their saddles and begin their journey home without her. She didn't weep—and it was a good thing else Connor might have been tempted to go to her—but she did look miserable enough to make him push off the wall.

Oxford reached her first.

When they turned to head back, Oxford's arm draped tenderly around her waist, Connor moved toward them. He passed Mairi without a word and took up his pace at his father's side behind her. He heard his mother say something about tennis but he wasn't sure what it was. His eyes dipped to Oxford's arm and he had the urge to rip his claymore from its sheath and cut it from his body.

"Captain." Two of his men greeted as they passed him, reminding him who he was. He couldn't go around hacking off English nobles' limbs. He would keep eyes on her and protect her against an unwanted suitor if he had to, but that was all. He would not lose his control—or anything else—because of her. He pulled his eyes away from her waist and looked to Colin being escorted by two of James's personal guards toward the stairs.

"He is granted another audience with the king."

"Aye." Graham nodded. "Last eve while ye were deep into yer cups, the king made an appearance at our table and told Callum and Kate that when he spoke to Colin earlier he found him to be a refreshing change from the dull, arse-kissing statesmen he was usually forced to tolerate."

"Did he mention what they spoke about?" Connor asked, returning to his father.

"Nae. Colin has not told ye then?"

"He has not."

They entered the palace and Connor almost forgot what he was just thinking about when Mairi's voice fell across his ears.

"Lord Oxford, truly, I am fine, but I think I will retire to my room fer a bit."

"Let me escort you there." The arm that Oxford had removed from her waist, returned.

This time, Connor removed it…with his fingers and not his sword, of course. His task was to see to her. That meant her reputation, as well as her safety, and that was all he was doing.

"Miss MacGregor needs no escort." He certainly hadn't meant to sound so threatening, but Oxford backed away nonetheless.

Mairi, however, did not.

"Captain," she said, fisting her small hands at her sides. Their size did not matter, for it was her tongue she wielded so expertly. "Do ye not have a wench to occupy yer attention, instead of aiming it here where it isna' wanted?"

"Aye." He offered her a smile riddled with amusement and challenge. "But ye are the only one here at the moment."

The spark of fire in her eyes tightened his guts, accelerated his heart

"Or mayhap," she said, smiling back at him, "ye still lack the wits to recognize when ye have been rejected."

Och, she hated him—and he freely admitted at present that it was his own fault, but she looked so ravishing standing there pulsing with barely concealed anger that he had to clench his jaw to keep from groaning.

Behind him, his mother cleared her throat and tugged on her husband's arm to keep him walking.

"Captain Grant, I must insist—"

Connor turned to Oxford and stilled the remainder of his words with a look that pierced as deadly as a sword. When he turned back to Mairi, she was gone.

"Stay here," he warned Oxford over his shoulder, and took off after her without looking back. He caught up to her as she rounded the hall of the Shield Gallery.

"Where are ye going? Yer lodgings are in the other direction," he said, slowing his steps at her side.

"I am getting away from ye." She didn't look at him but continued on at a brisk pace.

"Has the obvious suddenly escaped yer shrewd attention, Mairi?" He spared her a cool, brief side-glance. "We are stuck here in each other's company fer a while."

"Ye can leave."

He smiled at the delicacy of her profile, even as her words cut his flesh. He was immune to her barbs. At least, he told himself he was. "I cannot leave. Things have changed."

She stopped suddenly and glared up at him, a tendril of black hair caressing her cheek. "Nothing has changed. Ye remain a heartless, careless wretch."

For an instant that went completely out of Connor's control, he was tempted to reach out and touch the familiar curve of her jaw. But he knew that flare in her eyes too well. She would snap his fingers off with her teeth. He didn't marvel that the thing he found most alluring about her was the very same thing that kept him away from her for so long. Her passion, even in hating him, ignited his desire like a flame to dry timber. It tempted him to take up the fight for what was once his. But only fools continued to fight long after the battle was over.

And he was no longer a fool.

"I was speaking of the kingdom." He watched the knit of her brow and the shadows they cast over her eyes. Was it disappointment she was trying to conceal? She was difficult to read, innately mysterious, shrouding her emotions behind an alabaster face and lips that knew how to curl at just the right angle to make a man forget every moment before the one in which he saw it. The way she was doing right now.

"Aye, the kingdom." She looked away and picked up her steps. "Ye must be sadly disappointed that a Catholic now sits on the throne."

"A notion ye should be putting to yer suitor, Lord Oxford, instead of me. Or don't ye care anymore?"

"About what?"

He ignored her scathing tone and pressed on, following her around a bend in the hall. "Ye're aware that he's a Protestant, nae? Ye favor him with yer company much of the time." *Smiling at him as if ye truly might be considering him as a suitor.*

She came to an abrupt halt and turned on him. "And just what is that to ye? Who do ye think ye are, Connor Grant?" When he opened his mouth to answer, she cut him off with the sting of her words. "'Tis a wee bit late to concern yerself with the men in my life, d'ye not think?"

It wasn't true. He'd always been concerned. Always dreading Tristan's letters, and then always relieved to learn that Mairi had not married. "Nae, I don't. Whatever else ye have demanded I ferget ye're still a lass who needs looking after."

Her jaw clenched and her eyes narrowed on him like twin daggers forged from hellfire. Another man would have recoiled, not fit for the battle, but Connor welcomed it. She was a strong-willed, unbroken mare who would be tamed by no man. It was the first thing he had ever loved about her.

"I dinna' need ye to look out fer me, Captain. I am well equipped to handle whatever comes at me. Yer mother taught me how to wield a blade and *ye* taught me not to lower my shield."

When he moved to follow her, she slipped her hand beneath the split in her skirts. Connor saw a hint of her thigh and then a flash of a blade.

"Leave me alone," she warned, pointing a dagger under his chin as he caught up with her.

Connor held up his hands and took a step back, priding himself on his self-control for not disarming her and hauling her into his arms. But he had vowed long ago to do as she demanded.

He watched the sway of her hips as she walked away and disappeared into the next wing of the palace.

• • •

Mairi looked behind her. Connor was finally gone. She stopped and leaned her back against the wall to breathe. No other man ever made her so angry. He had always been rather arrogant, even boasting when he was twelve that he was born of two warriors instead of just one, thereby making him doubly skilled. But to put questions to her about Lord Oxford and then to insult her by claiming to look after her went too far. So, his was the face that tormented her dreams, so he'd grown older, taller, broader of shoulder. What did it matter when his false heart remained the same?

Lifting her skirts, she put away her dagger and the memory of Connor Grant. She was a MacGregor, made of stronger stuff than weak knees and a spine to match. If he chose to infuriate her every time they saw each other, that was fine with her. If she killed him, she would not be to blame.

The sound of men's voices speaking of the king drew Mairi into the shadows. It was Lords Oddington and Somerset. Mairi watched the latter pull a key from his waistcoat, look around, then slip it into a door a few paces away.

What were they up to?

When they disappeared inside, she left the shadows and tiptoed down the walkway. She came to the door and pressed her ear against it.

Chapter Five

The next two days were hell for Connor, and tonight didn't promise to be any better. Standing at the back of the Banqueting Hall, he sipped his wine and glared at the dance floor. He swore if he had to watch Mairi and Oxford laughing together for one more instant, heads would roll. They had eaten together, strolled the gardens together, and danced together every night for the past three nights. Connor wasn't jealous. He simply felt a tad... protective of her. He'd known her his whole life, after all.

He did everything he could to avoid speaking to her, but it wasn't enough. Her very presence at Whitehall was enough to distract him.

Thanks to his promise to her father to keep an eye on her, he noted that she appeared distracted most of the time, even while she giggled with her scar-faced admirer. Mairi giggling! She'd never giggled with him. He'd caught her gaze shifting to some of the other lords at court, mostly Oddington and Somerset. What was she up to? He'd seen her standing at Oddington's door, then scurrying away when the door opened. What had she heard? Why had she been listening?

"According to some," his mother said, appearing at his side and following his gaze, "you dance quite well. Why do you not ask Mairi—"

"Some other time."

Claire raised her eyes heavenward. "Then at least sup with us tonight. Your father and I have barely seen you in years and now that we have the chance to spend time with our eldest son, you disappear each night to a tavern. We've missed you Connor."

He looked into his empty cup, wishing it were full again. She was right. He missed his kin too. He missed his brother Finn. He missed Camlochlin. He couldn't continue to avoid his family because Mairi spent so much of her time with them. His eyes settled on her again, her hand aloft and close to Oxford's as they danced, her smile radiant, her eyes clear and vibrant.

"Lord Hollingsworth and his wife invited me to dine with them this eve." He felt like hell refusing his mother yet again, but he wasn't yet up to sitting with Mairi through seven courses and having to listen to her sugary compliments to a man whose head Connor wanted to smash.

"But, Connor—"

"I vow to dine with ye tomorrow and ye can tell me all about what's been going on at home."

Before she said another word to stop him, Connor lifted her hand to his lips and made a quick exit.

Two hours and three courses later, the fate of King Charles I, depicted in the painting over Connor's head, would have been a welcome reprieve from the company with whom he sat. What tragedy was losing his head if it removed him from both Lord and Lady Hollingsworth? The former, with his thick jowls glistening with the grease of his broiled duck and talking nonstop about who the bloody hell knows what. The latter, sitting beside her husband and licking her fingers while her heavy-lidded gaze offered to do the same to Connor.

Twice, he suffered the tightness her wanton gaze stirred in him. If he had any sense at all, he would meet her later and take what she offered him. It would do him good to release his frustration inside a warm and willing body—and judging by Lady Hollingsworth's heaving breasts every time his gaze met hers, he thought she would take as hard as he could give. But he had no sense. That had to be why, when the tables were cleared again after the fourth course to make room for dancing—and for more food in everyone's belly later—he cut across the hall to his family's table and snatched Mairi's hand as she offered it to Oxford.

"I beg your pardon, Captain," the Englishman sputtered with polite indignation. "Miss MacGregor and I were about to—"

Connor ignored him and pulled Mairi toward the dance floor. When she dug her heels in to stop their departure, he gave her a tug that hauled her into his back.

"What do ye think ye're doing?" she demanded, pushing off him with her free hand.

"I think 'tis quite obvious what I'm doing, Mairi. I mean to dance with ye."

"Well, I dinna' want to dance with ye."

"Noted," he said, not really caring if she wanted to or not. Only God knew how long she would be here, and he didn't plan on watching her blossoming romance with

Oxford the entire time. Her father would disapprove of such a union. It was his duty to stop it.

When they reached the other dancers waiting for the music to commence, he stopped and finally turned to face her fully. He tightened his hold and bent his face closer to hers when she tried to yank her wrist free. "There are things that need to be spoken between us once and for all."

It wasn't what he'd meant to say. He didn't know what to say to her that he hadn't already told her in more letters than he could count.

"I dinna' care fer anything ye have to say."

Her eyes seared into his with the promise of vengeance he knew she could deliver. It scorched his blood in a way Lady Hollingsworth, or any other woman, could not.

He shrugged his shoulders. "Unfortunately, ye're going to hear it nonetheless."

As if on cue, he released her wrist and tucked his arm behind his back as the delicate strum of a lute echoed off the high ceiling. He bowed to her, as did all the other male dancers to their partners, and used the moments until she fled to think of something new to say. But she didn't flee. She muttered something under her breath, looked around the hall, then sidestepped around him, as the first step began.

A small victory in what Connor was certain was only the beginning of Mairi's war. When she faced him again, he held out his hand and waited, his breath falling harder from his lips while she hesitated. If she ran from him, he deserved the humiliation that belongs to a fool. Duty or not.

Her skin against his charged his heart like a cannonball

through granite. Satan's balls, what kind of pitiful sot was he that a mere touch from her could weaken his resolve to resist her? He closed his fingers around hers the way he used to when she was his, and watched her take the same small inhalation of breath at their touch.

"Still practicing yer swordplay, I see," he said, rubbing the pad of his thumb over her callused palm, then gritted his teeth to keep any other inane declarations from escaping his mouth.

"Did ye haul me away to ask about my habits then?"

When she stepped under his arm, he assessed the shapely definition of her hips and her backside beneath the folds of her Highland plaid. He allowed the slightest smile to curl his lips when she turned to face him again. "Aye, ye've done much changing in seven years. Ye're not going to whip out another blade and point it at my throat, are ye?" He stepped around her and touched his back to hers.

"That depends on ye," Mairi told him over her shoulder. "But I must warn ye, I am tempted to do so right now."

He laughed softly, and facing him, Lady Amberlaine smiled back and tossed him a provocative wink.

"What would yer Lord Oxford think of yer unladylike tendencies, Mairi?"

She spun on her heel, ready to leave the dance floor and him with it. Hell, she was too easy to rile, especially when it came to her behaving like a lady. He only felt a wee bit guilty about using her weakness against her, mainly because it involved Oxford.

He snatched her back and hauled her close against him as the musicians changed their tempo for the *volte*. "I know ye loathe being a woman, Mairi, but, hell, ye're good at it." Ignoring her slight gasp and short, shallow breath, he took hold of her front lower hip with one hand and pressed his other palm to her back. She responded with a sharp glare aimed at an envious Lady Amberlaine dancing with her husband to their left. With reluctance, Mairi set her hand atop Connor's shoulder and readied for the turn.

"Yer lover hopes ye will drop me."

"I won't." Connor tried to sound as unaffected by their touch as she did. "And Lady Amberlaine is not my lover." He sprang with her onto his outside foot and lifted the inside foot forward.

"Mayhap ye simply dinna' recall bedding her, what with so many lasses lapping at yer heels."

She sounded jealous. Was it possible? Why would she be? She hated him. Didn't she? And if she was jealous, why in blazes did it please him? Could it be that she didn't revile him as much as she claimed? There was a way to find out. He would ponder why he cared to know later.

On the second beat, they stepped smoothly onto the inside foot and Mairi poised herself for the spring.

"If Lady Amberlaine was ever my lover," he said, lifting her into the air with both hands and smiling up at her murderous expression. "I would remember it."

He lowered Mairi back to the ground, her body pressed indecently close to his. Hell, she was bonnie. She didn't need red powder with which to paint her cheeks. The blaze in them came naturally. She took a step back and cracked him hard across the face.

Connor stood on the dance floor holding his cheek and watching his partner storm away. He felt Lady Amberlaine's eyes on him, along with every other dancer's around him. He didn't care. In fact, he couldn't keep himself from smiling.

Mairi did not return to her table when she left the dance floor. She needed to get away from the hundreds of eyes staring at her, from all the women who were either laughing at her or wanting to strike her for slapping Connor. How could he tell her that he would have remembered making love to Lady Amberlaine? What kind of cold, calculating bastard was he? Och, how she hated him! She hated his tongue that had become so sharp and cold when he spoke to her while his lips remained indecently full and inviting. She hated the way his brows knit together when he was angry at her, making those glacial blue eyes even more piercing. But when she looked down into those eyes, into the face she once knew better than her own, she did not care how cruel he was. For an instant she was tempted to do almost anything to be with him again.

Never! She did not want him anymore. She had been young and foolish when she fell in love with his wide, winsome smiles, the promise of her future in the depths of his eyes. But she was older now, with wisdom of how false a man's heart could truly be.

She stepped out into the Pebble Court. Broad walks above and below encircled the grass plot for promenading, though the walks were all but empty now. She lifted her face to the balmy drizzle that had begun, letting it cleanse her of Connor Grant.

But nothing ever would. She had done her best to rid her heart of him, but he remained. How could she truly forget him when everything about him reminded her of what she loved most? Home. Seeing him again was like stepping though time, into the past. Why last night, while

Lord Oxford droned on eternally about the different species of birds inhabiting the king's aviary, she found herself lost to the memory of Connor running along the pebbly shore of Camas Fhionnairigh. His laughter, as he looked over his shoulder at her chasing him, lost on the wind blowing in from the Cuillians. He had taken her doll and would not give it back. Tonight while she was supposed to be concentrating on steps Henry was teaching her on the dance floor, she was remembering a day, years later, when she and Connor raced together up the snowy mountainside on horses that flew against the bracing chill of winter. They wore furs that they used to soften the floor of their secret cavern, cut deep in the braes of Sgurr Na Stri. They made love for the first time while the wind battered against the walls, singing a song that belonged to the Highlands alone. A se'nnight later he told her he was leaving Camlochlin.

She had to remain strong. Those days were gone, never to be lived again. She had to resist him and forget what he had once meant to her.

"Leave me," she cursed softly, fisting her hands at her chest as if to tear his memory from her soul. She had withstood a lifetime of days tormented by images of him lying dead on a battlefield far away, or alive and vibrant, naked and poised over some harlot, ready to give her what belonged to another. She had withstood him. She had conquered him. She would not let herself think of going back.

"Mairi."

She turned around at the sound of his voice. He stood just inches from her, wet from the rain finally falling harder now, and as still as her heart. His hair dripped about his face, shielding her from the full force of his tender gaze. For a moment, she saw him as he used to be, free of England's salacious spell, a boy more beautiful than summer heather on the moors.

"'Tis time to put this terrible thing between us away."

She would not let herself go back. She swiped her fingers across her cheeks, freeing them of rain. "What is between us, Captain, is deceit and betrayal."

"As *ye* see it," he corrected softly, and moved a step closer. "I asked ye to come here with me many times."

"Ye knew how much I loved Scotland."

His jaw tightened around something he looked like he wanted to say. He fought it and, winning the battle, said, "Ye commanded my absence when I would have come home. 'Twas what ye wanted."

"Aye," she managed on the aftermath of a strangled sob. Saints help her, she did not want to be having this speech with him. Opening old wounds only made them hurt again. "And ye were only too happy to stay here, demonstrating year after year what I truly meant to ye."

He moved like a wraith caught between shadows and lightning, a phantom come to life from her dreams...and her nightmares. She did not move when he stood over her. She did not breathe when he spoke to her.

"Ye meant everything to me," he whispered in the rain. "How could ye not know that?"

"Miss MacGregor?"

At the sound of Lord Oxford's voice, she startled free of Connor's spell and stepped away from him. His eyes followed her, dark beneath the shadow of his brow.

Tipping her head around his body, she saw Henry raise a wide-brimmed hat above his wig and step out from beneath the protection of the upper galley.

"Is everything all right?" he asked, reaching them

quickly, the curls in his long wig drooping around his face.

The rain lightened but the air crackled at the deadly frost in Connor's gaze when he set it on Oxford. "Why wouldn't it be?"

A loaded question that any man with a spark of sense in his head would have declined to answer.

"My apologies if I've insulted you, Captain." Oxford smiled, straining the scar running vertically down his face. "But your reputation with the fairer sex precedes you. I am only concerned for the lady's honor."

Mairi was not sure which of the two she wanted to hit harder. Connor, for being such a cad that other men should fret over her honor, or Henry, for being a fool and provoking Connor to knock out a few of his teeth. Connor might be born of royal blood, but he fought like a Highlander. Smaller Lord Oxford would not stand a chance.

Connor's slow smile was anything but genial, but at least he didn't strike him. "We share a common goal then, Oxford. As fer my reputation, if I entertained every piece of gossip I've heard in my service to the king, I would have to arrest ye fer being in league with Covenanters."

Oxford made a sputtering sound beside her but Mairi did not spare him a second glance. Instead, she turned her frigid gaze on Connor. Damn him, what was he doing? He was going to ruin everything. If Oxford did know of any members of the prohibited Presbyterian religion, he would never tell her now.

"Really, Captain, I expected better from ye. Whatever ye heard about Lord Oxford is untrue."

"Ye defend him then?"

She hesitated, not because she trusted Oxford completely, but because Connor's rigid tone told her that

if she said she did, he would walk away from her and
never look back. But that was what she wanted, what she
needed, was it not?

"I do," she said, raising her chin with resolve.

He didn't move. He seemed not to breathe for a
moment while his eyes went hard on her. Then, "Verra
well." He turned without another word to either of them
and strode toward the gate.

Mairi watched him go. Some small, forgotten part of
her wanting to call him back.

"He cares for you."

She looked up, remembering Lord Oxford. "Nae,"
she said, and slipped her hand into the crook of Henry's
elbow, letting him lead her back to the Banqueting Hall.
"He cares fer England."

Lord, Mairi did not want to discuss him. Her knees
still felt weak from his words. *Ye meant everything to me.*
He used to tell her every day that he loved her. That he
wanted to wed her, and die in her arms. None of it meant
anything to him and neither did she.

"His eyes are always on you. It is clear that he—"

"I really should get out of these wet clothes." She
stopped him before he said something she did not wish
to hear. "I must look like a wet sewer rat."

He looked down at her and seemed to melt in his
boots. "You are a vision, Miss MacGregor."

Mairi smiled. Mayhap, she could find happiness with
someone else. Mayhap another man could love her even
more than Connor had. "My lord, ye are more than generous with yer compliments."

"Henry." He took her hand and brought it to his
lips. "And my veneration is the least I can offer you in
exchange for your company."

Hell, but he was sweet. Almost sickeningly so, but better, at least, than Captain Grant's fallacious responses.

She looked toward the gate one last time.

Ye meant everything to me. How could ye not know that?

She had thought she knew. But she had been wrong.

Chapter Six

The Troubadour was crowded with soldiers who had returned to England for James's coronation and found the palace halls a bit too refined for their liking.

Laughter rang out from the tables around him, but Connor did not join in the merriment. Why the hell had he danced with her? Tried to speak civilly to her? Oxford, he answered himself miserably. And it had nothing to do with her father. Satan's balls, he could deceive himself no longer. He was jealous. Worse, he had convinced himself that she might not revile him as she claimed. That mayhap she was also jealous of his attention toward the fairer sex. Pathetic. She was not only completely over him, but she had moved on toward different pastures. And why shouldn't she? Hell, why shouldn't he for that matter? But an Englishman? A Protestant? He hated to admit it, but it pricked him hard that Mairi had defended Oxford. How well did she know him that she would stand by his character when it was put to question? How much time had they spent together before Connor had returned to Whitehall?

Why hadn't he bothered to do a bit more investigating

into the earl and his son in the years he'd served Charles? He knew it was hasty to accuse the man of being in league with Covenanters, but it was better than punching Oxford's teeth into the back of his head.

He rubbed his forehead that was beginning to ache, downed his whiskey, then called for more. He had no claim on Mairi anymore, nor did he want one. She was still the same stubborn wench he had left when she was five and ten, believing that he'd deceived her...betrayed her. He thought of the women who had shared his bed in the last three years. Was he supposed to wait around for Mairi to decide if she could ever want him again? Hell, wasn't four years of waiting for her to forgive him enough? Betrayed his arse! It was she who had deceived him! Promising to be his wife, bear his bairns, live with him and laugh with him while they grew old together—and then banishing him from her life in a cold, uncompromising letter just six months after he'd left. Of course, he'd fought for her, foolishly holding out hope that she would come to her senses and realize that what they had was meant to be. He'd loved her since he could remember, before she began following him whenever he and her brother would wonder off on their childhood adventures. Aye, Connor had complained to have her tagging along, but he hadn't truly minded. She had a saucy mouth on her before she lost her first tooth and took her punishments as courageously as any lad when the three of them were caught stealing chickens from auld John MacKinnon. He remembered the first time he kissed her. He was twelve summers, she only nine. They laughed afterward, as if some unseen winged creature had wandered into their bellies and tickled them from the inside. No other kiss in his adult life had ever made him feel that same way.

He slammed his cup down on the table. If she wanted Oxford then he hoped they would be very damned happy together. There was nothing he could—or would—do about it. He certainly couldn't beat a guest of the king into a senseless bloody pulp—even a ruffled powder puff of a man whose smirk reeked of arrogance when he'd brought up Connor's past.

"Captain!" Young Edward Willingham slipped into the chair beside him. "Drinking without us?"

"What ails ye, Connor?" Richard Drummond straddled the seat on the other side of the table. "Ye've been brooding about since our return to Whitehall."

Connor smiled at them. They were more than his lieutenant and cornet. They were his friends, Drummond, fighting at his side when Connor had taken up finding out who was behind the Rye House Plot to kill Charles and James two years ago. Edward had joined his troupe only eight months ago and had attached himself to Connor's side ever since. Still, he would not tell them about Mairi. What he needed to do was put her out of his mind once and for all and concentrate on more important matters.

"I grow restless here also, Captain," Edward agreed, though Connor hadn't spoken. "It is too peaceful. The people are too damned polite."

"Peace is fleeting, Edward," Connor told him, and looked around the softly lit tavern. "The Dutch massacre at St. Christopher's Abbey is proof of that. But as taxing as being here is, we must remain." They couldn't return to Glencoe when Prince William sat at the king's table each night sharing wine and word with him. Connor was not just the king's captain, but his kin as well. He would drive Mairi from his thoughts and do what he'd been trained to do. Protect the throne. "Though there is peace at present,

I fear 'twill not last. Use yer free time to try and gain information on anything pertaining to the Dutch, the Duke of Monmouth, or even William of Orange. Report anything ye find to me."

"Can we begin tomorrow?" Richard asked him, catching the wrist of a pretty blonde serving wench and pulling her into his lap. She giggled at something he whispered into the crook of her neck.

Connor downed another cup of whiskey and looked away as a pang of desire shot through him. Hell, it had been a long time since he'd kissed the warm flesh of a woman's throat. There had been plenty of lasses in Glencoe eager to offer themselves to him, but he'd been there to protect them, not bed them. He cursed inwardly, meeting the sultry gaze of a woman standing in the shadows, close to the door. A lady of the night, here to give a man pleasure for nothing but a few shillings. He considered. And why the hell shouldn't he? What man with any sense in his head would grieve over something long dead?

He smiled at the woman near the door who wanted nothing more than to make him happy for the night. She stepped out of the shadows. She was lovely, with chestnut hair piled atop her head and dainty ringlets cascading over her forehead. Her eyes were just as dark and held the promise of sexual delights meant to make any man forget what truly ailed him. He pushed out of his chair with a brief word to his men that he would see them in the morning, and met her halfway.

"Good evening, lass."

She sized him up with the kind of satisfied, hooded gaze a cat might aim at a delicious morsel of food.

"Captain." She nodded, eyeing his coat. "Might I interest you in a walk? Some place less..." She lifted

her fingers to his chest and traced the buttons of his coat.
"…crowded?"

She wasted no time on coy formalities. Good. He
didn't want to talk or think. He wanted to get the hell out
of there with her before he changed his mind. He coiled
his arm around her slim waist and led her toward the exit.

"Ah, in a rush are you?" She looked up at him as they
neared the door and smiled at his dimpled response. "I
hope not too much."

Connor hoped not either, though he had to admit the
likelihood of his "quickness" seemed quite high thanks
to thinking on Mairi all damned day. He didn't think she
would appreciate his agreeing with her, so he laughed
softly. The way his father, the once infamous rogue of
the Highlands, might have laughed at such a preposterous
assumption.

"You're extraordinarily handsome, Captain Grant."

He slid his gaze to her, but it wasn't the lusty anticipation in her eyes that made him close his arm tighter
around her. He dipped his mouth to her ear and whispered
against it. "We're at a disadvantage, lass. Ye know my
name and I don't know yers."

She realized her error immediately. Connor had to
give her that much. As he suspected, her body went stiff
and her smile faded. She tried to pull away but he held
her closer, walking her out the door. Someone had sent
her to seduce him. Who? Why? He was going to find out.

He stepped out of the tavern and straight into an
oncoming fist.

Connor almost went down. Almost. He shook off the
effects of the blow, rolled his jaw, and gaped at Colin
before he snatched him by the throat. The lass broke
away and disappeared down the dark street while Connor

turned himself and Mairi's brother dangling from his fist and shoved him hard against the wall.

"What the hell did ye do that fer, Colin?"

Mairi's brother barely struggled against the hand cutting off his air. His eyes burned with anger and defiance. Likely, the fool would fall unconscious before he showed weakness. He would make a fine soldier.

"I told ye what yer reputation in the bedchamber did to my sister, ye heartless bastard. Ye would flaunt yer dalliances in her face?" Finally, Colin thrashed out to land a knee in his guts. He missed when Connor gave him a rigorous shake.

"Ye're not my keeper, pup." Connor moved closer until his nose almost touched Colin's. "Yer sister is not my bloody wife."

"Thank the saints fer that," Colin warned in a low growl. "Else I would have sunk my sword into ye long ago."

Connor had the urge to grin at such boldness in the face of a certain arse beating. He didn't want to hurt the lad and he surely didn't want to release him and find a dagger in his side for his trouble. "I'm going to let ye go. If ye swing that fist at me again, I'll kick ye all the way back to the palace."

"I'm eager to see ye try that."

Connor smacked him in the side of the head with his free hand, not too hard, just brisk enough to hopefully knock a little caution into him. "What the hell are ye doing here anyway?" he asked, releasing him and sweeping his eyes to the direction the chestnut-haired lass had taken.

Colin glared but did not move to strike him. The smack to the head had worked. "The king sent me to fetch ye. He's invited us to his table in the Stone Gallery fer the remainder of courses."

Connor turned back to him. "Why?"

"He invited us, Connor. I didna' ask him why."

Us, as in whom, precisely, Connor wanted to ask him, but didn't.

"Who was the woman?" Colin asked instead, pulling Connor's thoughts from where he preferred them not to be.

"I don't know, but she knew me."

"Interesting."

They continued on toward Whitehall in silence. Neither one noticing the bulky figure receding into the shadows.

❖❖❖

Chapter Seven

Mairi sat in the Stone Gallery at King James's table waiting for the two seats opposite her to be filled. She found no comfort in the luxuriously cushioned chair beneath her rump and little distraction unwittingly offered by Claire's whispered conversation with her husband beside her. Even Graham's tender smile did nothing to calm her nerves. She pushed away the cup of wine that had been set before her. After her earlier encounter with Connor in the Pebble Court, she knew she would need all the wits she possessed. Lord, he had moved so close to her. Would she have let him kiss her if he tried?

She breathed steadily and smiled at the king's wife, who sat watching her.

Hoping to fill her thoughts with something other than the night ahead, she looked around her. The Gallery was magnificent, hung with thick silver and crimson brocade, dividing three apartments. Wreaths of flowers and leaves enclosed the dining area, filling her nostrils with their sweet fragrance. The long table where she sat with the other guests was bathed in warm golden light from an enormous stone hearth carved with stags and horses. But she didn't want to be here. Connor had avoided sitting at her table since he'd returned to Whitehall, but that was about to change. She did not think she could get through four more courses looking at him, hearing his voice, his rich, contagious laughter. She missed the way he used to laugh.

"You are eager to return to your admirer, Miss MacGregor."

Pulling her eyes away from the entrance, Mairi turned to the king and offered him a polite smile. "I have no admirer here, Yer Majesty." She was still uncomfortable speaking directly to the leader of the three kingdoms and dipped her eyes to her lap.

"Ah, my dear, you have more than you realize." James turned to his petite wife, sitting to his right. The two shared a subtle look between them, proving they had discussed her previously. "Why do you think you are slighted here?"

"Because I am Catholic."

"True, but take heart." The king's dark eyes softened on her when she looked up again. "That poor opinion will soon be changed now that I am king."

Mairi smiled and wondered how he meant to do it. Her smile faded though, along with her thoughts, when she spotted Connor and Colin approaching the table.

"Pardon our tardy arrival, Yer Majesty," Connor offered with a reverential bow while he took his seat across from her. He spared her a brief, uninterested glance from behind a lock of hair that fell over his cheek as he sat.

"Thank you for joining us, Captain."

Thankfully, the queen's soft voice drew Mairi's attention to her. She was a wee thing, half the size and clearly half the age of her husband. Without a trace of guile in her large sable eyes, or a thread of superiority to mar the beauty of her thick Italian accent, she made all feel welcome. Mairi liked her.

"We haven't had a chance yet to meet properly," Mary of Modena continued. "Your uncle, the king's high admiral, has sent us word of your service to the previous king, has he not, my lord?" Her husband nodded and covered her thin fingers with his great paw. "We hope you will serve the new throne with the same dedication."

Mairi's eyes settled over him, waiting for his reply. He had been dedicated for certain, leaving all that he loved for a Protestant. She did not doubt he would double his years to serve a Catholic. Unless, of course he had turned traitor on his faith.

"'Tis my honor, My Queen."

Mairi looked away and caught the dark look William of Orange cast at Connor. She did not like the Dutch prince. In the years since she had taken up arms against her enemies, she had learned much about where schemes and whispers originated. For an instant, she wished she could go to Connor and tell him all she knew. He was not a king or a prince. He was the law, captain in the king's Royal Army. He sure as hell looked the part to perfection. Mayhap he could do something more than she to stop the men who had betrayed their original beliefs. Nae, she could never tell him without revealing what she'd been doing for the last six years. Other than that, she had no reason to ever speak to him again.

"We are glad to hear it." Again, the queen spoke for her husband, demonstrating to Mairi that despite her stature, she was no dormouse. "Were you caught in the downpour, Captain?"

"Aye, I fear I was."

Mairi did not need to look at him to know he smiled while he spoke. But she looked anyway, damn her.

"Fergive my appearance." His dimples flashed while he ran his fingers through his damp, golden locks to clear it away from his face. "I didn't—"

"You are forgiven," the queen granted, sounding just a little breathless. Not enough for her husband to take notice, or if he did, he made no show of it. But Mairi heard it. She recognized it and hated herself for feeling it too. "The rains are late this year. We are pleased that they finally begin, lest the crops suffer."

"Aye, but they ended too quickly."

Thankfully, the conversation moved away from Captain Grant and on to more pressing matters involving the kingdom.

Mairi gave the remainder of her attention for the next quarter of an hour to her supper. She listened to the conversations going on around her, inclining her ear in the directions of those that piqued her interest. When the king addressed Prince William, she stopped chewing.

"Do you know Admiral Peter Gilles? He holds command over one of your fleets." James gave his nephew a moment to consider his reply.

"I've heard of him, Uncle. I don't personally know all the men who serve under me."

Mairi did not look up from her plate at the king's reply but she could feel the snap in his voice. "I have reason to believe his men attacked an abbey in Dumfries and burned it to the ground, killing everyone."

"On whose account do you have reason to believe this?"

"On mine," Connor told the prince, involuntarily bringing Mairi's eyes to him.

"You saw him commit the deed then?" William asked skeptically.

"I didn't have to. The people who did are trustworthy."

"An abbey?" William did nothing to temper his mocking tone. "I can assure you if this is the truth, I will know of it when I return home and will deal with Gilles accordingly. But with respect, why ever would a man of war destroy an abbey filled with nuns?"

When King James remained silent, Mairi realized what the prince had done. James could not speak the truth—that one of his enemies had killed his true first-born, for no one was supposed to know of Davina Montgomery's existence.

"Mayhap, this Admiral Gilles simply hates nuns." Mairi quirked a brow at the king and then set her frigid smile on Prince William. "Catholic nuns."

Across the table, Connor smiled at her. Mairi ignored him.

The prince was not a very imposing man, though Mairi could not say the same about his nose. It was like an elbow jutting from between his eyes. She found it difficult to keep her eyes from going to it. He dressed in drab colors compared to the flamboyancy around him. Absent of wig, his hair parted down the center, dangling limply around a pallid face and loose jowls.

"Miss MacGregor," he spoke dispassionately, belying the flick of annoyance in his eyes when he turned them on her. "If Admiral Gilles is guilty of such a crime against *Catholics*, what would you have me do?"

Beneath the table, her hands balled into fists at the way he spat her faith off his lips as if it were poison. Everyone at the table was quiet, waiting for her response. She was speaking to a royal and there were a hundred different ways to answer with the respect and honor due his station. Mairi did not care about stations—or England—but she did care about her kin. Her behavior at this table was a reflection on the MacGregors of Skye. For that, she bowed her head gracefully before she spoke.

"With respect, Yer Grace, were I Admiral Gilles and guilty of such a crime, 'twould be God's punishment that brought terror to my breast. Not yers."

Unfazed by her slight insult, William leaned back in his chair and crossed one leg over the other. "*If* he is guilty," he parried, then jabbed, "I would suspect he does not give a damn what God thinks."

Mairi looked up from the dark veil of her lashes and slanted him a perfectly impassive look. She did not find his defense of an admiral he denied knowing an odd thing. She knew things about William of Orange. "Then he damns himself and there is nothing worse any man can do to him."

"Unless he has been appointed by God."

"Nephew." The king finally spoke, his voice thick with warning. "I'm tolerant of your Calvinist beliefs, but I will not have them discussed here. Put an end to it before you offend me."

William paled beneath his brown cap. He bowed his head to his father by marriage but not before he cast him and Mairi a steely glance. The moment the next course was over he excused himself and his wife and left the table.

Mairi wished she knew where he was off to and offered her brother a covert smile when he excused himself from the table soon after.

She ignored Connor for the remainder of the courses, though it was difficult when Lady Hollingsworth appeared at the table without her husband and bowed to the king. Every man present waited to see if her ample, creamy bosoms would fall out of her low-cut gown. But it was Connor's gaze the wedded wench sought.

Mairi practically leaped from her seat when Lord Oxford came to her rescue once again. She welcomed the escape, even though Henry began speaking and did not pause for a good quarter of an hour. They walked the length of the Stone Gallery, which was far indeed, extending from the Privy Gallery to the Bowling Green. The former, her escort told her, housed a Roman Catholic chapel and its vestry at the southwestern end.

"The principal staircase leading from the Privy Gallery to the garden is the Adam and Eve staircase. So called from a painting of Adam and Eve at the stair head."

"Interesting." Mairi did her best to quell a gusty sigh. Before she returned to Camlochlin, she would know more about Whitehall than any MacGregor ever needed to know.

"Is that the Duke of Queensberry, Marquess of Dumfriesshire?" She pointed to a small group of men gathered at the far end of the gallery. She hadn't been able to hear much listening at the door to Lord Oddington's lodgings a pair of days ago, but she did manage to make out the duke's name, along with the word "Cameronians."

"Yes, it is. Have you met him?"

"Nae, not yet."

"Well, come along then." Oxford looped her arm through his. "I'm sure he will find you quite delightful."

Likely not at first, Mairi thought as Henry led her forward, but being a woman sometimes had its advantages.

As she suspected, Queensberry, a tall, lanky lord, whose high, thick white wig added another two inches at least to his stature, was not at all pleased to make her acquaintance.

"MacGregor, you say?" He sized her up with a thin, wry smile and dark eyes that told her all she needed to know about what he thought of her name. "Your kin fought alongside the Marquess of Montrose back in '45, if I'm not mistaken."

"Aye, against the Covenanter forces outside of Selkirk," Mairi added with a graceful smile of her own. "Where the Scottish Royalists were soundly defeated."

"It must pain you to speak of it."

"Not really." She offered an indifferent shrug. "My mother is a Campbell. My uncle Robert Campbell was the 11th Earl of Argyll."

His smile went from sharp to genial in an instant. "A Campbell! My dear, why didn't you say so?"

"Yer Grace," she giggled, turning her own stomach at the sound, "I just did."

The men laughed, two of them, including Henry, appeared a bit short of breath when she graced them with a playful smile.

"Do you dance, Miss MacGregor?" the duke asked, taking her arm from Oxford's.

"I do, thanks to Lord Oxford's patient tutoring."

Queensberry eyed Henry and the pale scar marring his features. "I daresay, most women would not offer him the privilege."

Mairi's blood boiled at the unwarranted insult, but her smile remained cool as she looked up at the duke. "I am not most women."

She caught Henry's warm smile before Queensberry led her away.

"Indeed, I can tell," the duke said, leaning down, closer

to her ear. "You're intelligent and compassionate. Virtues not always found in one so striking."

"Yer Grace, ye are too kind." She patted his forearm wrapped over hers. "I must tell ye, I admire the same in ye. 'Tis why I asked Lord Oxford to introduce us."

"Oh?" His gaze on her went warm. His shoulders squared with pride. Hell, men were so easy.

"When ye allowed Richard Cameron to post on the town cross in Sanquhar the declaration renouncing King Charles five years ago, all I could think about was how courageous ye were."

His smile widened, revealing a row of yellow teeth. "I admit I wasn't aware that he'd done it until after. It stirred up his followers and got the fool killed at Airds Moss. It also put me at odds with Charles and even James. I had much to do to reinstate my good standing with the late king and his brother."

"Then ye did not agree with Cameron's preachings that a man should refuse to take the oaths of allegiance to an uncovenanted ruler?" Mairi looked up at him and pouted.

"I didn't say that." He reached up and pressed his index finger to her lips to quiet her. "There are others who would take his place."

Fighting the urge to draw one of her daggers and kill the duke where he stood, Mairi pressed in closer to him and smiled at his reaction. She would get a name before the night was through. Could the new leader of the Cameronians be here now, in her presence? Should she do anything about it, or save the information for her militia brothers in Skye? Where the hell was Colin? She looked around at the other men following her and the duke toward the Banqueting Hall stairs.

Her eyes found Connor almost instantly. Paused outside one of Whitehall's dozen grand gates (she didn't know which one, but Henry likely did), he smiled in the moonlight at Lady Amberlaine's upturned face.

Mairi's blood froze. She didn't realize her feet froze along with it until the duke said her name. She severed her gaze from Connor just as he began to look in her direction. She blinked instead at the lord and lady waiting for her to acknowledge them.

"May I present the Earl of Dorset and his charming wife, Antoinetta," the duke supplied graciously.

Mairi gave them the customary nod expected and answered a query or two about what she thought of the weather. Soon, she was forgotten in favor of the duke, giving her nothing more to do but wait until their speech ran out…and sweep her gaze about the long gallery.

A captain of the Dutch navy had replaced Lady Amberlaine's place at Connor's side. Sedley, Mairi recalled his name from having heard it whispered on the lips of over a dozen females, ladies and servants alike. A rogue, just like Connor, who presently tossed back his head with laughter at something Sedley said.

Damn him to Hades but he looked so irresistibly handsome when he laughed, so heart-wrenchingly haunting. He used to laugh that way with her.

Now, he did it with Protestants.

Chapter Eight

I did a bit of investigating into Admiral Gilles."
Connor pulled his gaze away from Mairi dancing with the Duke of Queensberry and looked at Nick Sedley sitting with him at the king's empty dais. They'd come in from the damp outdoors, mainly because Connor wanted to know what the hell Mairi was doing consorting with men who were long rumored to be Covenanters—even Cameronians.

"He has most definitely sworn his allegiance to the Duke of Monmouth. If you heard rumor that Gilles has landed in England, then it seems likely that Monmouth will be arriving sometime in the future."

Curious that Prince William hadn't used that pretext when questioned by James in the Stone Gallery earlier.

"I suspect that Monmouth will make a stand against the king," Connor told him. "He is King Charles's illegitimate son and believes the crown should have gone to him, but I heard nothing of Gilles raising an army to aid him."

Sedley eyed him over the rim of his cup. "What did you hear then?"

Connor shook his head. His gaze shifted back to Mairi. "That he attacked an abbey along the border."

"Your witness could have been mistaken."

"True," Connor allowed mildly. He'd known Nick for years but that was no reason to trust that he wasn't covering for the prince. 'Twas obvious that William of Orange wasn't being truthful when he denied knowledge of Gilles's involvement in the massacre at St. Christopher's. Hell, Connor didn't want to believe Sedley knew of it and did nothing to stop it.

His eyes followed Mairi when she stepped around the duke, her wool skirts swaying at her dainty feet. She'd been cheeky with the prince and it could be dangerous. He'd have to watch her more closely. He liked her fearlessness, admired her streak of brash Highland confidence, but William was a dangerous man. Connor was certain of it.

"That's the clan chief MacGregor of Skye's daughter, isn't it?"

Connor blinked and cut his gaze to Nick. "Aye, 'tis."

"If memory serves me," his old friend said, watching her, "she's the one you used to speak about every day when you first arrived here."

Connor shifted in his seat. "I was a peach-faced lad, even younger than Edward at the time."

"So nothing ever became of the two of you?"

"We've moved on," Connor told him woodenly.

"Your eyes have been on her all night."

"Her father asked me to watch over her in his absence."

"She's lovely." Nick studied her with the same smoky gray eyes that used to land a different woman in his bed every night.

"Stay away from her, Sedley," Connor warned. He had

enough men in her life to worry about. He sure as hell didn't want to add the rakehell Nick Sedley to the list.

"If I didn't know any better—"

"Ye don't," Connor cut him off. "There's Lady FitzSimmons. Didn't ye once tell me she had a lovely mouth and knew how to use it?"

"I did, and she does. I was with her last night."

"She eyes ye now." Connor smiled, looking at her, then turned it on his friend. "Mayhap ye didn't satisfy."

"Highly doubtful." Sedley rose from his chair, tugged on his military jacket to straighten it, then took off after her.

Alone, Connor gave his full attention to Mairi while the duke escorted her back to his table. He should be at The Troubadour with his men instead of sitting here by himself, wishing Mairi would look at him. What in bloody hell was wrong with him? How many times could a man vow to put things from his thoughts only to let them plague him over and over again? But it was more than just the memory of Mairi that weakened him, it was the sight of her now, proud, beautiful, bold. It was the spark in her eyes when she spoke to him that ignited his nerve endings. The fight she made him want to win. The feral mare he wanted to tame.

She looked up, as if feeling his eyes on her, and met his gaze across the crowded hall. He wanted to tell her that he missed her. A part of him always would. But it would do no good. Too much had changed between them. He wanted to tell her that her father had requested he look after her, that he wasn't the wretched sot he appeared to be, unable to control his own heart. She looked away first and returned her smiles to her host.

Seated at the other end of the table, Oxford didn't look too happy. That made Connor feel better.

He almost missed her departure from the hall when Lady Eleanor Hartley slipped into the empty chair beside him.

"If you dance with me, I promise not to slap you."

Connor suppressed a yawn and turned a playful grin on her. "Perhaps I deserved it."

He saw Mairi rise from her chair from the corner of his eye and turned toward her. Oxford nearly leaped from his seat to get to her the instant she was alone. She shook her head at something he said, then patted his arm and moved away from him. She was retiring to bed. Alone.

"Captain Grant?"

He remembered Eleanor and spared her a brief glance as he stood. "Pardon me. There is something I must see to." Mairi should not return to her lodgings unattended. Colin was nowhere in sight, so it was up to Connor to see her to her destination safely.

Before he left the hall, he eyed Oxford one last time to make certain he wasn't going to follow Connor following her. When he stepped outside, he looked toward the stairs and then up at the walkways that led to her door. At first he didn't find her and his heart drummed madly in his chest. But then he saw her creeping along the northern end, toward the nobles' lodgings.

Hell.

He raced up the stairs as quietly as his boots would allow, pausing and moving deeper into the shadows, when she stopped and looked over the railing. Certain once again that no one saw her, she continued on toward the duke's rooms. For an instant, Connor's blood scalded his veins. Was she meeting Queensberry for some nightly tryst? Had she stopped hating Protestants *and* Covenanters then? He narrowed his eyes on her as she lifted her skirts, pulled something he suspected was a dagger from beneath, and began working the lock.

He smiled, then scowled. She wasn't meeting the duke. She was breaking into his room! He didn't move, didn't breathe as she opened the door and took one more look around before disappearing into the darkness inside.

Was she mad? Had his fiery mare gone daft in the years since he'd last seen her? Why had no one in his family or hers told him? Thinking back, he did remember his mother mentioning something about there being much he didn't know since he left.

Damn it, why hadn't he pressed her further?

He made his way across the promenade and stopped at the door. He pressed his ear close and listened. Nothing. Cautiously, he fit his fingers around the iron handle and cracked open the door. He slipped inside and wished there was more light illuminating his way than the dull gray glow of the moon from the windows. He was about to whisper her name and demand that she get the hell out of here before she was discovered when he heard her shuffling about behind a slightly ajar door to his left.

He moved silently toward it, pushing softly on the cool wood. Soft silvery light fell onto a table in the center of the large study. Bookcases lined the wall behind it. A large, cool hearth to the right. But no Mairi.

He stepped inside, his senses sharp in the dim light. He smelled her before he saw her, heather and lavender, and all sorts of other wildflowers that clung to her plaid from their Highland home. He lifted his arm in time to block the heavy object coming for his head.

Moving in a flash of speed, he gripped her wrist and yanked her close. A knee close to his nether regions nearly dropped him to his knees, but he held fast to her arm, knowing she meant to do as much damage as possible. He tried to speak her name but her free fist to his jaw momentarily stunned him. Och, but she was a hellcat! She struggled viciously against him, even trying to sink her teeth into his hand that still held her.

With no choice but to subdue her as quickly as possible, he spun her around, hauling her spine hard against his chest. Her hand, still clutching what he guessed by the shape and length of it pressed into his belly was an iron candleholder, was twisted behind her and caught uselessly between them. He coiled his free arm around her waist, pinning her other arm to her side.

"I'm glad to see ye can take care of yerself, Mairi," he bent over her and whispered close to her ear.

When she realized who was behind her, her struggles ceased—for a moment. "What the hell are ye doing here?"

"A query I was just about to put to ye." Hell, she smelled good. Her hair against his nose, as soft and as thick as he remembered. Her body, captured in his unyielding embrace, set his blood to scorching. He wanted to whirl her back around to face him, feel her breasts against his chest, her warm breath upon his face, but she was too dangerous. And—she was no longer his. "What are ye doing snooping around in the duke's rooms?"

"Let me go, Connor, before I—"

Beyond the study door another door opened. Someone had entered the chambers. "Ssh!" He closed his hand around her mouth, risking a bite.

She heard the sound and obeyed, her body tensing and driving him a little more mad with desire. He finally released her but pulled her deeper into the shadows, listening to the sounds on the other side of the door. It had to be the duke. He was alone judging by the sound of his footsteps. Connor offered up a silent prayer that Queensberry had no business inside this room and would go directly to bed.

"Now look what ye have done," Mairi accused in a hushed voice turning on him.

"Me?" he asked just as quietly. "I wouldn't be here if not fer ye."

"I did not ask ye to follow me. Likely, I would have been done and on my way back to my room if not fer ye."

The floor creaked just outside the door and they both went still. Connor did his best to concentrate and think of a good excuse as to what they were doing in here if they were discovered, but Mairi had inched closer to him, her warmth seeping into his body, her scent enveloping him. He was glad he couldn't completely make out her face, her lips, or he might be tempted to kiss her. Aye, he was pathetic for certain.

"Done with what? What were ye looking fer?"

"It doesna' concern ye."

Everything she did concerned him. Satan's balls, he still cared for her. Denying it only made him a bigger fool.

"The idea of ye being tossed into prison concerns me, Mairi."

"Really, Connor, prison? Fer appearing in a man's room?"

He could hear the smirk in her hushed voice.

"A man with whom I spent the night dancing? Mayhap I was simply waiting fer him to arrive so that we could share a private moment together."

Connor considered how much noise throttling her would make. He shook his head, deciding against taking such a chance. "'Twould be difficult to share such a moment with him pummeled over the head with yer candleholder if it had been he who caught ye, rather than me, wouldn't ye say?"

She went silent catching his point. Finally.

They listened for more sounds beyond the door. Thankfully, it did not open. They waited, as seconds passed into minutes and the sounds grew quiet.

"So, what are ye doing in here? I'll not let ye leave until ye tell me."

She sighed, her sweet breath reaching his chin. "Verra well. I was looking fer something."

"What?"

"A name?"

"Whose name, Mairi?"

She sighed again and he knew they needed to get out of there quick before he hauled her into his arms and kissed her senseless. "Queensberry mentioned someone taking Richard Cameron's place. I was going to see if there were any parchments in here with a name that might look familiar."

Familiar? In what sense? How could anyone Queensberry knew be familiar to her? She lived in Skye, surrounded by mountains and water for hell's sake! What did she know about the Cameronians? He cursed himself for not writing home more frequently.

Now wasn't the time to question her. They had to escape the duke's lodgings. He would speak to her about it tomorrow though.

"I think he retired to bed."

In the dim moonlight she nodded and stepped toward the door. He reached his arm across her, stopping her and moving in front of her. She sidestepped and he bumped into her back.

Connor cast her a dark scowl she didn't see. He wouldn't have her go first. Someone could be out there waiting.

Taking her by the arm this time, he pulled her behind him, ignoring the soft, muttered oath coming from her mouth.

He opened the door slowly, listening to the silence. When he deemed it safe to proceed, he swung the door wider and reached behind him to take Mairi's hand. She wasn't there.

He felt her rush past him in a whoosh of heavenly scented wool, heard her light footsteps fall across the rushes, and watched her disappear into the night. All in the space of a breath, leaving Connor with nothing more than the sinking suspicion that she had done this before.

Chapter Nine

Mairi awoke the next morning to find the queen and seven guardsmen standing around her bed. Connor was among them. It took her a moment to clear away the effect of her dreams. When she did, she sat straight up in her bed and yanked her cover to her throat. "What...?" Her eyes darted to Connor, who at least had the decency to look away.

"The king is gone, Miss MacGregor."

Mairi shook her head, not sure she heard the queen correctly. Gone? Gone where? She pushed her curls away from her face and rubbed her eyes, trying to understand what the hell was going on. Why was Connor here in her bedroom?

"He has disappeared, and your brother has disappeared with him."

Mairi blinked at her, suddenly understanding it all very clearly. Colin. Och, dear God, he had done it. He told the king that his daughter still lived, and likely the king had insisted on seeing her.

"Do you have any knowledge of where they might

have gone…or been taken?" Mary of Modena's soft voice quavered at the last. She loved her husband. Mairi had seen the evidence of it last night in their tender touches. What should she tell her?

"Did anyone see or hear them leave?" She felt Connor's interest pique, felt his eyes on her, and avoided them. It would not take him long before he figured out what she already knew. Would he tell anyone else? Sedley, mayhap? She didn't trust him. How could she when he'd left so many broken promises scattered at her feet? Right now, it didn't matter. She had to ask her questions and know for certain that she was correct and her brother had not, in fact, been abducted along with the king.

"No one," the queen answered curtly. She was growing agitated, already suspecting that Mairi knew something and was evading the answer.

"Fergive my ignorance, please, Yer Majesty, but there are guards stationed around the entire perimeter of Whitehall and no one saw them?"

"That is correct, Miss MacGregor. Do you have any knowledge of how that might be?"

Mairi shook her head. "I am sorry, I dinna'."

For a moment, she thought the queen might shout at her. Her small hands clenched the folds of her skirts and her lips tightened before she turned to Connor. "Watch her every move and report them to me." She spared Mairi her briefest glance on her way out. "Good day to you, Miss MacGregor."

A dozen different protests fought to escape Mairi's lips, but she didn't get to voice a single one of them as the last of the soldiers filed out of the room and shut the door.

"Where are they?"

One remained. Och, she didn't care if the king himself

gave the order, she wasn't about to have Connor follow her around all damned day long. Last night was enough. When she'd returned to her room after their brief, but close encounter in Queensberry's chambers, she'd had to fight to keep from crying herself to sleep. Damn him!

She snapped the cover off her and swung her legs over the side. "Get out!" she ordered in her nightdress, marching toward the door to open it for him.

"Mairi!" His command stopped her. "Think about what ye just did. If ye know anything, ye must tell the queen. If she's fearful because the king has mysteriously disappeared, how do ye think the people will take the news? How long do ye think it will take Prince William to turn their heads against their Catholic king?"

"What d'ye care about that, Captain?"

For a moment, he looked about to throttle her. She was tempted to step back, but didn't. "Ye think I'm a Protestant then?"

"Why would ye not be? Ye have lived with them fer a long time."

The lines of his face hardened. "Believe what ye will of me. I know, however, that *ye* care, so tell the queen where her husband is."

"I dinna' know where he is."

"Does his disappearance have anything to do with why ye were snooping around in Queensberry's rooms last night?"

"I already told ye why I was there."

"Aye, ye did. And I would like to know what interest ye have in Cameronians."

Damnation, she'd said too much last night. "My life is nae longer any concern of yers, Captain."

His eyes bore into hers behind a few stray locks of

gold. He looked serious…and dangerous. "Verra well, then. I suspect I know where Colin is taking the king. I will tell the queen myself."

He pushed her out of the way, but she leaped back in front of him, stopping his departure. "Ye would risk the lives of my kin by telling her in the presence of her guardsmen?"

His jaw tightened and he muttered an oath toward the heavens. "Then they are indeed on their way home."

"My home," she corrected, surprised that he hadn't surmised it sooner. There was nothing she could do about it, save to warn him to keep silent. "The king of England is on his way to my home with little or no protection, as far as I know, save fer my brother. Ye must say nothing in front of the guardsmen. No one here can be trusted." *Not even ye.*

Lord, she prayed she was wrong. Mayhap he had converted his faith. That didn't necessarily mean he would betray her kin, did it? "I ask ye to remember that someone close to the king's daughter likely betrayed her. Colin told me that no one knew of Miss Montgomery's existence save fer the men who guarded her."

"Someone else knew as well."

"Aye, someone did," she agreed.

Her mouth went a bit dry at the way he looked at her, tilting his head a little to the side and smiling, as if considering what she knew and contemplating finding out how she knew it. She headed him off in another direction. Whatever his position on the Covenanters or on William of Orange was, it was safer if he didn't know what she had been doing in secret back home on Skye. "'Tis why Colin and the king left in the cover of night. 'Tis why my brother didna' tell ye he was going. Yer men have seen her."

"They don't know who she is."

"If ye took them along, they would find out, and they would know *where* she was. If even one of them has sworn allegiance to the king's enemy, how long do ye think 'twill be before he rides toward Camlochlin? Swear to me that you will tell no one."

"Do ye think me that foolish then?" While he waited for her reply, his gaze drifted over the length of her scantily clad body.

Her cheeks blazed and she fought the urge to cross her arms over her chest. Let him look. Let him regret leaving her, never being able to touch her again. "I dinna' think about ye at all," she lied. "Or is that too difficult fer ye to comprehend, Captain Grant?"

The arch of his brow and the amusement tugging at his mouth proved that he enjoyed going head–to-head with her. Or mayhap he enjoyed being the only man who could. "'Tis not nearly as difficult as trying to convince myself that ye're not the coldest wench in England, Ireland, and Scotland combined."

"Oh?" she asked mildly, refusing to give him the satisfaction of letting his grin goad her. "So ye admit then that ye are an expert on women?"

He had a way of lowering his head and looking at her from beneath his brow, or mayhap it was the smooth drawl of his voice, confident that he could parry whatever she threw at him that made her knees melt.

"Well, I haven't yet been to France, so I wouldn't call myself an expert."

At her sides, her fingers curled around her nightdress in an effort to keep them off his throat. "Dinna' be modest, Captain. Ye and I both know ye are an expert at bedding and then running from lasses." That was enough to wipe the glib smirk off his face. She should have felt victorious, but she didn't. "Now, if ye dinna' mind"—she continued on toward the door and swung it open—"gather up some of that decency ye once possessed and leave so that I may dress."

Relief washed over her as he made for the exit. Being in the same room with him, alone... again—was perilous to her good sense. When he reached the door though, he pushed it shut with one hand and coiled the other around her waist. "Stubborn lass," he groaned, dragging her forward. He bent his mouth to hers and snatched away the remainder of her protests on a hard, melting kiss that buckled her knees.

Hell, he might carry himself like an Englishman, but he kissed like a Highlander. Some fading part of her demanded that she fight him, but she could scarcely move, could hardly breathe. His tongue swept into her mouth like a brand, reclaiming ownership to what no man besides him possessed. The swift beating of her heart made her light-headed. Or mayhap, it was the scent of him covering her, the exquisite, possessive way he took her, as if he had never lost that right.

But he had. Last night she had been a fool to allow her old feelings for him bubble to the surface. She didn't miss him or the life she had always wanted, but was denied. She didn't want him back... or the dreams he'd once fired within her. She pulled away, tilted her head back to gaze into his face, and then slapped him so hard his head drew back.

For a moment, he did nothing but roll his jaw around the pain she caused him. Then, turning his scalding, hungry gaze on her, he swept her clean off the floor and into his arms. She pushed against him, afraid of how easily he quickened the embers of those dreams back to life. She had never wanted anything more than to be his, to wake up to his face each morning, and watch him play with their bairns at night. She had never wanted another man to kiss her, to touch her, not after Connor.

She had no defense against his masterful assault and even while her voice shouted in her head to stop him, she looped her arms around his neck. He hauled her back against the door, knocking the breath from both their bodies. Her fingers tunneled through his hair as he lifted her thigh around his waist, all the while keeping her wedged tightly between the cool wood and the length of his even harder body. How could she fight him when he tamed her so easily with just a few strokes? His lips devoured her until she groaned against his teeth, wanting him, needing him, missing him more than ever before.

Nae! She was stronger than this. He'd made her stronger. She had conquered the memory of him. Swore to herself she would never trust him again. She would not go back! No matter how right it felt to be in his arms, in his presence.

She pushed him away. He withdrew, his breath heavy, his eyes glittering as they moved over her face like jewels caught between light and shadow, robbing her lungs of air, her head of reason.

"Mairi, I—" Whatever else he meant to say ended when a hard rap on the other side of the door drew a tight curse from his lips.

"Miss MacGregor?"

Mairi closed her eyes at the sound of Lord Oxford's voice. When she opened them again, Connor's beautiful face was there, so close. How could she continue to resist him if she had to see him every day? He was the heather that swayed across the moors, the mighty wind that whistled over misty mountain ranges.

"Send him away," he whispered against her temple.

She shook her head. It was good that Oxford had come. Her body wanted Connor too desperately to deny him, but her heart would never survive losing him again. And she would lose him. He might remind her of home, but his heart belonged to England. "Let me go," she breathed along his jaw, choking on the words as they left her.

He pulled his head back to look at her as if he had never seen her before this day. She turned away when he stepped back to reach for the door.

Without giving her a moment to pat her hair back into some semblance of neatness, he pushed her behind him and tore the door open.

"Oxford, what the hell are ye doing at her door an hour after dawn?"

Blocked from sight, Mairi pressed her ear to Connor's back to hear more sputtering from Henry. Poor Henry. How was any meager man expected to stand against such a force? She jabbed her elbow into Connor's spine.

"I came to escort her to breakfast." She heard more clearly once the brute before her jerked a bit to the left after her poke.

"I'll be doing that." Connor informed him. "Good day to ye." He slammed the door shut in Henry's face and turned to her.

"Does he escort ye to breakfast every day then?"

Another rap on the door halted her reply. This time, Connor did not bother with concealing her when he swung open the door. He did not bother addressing Lord Oxford either, but looked over his shoulder and motioned to another man. "Lieutenant Drummond, escort this man below stairs and see that he doesn't return to this door. If he refuses, take him to the queen."

Mairi watched him lean against the door after he closed it, his gaze settling on hers again. "Ye can do better than that, Mairi."

She turned away. She did not want to fight with him now. Her emotions were too raw after their kiss. Her lips still burned, along with every other part of her body. The bastard! How dare he try to push his way back into her life? What right did he have to make every other man feeble and obsolete when compared to him? She wanted to move on. She needed to, and now he was back to ruin any chance she had to be happy with Lord Oxford—or any other man.

"Get out."

"Nae."

Nae? The arrogant son of a—! Clenching her fingers at her sides, she stopped and pivoted around. "What do ye mean, nae? Do ye want a dagger in yer eye?"

He grinned with such casual delight; she was tempted to leap back into his arms. "I was commanded to watch yer every move, if ye recall."

She quirked her lips at him, giving him the point. "That is about to end when I go to the queen and tell her what she wants to know."

He shrugged, "Until then…"

She bit her tongue and whirled on her heel, away from him. "Verra well, Captain. But I never took ye fer one whose pleasure relied on forcing a woman to do his bidding."

He laughed and the sound seeped through her like a song that haunted the moors. "How did I manage to escape *that* assumption during all these years of betraying ye?"

She reached her trunk and pulled out a fresh plaid woven in shades of sapphire blue and crimson and a blue sleeved vest to match. "Nae doubt, ye have become quite adept at keeping yer darkest traits hidden." It was difficult to keep her tone casual with the memory of his sensual, demanding mouth and wicked touch so fresh in her mind. Och, he was dark, aright. Before she could stop herself, she wondered if the other women he took to his bed enjoyed the dominating force of his passion. He had been gentle with her the first time she'd lain with him, but they had been young, inexperienced. He had taken her again before he left Scotland, making certain she would not forget him while he was away. She had ached for him for weeks... and she had not forgotten.

He remained leaning against the door, his bold gaze dipping to her calf while she lifted her nightdress. He truly was going to watch her undress! She slid the soft fabric upward and glared at him when his smile faded into something harder. How would he take her now if she let him? She was not about to find out, though, damn her, a part of her wanted to lie with him again. To feel his rough hands on her, to hear that deep, languid voice tell her that she was his while he buried himself inside her and made it so. Her hand shook as she reached for the dagger tied to her thigh.

Thankfully, his reflexes were as quick as she remembered them when her blade flew and landed in the door inches from his head.

He cast a worrisome glance at the hilt above his shoulder, then at her. "Yer aim has improved."

"Turn around or the next will not miss."

Hell, he looked like he was about to spring at her. The rest of her knives were hidden in her trunk. She would never get them out in time. She did not want to. Fortunately, he turned to face the door without another word.

She undressed quickly, watching his back the entire time. Her fingers shook while she slipped her arms into her sleeves and worked the small stone buttons at her chest. Her long earasaid was a bit harder to manage but she clipped the brooch to her shoulder without drawing blood and hastily fastened the belt to her waist.

"I am done," she called out a bit breathlessly, and sat on the edge of the bed to put on her boots while he yanked her knife from the door.

"Yer modesty pleases me, Mairi," he told her, handing her weapon back to her. "I hope ye're as zealous with Oxford if he tries to have his way with ye."

She picked up the closest thing to her and threw it at him. He caught the nightdress and held it up to his nose.

"Now this," he said, inhaling the fabric and then setting his smoldering gaze on her once more, "is a deadly weapon, indeed."

Chapter Ten

I had hoped that forcing Captain Grant's attention on you would hasten your confession. But less than an hour?" The queen watched Mairi curtsey before her and then looked over her guest's bent head at Connor standing behind her. "She does not like you overmuch."

They stood in Mary of Modena's Privy Chamber, alone at Mairi's request. Connor's bonnie spitfire had requested that he, too, remain outside the door, but he had refused. He worried over the queen's reaction to discovering where Mairi's brother had taken the king. He was there to stop any MacGregor heads from rolling, especially Mairi's.

"Nae, not overmuch, Yer Majesty," he agreed.

"I wonder why?" the queen puzzled, more to herself than to either one of them. She didn't expect an answer as she took her seat opposite theirs and waited while they did the same. "My husband," she said an instant later, turning her full attention to Mairi. "What do you have to tell me about him?"

Mairi didn't flinch under the Queen of England's

scrutiny. Connor wanted to smile at her. "More than ye may want to hear, I'm afraid."

The queen blinked, but whatever fears Mairi's warning had birthed within her remained in check. "And how do I know that what you tell me is the truth?"

"Ye will have Captain Grant's confirmation to every word I speak, or I shall not speak it."

Connor met the queen's arched glance, but before he could nod his head, she returned to Mairi.

"I don't know if that is enough, as I hardly know him. You do, however, and your low opinion of him causes me to doubt that one of you is trustworthy."

Aye, Connor didn't like Mairi's low opinion of him either, but now was not the time to concern himself with such matters. Or with the titillating memory of her leg coiled around his waist and the sweet taste of her mouth, as hungry for his as his had been for her.

"Why did you try to keep this information from me when I first came to you?" The queen's question to Mairi pulled his thoughts back to the present.

"Because we were not alone, and what I tell ye must remain secret. Only a verra few among us can be trusted."

"Speak then, Miss MacGregor."

"Verra well. Yer husband is on his way to Camlochlin."

"Camlochlin?"

"My home," Mairi clarified.

"Why is the new king on his way to the Highlands of Scotland?"

Finally, Mairi shifted in her seat. "That is where it gets a wee bit more...delicate. Ye see, yer husband travels to the Highlands to meet his daughter."

"His daughters are here in Whitehall, Miss MacGregor.

Captain"—the queen turned to him—"you brought her to me for games?"

"Nae, My Queen," he said gently. "Miss MacGregor speaks of the king's true firstborn. She's been kept in seclusion in an abbey her entire life, raised in secret as a Catholic."

Something dawned on her while she stared at him. Her eyes widened and her complexion paled a bit. "The massacre at the abbey. James has been so terribly somber since word came to him of it."

"He believed his daughter to be among the dead." Mairi continued. "But she was not. My eldest brother saved her from Admiral Gilles who was sent to kill her. My brother's party met up with Captain Grant who was on his way here. Together, they concluded who the novice was."

"You saw her then?" the queen asked Connor. "Is it true? Is she the king's daughter?"

"I believe she is, though she did not confirm it to me."

"Yer husband confirmed it to my brother."

Hearing this for the first time, Connor turned to Mairi. Hell, Colin hadn't told him. Why?

"Why did he not tell me?" Mary of Modena's voice grew soft, almost silent.

"No one knows of her."

"Then how did her enemies find her?"

Mairi looked at Connor for the first time since they had arrived in the chamber. "One of her guardsmen must have betrayed her."

"I see," the queen murmured, sinking farther into her chair. "You were correct not to speak of this earlier. But how do you know for certain that the king hasn't been abducted? Your brother may have tried to stop it and been taken with him."

"If my brother meant to stop something, he would stop it," Mairi assured her. "Nae, I know they left of their own accord because no one knows they are gone. My brother is verra stealthy. My only cause fer doubt is that they left alone. Colin knows the dangers of the road, as does the king—"

"They did not go alone," the queen interrupted. "Thirty of my husband's men are with them."

"Then, fer certain Camlochlin is where they went."

"Will the king be safe there?"

"There is nae place on earth that is safer, Yer Majesty," Mairi said with a measure of pride in her voice that drew a smile to her lips.

"That is good to hear," the queen said with a sigh of relief. "If all that you have told me is true, my husband is going to need friends who are loyal to the throne."

"He has them in the MacGregors," Mairi promised.

"And in the Grants, as well," Connor followed, cutting a glance to Mairi and finding her looking back at him. He winked. She turned away. Damn him to Hades, but he couldn't rid her from his thoughts. He shouldn't have kissed her, touched her. Not when he knew she could resist him. She sure as hell had proven her steely resolve over the years. But to be discarded for Lord Oxford? Satan's balls, the moment she heard the man's voice she'd grown as cold as a wife discovered with her lover.

"I have another question to put to you, Miss Mac-Gregor," the queen said, capturing Mairi's attention, and then Connor's. "To both of you in truth. If no one here can be trusted, how do you know that you can trust me with this, when the king himself did not?"

"Because ye love him," Mairi told her simply. "I saw it in yer gestures toward one another, in the way ye looked at him at supper last eve."

The queen smiled for the first time. "You know of love then?"

Mairi cleared her throat and shared a sidelong glance with Connor. "My sire and my mother share the same look."

"I see." The queen's smile remained while she turned to have another look at Connor. "We understand that you were raised in the Highlands, Captain."

"That is true," he admitted. "My family resides at Camlochlin."

"With the MacGregors."

Connor wasn't sure where her questions were leading, but judging by her piqued interest in him and the shrewd smile she aimed at him, he suspected they were heading in Mairi's direction. He hoped he was wrong.

"So then it is safe to assume that the both of you grew up together."

"Aye," he admitted, rather reluctantly. He didn't like this turn in the conversation. While she posed her earlier questions to her guests, Connor had been pleasantly surprised to find her as clever as Mairi, for a king with many enemies needed a bold, intelligent wife. But when it came to him and Mairi, he didn't want to be scrutinized.

"I think 'tis best fer now," he said, trying to steer her away from the current topic and back to the previous one, "if Yer Majesty told her subjects that the king left fer Edinburgh to meet with the new Royalist Parliament."

"Yes." She smiled brightly. "It is a few weeks early, but no one will question it. You have my gratitude in this, Captain. And you, as well"—she turned to Mairi—"for telling me that the king is safe when you could have remained silent. I just have one more query to put to you both before Captain Grant tells me about the king's daughter."

Mairi nodded and waited for her to continue.

"Why was your captain here excluded from going to Camlochlin with the king, or even told that they were leaving?"

Mairi smiled darkly. "That would likely be Colin's doing." She clarified further when the queen arched a curious brow. "My brother doesna' like him overmuch either."

"Hmm." The queen's astute gaze settled over Connor. "Interesting."

They left the chamber together a quarter of an hour later. Mairi strode toward the queen's backstairs while Connor closed the door behind them. Neither spoke a word. He picked up his steps behind her and took his pleasure in the view. So far, the day wasn't going so badly. They had just spent more time together than they had in seven years, and she hadn't killed him. Aye, she'd flung a dagger at him, but she hadn't been trying to end his life. There was a difference. Mayhap, his foolish heart told him, being together each day would not be so difficult.

"Ye nae longer have to follow my every move, Captain Grant," she called out to him without turning around.

Or not.

"Do ye know another route to the Banqueting Hall then, Miss MacGregor?"

"Through the dungeons, mayhap? Why dinna' ye go look?"

He smiled behind her and folded his hands behind his back while he walked. "There are no dungeons here. They put people in prisons now. Remember? We spoke of it last night. Which reminds me, what—"

"Well then, ye dinna' need to speak to me on the way," she cut him off.

"I'm not. Ye're speaking to me."

She stopped and swung around to stare at him. Many a time in his life had he watched those eyes peer into a man's soul and send him shrinking away at his own inadequacies. She was a strong-willed, pigheaded lass, as loyal to Scotland as his heart was to her. From her clever mouth and succulent tongue, to the small arsenal she kept hidden beneath her skirts, everything about her enchanted him beyond his resistance. It always had. She'd claimed his heart long ago and never let go.

He walked toward her, unclasping his hands as he reached her. Her jaw tightened on his slanted grin. He moistened his lips and adjusted the full weight at his groin. Hell, the spark in her eyes drove him to want to conquer her. No matter how he tried to fight it, it returned every time she fought him.

"What happened between us in my room was an err I will regret until I am an old woman."

He didn't realize he'd snaked his arm around her until her saucy mouth dangled just inches from his. He *had* to take it. When she pulled against his embrace, he yanked her back and slipped his hand around her nape to hold her still. His tongue dashed between her teeth and plunged with undeniable possession into the sweet warmth within. It amazed him that such poisonous lips could taste so fine. He wanted more, and stroked his tongue across hers like a hungry flame.

The sound of many footsteps approaching at his rear jarred his attention. With regret, he broke away from their kiss and turned to see the queen and four guards, three of whom he knew well, round the curve of the hall. He let Mairi go as Mary of Modena's large dark eyes settled on him. He was vaguely aware of Mairi's hands on his shoulders until she turned him to face her again. And then she bent her knee and drove it hard between his legs.

He thought he heard one of the men laugh as he crumbled to the floor. Nick Sedley, most likely.

"Come, Captain, on your feet." The queen paused over him. "I am making an announcement over breakfast and I want you there. Miss MacGregor"—she moved on mercilessly to Mairi before he could obey—"it appears you need an escort to protect you from your escort."

Protect her? Wasn't he the one squirming on his knees?

"You will have to tell us more about your 'old friend' later, Grant."

Connor looked up at Sedley's rather lecherous wink. Like hell he would. He refused when his lieutenant offered him a hand to help him up.

"Who is she?" Richard asked while Connor groaned to his feet.

"She's the MacGregor chief's daughter," Edward answered for him. "Don't you remember her sitting at their table a few nights ago? Tell him, Captain Sedley"— he poked the captain—"you remarked on the color of her eyes."

Straightening to his full height, Connor aimed his darkest glare on Sedley. "Her eyes are no concern of yers."

"Oh?" Sedley challenged as Connor stepped around him. "Is she yours then?"

"Aye," Connor growled. "She is mine." It wasn't true, not anymore, but if it would keep Sedley away from her, then to hell with being truthful.

Chapter Eleven

By God and all His saints, the day simply could not get any hotter. Mairi squinted up at the sun and was glad for Lord Oxford's arm supporting her when the glare made her light-headed. She nodded at something he said, then looked longingly toward the shade. How the hell did anyone live here year-round? She missed the cool breezes that swept through the braes, and her heavy woolen blankets that kept her warm on frigid nights. When she had first arrived in England, she thought the silken fans the ladies fluttered against their faces a silly deception at being coy. But now, she waved her own before her. It did not help matters any that she had spent the entire day in battle with her own thoughts. She was exhausted—and she had Connor Grant to thank for it. How dare he kiss her, not once, but twice, and as if he owned her? She should have fought him harder the first time it happened in her room. But how in damnation could she fight when the hungry gleam in his eyes consumed her in their fire? God have mercy on her, but kissing him was like...like waking up in Camlochlin on the first day of spring when colors burst forth on the misty moors and the fragrance of wild heather filled the cool, crisp air. It awakened her senses in a way that felt like she'd been asleep until the moment his lips touched hers. Och, how she had adored him, following him about from the day she had taken her first steps. She thought she would never be happy again after he left, but she'd found her strength in her blade, renewed her passion, not for a man this time, but for a cause.

And now he was back, stirring to life her old dreams, her forgotten desires. It terrified her how quickly she had succumbed to him, ready and willing to give herself up to him again. She had succeeded in keeping herself composed while in audience with the queen. A feat worthy of praise since he was in the room, his presence charging her nerve endings.

She would never admit it to him, but she was glad he had been there with her. Not because she had been anxious over sitting with the queen, but because she worried about speaking on her kin's behalf. He'd supported her words, much like he had done so many times when they were children and she had to stand before her father for some trouble she had caused with him and Tristan.

He may have betrayed Scotland, but he would not betray her kin. She was a fool to think otherwise. Besides, he already knew the king's daughter had been taken to Camlochlin. He was the one who brought the news to her father. Still, she would have preferred it if he had remained outside while she'd spoken to the queen.

The battle started up again while he told the queen of the stepdaughter she had never met. His smile, as languid as a summer breeze, stirred her blood and quickened her heart. His profile against the firelight was as beguiling as the rest of him. With a straight nose and strong golden chin—carved from some likeness of an ancient Grecian god—he was masculinity personified. Just looking at him made her feel delicate and feminine. By the time Mary of Modena had exhausted all her questions, Mairi was ready to spring from her seat and sprint to her room.

"Miss MacGregor?"

"Aye?" she turned back to her escort. Why could she not fall in love with a sweet man like Henry?

"You asked me about the Earl of Essex and I don't think you have heard a word I've said. You look a bit flushed. Are you unwell?"

"Mayhap we should go inside," she suggested when the image of Connor standing over her, moistening his lips before he kissed her in the hall, declared war on her.

"I'm afraid"—Lord Oxford paused to bow at an older couple passing them on the lawns—"it will be even more stifling inside, dear lady."

"But the sun—"

"Look there!" He pointed toward his father and the young lady escorted on his arm. "It is my sister, Elizabeth! Do you remember? I told you she was arriving today." He did? Mairi did not recall as he tugged on her arm. "Come, I want her to meet you."

He would have been charming if he were not pulling her to move faster in the bloody heat, and if he were not wearing a wig that had to feel like a damned sheep resting on his head.

"Isna' all that hair hot on yer scalp?" she felt light-headed again looking at it while being toted forward.

"Lizzy!" Lord Oxford let her go so suddenly that she nearly spun in the opposite direction. "When did you arrive?"

Mairi righted herself, pulled her earasaid away from her neck, and swatted her fan down the front of it. She would have given anything to be standing in the rain like she had been with Connor after he'd forced her to dance.... She looked up, cursing Captain Grant for invading her only refreshing thought.

Henry, Elizabeth, and their father were staring at her—waiting for something. She blinked. Had Henry introduced her and she had not heard it? "My lord." She gave the earl the courtesy of a bow for her rudeness. Her head spun as she straightened. "Lady Eliz—" Her legs gave out beneath her but she managed to stay conscious as she collapsed into Lady Elizabeth de Vere's arms. In truth, Henry's sister did not catch her but thrust out her palms to keep Mairi away.

"Do get off me!" Lady Elizabeth screeched in Mairi's ear, and shoved her off. "Henry, is she drunk?"

"Of course not, Lizzy. She's—"

"'Tis the heat." Mairi wanted to glare at her but the sun was shining in her eyes, nearly blinding her.

"I don't care what it is!" Lady Elizabeth's perfect yellow ringlets bobbed around her ears when she swung to her father. "I won't be pawed at by a heretic!"

Mairi's eyes opened wide and she prayed to God not to let her pass out. A shadow moved over her, and, for a blessed instant, she forgot her retort and took delight in the shade it provided. Until she looked up and saw who provided it.

"And who, pray tell, is this?" Lady Elizabeth's huge golden eyes softened on Connor and then followed his hand as it swept behind Mairi's back.

"Captain Grant." Connor told her with a slight bow.

"Ah, the Earl of Huntley's son."

Mairi wanted to slap the honeyed smile off Elizabeth's face. If she knew who Connor's father was, then she also knew that Connor was a Highlander. How convenient for her not to consider *him* a heretic. Then again, mayhap he wasn't one anymore.

"A title gained by marriage," Henry pointed out dryly.

Mairi felt Connor go stiff at her side, but when she tilted her head to look at him, she found his smile as bright as the sun. "A title gained after my father helped restore King Charles to the throne."

"Yes," Elizabeth gushed. "You are the king's cousin! Perhaps you would care to show me around the grounds. I've only just arrived and I—"

"Perhaps another time, my lady," Connor cut her off, much to Mairi's delight. "After I get Miss MacGregor out of the sun." Without sparing any of them another word, he leaned down and scooped Mairi up in his arms.

The swift ascent almost shattered her last store of resolve to remain conscious. But, damn her, she would not faint in front of Elizabeth de Vere. Though being carried away was no better.

"Connor, put me doun fer heaven's sake." She hoped he wouldn't listen and it had nothing to do with how perfectly she fit in his arms, or how tenderly he was holding her. Aye, well that was part of the reason. The other was that she couldn't breathe in her woolen earasaid and her bones felt a wee bit like thick honey. She was afraid if he did as she bid him, she would not be able to keep herself up and might crumple to the ground. Still, to be carted off like an invalid...and with that golden-haired witch watching. Och, it was enough to boil her blood. She fanned herself, cursing the sun and her weakness to it. "I am perfectly fine and can take care of myself."

"Ye're not fine." He looked down at her, only inches away, and Mairi decided he was as detrimental to her health as the blazing sun. "Quit being such a stubborn wench and thank me fer rescuing ye from that unholy threesome."

"Thank ye," she said in a soft voice. When he smiled, she looked over his shoulder at Henry's sister still watching them. Mairi didn't like her. Did Connor?

"Lady Elizabeth seemed to take a liking to ye."

He shrugged, a lazy ripple of muscle that Mairi felt all the way to her toes. "I hadn't noticed."

What kind of bloody answer was that? Was he blind? She wished he would put her down so she didn't feel like a child when she called him a liar. "She is verra bonnie, Connor." She narrowed her eyes on him waiting for his reaction.

He looked over his shoulder at the wench. "Do ye think so?"

Did she think so? Even when the woman was shrieking at her, Mairi could not deny her exquisite face and form. Why, she likely had to do little more than bat her luxurious lashes to make any man fall to his knees. And, hell, but what woman with a pair of working eyes in her head wouldn't want Connor?

"Well, I dinna' care what ye think of her." She folded her arms across her chest and turned away from the amusement lighting his eyes. She wanted to bury her face in his chest a moment later, when she saw a goodly number of the king's guests staring at her with both concern and contempt.

"Why are ye not guarding the queen?" she asked, squirming to get out of his arms.

"She already informed the people of the king's departure fer Edinburgh. She has nae more need of me."

"Nor do I, so quicken yer steps before I am tempted to hurl another dagger at yer head."

Her heart flipped in her chest when his laughter settled over her and his arms pulled her in a bit closer.

"How did I ever survive ye, woman? Do ye remember that time when we were babes—ye were barely five summers old, I think. I had snatched the doll ye had been playing with and ye chased me and then began to cry when ye couldn't catch me."

Och, damn him to Hades, why was he bringing up their childhood? "If ye dinna' mind, Connor, I would prefer not—"

"Feeling terrible fer what I had done, I walked back to ye and handed ye back yer treasured doll. Ye took it gently, kissed its head and then whirled it around yer shoulder and smashed it into my face."

"I never struck ye with a doll," she insisted, refusing to drift off into the past with him. "You are a liar and have always been one."

"I lost two teeth."

"So? Ye grew more, didna' ye? I was sent to bed with no supper because of ye."

"I didn't know that," he admitted softly, deeply. She thought he was going to apologize. "That makes me feel better, at least. That doll was fashioned of wood and my mouth was so swollen I couldn't eat and could barely speak fer two days."

Against her will, Mairi smiled—very slightly. But Connor's keen eyes caught it. "Ye do remember it then."

"Nae. I was just wondering if I have anything fashioned of wood in my room that I could hit ye with now. To render ye speechless would make me ecstatic."

His wide, open grin fell over her like a rush of

northern air, exhilarating her senses, bedazzling her heart.
Blast him.

"Come now, Mairi," he said in a low, gruff whisper
that made her muscles tremble. "If I stopped conversing with ye completely, who would ye have to help ye
sharpen yer tongue?"

"'Twould be worth the sacrifice."

"Ye don't mean that."

But she did. She did not want to think about those
long summer days filled with his laughter. When he was
hers. Whether he was practicing in the field or bringing
in the sheep with her brothers, his eyes had always found
hers, silently, tenderly telling her that he would rather be
with her than with anyone else.

But it wasn't true. She didn't want to remember. They
were children. Foolish, innocent children. What was she
doing in his arms, her ear pressed to his heart? She should
be in Scotland, leagues away from him. Forgetting him.
But even as her mind resisted him, being crushed up
against him felt so perfectly right.

"Satan's bloody arse, Connor! What's happened?"

Claire's voice saved Mairi from emitting the delirious
little sigh about to fall from her traitorous lips. Her relief
quickly turned to mortification though when she peeked
over his shoulder to see her dearest friend and the queen
with her, the latter looking quite amused at Lady Huntley's oath.

"'Tis nothing to fear." Connor assured as they hurried
to catch up with him. "She is suffering from the heat."

Mairi caught the way the queen looked from her to
Connor, a small smile tinged with speculation curling
her lips.

Damnation, she liked the king's young wife. She was

clever and passionate, and remarkably poised at both. Mairi detested looking like a weak, wilted woman in her eyes. "Thank ye, Captain Grant." She squirmed in his arms. "I am feeling much better. Ye can put me doun now."

He did not so much as slow his pace, but instead tossed their companions a frustrated sigh. "She's stubborn."

Dear God, she was going to kill him. Slowly. Painfully.

"You do look a bit pale, sweeting." Claire reached out to touch her clammy cheek.

"She needs to come out of that heavy woolen blanket she's wearing," the queen noted. "Bring her to my chambers. I will have my seamstress fit her for some new gowns."

"Nae," Mairi refused. "Truly, Yer Majesty, that is not necessary." There was no way in hell she was going to don an English gown. From the corner of her eye she saw the twinkle of Connor's dimple. The bastard. He was enjoying her humiliation.

"Mayhap," he said with a challenging grin she wanted to slap off his face, "Miss MacGregor would prefer it if I carried her inside each day."

"I would rather be dipped in boiling oil," she murmured, not really caring anymore who heard her.

When he laughed, she elbowed him in the guts and said a silent prayer for God to grant her the patience not to murder Claire and Graham's eldest son, the wisdom to remember that he was no good for her, and the strength to resist his familiar, maddening charm.

Chapter Twelve

$\mathcal{M}$ airi stood perfectly still while one of the queen's personal handmaidens hooked the endless buttons trailing down the back of her borrowed three-piece gown. She would have preferred dressing herself, the way she did at home, but her royal hostess had insisted on sending her aid, and rightly so, since English gowns were nearly impossible to get into without at least one extra pair of hands.

She took no joy in being primped and prodded like some self-important English snob, but she had to admit the fabric was divine, even softer than her wool, and so much thinner.

She ran her hands down the fine folds of her skirts and clenched her teeth. What was she doing allowing herself to be dressed like one of them? Liking the queen was one thing, letting England change her was another. Connor had succumbed to her grand halls and elegant lifestyle. She would not. But then, why was she here instead of in her own chamber, clipping her brooch to her plaid? She could not let herself begin to suspect that she was here for Connor, and the hope that he might find her bonnie in her English garb. Nae, it was the heat. Her Highland earasaid was too heavy to wear beneath the southern sun. That was all. Dressing like the women Connor preferred had nothing to do with it.

She spread her palms across her belly and struggled to inhale. "Mayhap," she gasped, turning to the handmaiden, "ye could leave a few buttons open. 'Tis a bit snug."

"But, m'lady, there is plenty of room. It is not tight at all."

Mairi narrowed her gaze on the face looking back at her. Of course it was too tight. She could barely breathe and she could not allow Connor to be the reason.

When the handmaiden lowered her eyes to her feet, Mairi studied her more closely. She looked to be younger than Mairi by a few years. Her saffron gown was finely crafted but simply cut. Caught up beneath a plain matching caul, her amber hair lacked both adornment and the fashionable curls of the time. She was not like the other witches roaming the halls. "What is yer name?"

"Judith, m'lady." She performed a well-practiced curtsey. "I am the second daughter of Viscount and Lady Astor."

"Judith," Mairi said, unimpressed with her title. "I am Mairi MacGregor. Ye are not my servant, so please stop calling me m'lady. It makes me feel old and wrinkled."

The door to her chamber sprang open, saving Mairi from the pearl hair clips Judith was reaching for.

"Whatever is taking…" Claire's voice halted along with her steps when she looked into the room. "Mairi, you look lovely."

"I knew the scarlet silk would suit her well." Queen Mary smiled, entering the room next. "Look how well it fits."

Mairi was not surprised to find the two of them together since this afternoon when they had accosted her and Connor on the way in from the garden. Like the queen, Claire was a strong woman, in control of her life, of her heart, and her happiness. It was natural that they would get along so well, especially since the queen likely did not have a friend in the entire palace—though Mairi had not noticed the bond between them before this afternoon.

She smiled when the queen went to her and gave the soft silk on her hip a tug. Really, they were all wrong. The gown was too damn tight.

"I'm still astonished that she agreed to wear it." Claire came to stand on the other side of her, licked her index and middle finger, and smoothed back a stray curl that had fallen over Mairi's forehead.

"Perhaps it is the handsome Lord Oxford who compels her to abandon her cumbersome, less flattering clothes." The queen tossed Claire a teasing wink and stepped behind Mairi to close the remaining buttons.

Mairi clamped down on her teeth and avoided Claire's tender smile. Connor's mother had so wanted him to marry Mairi, mayhap as much as Mairi had. She had tried to defend her son over the years, but it became too hard to speak of him, so they both stopped.

"Lord Oxford has already asked to escort you to the theater tonight," the queen pressed on. "He certainly does fancy you."

"The theater?" Mairi asked woodenly. Another of England's lures she fought to resist. "I have never been to a performance before."

"Well, you will be attending many from here on out. Miss MacGregor." The queen took her by the shoulders and turned her around to face her. "If you hadn't told me where my husband had gone, I would have spent each day in terror that his enemies had taken him, perhaps killed him. You trusted me, and for that I owe you something. If you fancy Lord Oxford, I have but to speak a word to my husband when he returns."

"Gratitude, Yer Majesty." Mairi shook her head and looked away. "But I do not want a husband."

"Nonsense." The queen smiled and clicked her tongue against the roof of her mouth. "You are not getting any younger, dear girl. What is your age?"

"A score and two."

The queen's large eyes opened wider. "We must find you a husband soon! Perhaps the Baronet of Aylesford's son. His name escapes me at the moment." She looked around Mairi's arm at Claire. "Lady Huntley, do you recall what it is?"

"Captain Nicholas Sedley. He's quite handsome."

Mairi turned slowly to look at her. Was she out of her mind? Captain Sedley was a naval officer in Prince William's royal fleet. He couldn't possibly be a worse match for her.

"That's correct! Sedley!" The queen stepped away to take in the full sight of the girl before her before deciding what else needed to be changed about her. "He comes from very fine stock I am told," she said more to Claire than to Mairi. "Of course, once the engagement to either him or Lord Oxford is announced, she will have to cease contact with your son, Lady Huntley. His ease with her is unseemly." Her eyes settled on Mairi's again. "Even more so since you have made it quite clear that you don't like him. You agree, no?"

Mairi blinked. Cease all contact with Connor by

order of the throne? It was what she needed. She should be rejoicing. "Nae...I mean...I dinna' want to marry either of those men." But hell, she *was* getting older. She hadn't thought about marriage until she saw Connor again. She had been perfectly happy living as she was: a warrior—at least, a warrior in secret. She didn't want her mother's life anymore. She wanted Claire's. But even Claire had wed the man she loved...and who loved her in return.

"We should let you finish dressing." Claire moved in to kiss her cheek, then motioned for Judith to resume her work. "Don't take too long, sweeting," she called out as she made her way toward the door with the queen. "We are having iced cream with supper tonight and it will melt if you are late."

When they were alone again, Judith reached for a comb and commenced tugging on Mairi's long tresses. "The queen is correct, m'lady," the handmaiden said behind her.

"Mairi," she corrected.

"The scarlet does suit you well...Mairi. You look lovely, but...may I speak freely?"

"Of course."

"I fear the gloom in your expression is all anyone will see."

God's mercy, was she that transparent? She did not want to wed simply because she was getting on in years, and she was not about to be forced to do so. She wanted to go home, mayhap wed a Highlander...one who would never choose England over her. If there were none to be had, then she would continue to be content fighting for the preservation of her religion and the Highland customs.

"Sara, the Baron of Pembroke's daughter, and I have been watching you," Judith shyly admitted while she reached for the pearl hair clips on the table beside her to match Mairi's borrowed earrings.

"Is that so?" Mairi turned and arched a curious brow at her.

Judith nodded, her large green eyes traipsing over Mairi's hair, deciding where to begin pinning. Finally she threw up her hands. "There's so much of it! It hangs to your waist! But as I was saying—you are not like the other ladies who are visiting."

"Nor are ye."

Judith exchanged a smile with her. "You do not powder your face or paint your lips. Your clothes are a bit drab and a tad threadbare. And we have yet to see you disheveled by a forbidden kiss from someone else's husband."

"Nor shall ye ever," Mairi vowed, and marveled at the handmaiden's transformation. She had gone from a dormouse to a chatterbox in the space of a breath. Mairi almost wished she had not tried to make her feel so comfortable. But at least the bolder Judith provided a distraction from her more troubling thoughts, like how Connor might prefer her hair. "'Twill take too many clips," she said as Judith began fastening her hair to her head. "I am afraid there is no time fer that." And, Lord, but they pinched.

"You are fortunate that the queen has chosen *two* possible husbands for you, and both of them young. Captain Sedley is quite handsome, if I might be so bold. But like his father, he has a bit of the devil in him, and he does reside in Holland. Were I you, I would choose Lord Oxford, despite his misshapen face." Judith let out a dispirited sigh of her own before Mairi could reply. "I fear she will choose someone old and weathered for me."

"Whom would ye choose then?" Mairi asked, feeling terribly sorry for her having to live with the prospect of wedding a half-dead noble. "My friend Lady Huntley seems to have the queen's ear. Mayhap I could suggest someone to her and she could put it to the queen."

"Oh, that would be most kind of you!" Judith looked like she might toss her arms around Mairi and kiss her. "Now let me see. I haven't thought on it overmuch." She tapped the comb to her chin for a moment or two and then smiled brightly. "Captain Grant would be lovely."

Mairi swallowed. She tried to take a breath but her damned gown was suffocating. "Captain Grant? But surely ye are aware of his fickle heart. He will never love ye as much as he loves his duty. He is infinitely more handsome than Captain Sedley and has likely enjoyed many more women in his bed."

"I wouldn't know about that. He's been away in Glencoe for some time. Before that though, I don't recall him being all that lecherous with any of the handmaidens here. But you are correct about his devotion to his duty. He seems to care more about the king and his safety—at least when King Charles was alive—than who is in his bed. I cannot speak for anyone else, but he has never tried to seduce Sara or me. In truth, now that I think on it"—Judith set her eyes on Mairi—"you are the only lady I have seen him give so much of his attention to."

Mairi did not blush, and she was not about to begin now. But her palms did grow moist and the room did feel warmer, a bit stifling. He did seem to be hovering around her often, following her when she thought she was alone, refusing to leave her room after he'd kissed her. Dear God, that kiss…"He is simply a rogue who wants what he canna' have. Mark my words, Judith, fer I know him well. Captain Grant is a devil. He might not be as open about it as Sedley, but he is one nevertheless. He isna' content to simply lure ye to his bed. He will steal yer heart and make ye feel more alive than ever before, and then he will leave ye as easily as a soldier leaves his dead enemy on the field. Ye would do well to stay as far away from him as ye can. Now let us stop speaking of him and tell me about this iced cream we are having with supper."

A quarter of an hour later, Mairi left the queen's private chambers and strode down the hall alone. She did not look at the faces of the lords and ladies who passed her. She did not want to see them laughing at her, or hear their mocking whispers about how a Highlander was trying to fit in with the graceful swans around her. Hell, she felt more out of place in her silk gown than she did in her plaid. With only two of her daggers secured to her calves and thighs, she felt infinitely more vulnerable as well.

When she spotted Lord Oxford and his sister at the end of the hall, she girded up her loins and proceeded forward.

"Miss MacGregor." Henry captured her hands and brought them to his lips while his sable eyes scored over her. "You look ravishing. Does she not, Lizzy?"

Lady Elizabeth tossed her a brief, inconsequential glance before finding more interest in her fingernails. "I was not aware that Highlanders owned anything as fine as silk, but if it keeps her from falling on top of me again, I will be the first to thank whoever loaned it to her."

Mairi sized her up with a tight little smile. Och, what

she wouldn't give to get Lady Elizabeth in her father's training field. "Ye may thank the queen when next ye see her then."

Her reply garnered the desired effect on Henry's sister. She stammered while Mairi turned to the viper's brother. "Lord Oxford, have ye come to escort me to supper, or yer sister to the privy? She does look a wee bit ill."

"Oh, Lizzy, are you?" Oxford tried to take her hand but she slapped it away.

"No, you fool! Go! Take her and leave me alone! I will find my own escort!"

Goodness, but the woman certainly knew how to seethe. Satisfied to have affected her so, Mairi looped her arm through Henry's and smiled as he led her away.

"You mustn't mind Lizzy," Henry told her gently. "She can be a bit too tightly strung at times."

Nothing a dagger would not fix. "I dinna' mind her," she said with a pleasant smile she did not feel. Satan's arse, she had to speak to Claire. Henry was a nice enough fellow, but if the queen tried to force her to marry him, she very likely would end up killing his sister. And, hell, but she didn't like the way he nearly shook in his high-heeled shoes when the shrew screeched at him.

Connor certainly would not have backed down, but she refused to let him haunt her thoughts again. Not even when she stepped into the Banqueting Hall and did not see him among the guests did she let herself wonder where he might be.

Henry was courteous to Connor's father, who was less likely than her own to gut him down the middle for being so bold as to sit at their table yet again. He droned on for an hour about how the Roman emperor Nero had ice brought down from the mountains and combined it with fruit toppings, and, later, how the caliphs of Baghdad were the first to use milk and sugar as major ingredients.

Mairi wished he would shut up and eat it.

By the time supper was over and everyone rose to follow the queen to the theater, Mairi found herself missing Connor's quick banter.

Damn him. Damn him to Hades.

※

Chapter Thirteen

The king's theater or, as it was sometimes still called, the Cockpit, because of the cockfighting once done here, was smaller than Mairi imagined. There were tiers of balconies all around the structure to give all a favorable view of the stage and its players. The clamor of excitement among the guests was contagious and soon Mairi was able to put Connor out of her mind.

The queen sat in a tier above on the opposite wall, in a private booth with the king's daughters, Mary and Anne, and their husbands. Mairi looked around at the hundreds of faces and spotted someone who had piqued her interest in the last few days. "There is Lord Hollingsworth. His wife is striking, but she does not seem verra interested in her husband."

"Most likely that is because Lord Hollingsworth favors food and men over her."

Goodness, Mairi eyed the buxom trollop. It was no wonder why she had followed Tristan around for three days and then followed Connor after that.

"It was rumored that he and the exiled Duke of Monmouth were lovers."

Mairi raised her brow while Hollingsworth and his wife gained their seats. "The Duke of Monmouth ye say?" Another bit of interesting information to bring home to her militia brothers. She was about to ask Henry more questions when her gaze fell to one of the lower balconies beneath the queen and she saw Connor taking his seat in a booth already occupied by a group of his soldiers. Where had he been all evening? A flash of yellow drew her eyes to the person sitting at his left. Her heart stopped beating. It had to have stopped, for she could not take in any air or let any out. She went deadly still taking in those golden ringlets, those lion-colored eyes with the fangs to match. Nae, not Lady Elizabeth. Not her.

"Miss MacGregor, are you falling ill again?"

She sucked in a gasp of air and expelled a sound so pitiful to her own ears it made her want to weep for herself. But she wouldn't. She would never shed another tear that had anything to do with Connor Grant. "I am fine," she remedied with perfect serenity in her voice.

"There's Lizzy." He waved and Mairi was tempted to toss him over the side. "She looks well recovered."

Did he honestly care so very much about her "high-strung" nature that he would voice her improvement with such relief? Or was there another reason completely why he felt the need to point out the obvious? She turned to him, curling one corner of her mouth and pinning him with a stare that made most men wilt in their boots. Henry de Vere was no exception.

He was trying to point out his adversary's faults by flaunting Connor's latest conquest in her face, trying to test her feelings for the scoundrel. He probably did not deserve the force of her strike about to come but she didn't care. Connor wasn't beside her to take the blow, and Henry was.

"Mayhap 'tis just ye who does everything to displease her. Or"—she blinked, releasing him, and brightened her smile as she turned back to his beloved sister—"mayhap, like most of the other *ladies* at court, she requires half a company of soldiers to pleasure her."

"Miss MacGregor..."

She ignored the quaver in Henry's angry voice and gave his hand a gentle pat. "Either way, my lord, I am pleased that she is happy again."

Her false smile faded when he pulled his hand away from hers. He did not begin speaking to her again until the second act. She didn't hear him when he did—or the actors for that matter. She did watch the stage on a number of occasions when a colorful costume caught her eye, but her eyes always drifted back to the balcony below. She noted every smile the players brought to Connor's face, every moment of concentration that dipped his brow. Her scathing glance did not miss Lady Elizabeth's soft touch to his arm, or the way she smiled up at him like some besotted milkmaid.

Connor caught her watching him more than once, but she turned away, breaking eye contact. Had he been with Lady Elizabeth earlier? Had he missed supper and iced cream to be with her? Why had she not looked toward the de Veres' table to see if Elizabeth was with her father? Och, God, she didn't want to think of them together, naked, sweating...But she did, and it near drove her mad. But truly, why was she surprised that Connor had kissed her...twice...and then bedded Elizabeth de Vere the same night? He likely had a dozen women waiting for him at his door each night when he retired to his bed. She wanted to stand up and scream at him over the players, or sink into her seat and curse herself for caring. She could not stay here and watch whatever grew between him and his current lover. But where the hell could she go? She did not know how to get home from England, and even if she did, she could never travel alone. She cursed Colin for not bringing her home with him.

"...and so I have decided to forgive you. Miss Mac-Gregor? Mairi?" Oxford's use of her familiar name drew her attention back to him. Hell, she had not heard a word he had said.

"Fergive me, I was thinking of my home."

"Mairi, I said you have become very dear to me and so I have decided to forgive you."

"Thank ye, my lord." She smiled and began to turn back to the stage when he took her hand and crushed it to his lips.

"Walk with me later in the garden. There is something I wish to ask you."

Ask her? Saints, he was going to ask for her hand in marriage! Her gaze swept immediately to Connor. His eyes were already on her, dark and murderous on her knuckles pressed to Henry's mouth, watching each kiss he placed there.

"My lord, I..."

"I have been patient and courtly, Mairi." His scar burned red against his skin. "But if you refuse to walk with me alone, I will be forced to kiss you in front of everyone."

Her eyes darted back to Connor. What would he do if Henry kissed her? Would he care? She should let Henry do it, mayhap even kiss him back and show Connor, rather than continue to tell him, once and for all that he no longer meant anything to her. But she couldn't. She would worry about what that meant later.

"Ye would be risking too much, Lord Oxford, I assure ye. My faither's closest friend would be one of those watching. If Lord Huntley does not call ye to the yard, my brother will upon his return. I could not let ye take such a risk. If ye wish to court me, ye must ask my faither."

She knew Henry would never agree to such a thing. The last time her father had cast him an askew glance, he nearly tripped on his own feet in his rush to be away from him. Not that he would ever find Camlochlin, and even if he did, her father would never agree to her marrying a Protestant.

"Mairi, I—"

Good Lord, it was not going to work. She had to employ a different tactic, one that disgusted her to her very marrow, but necessary, nonetheless. She only hoped he possessed the decency to react appropriately. "Please, my lord. Ye are frightening me."

When she pulled her hand away from his face, he let her go without a fight and looked suitably remorseful. "It was not my intention to cause you alarm. Forgive me."

Hell, why did he have to be so kind? She nodded and flashed him a brief smile before turning her attention to the stage. She breathed a sigh of relief after narrowly avoiding his proposal and found her gaze returning to Connor once again. He had looked angry before, but now he smiled at her while he slipped his arm around Lady Elizabeth's shoulder and bent to speak against her trembling curl.

Mairi's hands fisted in her lap and she looked away from him for the last time.

Mayhap, she could convert Henry and grow to love him after all.

The play was a blur of dramatics and bright colors and when it ended, Mairi cursed Connor for spoiling it for her with his attendance. She was happy to be leaving the cramped theater, eager to get to her chamber, away from Connor and Henry, and out of this blasted, tight gown.

She made it to the exit with her arm curled through Henry's when she came face-to-face with Connor and his men. Lady Elizabeth was with him, of course, with one arm looped through his and her other hand placed possessively on his forearm. Mairi fought the urge to claw out her eyes...and Connor's next.

Not surprisingly, Henry broke away from her and rushed to Elizabeth's side. Mairi barely heard their brief conversation, so fixated was she on thinking of a scathing comment to fling at Connor. Nothing came to her, and it was just as well, for he looked like he wanted to toss a few choice words at her, as well. She tightened her jaw and stared at him while the others around her discussed the play.

Here was the only man who did not wither or shrink away at her piercing, penetrating gaze. Instead, he smiled slightly, ready for the battle to commence, confident that he would come out the victor.

Bastard. She ached to strike him hard and fast for making her sit through two hours of watching him enjoy himself with Elizabeth de Vere, of all people. But God and all His saints help her; he made every other man in the theater insignificant. He stood his position, long, lean, so elegantly garbed. A beautiful facade. For what lay beneath was purely savage. Raised to manhood in the cold, hard mountain ranges of the Highlands, his body pulsed with the power of it. He had been everything her heart desired. How long could she keep up this fight before she surrendered?

He held her there, still, breathless, while, with a slight flare of his nostrils, he took her in from foot to crown. He did not need to say a word. His eyes ravished her in her borrowed gown, sapping her of her will to defy and resist him. He was a force she could never defeat and she stepped back, not because she did not want to throw herself into his arms, but because she did. His dimples faded. His eyes smoldered with determination and desire, his muscles resisting both in the subtle shift of his shoulders, the slight change in his breath. He wanted to follow her, but he stopped himself.

Captain Nicholas Sedley, on the other hand, did not. "I do not believe I've had the pleasure of a formal introduction." He swept around Connor with the grace of a cat on the prowl and reached for her hand.

Connor watched him silently, his eyes hooded and deadly, while Captain Sedley planted a soft kiss on the top of her hand and introduced himself.

Mairi sized him up cautiously. So, this was the queen's second choice on her list of husbands well suited for Mairi. He was quite handsome, with hair as black as coal and eyes the color of a twilight sky, but the queen was mad if she thought Mairi would marry him. Not only had he sworn his fealty to England's enemy, but his seductive charisma instantly reminded her of Connor. This man's heart was loyal to no woman.

Still, she thought returning her gaze to Connor. He

possessed no feigned airs about him meant to purposely lure women to his bed. He did not need any. He beguiled the senses with the natural ease of his resplendent grin, his unflappable self-confidence, and the supreme control he wielded over his heart. Connor Grant did not chase skirts. If one rejected him, there would likely always be another waiting in the wings.

"There will be dancing in the Banqueting Hall upon our return," Captain Sedley reminded her. "I pray you will do me the honor of—"

Connor shoved him out of the way with little effort and, disengaging himself from Lady Elizabeth, moved into Sedley's place before Mairi. "I want to speak to ye."

"I dinna' care to hear anything ye have to say."

"I didn't ask ye if ye cared, but ye *will* listen."

She laughed, but it sounded hollow to her ears. Against her will, her eyes scanned the small crowd around them. Lady Elizabeth appeared to have reverted back to her fitful, pinched-lipped self. Connor's friends, including Captain Sedley, all wore the same curious, somewhat surprised expression. She half expected his lieutenant to pound him on the back and shout *huzzah*! Henry's face was as red as the deep scar marring it. He looked about to say something he might regret. Mairi would have to give him credit if he did, for Connor was bigger and more threatening at the moment than a hundred men readying for battle.

She spoke before Henry opened his mouth. "I wouldna' want to drag ye away from yer…." She veered her own lethal gaze to Lady Elizabeth. "…other pursuits."

Connor's dangerous expression transformed into sheer amusement in the space of a breath. Mairi had the sinking feeling that he read her as easily as the books her uncle Robert used to read to them. She was jealous, and he knew it.

Desperate to escape before she was forced to admit to herself that he was correct, she pushed past him, forgetting Henry and everyone else. "Good night."

She left the theater with Henry hot on her heels. But it was Connor's eyes following her that almost pulled her back.

Almost.

Chapter Fourteen

The morning sun beat down on Connor's shoulders as he strode into the tiltyard and called Edward to his side. "Where's Drummond?"

Running beside him to keep up with his captain's formidable gait, Edward looked around the list field, his dark eyes squinting against the sun and the dry dirt kicked up around them. "He was here a moment ago. He must have seen you coming."

"Ye'll practice with me then."

Edward swallowed audibly, "Me?"

Connor looked down at him and gritted his teeth. Damnation, Edward hardly had any damn hair on his face. But Connor needed to fight, to train hard and work out some of the frustration that was eating him up inside. He'd spent the entire night tossing in his bed and fighting his damn pillow; plagued by the image of Henry de Vere taking his time kissing Mairi's hand, as if he had all night to do it with no one to stop him. Without *her* stopping him. Plaguing him with the dreaded certainty that there was nothing he could do about it either, short of beating

Oxford to a bloody, half-dead pulp. He'd be put in the Tower, or mayhap thrown into Newgate prison, where he'd have to live with the knowledge that he'd surrendered his control, his life, and everything he had trained to become, to jealousy. He knew himself well enough to admit that he was, indeed, jealous, but he wouldn't act on it. He couldn't, without shaming his kin, his king, and himself.

But he still needed to fight someone who could give him a decent go. All his men were well skilled with the sword, but this was a day when Connor wished for someone like Rob MacGregor to take up swords with. Hell, he missed fighting with Highland men.

He almost smiled for the first time that day when he spotted Drummond, a Scotsman, at least, entering the lists.

"Lieutenant!" he shouted across the dusty distance. His suddenly reluctant opponent waved at him. Connor motioned him to come forward, yanked off his military coat, and rolled up his ruffled sleeves. "Quicken yer pace, Drummond," he ordered, dragging his claymore from its sheath. "And let's begin the day."

"I have not even broken fast yet."

Connor cast the heavens a brief sigh, then swung his flashing blade at his lieutenant's head. They fought for a quarter of an hour—with Connor landing the more devastating blows—before Drummond lifted his hand for a rest.

"If 'tis Sedley or that Oxford fellow who angers ye"—his lieutenant leaned against the short wall that separated the tiltyard from the courtyard and rubbed his shoulder—"then why the hell did ye choose my arse to pummel to the ground this sunny morn?"

Connor laughed, pushing off the wall, ready for the next set. "Ye're here. Sedley is not." He pointed his sword at his soldier and friend, and gestured with it for him to get back on his feet. "As fer that Oxford fellow"—he blocked a strike to his left and countered with a chopping blow that would have gutted Drummond's middle if he hadn't leaped back—"I've no idea why ye bring him up."

"Tell me if this sounds right to ye then." His lieutenant swung low, missing Connor's legs. "Oxford has attached himself at the hip to the woman ye love." He arched his blade upward and caught Connor on the upper arm, slicing his shirt and the skin beneath.

The burn of his wound and the blood it produced were nothing new to Connor. He'd been cut a hundred times while training with his father and Callum MacGregor. But it didn't bode well for him to get cut by Richard Drummond.

Damn Mairi.

With one more crushing blow, meant to end the fight, Connor tore Drummond's sword from his hand and stepped back, victorious.

"I don't love her. I haven't seen her fer more than a few days at a time in seven years."

"And before that?" Richard asked, bending his palms to his knees to aid his breathing. "What was she to ye before that?"

Connor pushed his blade back into its sheath and stared at the man who'd worked and fought beside him for the last seven years. Ah, hell, he was tired of denying it. "She was everything."

Straightening, Richard nodded then cracked his back. "Ye never told us of her."

"I needed to forget her."

Drummond beckoned him back to the wall and rested his backside against it. "Is she the reason then that ye havena' taken a wife? Most would have ye, ye know."

Hell, he didn't want to be having this conversation with Drummond, or with anyone else. He didn't want to admit to himself that she was indeed the reason he chose to go to battle while other men stood before priests, pledging their lives to a lady who came first in their hearts. He hadn't been given that gift. For his heart, he could no longer deny, belonged to one who had rejected him. How could he admit such a thing to his friend? He looked away, toward the tiltyard instead.

"Come now, Captain, we've known each other long enough." Richard smiled and patted his back. "'Tis not as bad as all that."

Aye, it was worse.

"We all fall like wounded men on the battlefield over a lass at some point in our lives."

"I haven't fallen, Drummond." When his lieutenant offered him an encouraging smile, Connor was tempted to fling him over the wall. "I could beat yer arse all over this yard to show ye."

Drummond shrugged his shoulders. "'Twill not change anything. Ye still love the gel. Hell, 'tis plain to see on yer face every time ye see her, Captain. Now what are ye going to do about it?"

"I don't—"

"There's the esteemed Captain Grant!"

Connor looked up to see Sedley entering the lists with Lady Elizabeth de Vere on his arm. When she saw Connor, she waved and broke away. Damn it, the last thing he needed was her constant chattering in his ear, especially when most of what she said revolved around her. And what in bloody hell was Sedley doing bringing her inside the wall? There were other men practicing in here, some on horse, all with a weapon.

"Get her out of here, Sedley!"

"Oh, but, Captain," she cried, rushing toward him. "I have been looking for you all morning!" She reached him breathlessly and pressed her palms against his damp shirt. "I was hoping you and I could take a ride to St. James's Park. I would love—"

"Lady Elizabeth." He took her hands and gently removed them from his chest. "Ye cannot be inside the lists. Ye could be injured." He glared at Sedley over her shoulder. "Fer the last time, Captain, take her somewhere else." It was the second time Nick brought her to Connor and left her with him. He wouldn't get stuck with her again as he had last evening.

"After tea then?" She blinked her huge topaz eyes at him and quirked her full lips as someone's sword sailed over her head.

Connor watched the blade fall harmlessly to the dirt a few feet away from her, then, a tad pale, he bent to haul her over his shoulder and carried her out of the lists. He set her down with a bit more force than he'd intended and was about to send her on her way, when he saw Mairi watching him with his mother and the queen on either side of her. None of them looked happy.

"Captain," the queen spoke first, and moved forward. His mother followed, but Mairi remained in her spot a few feet away. "You seem to enjoy toting ladies around with you."

He looked at Lady Elizabeth, who smiled up at him

in return. "Yer Majesty, I was just escorting the earl's daughter out of the lists."

Mary of Modena raised a sharp brow at both of them. "A dangerous place for a lady to be, indeed."

"Foolish twit," his mother, who never failed to speak her mind, muttered loud enough for all to hear.

Elizabeth took immediate offense, though she managed to keep her voice an octave below a screech. "Lady Huntley, I—"

"Lady Elizabeth," the queen cut her off. "You will retire to your rooms immediately. Lady Huntley and I will escort you there so that on the way we may speak to you with more privacy about the hazards of your actions."

"Yes, Your Majesty." Elizabeth bowed her head and followed the two women without another word. Before she left, she turned her most scathing look on Mairi.

"Miss MacGregor," the queen added when Mairi picked up her steps to go with them, "ye will wait here with Captain Grant until we return."

"But I—" Mairi called out as the queen left the tilt-yard, unconcerned with her protest. Mairi finished voicing it anyway, albeit, in a fading, defeated tone. "—dinna' want to wait here."

Connor didn't know whether to smile or fix her with the scowl she deserved. Satan's balls, how did she manage to look even more bonnie than she had last evening? Than she had in her cherished Highland earasaid? "Mairi, ye look…" He paused, as if the words were stuck somewhere between his heart and his lips. They were, for he hadn't spoken them to her in so long. "…beautiful." Hell, when would the sight of her quit stalling his breath?

She wore a simple chemise beneath a low-waisted

coral-colored *nightgown*, casually unfastened at the breast, as was the latest fashion of *undress* among English ladies. His eyes lingered there for a moment before moving on slowly up the column of her sweet neck, exposed and ripe for the kissing thanks to her thick, dark waves being swept off her shoulders and pinned atop her head. Hell, he needed a bucket of cold water to pour on himself before he hauled her in his arms and promised her the world.

He'd already done that, and she had refused him.

"Ye're making me verra uncomfortable looking at me like that."

He laughed softly. "Like what?"

"Like I might be as hideously dimwitted as the last trollop who offered herself up to ye." She set her cool blue gaze on Lady Elizabeth in the distance.

His heart nearly soared right out of his chest at her obvious scalding jealousy. He'd seen it last night in the theater, but he'd been too preoccupied by his own anger at Oxford's mouth all over her hands.

Hell, but he was pitiful.

He looked over his shoulder at his lieutenant, who caught his eye and tried to look busy wiping the dirt off his blade.

"Ye are looking…damp," Mairi said, pulling his attention back to her.

He looked down at his sweaty shirt clinging to his torso. "I was practicing."

"He was trying to kill me, is more like it!" Drummond contended, then hurried on his way when Connor glared at him.

"Ye must have put on quite a display." Mairi's eyes glittered beneath her lashes, but her smile remained as cool as a Highland winter night. "Yer new interest couldna' keep her hands off ye."

Ah, there it was again. That delightful spark she had unwittingly revealed yet again. She did her best to hide it from him, but he no longer doubted what he'd suspected the night he danced with her. But did it mean that she still cared for him? Or was she simply being possessive of what was once hers?

"I'll admit, she's fairer than I first found her." He watched, doing his damnedest not to grin at her clenching fingers. "She wants me to take her riding in St. James's Park after tea."

Unlike himself, Mairi was a master at disguising on her face that which was on her mind or in her heart. But he had always been able to read her better than most and presently she was livid.

"And are ye taking her?"

"I haven't yet decided," he replied vaguely, enjoying her discomposure and the reason for it too much to stop. He watched her gather herself up and couldn't help but smile at her. His Mare never stayed tamed for long.

"I agree that decisions involving our suitors should be made with care," she said. "Fer I have one to make, as well."

"Do ye?" He wanted to take her in his arms and kiss the fire from her lips.

She nodded. "The queen has chosen two possible husbands fer me, and I must decide which one I would prefer. Lord Oxford or yer friend Captain Sedley."

Connor wanted to laugh and give her the point, but something in her expression stilled his heart. She was speaking the truth. No! No way in hell!

"Sedley!" he roared, startling two horses being led

away by their grooms. Mairi, too, took a step back, but he reached out and snatched her back. When Sedley appeared at his side, he ordered him to follow while he pulled Mairi toward the palace doors.

"Where are we going, Grant?"

"To the queen."

Chapter Fifteen

Connor didn't slow his pace until he found his father in the Shield Gallery and deposited Mairi into his hands. At least, his father would keep Oxford away from her until he returned. When he reached the queen's Privy Chamber with Sedley, he commanded to the two lesser-ranked guardsmen at her door to announce him—and be quick about it.

After a moment, he was admitted an audience and strode inside, pulling Sedley with him. Both bowed before the queen's table, where she sat penning a letter.

"You look agitated, Captain Grant," she said after sparing him a glance and blowing on her parchment. "What troubles you?"

There was no polite way around this—or, at least, he hadn't thought of one on his way up here. He folded his hands behind his back and harnessed the storm roiling within him. She was the queen and he would conduct himself with courtesy. "Yer Majesty, I would speak to ye about Miss MacGregor and her future."

"Continue."

"I understand that ye are considering giving her hand away in marriage to either Lord Oxford or Captain Sedley."

Sedley looked stunned and mildly ill when he looked up at him.

"That is correct."

Connor felt like a cannonball had blown a hole through his middle. "Captain Sedley respectively refuses."

Mary of Modena didn't even try to suppress the smile creeping over her lips. "Why would he refuse? She is a lovely woman with—"

"Because he is already betrothed."

When Sedley looked about to laugh at the ridiculous falsehood, Connor's hard gaze warned him not to.

"I was not aware." The queen offered Nick an apologetic smile. He was about to open his mouth, but Connor spoke for him.

"Aye, to a kindhearted lass in Holland. She eagerly awaits his return."

Sedley shrugged, and then nodded his agreement.

"Well, that makes things a bit more difficult, does it not?" The queen reclined in her seat and picked a mote from her puffed, elbow-length sleeves. "The matter is settled then. Miss MacGregor will wed Lord Oxford."

"She cannot wed him either."

Mary of Modena stopped grooming herself and cast him an impatient look. "Captain, is the Earl of Oxford's son betrothed, as well?"

"He's a Protestant. Mairi hates Protestants. She will not find happiness with him."

"She appears happy enough to me when she is with him."

"She does not love him."

Now the queen laughed and shook her head at him.

"What does love have to do with marriage?" Before he answered, she narrowed her eyes on him. "Did she ask you to come to me and plead on her behalf?"

"She did not."

"Then why, Captain Grant, are you here in my chambers, out of uniform…"

He realized only then that he had left his military coat in the tiltyard.

"…arguing with the queen about something that does not concern you? You are dismissed."

"Yer Majesty—"

"Good day, Captain." She picked up her quill and went back to her letter.

"Come, Connor," Sedley said softly, placing his hand on Connor's forearm. "Come now."

Nick closed the door behind him and tossed his arm around Connor's shoulder. "Betrothed, eh? What a terrifying thought. You couldn't have simply told her the truth then? That I'm a rakehell who will only break your Miss MacGregor's heart?"

Connor shook his head while they walked the long corridor. "Not a sound enough reason. And just so ye know, she is not my—hell, there's Lady Elizabeth." He ducked behind the stairs to avoid her seeing him.

Nick laughed at him when he reappeared. "Then you're not escorting her to St. James's Park?"

"Ye take her."

"But I'm betrothed!"

Connor was tempted to hit him over the head with his sword.

"Let's go to the tavern and have a drink. I'll pay since you saved me from having to wed the woman you're still pining over."

Connor thought about arguing that last point over with him, but what was the use. It was the truth. "Later," he said instead. First, he wanted to find Mairi and tell her she wasn't marrying Sedley or Oxford. If she did, it would be over his dead body, or more likely, over theirs.

"He is going to hate me." Claire Stuart left the concealment of a thick brocade curtain and dropped into the nearest chair.

"Not if all goes as planned." The queen crumbled her parchment and tossed it into the hearth fire. There was nothing but scribble on it anyway.

"And if it doesn't? What if he decides he doesn't want to fight to win her back? If he believes there is no purpose in it, he might—"

"He will fight for her."

Claire smiled at the door, thinking of her son and knowing him well. "Aye, I knew he loved her still. I tell you I've never heard such fear in my son's voice as when you dismissed him." They both giggled. "He is so stubborn. He will not tell her how he feels, and yet he can't let her go. She is the same."

"That is where Oxford and his sister will aid. We need not do anything to foster Henry de Vere's affections toward Mairi. He is already taken with her. Very soon now, Captain Grant should make a bold move. As for your Miss MacGregor, did you note the rage in her eyes when she saw Oxford's sister flung over the captain's shoulder?"

Claire nodded, and they laughed again before the queen continued.

"Captain Sedley did what I asked of him and twice brought Elizabeth de Vere to your son. The girl did the rest on her own."

"She is already chasing Connor," Claire agreed.

"Your son is a very handsome man."

They exchanged a smile. "I was truly astonished," Claire said a moment later, "by Captain Sedley's ability to pretend surprise when he learned of his intended marriage to Mairi. I wasn't sure he would help us. He has known Connor for many years, but it's difficult to trust completely anyone who lies so effortlessly."

"But, Lady Huntley," the queen pointed out, her dark eyes gleaming with mischief. "We are no better, and to your own son!"

"Hell, that is true," Claire agreed again. "But it is for his own good. He and Mairi are meant to be together."

"And we will help them see it more clearly."

Och, but Claire was glad she had come to England, glad she had met this pleasant, clever woman who was willing to help her and enjoying it immensely. If all went as planned, in a few months she would be planning the wedding of two of the people she loved most in the world.

Relief washed over Connor when he found Mairi where he'd left her—at his father's side. At least she wasn't with the man who could possibly be her future husband. Like hell, he told himself, forging on toward her.

"I wish to have a word with ye," he told her when he reached them. He spared his father a brief nod of thanks for not letting her wander off then turned his gaze on her once more. "'Twill take but a moment of yer time."

She looked about to refuse him but then reconsidered when he hardened his jaw, daring her to do so.

"Verra well, speak."

"Not here." Without another word, he grasped her

hand and pulled her toward a shadowy alcove a few feet from the strolling guests.

He hadn't thought of what he was going to say to her on his way there, which was why, the instant they were alone he foolishly said, "Ye're not marrying Oxford."

He knew when her raven brow arched that he had begun the wrong way.

"I spoke to the queen."

"Did ye?" Her lips curled into a rapier thin smile. "And what about Captain Sedley?"

He shook his head, certain that opening his mouth would only cause further damage.

"Should I thank ye then fer sentencing me to the life of a maiden in my old age? Will ye ride off to Skye next and ask my faither not to let me wed Hamish MacLeod or Duncan MacKinnon?"

Hamish MacLeod? "Duncan MacKinnon asked fer yer hand?" he asked, unprepared for the rush of fury—and raw panic—that washed over him. "How long ago? Why didn't yer brother tell me in his letters?"

Her eyes opened wider on him. "Tristan penned ye letters?"

Hell, he should have thought this speech through before engaging in it with her. But since when could he not control his mouth? "Not fer a while now," he amended.

"Letters about me?"

This time he took a short breath, trying to proceed more delicately. The last thing he wanted her to know was that he'd never stopped asking about her. "They were not always about ye." When her eyes narrowed on him, he dipped his gaze to her hands, expecting to find a dagger in each one. "I simply wanted to know if ye were happy."

"Ye lost that right to know. Just like ye have no right

to try to step into my life now and make decisions fer me that dinna' concern ye!" Her voice rose as she spoke, drawing the attention of the Earl of Essex and his wife while they studied a painting at the end of the hall.

She spoke more quietly but with even more conviction when she continued. "I will wed who I want and neither ye nor the queen will change that."

"Ye would wed a Protestant then?" he challenged, truly wanting to throttle her pretty neck. She likely would wed anyone simply to anger him. "Because if ye would"—he cut her off when she would have answered—"then 'tis ye who betrays Scotland, not I."

Her mouth opened, but for a moment no words came out, then, "Me? A traitor to Scotland? I am the one who fights to preserve it while ye fight to preserve kings who refuse to do—"

"What do ye mean, ye fight?" Hell, the daggers, the spying... When her lips snapped shut his heart crashed to his belly. He repeated his question, hoping for a different reply from the one he suspected. "Does yer faither know about this?"

"I am through speaking with ye, Connor."

His fingers around her arm stopped her when she tried to step around him to leave. The warning glare in his eyes prompted her to give him an answer.

"All right then," she said, yanking her arm free. "I've been in a few skirmishes with some Cameronians, that is all. Nothing that would do him any good to know about."

Och, hell. He rubbed his hand over his stubbled jaw and closed his eyes to gather back the control he needed not to shout at her. "Skirmishes involving weapons?"

"Ye wouldna' go into one without a weapon, Connor," she said as if he should know, being a captain after all, then let out a slight, frustrated sigh. "Nothing overly dangerous...or frequent. There are not many Cameronians left beyond Edinburgh. The last time I used my blade was this past spring outside of Glen Garry."

Connor couldn't believe what he was hearing. She'd always been interested in the sword, even training under his mother's tutelage. But never, never would he have imagined her to be so foolish as to...He couldn't even think it. Mairi, fighting against men bent on killing her. Satan's balls, she *had* gone mad.

Chapter Sixteen

*H*enry de Vere leaned his back against the cold stone wall a few inches from where Mairi and Captain Grant whispered in the shadows. His heart beat frantically in his chest, and, with each beat, it broke again and again. He touched his fingers to the scar disfiguring his face. No, he had to have heard wrong. Mairi could not have done this to him.

He had to move. He no longer cared to hear what they were saying to each other. He had to flee before they saw him. He had to think, to consider what it meant and what he should do about it.

Leaving the Shield Gallery, he made his way slowly toward the stairs. His legs felt weak, his arms heavy, his face...

She had beguiled him with smiles no other woman would bestow upon him. Because of her. Oh, how could he not have recognized that silky, husky voice? He thought he would never forget it—or her eyes, so vividly blue and cold as she sliced open his face in Glen Garry last spring.

On his father's orders he had attended a secret meeting held by a group of Cameronians who had begun to fear that Charles might grant the kingdom to his Catholic brother, James. They had been correct…and they had also been discovered.

The night had been black and the road even darker, but he had sworn to himself that he would never forget those eyes below her hooded and masked face. Poor Edgar, his coachman, had reached around his shoulder and shone down his torch on the small group that had come upon them. She flung her blade and killed Edgar instantly. Henry knew he should not have left the carriage. He regretted his bravery every day since.

He'd moved quickly in his rage, knowing exactly where she stood when Edgar's torch died with him. In the darkness he reached her before she or her comrades could stop him and slapped her face hard with his glove.

She couldn't see him else the second dagger she produced would not have missed when she swung at his throat. Though the strike was not a lethal one, he went down clutching his bloody face.

"Traitorous dog," she had spat at him before she hurried away. "'Tis a shame ye willna' live to warn the others that we are coming fer them next."

She thought she'd killed him. He wished she had, instead of leaving him mangled and terrifying to look upon.

Mairi.

He'd wanted her from the instant he saw her at Whitehall, so proud and confident, while the other women in the palace reviled her and her Highland dress—just as they reviled him. She was the most beautiful woman he'd ever seen, and when she smiled at him, unfazed by his ugliness, he'd nearly dropped to his knees before her.

"No," he croaked, tearing his wig from his head. It

couldn't have been his kind, compassionate Mairi who had done this to him.

"Henry?"

He turned at his sister's voice. He didn't want to speak to her now. No doubt she would do all the talking—about her handsome Captain Grant. That bastard had had his eyes on Mairi since he'd arrived.

"You look terrible."

He didn't need to be reminded. "I'm off to bed, Lizzy."

"But it's the middle of the day!" she called out as he turned from her again. "Are you ill? I hope you have not picked up some malady from that little Highland trollop of yours."

"She's not a trollop," he defended rather weakly, since Mairi did swoon over Grant the way the rest of them did. She claimed she didn't care for him, but every time he was in view—which was all the damned time—her eyes always darted back to him. And who the hell did Grant think he was carrying her out of the sun and away from his family yesterday? Why, Henry wanted to strike him for being so bold. Why hadn't Mairi done it for him if she didn't like the bastard as she claimed?

"Henry, are you going to answer me or just stand there looking miserable?"

He blinked at Lizzy. Should he tell her that it was Mairi had who scarred him? He needed someone to talk to, someone he trusted to give him advice as to what to do about it. Should he go to his father and tell him that Mairi MacGregor killed Cameronians in her spare time? Perhaps tell the Duke of Queensberry? Pen a missive to the Duke of Monmouth himself? What if they wanted him to kill her? Could he do it? "Lizzy, there is something I wish to speak to you about. I need—"

"Have you seen Captain Grant?" she asked, interrupting him, her eyes scanning the gallery below. "He was going to take me to St. James's Park, but he seems to have disappeared."

Henry's expression darkened on her. Even his sister couldn't keep her thoughts off the golden-haired rogue. It fired his blood and made him clench his jaw. He knew his scar appeared more pronounced when he was agitated. He didn't care.

"Elizabeth, I think your captain favors another."

Her eyes opened wider and grew moist instantly. He felt only mildly remorseful at his words. Why should he be the only one to suffer? Lizzy would get over Grant. She was still beautiful, after all. Unlike him.

"Who?" she demanded, her lips tightening. "You will tell me this instant who he favors." Her voice rose to a quivering pitch. When she took a step toward him, he dropped his wig to the floor, freeing his hands if he had to defend himself. His sister sported a hellish temper and had struck him before when she didn't get her way.

"It is Miss MacGregor," he blurted. "They are together right now."

She stopped, her jaw falling open and then growing taut again. For an instant, Henry thought she might fling back her head and commence screaming. She seemed to pull herself together instead and offered him a steely smile.

"That is the reason for your gloom, is it not?" She shook her head at him in disgust. "You care for her and this is how she repays you? What are you going to do about it, Henry?"

"What can I do?"

She bent to pick up his wig and handed it back to

him. "Poor Henry. You lost so much more than your handsome face when you were attacked. You used to be so cocksure and determined to get what you wanted." She moved closer, her breath falling against the sensitive flesh of his scar. "If there is still the heart of a man beating somewhere within you, brother, then take her to your bed and show her, and if she still doesn't want you after that, kill her."

He drew back with a short breath. How many nights had he dreamed of killing the bitch that had done this to him? Dreamed of finding her and peeling off her mask to behold her face before he ran his blade over it and then snapped her neck?

"Come now." His sister chuckled against his ear. "I know what you did to that peasant girl in Nottingham two winters past after she told all that she carried your bastard."

He closed his eyes, remembering. He couldn't do the same to Mairi. She may have done this to him, but she was kind to him. She favored him. He was certain of it. Him and Grant. Perhaps Mairi wasn't the one who needed killing.

"Do something about her, Henry," Lizzy warned quietly, and placed a soft kiss on his face before she stepped away. "Or I will."

Connor stopped Mairi before she entered the Privy Garden. He wasn't finished speaking with her, even though she believed otherwise. She hadn't promised him not to wed Oxford—or either of her Highland suitors, but worse than that, she didn't seem concerned in the least about the possible consequences of facing men in battle—or here in Whitehall for that matter. His skin grew cold at the memory of her laughing and dancing with Queensberry and then stealing into his room to rummage through his possessions.

"Who else knows that ye've been ambushing Cameronians in their own homes, Mairi?"

"Homes where they were holding secret meetings with members of the old Parliament. Might I remind ye that under Richard Cameron, they renounced their allegiance to Charles and denounced James as a papist. Now they are trying to gather recruits in the north. Someone has got to stop them, Connor."

"Was levying fines upon those who did not attend government-approved churches, or hiring Highland mercenaries to plunder their shires, not enough then, Mairi?" Connor asked her forcefully. "Was it right to authorize field executions without trial?" He looked away and lowered his voice so that she almost did not hear him. "Leave the extermination of an entire populace to the king and his army, lest ye stain yer hands with blood that can never be removed."

"Ye sound compassionate to them, Connor. I wonder, does the king know that ye side with his enemies?"

Damn her, how could she think so little of him? "He knows that I took part in the executions, Mairi. A part I regret, whether ye like to hear that or not."

"But they were traitors to the king ye served fer seven years!"

"Aye, they were," he agreed quietly. "But they were also men who simply believed another way. That made them outlaws, and as yer father and mine know all too well, outlaws are not tolerated by the government."

"But this is different," she argued. "My kin fought fer their basic human rights, they didna' seek to change the church. We are hated because we are Catholic."

"Aye, and our hatred fer Protestants makes us no better."

She was quiet for a moment, as if considering his words. He prayed she listened to him. She had no idea what having so much blood on her hands would do to her heart. Worse, she would be killed eventually if she continued fighting. Hell, when had she become so hard? What had become of the lass who wanted nothing more than a quiet life with her kin and a husband who adored her?

"Why did I tell ye anything?" She moved to leave him, warning him over her shoulder, "If ye breathe a word of it to anyone, I swear I will kill ye while ye sleep."

"Unlike ye," he said, reaching her again, "I would never put yer life in jeopardy."

"Not even to the Prince of Orange?" she asked, flicking him a brief scalding gaze.

That did it. He snatched her hand and pulled her to a skidding halt. He was tired of her accusing him of betraying her, betraying Scotland. "Though I sympathize with any who are persecuted fer what they believe, I am not in league with William, Mairi. Hell, ye know me better than that."

He felt his heart skip in his chest when she turned to face him fully, her eyes wide, haunted by memories she tried to forget.

"I dinna' know ye at all, Connor."

"Aye, ye do. Ye're just too damned stubborn to realize it. I would never do anything to hurt ye."

"'Tis too late fer that, is it not?"

"And what of ye?" he charged just as meaningfully. "Do ye think I've been happy all these years without ye?"

Something in her expression changed, softened on him just enough to make his heart exalt in it. But he wouldn't admit anything else to her. She would likely laugh in his face, knowing with the same certainty that was beginning to plague him every time he was near her, that he was foolish enough to still love her.

"Who else knows, Mairi?"

Her gaze on him narrowed and she pulled her hand free of his. "Yer mother knows, so if ye mean to tell anyone, including my faither, remember that, I pray ye."

He watched her storm away, wanting to call her back, wanting to tell her that she had meant more to him than any king or any damned patch of land he ruled over.

She still did.

He turned instead toward the sundial where his mother stood speaking with Lord Douglas of Paisley. There was much he didn't know about Mairi since he had left Camlochlin. He was about to change that.

Chapter Seventeen

*M*airi despised weeping. She hadn't done so in almost seven years. After six months of crying over him after he left, she'd vowed never to shed another tear over him. But, and by God, she couldn't believe her own weakness, there were tears streaming down her face. And all because Connor had asked her if she thought he was happy without her. Because in that moment he looked as wretched as she'd felt for a year after he left. She had never considered that he wasn't happy here... without her. She swiped her cheeks. He'd chosen this life, duty or not. Aye, it was true that she had commanded him to stay away, but she'd never expected him to truly do it. Was he unhappy? Why didn't he tell her if he was instead of going back to ordering answers from her she didn't want to give him? What if he spoke his pretty words only to soften her into telling him about the militia? Och, God, he sympathized with Covenanters! Still, his reasons why were understandable. She'd heard about the field executions decreed by late King Charles. They were said to be so bloody that even James disapproved. Connor had taken part in those massacres. She shivered, admitting to herself that murdering entire shires of people, whether Covenanters, Cameronians, or Catholics, was wrong. Was Connor tired of fighting and killing? Was he finally ready to end his service to the Stuarts and come home? And God, what if he did return to Camlochlin? How would she live every day with him there, dressed in his plaid, his smile wide and resplendent while the wind streamed through his hair and carried his laughter across the braes? What if he took a Highland wife? What if he wanted her back?

Why hadn't Tristan ever told her that Connor asked about her in his letters? Would it have made a difference? Och, how was it that she could face a dozen sword-wielding men but a few simple words from Connor, the thought that he could love her again, could still bring her to her knees?

Her head was beginning to pain her from all the questions swirling about within. She didn't want to think. She didn't want to lose herself to him again. Losing him had been too painful. It frightened her...and she hated being afraid. She hated weeping even more.

She heard the muffled sound of men's voices coming from behind a tall, gilded statue of a winged angel. The Dutch inflection was hard to miss. Prince William. Here was what she should be contemplating. Thanks to visits to Camlochlin from Claire's brother, High Admiral Connor Stuart, she and Colin had learned much about King James's son by marriage. William, a sovereign prince by birth, governed as stadtholder over Holland and many provinces of the Dutch republic. While he had outwardly maintained goodwill with his uncles, Charles and James, there had been much dissention between them. Their battle was a religious one, with Anglican England and France the victors of most. A staunch Calvinist Protestant, William had not surrendered his faith but rebuilt his army and stood alone against two of the world's greatest powers.

Mairi had overhead some at Whitehall whispering of his courage and determination. Aye, she had to admit, he deserved such accolades, but he was clever, as well. For he had put an end to the war by marrying his uncle's daughter and establishing a pact between the Netherlands and England.

But William did not attend his father-in-law's coronation to celebrate. Holland's faithful had suffered harshly at the tips of Catholic's blades, and now there was a Catholic king on the throne. William had much to fear, but it was French King Louis who at present remained the sharpest thorn in his side. William hoped to gain James's support in an anti-French alliance. It was likely never going to happen, especially after the attack on the abbey.

She moved closer to the statue, pretending to examine it.

"...doesn't know anything about the meeting with Parliament being called early."

Was that Lord Oddington's voice behind the angel's foot? It didn't matter. The queen's defense of her husband's disappearance was being investigated. This didn't bode well for Colin and the king on their way to Camlochlin.

"The tracks disappeared just outside of London, so we don't know which way they rode."

It was Oddington, the treasonous bastard, Mairi decided while she smiled at Colin's craftiness at covering his tracks. At least William didn't know where they were heading.

Inclining her ear, she moved closer to the angel, and

then stopped abruptly and looked up into Prince William's dark eyes.

"Miss MacGregor, did you misplace something?"

She shook her head no and smiled at him. "I was—"

"How long have you been standing here?"

Mairi had faced many of her enemies over the last few years, but none of them was as dangerous, or as intelligent, as this one. His thin lips were taut beneath his enormous nose, the threat in his eyes unmistakable. She tried to slow her pulse, but this man had very well likely ordered nuns to be burned to death, and presently he looked like he wished she were among them.

"There ye are, Miss MacGregor. I hope I didn't keep ye waiting too long."

She turned, more relieved to see Connor than she would ever admit. "Nae, Captain, I just arrived."

His dimples flashed when she offered him a pleasant smile, and made her pulse race all the more.

"Yer Grace," Connor greeted, coming to stand in between them. "How are ye enjoying yer stay here at Whitehall?"

"In truth, Captain," the prince said, taking a step back so that he wasn't craning his neck to look up at the Highlander practically looming over him, "I would enjoy a bit more privacy."

Connor flicked his gaze around the statue, but Oddington was gone.

"Good day," William bid them, letting his gaze linger on Mairi positioned slightly behind Connor's back, before he turned and left.

When they were alone, Connor inhaled a deep breath before turning to her. Mairi looked up into his eyes, reading the fear and anger in them clearly enough to know he was summoning his control before he spoke to her. If he was in cahoots with the Dutch prince, he certainly didn't look like it now.

"What the hell are ye trying to do?"

"I am not trying to do anything. I stumbled upon them."

"Who?"

"The prince and Lord Oddington."

He scowled, looking even more beguiling. "Ye were eavesdropping. I was watching ye—"

She stopped listening and considered him for a moment. He watched her often. No matter what she was doing, she could feel his eyes on her. At first it had angered her, especially after he'd followed her into Queensberry's rooms. She didn't need looking after, but was there another reason his gaze followed her wherever she went? Mayhap her snug-fitting English attire? Her heart flipped in her chest and she cursed the madness of her thoughts.

"I dinna' like being spied upon," she said, before she said something else like "Why did ye leave me? I nearly perished without ye!"

"Neither does the prince."

She nodded, giving him the point. Hell, he was big, and so virile standing there with the sun gleaming off the golden strands of his hair. She would have been insulted if any other man had stepped in front of her as if to protect her, but Connor made her feel delicate—he always had—and she missed feeling that way. Damn her.

"He looked angry."

Mairi blinked, gazing into his eyes. "Who?"

"The prince." His lips curled just enough to aim his right dimple at her.

"So did ye."

"I was smiling."

But she knew each one of his smiles and the one he offered William was anything but amiable. What would he have done if the prince had laid hands on her? She shook her head to scatter her childish fancies. So mayhap he wasn't secretly aligned with Protestants. That was no reason to smile at him now.

"They suspect the king didna' go to Edinburgh." She looked away from the need she told herself she saw in his eyes, or mayhap it was the need in her own eyes that she didn't want him to see.

"What did ye hear?" His tone went serious instantly, drawing her gaze back to him.

"Oddington told him they searched fer tracks. They didna' find any," she added when his jaw tightened. "But at least we know fer certain that Lord Oddington stands with William."

"In what?" Connor pointed out. "Suspecting that the queen was untruthful? It means nothing."

"Then we can—"

"Nae," he cut her off. "*We* can do nothing. Ye will quit whatever ye're doing here and leave the king's enemies to his men."

She did not hear what he said after that. She stood there staring at him, feeling her blood boil in her veins. If there was one thing she despised even more than Cameronians, it was being told she could not or should not do something because she was a woman.

"Would ye have me sew ye a pair of hose fer the remainder of my stay then?"

If he heard the sting in her voice, he seemed not to care in the least. When he nodded, she looked around at the ground for something to fling at his head.

"Fighting a few Cameronians is bad enough, Mairi,

but traipsing around the toes of a man who we both believe ordered the death of over a score of nuns is quite a different matter."

"Because I am a lass."

His gaze fell to her fingers clenched tight at her sides, then returned to her steady, challenging stare. He grinned, making light of her anger—which angered her all the more. "There is nothing wrong with being a lass, Mairi, especially when ye do it so well."

"Mayhap I would mind being a lass less if I spent more time around a man who was at least *aware* of his knuckles when he tripped over them."

His smile deepened into something more primitive and dangerous as he moved toward her. "Do ye wish me to apologize fer worrying over ye then?"

He moved toward her, a powerful force robbing her of breath, of reason. She would not step back. "Why would I want that when yer apology is laced with more insult. Honestly, Connor, being in England has turned ye into an antiquated—"

His hand closed around her upper arm and in one fluid movement he swung her around the back of the statue and into his arms. He kissed her, quieting her protests, angling his head to deepen the thrust of his tongue. In an instant she was lost. Och, she did not mind being a woman to a man who kissed like this. She was still angry with him though and bit his lip to remind him that she was not completely defeated.

He pulled back, dragging his hand across his bloody mouth. His eyes gleamed with an unholy fire that promised he was about to do much more than kiss her. This time, she stepped back and held out her palms when he came at her again.

"If ye kiss me again without leave, I swear I will—"

The remainder of her threat was vanquished by his mouth, his tongue, his strong arms closing around her. She couldn't fight him. She didn't want to. Mad, pitiful fool that she was.

Chapter Eighteen

The Troubadour was less crowded this afternoon than it had been the last time Connor was here. The stench of stale wine and ale so early in the day assaulted his senses and made his stomach tighten, but he needed an hour or two to figure out what he should do, what he *could* do, to stop the queen from wedding Mairi to Oxford. Hell, he had to do something. He wanted her back in his life, and this time he wasn't letting her go without a fight.

She still hadn't agreed not to wed the bastard, even after their passionate kiss yesterday in the garden. He smiled recalling how furious she'd been when he pulled her out of sight and kissed her. She hadn't seemed so angry the second time. He might be a fool, but he didn't believe that she hated him, at least her mouth didn't give any indication, nor did her arms when they coiled around his neck and nearly buckled his knees.

He sat at one of the empty tables stained by wet cups and spilled drinks and gave the place one last looking over. He smiled at Vicky, then looked away from her to stop her advance. He didn't see the woman who had offered him a night's pleasure the last time he was there. He didn't know her or how she knew his name, but he couldn't keep his thoughts on her longer than an instant before Mairi pushed her way into his head again.

He still wanted to strangle her for taking up arms in one of England's many religious wars, but at least, according to his mother when he questioned her, Mairi was well skilled with a blade and had always returned from her skirmishes unscathed.

Connor had nothing against women wielding a blade. Almost every woman at Camlochlin knew how to swing one, thanks to his mother and Mairi's, both being skilled swordswomen before they knew how to sew. But the thought of Mairi in real combat stilled the blood in his veins.

How the hell could she hate Protestants so much and still consider marrying one?

"Here you are!" Nick Sedley swept into the chair beside him and called out for two ales. "I looked for you in the tiltyard. You used to train everyday. Peace is softening you."

Connor laughed and pulled at the damp military jacket clinging to his chest. "I've been practicing since dawn, while you were still dreaming."

"Ah, but I wasn't dreaming at dawn," Sedley countered, reaching out for and missing the serving wench laying down their drinks and then scurrying away. "I was actually engaging in what you were thinking about when you laid down your head alone in your bed last evening."

Connor raised his cup, giving him the point. "Why were ye looking for me?"

"Ah yes, that." Sedley took a hearty drink from his

cup and then sat back in his chair. "I was curious about something and I thought you might aid."

"Curious about what?"

"I thought since you are acquainted with Miss Mac-Gregor you might know why the king took her brother to Edinburgh with him and not his own captain."

Connor looked at him. Hell. Had William of Orange sent his captain to question him? Since when was Nick curious about anything other than the next lass in his bed? And why did he assume Colin had gone with the king? The queen hadn't mentioned it, though William likely suspected it since Colin was gone. That would mean the prince was more aware of Whitehall's guests than he let on.

No one can be trusted here. Mairi's disturbing warning rang through Connor's head again. As much as he didn't want her to be correct, he knew that she was. She would have made a fine tactical soldier were she a man.

"'Tis peacetime," Connor told him benignly. "The king travels with another captain and General Gilbert's men. Should he have taken his entire army to meet with Parliament?"

Sedley chuckled. "It might be amusing to watch all those lords soil their breeches at the sight. It is odd though…"

"What's that?" Connor asked, watching him more closely now and hoping he was wrong.

"There are some here who should be at that meeting with Parliament, but are not."

"Aye, that is odd." Damn it, Connor thought sourly, his old friend was indeed doing William's bidding. "I cannot presume to know the answer to that. You will have to ask the king when he returns."

This time, Sedley raised his cup to Connor, giving *him* the point. They both knew full well that soldiers didn't question kings. "Oh, by the way," he said behind the rim of his cup, "I thought you might like to know that your Miss MacGregor left Whitehall."

"What?" Connor sat forward in his chair, about to leap from it. "Where did she go?"

"To St. James's Park, I believe. With Lord Oxford."

The table screeched against the rushes as Connor pushed it out of his way and ran for the door.

Connor wanted to smash his fist through a few heads as he strode toward Whitehall's stables to retrieve his horse. How could she do it? How could she go with him? He knew the last thing he should do was follow her. It would only prove to her what a jealous fool he was. Unless, of course, Oxford was kissing her. If he was, Connor didn't care what Mairi thought of him. Oxford was going to lose his teeth.

He narrowly avoided Lady Hollingsworth on her way out of the stables and leaped upon the first horse he found saddled, drove his heels into the beast's flanks, and flew past the East Gate.

It didn't take him long to reach the fifty-eight-acre private park. Finding Mairi without her seeing him would be more difficult. He didn't intend to spy on her. Not really. He simply wanted to discover if she'd truly given her heart to the English noble. Watching them alone would tell him. But did he want to know? He swore if she was giggling with Oxford on some cozy blanket he would walk away from her forever. Saints strengthen his pitiful heart but he hoped, he prayed he wouldn't find her giggling.

Almost reluctantly, he searched for her along sunny paths and through thick columns of walnut and majestic oak trees, vaguely aware of the jays singing overhead or the laughter coming from any of the blankets laid out in the grass that did not belong to Mairi.

Just when he thought he might not find them, he did. They stood at the edge of a small bridge, just beyond the trees that gave him cover, looking over the side into the narrow canal below. Careful not to make a sound, he dismounted and moved a bit closer, keeping out of sight behind a tree.

Oxford was pointing at something in the water that made her smile. Damn it to hell.

What was he doing there? How could he allow her to turn him into some watered-down dolt? He led men into battle, for hell's sake! Kings trusted him to face their enemies with a stout, courageous heart, a mind and body in complete control. The three had never failed him, until Mairi stepped back into his life.

He should leave. If she was happy and Oxford was whom she wanted, he should go and wish her well. But he couldn't bring himself to move. He watched her as if she were a dream that had come to life. How many times had he gazed at her profile against the backdrop of an azure sky or a wild, open glen painted in purple? He knew the curve of her pert nose, the tantalizing dip of her full lower lip, better than he knew the path home. When she leaned over the edge, his gaze slipped to her backside and he drew in a silent, starving breath. Every woman he'd been with after he left Camlochlin had left him cold. But Mairi sparked his passion with a simple quirk of her lips, the bite of her tongue...and her teeth. He brought his fingers to his lower lip, still a bit swollen from where she drew blood yesterday. He loved her vivacity and her sharp, sometimes merciless wit, but he missed her laughter. He missed the way she used to look at him, as if the sun rose when she saw him. Could he win her back? He smiled when she moved her arm away from Oxford's touch. To hell with being a fool. She was worth it.

The sharp snap of a twig behind him made him turn, but it was too late. He saw only a shadow and then darkness as he slumped to the ground.

"Are you certain 'tis him. Linnet?" The man standing over Connor's fallen body looked at his sister and dropped the rock he'd used to hit him. "There are a lot of captains here."

Linnet slipped her hood off her head and bent quickly to have a better look at him. God's teeth, but he was handsome. She remembered the way he'd smiled at her that night at The Troubadour, those deep dimples beguiling her senseless. Pity, she sighed and rose to her feet. "It's him."

"What should we do with him?"

"Kill him, as we were paid to do." She looked through the thick tangle of branches at what the captain had been looking at before they came upon him. "We cannot leave him here. Bring him to the alley behind The Troubadour and dump him there. Check his clothes. If he carries anything on his person, take it. It will appear to have been a robbery."

"What if he has no coin?"

She gave her brother a look of impatience. "Then take his boots. And, Harry," she said before she left him, "have a care."

She didn't remain behind to watch her brother sink his

dagger into the captain's belly. She wasn't at all happy about what they had done, despite the amount of coin they'd received to see the task through. Killing a soldier in the king's Royal Army was punishable by hanging. Oh, God, please, don't let her get caught. She knew the man who'd paid her would not come to her rescue if she was. She was not foolish enough to believe his whispered words of affection while she lay with him were true. He'd used her to do his bidding. But she had used him, as well. She needed coin to get Harry out of London before the bodies of the two prostitutes he had killed were discovered. Damn him anyway for his depraved sexual appetite. She should leave London alone and let him suffer the consequences of his deeds, but she had promised their father that she would look after him.

She sighed, thinking of the purse hidden beneath her skirts, and smiled at the tinkle of coin. It could take her to France if she traveled alone. She thought about it as she left the park. She wasn't Harry's mother, after all.

Chapter Nineteen

Tennis was an odd game, Mairi thought, while she fanned herself in her seat. There was nothing like it played at Camlochlin. It appeared quite strenuous, with players running to receive a ball that was tightly wound with cloth strips and driving it back again with strange little rackets fashioned from ash wood. While he was here, her father complained that the game served no purpose but to make a man sweat, and he would rather do that while honing his battle skills.

Hell, but she missed him, and her mother too. She missed Rob and her aunt Maggie—and even Tristan.

She smiled when Claire earned a point over Lady Margaret, Lord Ashley's daughter.

"Are you enjoying the game, my dear?" the queen, sitting beside her, asked.

"Aye, but it seems unnecessarily taxing in this heat."

"It's the high walls," Mary of Modena agreed, looking up. "They block the spring breeze. You are not going to fall faint again are you?"

Mairi shook her head, mortified all over again by the

memory of Connor carrying her out of the sun. Where was he anyway? She had not seen him since this morning in the lists. She knew he wasn't with Lady Elizabeth because the pinched-lipped little trollop was sitting at the other end of the court.

Dear Lord, but it had been a trying afternoon. She had agreed to ride to St. James's Park with Henry after he practically begged her for over an hour. She hadn't wanted to go, but she conceded, deciding it best to tell him away from court that she didn't favor him the way he so obviously hoped. She hadn't been able to do it though, not when he spent the entire afternoon telling her how his life had changed after his accident. She'd never thought to ask him how his face came to be so disfigured. It didn't bother her, since many of the men at home bore similar scars. But poor Henry hadn't earned his scar in battle. His cousin had inflicted the wound in practice. Thankfully, there resided a skilled healer at his father's castle, and she'd put Henry's face back together as best she could. Sadly though, there was little she could do about the ladies who spurned him from then on or the feelings of inadequacy he suffered. Mairi was the only one, according to Henry, who showed him kindness. How could she break his heart after that?

She had to tell him soon though. She wouldn't tell him that she would likely spend her later years as miserable and alone as he, or that Connor Grant was the reason for it. How could she wed another after Connor had kissed her, held her, loved her before any other? Dear God in heaven, but his kisses ignited fires in her that were a thousand times more deadly than they had been before he left Camlochlin. He was no longer a boy and he no longer kissed like one. The question that pricked her like an irritating nettle caught in her boot was how many lasses had he practiced on? Och, but when he kissed her, she didn't care.

She knew, after only a se'nnight with him, that no other man could ever make her happy. No other man would stand up to her the way Connor did, so confident and cocksure of himself. Damnation, it was attractive. As much as she hated to admit it, and, och, she hated to, part of her heart still longed for the bastard.

"Are you certain you are well, my dear?" the queen asked her, pulling Mairi's attention back to the game. "You are fanning yourself hard enough to strain your wrist."

"I am fine, truly," she assured her hostess with a gracious smile. "The thinner gowns help. I fear, though, that they will be of no use to me when I return home."

The queen clapped her hands when Claire earned another point. "She's quite good."

Mairi agreed, watching Claire swing her racket around like a blade going for a Royalist's throat. Compared to their petite queen, who took more enjoyment watching her guests play tennis and bowl on the green than actually competing in the games herself, Claire Stuart was a force to be reckoned with.

"Ye should see her wield a sword," Mairi said with a measure of pride squaring her shoulders.

"Yes, I heard that she once fought alongside her brother. It is not so difficult to believe when I see her vigor with my own eyes. With all the practicing her son does in the lists every day, it is obvious that he shares the same love of the blade."

Mairi shifted slightly in her seat. "His father, along with my own, made certain that he practiced daily. He is an excellent swordsman."

"Thankfully, I have yet to see him fight. The king, however, remembers him during the Rye House Plot, when conspirators planned to murder him and his brother Charles. Captain Grant was the first to capture and arrest Lord William Russell, one of those implicated in the plot. The late king thought very highly of him."

Word had reached Camlochlin two years ago about Connor's prowess at catching one of the conspirators. It had not surprised Mairi that Connor risked his life to protect his royal cousin. It had angered her though. Whether she hated him or not, she did not want him to die. The mere thought of it had near set her to tears for a full two days.

"He is loyal to the throne, Yer Majesty." Should she have told him about the militia? Hell and damnation, why couldn't she keep secrets from him? It was the same when they were children, he, her best friend and the one she trusted more than the next day's sunrise.

She looked away when the queen turned to smile at her, her fan flapping faster. She did not want to speak of him. Every time she did, his face, his smile, his kisses invaded her thoughts and made her feel hotter.

"You must know him very well. Tell me," the queen went on mercilessly, "what kind of woman would he prefer for a wife?"

Mairi's fan stopped along with her heart. She turned back to her hostess, knowing her face had gone pale and not caring. "A wife? Fer Connor?"

"Yes." The queen nodded. "For Connor."

"He..." Dear God, she had to get a hold of herself. She had to think, to say something other than sputtering. Lord, she hated sputtering. "I...He..." Her fan picked up its frantic pace again. "Has he requested one?"

"Why no." The queen laughed. "But he is a score and

five. Goodness, what is this aversion you Highlanders have toward marriage?"

What was this preoccupation the queen had for marrying everyone off? "I dinna' think anyone here is right fer him." Mairi looked across the court at Lady Elizabeth and scowled.

"Oh? Why ever not?"

Mairi gaped at her for a moment before snapping her mouth shut. How in blazes was she to answer that? "Yer Majesty, yer guests are all overindulged harlots" wouldn't sit well, she was sure. She could not tell her that she did not want Connor to marry anyone without providing a reason why. And *that* she certainly would never admit to the queen. It was hard enough to admit to herself.

"Should I choose a Scotswoman for him then?"

"With respect," Mairi softened her voice, and it was a difficult feat to accomplish when what she wanted to do was scream. "Why choose anyone at all? At home, we are permitted to pick our own husbands or wives."

The queen shook her head and patted Mairi's knee. "This is not the Highlands, my dear. Lady Huntley is my friend, and the king's relative. It is my privilege to see her son wed to someone well bred and right standing. He should have a wife to come home to, a dozen children at his feet…"

Connor, a father to children that were not hers? Satan's balls, she was going to faint in front of the damned Queen of England.

"Pardon the intrusion, Yer Majesty."

Mairi looked up and shielded her eyes to Richard Drummond standing over them.

"I beg a word with Miss MacGregor."

The queen nodded her head, permitting him to speak.

"'Tis about Captain Grant, my lady. I'm afraid no one can find him and I was hoping ye might—"

"What do you mean no one can find him?" the king's wife snapped at him.

Connor's lieutenant didn't appear overly worried, but Mairi noted his white knuckles clenching the hilt of his sword at his side.

"He has not been seen since early this afternoon, Yer Majesty. According to Humfries, who was the last to see him in the stables, he was on his way to St. James's Park."

"Alone?" Mairi's gaze cut to Lady Elizabeth watching her.

"He was looking for ye."

Mairi wasn't sure what it was that set her heart to pumping, the idea that he would go after her and Henry, or the fact that she had returned hours ago, and he hadn't.

"Where have you searched for him?" The queen rose to her feet and beckoned Claire to her.

"Everywhere, ma'am," Drummond told her. "My men search even now. I have over forty combing the park and the rest have gone through the palace, but to no avail. I take it then, Miss MacGregor, that ye have not seen him."

"Seen who?" Claire asked, coming to them short of breath.

"Your son," the queen informed her. "He appears to be missing."

Mairi knew and understood full well the look of fear and dread that came over her dearest friend as the lieutenant repeated everything to her. He was safe, Mairi told herself. Somehow they had simply missed him. He had to be somewhere. He had to be all right.

"Have you checked The Troubadour?" Claire demanded. "He has been spending time there recently."

"My men searched the tavern an hour ago, Lady Huntley. He was not there."

"Search again! If he is not in the palace or on the grounds—Oh, to hell with this," Connor's mother growled and pushed past Drummond. "Find my husband and saddle our horses," she shouted over her shoulder. "And someone get me a sword!"

Connor opened his eyes, then wished he hadn't. Pain shot through his skull like a fireball, exploding behind his eyes. Everything was dark around him and he wasn't sure if night had descended, or the splitting ache in his head had made him blind. He was lying down on top of something that jabbed into his back like a blade. Where the hell was he? His mind cleared just barely enough for him to remember looking at Mairi in St. James's... Hell, someone had hit him. He tried to move and something under him jabbed him in the back like a blade. Reaching behind him slowly, he uncovered what felt like a fishbone. Without warning, the stench of piss and rotting meat assailed his senses. He gagged and attempted to sit up. He became aware of a whole new pain. He clutched his belly and groaned at the sticky fluid that covered his hand. Blood. He'd been stabbed and left for dead.

Hell. Someone was going to die for this. But first he had to get back to Whitehall. Calling up every reserve of strength he still possessed, he slid his body to the left. A little more. A cat screeched and darted away from him, knocking over something that clanged to the ground. At least he hoped it was a cat and not a very big rat. He moved a little more and a wave of nausea washed over him. His head throbbed and his belly burned but he managed to pull himself out of the pile of garbage he'd been tossed into. Who the hell had done this to him, and why? It was his last coherent thought before his eyes closed again and his mind slumped back into blessed unconsciousness.

"He's here!" Richard Drummond shouted into the darkness, and held his torch closer to Connor's face. He was about to check for breathing when the captain's parents and five other guardsmen rounded the corner of the dark alley behind The Troubadour.

"Oh, dear God in heaven." Claire drew her hands to her mouth when she saw her son lying still beside the day's refuse. "Does he live?"

Her husband pushed past her and skidded to a halt above his son. His face, ashen, his breath suspended, too afraid for a moment to know the answer.

"He lives!" Drummond told them, lifting his cheek from Connor's parted lips. "His breath is shallow. Merciful God, he's been stabbed."

Graham didn't wait for any other discoveries, but bent to his knees and hefted his son in his arms. "We need to get him back to the palace. Drummond, bring me your horse. Hurry!"

Chapter Twenty

The silence that clung to the great lawns leading to the entrance of Whitehall was shattered by the thunder of many horses. Captain Sedley led the charge, but Mairi leaped from her mount first and ran for the doors. She had been searching the park when Connor's cornet, Edward Willingham, had found them and given them the news that Connor had been found—barely alive.

Informed that he had been taken to his parent's guest chamber, she raced up the stairs, all the while praying to God for his life. He could not die! She could not imagine her life without him alive in the world. It did not matter where, or if, they were together, as long as he lived. When she reached the second landing she stopped upon seeing over a hundred of Connor's men lining the cavernous hall. She took a dreaded moment to note the somber lines creasing their faces. The queen sat in a heavy chair off to the side, engaged in quiet conversation with Richard Drummond. Mairi took off toward her.

When the queen saw her, she rose and met Mairi halfway.

"Does he live?" Mairi moved toward the door, but the queen stopped her.

"My private physicians are with him. He was stabbed, though not fatally. But he now suffers a fever."

"I must see him!" When the queen looked about to refuse, Mairi pressed on. She could not lose him without saying farewell. *Och, God, dinna' let him die.* "I beg ye, Yer Majesty. Please, let me see him."

"Very well." The king's wife motioned to the men standing guard at the door to give her entry.

"Thank ye." Mairi took her hands and kissed them both. "Thank ye."

She was directed to the bedchamber, where light from the hearth bathed the room in soft amber hues. The air was heavy and scented with sage and thyme. Two of the queen's physicians stood by the bed, blocking her view. Graham and Claire were there also, and when she saw Mairi, Connor's mother left her chair by the bed and went to her. They embraced, both with more to lose than they could bear. After Graham gathered her in his arms next, Mairi wiped her eyes.

"What happened?" Even as she spoke, she turned toward where Connor lay, drawn by the need to go to him.

Graham filled her in on everything they knew so far while the physicians parted and allowed her near.

He looked peaceful and so very handsome, this face she had known since birth. His head was bandaged, the wound at his belly dressed loosely to allow draining.

"They will suture him tomorrow if all goes well," she heard Claire, somewhere behind her, say.

If all goes well. Mairi's hands shook as they moved to touch his cheek. His skin was so hot she thought he must be burning inside. "Ye must get well, Connor," she said softly. "We are not yet done, ye and I."

"We believe 'twas a robbery," his father said, coming to stand at her side. "Fer his boots. He..." He paused as if the words were too unbearable to utter. They were. "...was left to die in the filth and debris behind the tavern."

Mairi closed her eyes at the fury scalding her veins. "Then whoever took his boots will be wearing them." If she saw them, she would take them back, and the robber's legs along with them.

She'd spent so many years angry with him, but now her reasons seemed trivial. Och, why had it taken the possibility of losing him forever to make her open her eyes to the truth? She still cared for him. Had she been a fool for pushing him away for so long, too blinded by the ache in her heart to give him a chance to repair it? Could he repair it? Could she ever trust his promises again? What if he no longer wanted to promise her anything? What if he cared for Lady Elizabeth? Och, Dear God, she would worry about that later. Now, she only wanted him to open his eyes and cast her one of his casual smiles. Saints help her, but she could not live in a world void of his smiles, even the ones that infuriated her.

"Connor"—she leaned down close to his ear—"ye will recover. Ye are a Highlander, dinna' ferget. Ye are strong and fit. Ye will not allow some meager dagger to end yer life. D'ye hear? Ye must come back to me, Connor."

"Come, sweeting." Claire took her by the hand. "Sit and pray with me. Together, we will fight the death angel that stalks him."

Their vigil continued long into the night, with both Mairi and Claire taking turns applying cool compresses to his head. The queen sat with them for a time, promising to use every man available in their search for the robber. Thankfully, she kept all talk of marriage out of the conversation. For the most part, she remained quiet with the rest, praying for Connor's swift recovery and watching Mairi with a knowing smile while she tended to him.

Sometime during the night, after the queen left them, Mairi closed her eyes to sleep for a bit. She'd refused her bed when Claire, and even the queen, suggested she retire to her room and get some rest. Not until he opened his eyes. Not until he spoke to her and promised to live. She didn't know if what they had before could ever be reclaimed, but she wanted him in her life. He was more than her first love. He was her friend, and she missed him.

She slept for a bit before a sound pulled at her dreams of Connor's passionate gaze, his full, inviting lips telling her every day how bonnie she was to him. She opened her eyes, not knowing how long she had slept, and looked at him. He remained still, his body covered by a thin blanket from the waist down. Above that, he was bare. She took her leisure appraising the hard, lean muscles rippling his abdomen, the width of his shoulders. His body had changed. The boy was gone.

He moved. More precisely, his body twitched slightly and then his lips parted as if a word sought to escape him before being burned by his fever.

Mairi sprang from her chair and took his hand in hers. "Connor?" she whispered, waiting, hoping he would answer. "Wake up. I have cried a hundred oceans fer ye, Connor Grant, and ye know how I hate to weep, so wake up."

He didn't move. She didn't know how long she watched him, or when she fell back to sleep in the bed beside him.

Connor opened his eyes just before dawn and looked up at the ceiling in his parents' room. He had no recollection of how he'd arrived there. He felt like hell, but he wasn't dead—and he was thankful. He tried to move, but something atop his arm stopped him. He looked down at a head of dark, glossy waves, the ends of which were spread across his chest. His mind told him it was Mairi, but he could still be dreaming. He kept his arm still, becoming aware as the seconds passed that it was completely numb. If she was real, he didn't want to wake her. If she wasn't, he didn't want to wake himself. She shifted, cuddling deeper into his side, and lifted her face just enough for him to catch his breath at the sight of it so close, so peaceful.

Mairi. What was she doing here in bed with him? He had to be dreaming. Either way, he had to touch her. Lifting his free hand, he traced his fingers down the silken tendrils curling at her temple, softly across her cheek. She opened her eyes and he smiled looking into them.

"I dreamed of ye," he whispered, stroking the sweet curve of her jaw.

She didn't move away. She didn't move at all. She simply stared into his eyes the way one might look at their beloved childhood home after years of being away. Then she smiled at him and his heart came undone.

"Ye are alive."

"Why, Miss MacGregor," he whispered, cautious against speaking any louder, lest he awaken. "Is that relief I see on yer bonnie face?"

"Aye. 'Tis relief ye see."

He watched her lashes dip as he bent his head to kiss her, ignoring the pain of his wound. She would not deny him, nor would he be denied.

"I couldna' let ye die without telling ye what I thought of ye, Connor Grant."

He laughed softly against her lips, but he would hear his faults later. Now, he wanted to taste her and welcome her back.

"Connor"—she moved her head away and covered his mouth with her fingers—"ye were breathing in garbage fer quite a few hours."

When he blinked at her, not quite getting what she was hinting at, and not sure if he cared, she avoided his gaze and clarified. "Ye are less than fresh."

Of course. The most important kiss of his life and his breath was foul. He had to laugh, and resting his head back on his pillow, he did.

"Welcome back, my son." When he heard his mother's voice, he turned to her and smiled as Mairi fled from his arm, and his bed. "It pleases me that you were greeted by someone so dear to you."

He watched Mairi take the seat beside her, flushed, but suddenly curious for his reply. "Had I known what awaited me, I would have gotten myself stabbed long ago."

Both women offered him the same pained smile.

"Do ye recall what happened?"

Connor turned to the other side of the bed just as his father was leaving the chair he'd been sleeping in. He rested his hand on Connor's shoulder and gave him a loving pat. "We will celebrate yer recovery later. Tell us what ye remember while 'tis still fresh in yer mind. Ye went searching for Mairi in St. James's Park. How did ye end up behind The Troubadour?"

"Is that where ye found me?" Connor asked him as the attack returned to his thoughts. He told them about finding Mairi with Oxford and watching from a hidden position to see if Oxford was honorable. He had been about to go to her when his assailant came upon him.

"Ye were stabbed in the park then?" his mother asked.

"I don't know. I was struck in the head first and blacked out. I didn't see his face," Connor told them, knowing their next question. "But I'm certain 'twas a man. A woman reaching up could not have hit me as hard."

"And it had to have been a man," Mairi added, "to have moved yer body to the tavern."

"Someone must have seen such a sight," his father said, "whether ye were on his back or on yer horse." He went for the door. "I'll have Captain Sedley send the men out to question everyone."

"Father," Connor called, stopping him, "have Lieutenant Drummond see to it instead."

His father nodded and left the room.

"What is it, Connor?" Mairi asked, reading him like one of her late uncle's beloved books. Looking at her, he marveled at how easily she could make him forget, if only for a moment, the worst part of all this: that his friend could be behind trying to kill him.

"My mother and her brother were betrayed by their dearest friend. No one can be trusted."

"But what reason would Sedley have to cause ye harm?" his mother asked him. "What would he gain by killing ye?"

"He is William of Orange's man. He lied to me about Admiral Gilles. I'm certain of it, and he questioned me about Colin going to Edinburgh with the king."

"How does he know my brother travels with the king?"

"I don't know."

The door opened and two physicians entered the room and went directly to the bed. "Lord Huntley informed us that you have awakened." They each took turns poking and prodding him and when he yawned they insisted his visitors leave so that he could sleep.

"Is there anything you need?" his mother asked him when she kissed his bandaged forehead, readying to leave.

"Aye, a sprig of mint." He winked at Mairi, then yawned again when his mother promised to return later. She left before Mairi did, giving them a moment to themselves.

"Have I told ye already today that ye look bonnie in that dress? England suits ye well, Mairi MacGregor."

He didn't know why her smile faded. He would have commented on it, but his eyes were already closing. Hell, he didn't want to sleep. He wanted to stand from this bed and drag her into his arms.

He heard her say something but he wasn't sure what it was, and then he thought he heard the door close. Was she gone, or had she been a dream after all?

Chapter Twenty-one

$\mathcal{M}$airi walked slowly across the long Shield Gallery, unsure of which direction she should take. Should she go to supper, alone at her kin's table, or to Connor's room, where he would no doubt beam with joy that she was fitting in so nicely here in England? She wished she had not let the queen take her earasaid and boots for cleaning. Now she had nothing to wear but whatever the queen supplied. Today it was a brocade gown of cobalt blue, shot through with emerald lace. It was extraordinarily beautiful, but England would never suit her. It broke her heart that Connor thought it did. She remembered his letters asking her to join him here. He had to have known she would never leave Scotland. The very idea of it seemed traitorous to her. This was not the life she'd wanted with him and being here only proved it to her more. She didn't fit in with the capricious noble lords and ladies who powdered their faces and smiled while they pricked a knife into each other's backs— who saw her as nothing more than a barbarian because of her name and her religion. Theaters and iced cream were lovely, but they meant nothing to her compared to fiery sunsets over a vast expanse of mountain peaks, and cool, heather-scented wind in her face, and kin who loved her.

She could never be happy anywhere else. England was Connor's home, but it could never be hers. Mayhap, she thought, swatting a blasted tear from her eye, it was not Connor that she wanted back as much as the dreams he had taken from her.

"Miss MacGregor."

She turned to watch Lord Oxford hurrying to catch up with her. She was going to have to speak with him sooner or later about her feelings. It might as well be now. She smiled when he reached her.

"I missed you last evening," he said, taking her hand. "I do hope you are not going to spend the entire day at Captain Grant's bedside."

It irritated her that he did not query about Connor's condition. Then again, Henry cared for her and having such a striking captain always at their heels would be enough to drive any man mad, especially one who believed himself to be so homely. Henry was likely relieved to be getting rid of Connor for a few days. "My lord, he was stabbed and left—"

"Yes, I know. Everyone in the palace knows. My poor sister is beside herself."

Mairi frowned at him. Och, she didn't want to hear how Connor's lover wept over him. They had to be lovers. Why else would Elizabeth practically hiss at her every time they passed each other in the halls? Thinking of it angered her. How could Connor care for such an overindulged brat? She was beautiful, Mairi answered herself. And English.

"I was hoping that you might break fast with me."

Mairi looked at Henry, and then at the stairs leading to Connor. Despite whatever feelings he had for Elizabeth, she really should go check on him.

"Have you heard of Tomas Marshall?"

She shook her head no. "Should I have?"

"Probably not, but I recently discovered some interesting information about him."

Good Lord, not another hour-long lesson on some dead English patriot. Thanks to Henry, she already knew more useless tidbits about England than she would ever need to know.

"I really should—"

"He has taken up Richard Cameron's cause in the Lowlands. Do you know about the Cameronians, Miss MacGregor?"

She nodded, taking the arm he offered her. "I have heard of them." Her heart beat wildly in her chest. Finally, he had some information she wanted to hear. And it couldn't get any better. Marshall, the new leader of the Cameronians! Wait until her militia brothers heard this!

"Come," he said softly, beckoning her away from the stairs. "I will tell you what I know, though you may stop me if I bore you. I know I tend to blather on about things others find inconsequential."

"Och, my lord," Mairi said, giving one last look toward the stairs. Connor would be fine for a few hours. This information was too valuable to let slip by. "Ye never bore me. Ye are a man of high intelligence. Anyone who doesna' see that is a fool."

"Yes," he agreed, smiling at her and patting her hand as they made their way to the Banqueting Hall. "I agree."

• • •

When Mairi reached the door to the Grant's bedchamber two hours later, she smoothed her long waves over her shoulders, checked the pins in her hair holding strands away from her face on either side of her head, and knocked.

"Come." Claire's voice ushered her in.

Upon entering the bedroom, Mairi's eyes settled on Connor first. She was relieved to see him looking much better. In fact, he looked so good her knees went a wee bit soft.

Propped up against a mountain of pillows, his hands resting comfortably on his covered hips, he turned to spare her a brief, somewhat irritated glance.

Mairi paused on her way to him but not because she felt badly about not visiting him sooner, or because she had been doing something he disapproved of, gaining information that would aid her in her battle against the Cameronians.

It was the bounce of a golden curl against the firelight that stopped her in her tracks.

"Miss MacGregor." Lady Elizabeth looked equally stunned to see her standing at the door. "You are supposed to be spending the afternoon with my brother."

Mairi set her hands in front of her and quirked her brow. "Since when do ye know what I am supposed to be doing, Lady Elizabeth?"

How the hell *did* she know? Had she set her brother to the task of keeping Mairi away from Connor so she could tend to him? Sly bastards, both of them. Damn Henry for doing his sister's bidding like a sheep at the end of a stick, and for doing his part in trying to bolster his sister's relationship with Connor.

"Did he take ye on another romp to St. James's Park?" Connor practically growled at her from the bed.

She shot him a look of surprise at his tone, then blinked as the truth settled on her. *That's* what he was angry about? That she had been with Henry? Her belly flipped and made her clutch the folds of her gown. Her anger toward him had blinded her to what had been right in front of her since the first time she had danced with Henry. Connor was jealous. Aye, she may have suspected it when he informed her that he'd gone to the queen about her wedding Oxford or Sedley; she was not a lackwit, after all. But she'd discounted it as nothing more than a false sense of possessiveness on his part.

He certainly had kissed her as though he had a right to. Hell, but this room was hot. Quickly, she chased the memory of his mouth on hers away. It would do her no good to lose her wits with Lady Elizabeth in the room.

But it was more than possessiveness. Connor had nearly lost his life looking for her at the park. Did it mean he still cared for her? And what would she do if he did?

"Lord Oxford wished to speak with me about something," she told him truthfully. "We have spoken, and now we are finished."

"What was so important then?" he tossed at her. "Did he speak to ye about the queen's wishes?"

Marriage. Och, he was fuming. She almost smiled at him, but Claire stood from her seat and interrupted them.

"Connor, there is something I wish to tell you. In private," she added, glancing at Henry's sister.

"Later." He held up his palm to stop her. Then, without taking his eyes off Mairi, asked his mother to leave and take Lady Elizabeth with her.

If anyone else had tried to remove Elizabeth from the room, it would have required moving her bodily, but

Claire Stuart had but to cast her one warning look to get the trollop moving.

When they were alone, Mairi walked around the bed, pulled the nearest chair closer, and sat in it. "We didna' speak of marriage."

"Why not?"

She shrugged and folded her hands in her lap. "Mayhap he doesna' wish to marry me?"

His jaw, shadowed by a few days' worth of dark golden whiskers, tightened, defining that blasted right dimple. "Ye're being evasive. Why didn't ye tell him—"

"What? That I willna' marry him because I love *ye*?"

She smiled when he looked away and cleared his throat. "I didn't say that."

"Wise."

He looked at her from under his brows, but said nothing.

"Why did ye not tell Lady Elizabeth to leave this room and never return?"

"Because," he said, aiming another cool stare at her, "I was too interested in hearing about the afternoon ye'd be spending with her brother. 'Tis pitiful, I know," he drawled when her smile widened. "Don't gloat about it."

"Fergive me." She lowered her eyes but her smile remained. Damnation, she was the pitiful one taking such enjoyment in his discomfort. Was he truly so interested in what she was doing that he would suffer Elizabeth's company?

"I was stabbed, Mairi."

She looked up. He looked too damned healthy to have almost perished. The thought of it made her close her eyes and take a deep breath.

"Aye, Connor, I know."

"Then why did ye spend the morning with Oxford? Do ye care fer him, truly?"

She could tell him she did and he would ask her to leave. Part of her told her she should do it. She couldn't bear falling in love with him again, dreaming of her life with him in the Highlands, and his choosing England over her yet again. She should listen to her head and walk away from him before he hurt her again, but her heart told her to stay.

"Nae, I dinna' care fer him. I went with him because he had information about the Camer—" She stopped as something she'd missed while speaking to Elizabeth dawned on her.

"He knew what to say." She hadn't realized she spoke aloud and looked up at Connor to find him waiting to hear the rest. Och, he wasn't going to like it.

"About the Cameronians," he said before she did.

She nodded and watched as the same conclusion, along with a sickened look, settled over him.

"His sister wanted time with ye, Connor, and she used him to keep me away. He found me on my way to ye and he knew what to say to make me go with him instead."

"But, Mairi"—he leaned up in the bed and looked at her gravely—"how could he know who yer enemies are? What have ye told him?"

"Nothing. I have never even mentioned the Cameronians to him."

"Are ye certain?"

"Aye. I have only spoken of them to ye." She thought about it for a moment. Then, "He may have overheard us. Or he may have taken notice of my interest in them when I spoke with the Duke of Queensberry."

He was about to say something when a soft knock

came at the door. They both looked up at Claire as she stepped into the room.

"Is all well?" She smiled at her son, and then at Mairi. She waited while they nodded before she regained her seat. "Good. Now, I have something to confess to the both of you." She sat up straighter and folded her hands in front of her. "I am guilty of doing something quite wicked, and the queen has been my accomplice."

Chapter Twenty-two

*M*airi left the Huntleys' lodgings an hour later feeling a bit bewildered and not all that pleased with Claire, or her confession.

She knew Claire loved her and had wanted her to reunite with Connor, but to plot with the queen of England to see it done? It was devious! Why, they had even gone so far as to involve Captain Sedley in their schemes to make them jealous of each other. Ridiculous. Mairi didn't posses a shred of jealousy in her body. Well, mayhap, she did if wanting to take a dagger to Elizabeth de Vere counted for anything. She thought of Connor, propped up in bed, looking rather slighted when he asked his mother if all her scheming meant that Lady Elizabeth was not as taken with him as he thought, and then his bemused smile when he caught Mairi glaring at him. He was, though, genuinely pleased with the news that she wasn't truly going to be promised to Lord Oxford.

And what of that wee worm of a man? How did Henry know to distract her from visiting Connor by using the Cameronians? Had he heard her interest when she was speaking to Queensberry? If so, why had he not said something sooner? She paused in her steps as another thought occurred to her. Did Henry somehow suspect her of fighting against Richard Cameron's Lowland followers? How could he? She hadn't put a single question to him concerning them or the Covenanters.

Nae, he didn't know about her belonging to the militia. No one did save for Colin, Claire, and, now, Connor.

Och, Connor. Mairi was happy that he lived—so happy, in fact, that she felt giddy. A disgusting trait and one she hadn't felt in seven years. She had learned to guard her heart well. Never again would she allow a man to make her so happy that she would be completely miserable without him. But nothing could have prepared her for seeing Connor again, hearing his slow, thick drawl when he told her that she had meant everything to him, for being kissed by him again, and now to discover him jealous after so many years. Damnation, how could she let him dissolve all her defenses with nothing but a smile cast her way? She needed her defenses, had relied on them to see her through the long days and even longer nights alone in her bed when other lasses her age were already wed with a bairn under each arm.

She didn't want to love Connor Grant again, but she no longer wanted to hate him either. So what if he loved England? They could somehow find a way to remain friends. Couldn't they? Then again, did friends want to spring from their chairs and kiss the other's dimples, his chin, his lips while thanking God over and over for sparing his life? Did friends take such absolute pleasure in the other's jealousy?

She sighed on her way down the stairs, unsure if it was joy or dread making her heart crash within her. If Connor thought to win her again, should she let him? Could she ever trust his promises again?

"Miss MacGregor?"

She turned and reached for the banister when she saw Prince William behind her. Would he push her down the stairs in front of the king's guests?

"Yer Grace?"

"How is Captain Grant faring?" He offered her a cordial smile beneath his nose. "Any better today?"

"Quite."

"That is good news," he said, reaching her and extending his arm. "Where are you off to?"

She looked at his arm warily. He didn't like her, but he wasn't so foolish as to cause her injury out in the open. And she sure as hell didn't want him to think her afraid of him. She accepted with a polite smile.

"Just off fer a wee bit of fresh air. 'Tis overly warm in Captain Grant's sick room."

"Ah, to the garden then?" Before she had time to accept or decline, he picked up his steps, taking her with him. "Allow me to escort you. I could use a bit of air myself."

Now, why would he want her company? Did he think she knew something that would aid him in his quest? Did he think her fool enough to tell him? She went along, deciding his queries could be quite telling. Besides, there were more pairs of eyes in the Privy Garden than anywhere else in the palace. If the prince meant to harm her, he would likely send someone else to do it for him, the same way he had likely sent Admiral Gilles to kill the king's daughter. Coward. If he meant to sit on the throne, she meant to stop him.

"I would be honored by yer company, Yer Grace." *And mayhap learn a thing or two more about ye.*

"What think you of London?" he asked her as they stepped outside together.

"Everything here is verra structured and proper. Even the trees grow in tall orderly rows." They shared a chuckle looking at the trees on either side of the path. "'Tis warm and there are not verra many hills." She could think of a dozen more things, but refrained, preferring him to do the talking.

"I daresay, my homeland is not as balmy. You though," he added in a softer tone, bending his lips to her ear, "are like a refreshing spring."

So surprised was she by his intimacy, she nearly stepped back. What in blazes was he about? "Yer Grace, ye flatter." She angled her head up to look him in his eyes and curled one tip of her mouth.

Aye, she'd learned over the years that being a woman had its advantages, even if they were a bit demeaning. Still, they served in gaining her information from men who had reason to be tight-lipped. She almost hated herself for wielding her wiles so well.

"I speak true." The prince grinned, thinking he had her as easily as the English trollops sneering at her with her arm coiled around royalty. "It is not every day that I find someone who will give me an honest opinion on matters of the church—and never one so lovely as yourself."

She turned back to the path before them, unable to gaze at him one more moment than she had to. "Perhaps I can offer ye more forthright opinions then. Ye have but to ask."

"Indeed." He stopped when they came to a brook that ran into the Thames, partially shielded from the sun by a stand of tall oak. "Tell me, what do you think of the French?"

She blinked her eyes at him. "The French, my lord?"

"Yes. You spoke of God at the king's table a few nights ago and I was curious what you might have to say about King Louis's Declaration of the Clergy of France? Surely, you have heard of it? In which royal authority is increased at the expense of papal power?"

"I am afraid I know nothing of it," Mairi admitted, having no idea where this talk was headed, but guarded and certain that it was headed somewhere.

"I assumed that with you living with Admiral Stuart's sister, Lady Huntley, you might be familiar. Of course you are aware that he has been living in France for some time now."

Was this what he was after? Information that might aid him in his fight with the French? It was clever of him she had to admit. If anyone could supply him with what he wanted to know about his enemy, it was Claire's brother. But, she reasoned, why did he not simply question Graham, or even Claire? She remembered why a moment later. He thought her rash and foolish, easily won over by pretty words.

"Sadly, we havena' seen the high admiral in many years."

"Lady Huntley receives no letters in…where is that your family lives in the Highlands?" he inquired innocently.

Now why would he want to know that? No one in England, save for Connor Grant, knew of Camlochlin or its whereabouts on Skye, and since she had arrived, no one seemed the slightest bit interested in where they might find the MacGregors. She tilted her head, assessing William before she answered. Could he have somehow found out that his schemes to kill the king's firstborn daughter had failed and that she was now in the MacGregors' care?

She felt the urge to look around her. Had any of these people arrived at Whitehall recently? Had they heard rumor that not all had perished in the flames of St. Christopher's?

"Alas, my lord," she said placidly, "my kin have little or no land. During the proscription we lost ownership of our territories in Glen Orchy.

"In truth, we are nomads and have never settled in one particular place. Admiral Stuart doesna' send letters because there is no place to send them."

William stared at her archly. "Lady Huntley does not strike me as the type of woman who would be satisfied without a roof over her head."

"Lady Huntley, as I am certain ye already know, spent many of her earlier years living in the forest."

"Yes." The prince crinkled his enormous nose as if a sudden and unpleasant odor just wafted across it. "I had heard that about her." He folded one arm behind his back and with the other twirled the fringes of his lace lapel. He picked up his steps again, seeming to be mulling things over in his mind, weighing different possibilities...or strategies on how best to proceed with his next question.

Mairi walked beside him and waited patiently. She watched the swans glide across the surface of the lake, then looked up at a bright red bird fluttering from one tree to the other. She had to admit, partly because she was friends with Connor again and her heart felt light enough to fly, that parts of England were rather pretty.

"Miss MacGregor."

She stopped walking and then realized that the prince had stopped before her.

"I wonder," he said, moving toward her, "if you know why King James took your brother with him to meet secretly with Parliament?"

She caught her smile before it faded. Here's what he was after. Of course! Then he *was* involved with the massacre at the abbey! "I wasna' aware that the meeting was a secret."

"Yes, they were to meet next month."

"Well, that I canna' answer, my lord, but I suspect that the king took my brother with him because he recognized that Colin could likely beat any one of his men in the lists."

"Hmmm," the prince agreed. "I've seen the young man in the tiltyard. His skills are impressive, if not a bit brutal. But I wonder..."

Whatever else he meant to ask her was halted by the sky opening and spewing its torrent down on their heads as suddenly as the cool breeze that preceded it.

Mairi gasped and smiled as the cold droplets soaked her and the guests around her ran for cover. It was the same rain that fell at home, just as abrupt, just as hard. She inhaled the fresh fragrances of the earth coming awake. Finally, it rained in England in the spring.

"I daresay, Miss MacGregor," the prince said, looking around for one of his men to cover him and finding none, "perhaps we might finish our speech another time?"

She smiled at the raindrops dripping off the tip of his nose and nodded an instant before he fled back to the palace.

Chapter Twenty-three

*M*airi spent most of the dark, dreary day with the Grants, visiting Connor, and no matter how gloomy the weather, his laughter brightened the room.

She watched him when his men visited his bed and teased him about being clopped over the head and rendered helpless like that night's supper. She watched the way he lifted his brow with a flash of unexpected humor. How he opened his mouth and tossed back his head when he laughed. She loved his face and the speed at which it changed with a dozen different emotions, all while his smile and his voice remained as languid as a summer day. She realized, quite happily and with a bit of astonishment, that he was not nearly as open and charming with the women who visited him. Och, the dimples were there—they always were—but his smiles were tempered with...boredom.

Even the queen saw in him only what he wanted her to see—a dutiful, loyal captain. Still, it did not stop Mary of Modena from innocently flirting with him. Mairi did not mind. He was growing stronger each day, more vibrant in his bed. No woman with blood in her veins could ignore even his slightest, most casual glance. Lady Elizabeth certainly could not, in spite of her seething anger over Mairi's presence when she visited—which was often. Lady Hollingsworth practically had to be hauled out the door two long hours after she had arrived. Connor did not tease or seduce either of them but kept his smiles polite and his words brief.

"They hate that I am here with ye," Mairi told him on the second night of the downpour. They were finally alone and now that they were, she was having a hard time remembering what she had been waiting two days to tell him. She walked around the room, touching this thing and that, trying not to look at him.

"So?" He lay there, his bedsheet riding down his bare, hard torso, one arm tossed casually behind his head like a sinful angel come to tempt her to his bed.

"So." She picked up one of his medicinal bottles and held it to her nose. "They are angry that ye dinna' show them more interest because I am here."

"Mairi," he said, hooking his mouth and forcing her gaze to the other side of the room, "I don't show them interest when ye're not here either."

He made her heart flip with a few mere words. Against her will, for she didn't want him to see how he affected her, she turned back to him. "How many times have they visited in my absence then?"

An intimate smile teased his lips and she knew she failed. Oddly, it made his victory even more alluring than the weapon that was Connor Grant's tongue. Ah, but he wielded it like an expert against her, whether in challenge, or humor, or to utter so casually words most other men might find difficult to admit.

"Well, now that 'tis a wee bit cooler inside, ye won't be leaving so often."

"I might not," she conceded. "Then again, wandering about the palace alone has afforded me an opportunity to speak privately with Prince William, so, I might."

He sat up and her eyes moved of their own accord over the ripples in his hard belly. "Ye spoke with him alone?"

"Aye, and please dinna' look so angry. 'Tis insulting."

His mouth opened then closed again an instant after he visibly rejected what he wanted to say. Mairi hoped it had nothing to do with her being a lass.

"Really, Connor, ye mustna' fret over it. I said nothing that would put me or my kin in jeopardy."

"He's clever, Mairi."

"He was desperately inadequate."

When he grinned at her, it was thankfully recognizing her for the warrior she was—either that or he was laughing at her claim. When she backed away from the bed, he beckoned her back by patting the mattress beside him.

"Tell me how ye slew him, Mairi."

She didn't realize she was smiling until she went to him and sat, forgetting everything else but the joy of sharing her secrets with him. "Swear to me yer fealty to our Catholic king first."

He rolled his eyes, but did as she asked.

"Connor, he was involved fer certain with the massacre at St. Christopher's."

"How do ye know?"

"He practically told me," she said, eager to tell him all. "He thought he was being clever, but his queries were as obvious as the nose on his face."

He laughed, and so did she. Hell, she had not laughed

with him in so terribly long. It was like dancing without her feet touching the ground. She told him about the prince's queries having to do with France and his uncle, and how he tried with failed subtlety to find out where their kin lived, and finally why Colin had accompanied the king to Edinburgh.

"It had to be him, Connor. It all makes sense. Why is he so curious about my kin? Dinna' ye see?" she asked, then continued before he could agree or not. "Rob feared Miss Montgomery's enemies might be among the king's guests. That is why he asked ye not to tell the king of his daughter's rescue. When ye arrived and my kin picked up and left, it likely roused William's suspicions that something was amiss. Then, when James fled in the cover of night with another MacGregor supposedly to meet with Parliament a month early, he feared the worst. The king's daughter had to be alive somewhere with the Mac-Gregors. 'Twas the only thing that would make James leave England without explanation."

Her eyes followed him when Connor leaned back on the bed to allow her words to seep in. Silently, she took in each nuance of muscle that graced him. After the excitement of telling him what she had discovered was exhausted, her thoughts shifted back to baser curiosities. Did he want to kiss her again? How would the golden bristles on his face feel against her throat, her breasts? She blinked realizing that he was looking at her.

"Ye're a clever lass, Mairi MacGregor."

She smiled, feeling even better than she felt two winters ago when she and Colin figured out that Kevin Menzie of Rannoch was a Cameronian.

"I wasna' sure if we should tell the queen, or wait until the king returns," Mairi said. "If her demeanor changes toward the prince, he may suspect she knows and act upon it."

"We will wait then," he agreed, moving his fingers over hers and shaking her to her core. "Ye'll tell me later what else ye know about William of Orange and how ye know it. Fer now, let us speak of us."

"What about us?" she asked, feeling her blasted breath stall and her face go warm.

"I miss ye, Mairi. I've missed ye fer a long time."

She closed her eyes and tried to recall all the times she had wished to hear those words from him. But how could he have missed her and still stayed away? "Ye didna' fight fer me."

He laughed but for once, there was no humor in it. "Fer four years, I did. How long would ye have me try to win ye back?"

"Fer as long as it takes."

His slow sensual smile made his eyes gleam with heat and made her excruciatingly aware of his closeness. "Then I shall begin again."

The morning of the fourth day of the storm had started out quite nicely, though not due to anything Connor had intentionally done. At least, Mairi did not think he intended to look so ridiculously appealing simply by sitting up in his bed, his sheet cast carelessly aside, and his legs, encased in nothing but snug-fitting cotton breeches, tossed over the edge. He could not have known she was about to enter the bedchamber when he decided he had spent enough days abed and began flexing and stretching his unused muscles.

He looked up from his bandaged wound and grinned at her when she opened the door. The sight of him scattered every thought in her head, save one. How the bloody hell did he manage to look so virile and revived so soon after being stabbed in his guts?

"'Tis too soon!" She went to him, meaning to convince him to lie back down, but he captured her hands in his and used her weight to lift himself to his feet. The heat from his body almost touching hers thrilled the breath right out of her. His height, when she tilted her face to look into his eyes, and the breadth of his shoulders made her feel small and so much like a woman she nearly groaned with an ache she had not felt in seven years.

"I've much to do to prove to ye that 'tis not too late."

His fresh, minty breath washed over her while the husky timbre of his voice made her own mouth go dry.

"Then ye had best start walking." She smiled and stepped away, letting go of his hands. She watched him take his first tentative steps away from the bed, admiring his strength and the shapely curve of his buttocks so well defined in his breeches—breeches that left little to the imagination when he turned to her again.

It occurred to her, when his lips curled at the direction of her gaze, that her first assessment may have been incorrect, and that he had planned every movement for her pleasure.

"It feels good to be on my feet again."

Likely not as good as he looked on them, Mairi thought, then chastised herself for her wanton thoughts. God help her, but she wanted to run her tongue down the rippled contour of his belly. "I should have yer clothes returned to ye."

He laughed behind a few silken strands of gold that fell over his eyes, knowing full well what the sight of his half-naked body was doing to her and enjoying it.

"If ye wish, Mairi."

The way her name rolled off his tongue produced tiny droplets of perspiration along her brow. How could one man do this to her, and so quickly? And one whom she had convinced herself she hated? The only man to ever break her heart. He deserved the challenge she wanted to give him in trying to win her back. She didn't want to make it easy for him, but she was failing miserably.

"I was going to request them since I'll be joining ye fer supper tonight and I'd hate to see ye claw out Lady Hollingsworth's eyes if I attended like this."

She scoffed at him, determined to prove to him that she was not jealous. "Wear whatever ye like. I will be too busy with Lord Oxford to notice all yer lady friends falling at yer feet."

He grew serious instantly. "Are ye going to start spending yer time with him again?"

"Nae, but I am curious as to what he thinks he knows about me and I havena' had the chance to speak with him about it."

"I don't want ye to speak with him about it."

Och, hell, why did he have to go and ruin a perfectly nice morning by ordering her about? "What d'ye mean ye dinna' want me to speak to him about it?"

"'Tis too dangerous. If he does know something…"

"…then I wish to know what it is. And I also wish that ye would quit insulting me. Ye, more than anyone, know how I detest being thought of as weak because I am a lass."

"I didn't say ye were weak, Mairi."

"Good, because I can wield a blade as well as any man."

He smiled as if she amused him and she had the urge

to slap him. He moved closer to her until she could feel the heat of his bare chest. "I cannot help wanting to protect ye." His voice fell in a husky whisper across her temple. "If anything were to befall ye—" His fingers lifted to capture her face and tilt it toward his.

She wanted to tell him that nothing would befall her. *She* was not the one who was stabbed in the park with dozens of people nearby! But she couldn't speak. She closed her eyes instead, waiting for his kiss and bracing herself against the crashing of her heart against her breast.

The door opened and the queen entered the room with Claire behind her. A moment of stunned silence passed before Connor moved away from her and Mary of Modena blushed to her roots.

Mairi was not sure if the queen was embarrassed from barging in on them and interrupting what was clearly a very intimate moment, or if her cheeks flushed at the sight of Connor in his breeches.

Mairi did not stay long enough to find out.

Chapter Twenty-four

Connor stood at the entrance of the Banqueting Hall alone and without the aid of the walking stick the queen had insisted he use. The white-hot pain of his wound had lessened into a dull ache over the last pair of days and he actually felt quite fit as he set his gaze over the inhabitants of the hall. He found Mairi sitting at her table with none other than Lord Oxford at her side, blathering on in her ear. She looked immensely bored and Connor smiled, despite being angry with her for not staying away from Oxford as he'd asked. Well, perhaps he'd ordered rather than asked.

He swiped the raindrops from the shoulders of his justacorps as he stepped inside. Besides his military coat, this was the finest coat he owned. Made of deep blue brocade with a silk silver lining and buttons to match, it was cut to fit close and hung to his knees. The intricate loops of wide blue ribbon at his throat felt a wee bit suffocating, but the queen had nearly squeaked with delight while his mother tied them around his neck. He hadn't minded their aid in choosing what he should wear after he'd requested his own room back and a private bath to go along with it. He was trying to win Mairi back and they were both more than happy to help him look his best while at his task. He flatly refused to wear a wig, hose, or heels though. He might reside in England, but he was still, and always would be, a Highlander.

"Aw, hell, is this what love does to man then?"

Connor smiled when his lieutenant appeared beside him with a drink and gave him a pitiful looking over. "'Tis what two meddlesome women do to a man, Drummond."

"'Tis worse than I feared if ye're letting women dress ye." The lieutenant looked around Connor's chest and took a sip from his cup. "Where are ye sitting?"

"There." Connor pointed to Mairi's table. "Why? Do ye want to join me? There are empty chairs and there will be one more before the hour passes."

"I'll sit with ye." Drummond pushed him forward. "But ye'd best get moving. Lady Elizabeth approaches with a determined look in her eye and some extra sway in her skinny hips."

Connor caught the flash of yellow curls as he and his lieutenant cut through the crowd and escaped, though just narrowly.

When he reached his family's table, he greeted Mairi first and then his parents.

"Oxford," he said last, turning to the English nobleman, "yer sister was looking fer ye. I assured her that ye would be returning to yer own table momentarily."

Oxford studied him for a moment with an arched look, then smiled. "Perhaps Lizzy can dine here with us."

"Another time, perhaps. I've already invited my men to sit with us—to celebrate my return—ye understand. I'm afraid there won't be room here fer even ye."

Mayhap it was Oxford who had tried to have him killed. The blatant fury on his face as he looked at Connor's parents and then at Mairi was telling enough.

"Of course, Captain. I'm pleased to see you well again," he lied, and rose from his seat. "Miss Mac-Gregor," he said, taking her hand and bringing it to his lips, "I hope to see you later."

Not if Connor had anything to say about it. He watched Oxford leave the table, then turned his most vibrant smile on Mairi, ignoring her stony gaze. He didn't care if she was angry or not. He didn't like Oxford and now he had a reason to mistrust him.

"Ye look bonnie this eve, Mairi," he told her, taking the seat opposite hers. And hell, but she did. She wore a pale yellow gown, spun it appeared, from the finest silk, with deep golden lace peaking up from her low-cut neckline. The pearls around her throat and woven through her hair added to her creamy complexion, but she needed no adornment to accentuate her beauty. He wanted to pluck each clip from her hair and watch while her tresses spilled over her breasts. He wanted to kiss her and taste the fire of her tongue. She was his and he wanted her to know it. If she wanted to be won, he was more than happy to oblige. And win, he would.

"Yer treatment of Lord Oxford was quite rude," she said, veiling her gaze beneath her black lashes after appraising him in his justacorps.

"He will survive it, though I wonder if I will."

Mairi gave him a curious look and then turned to eye Oxford making his way to his own table. "Ye dinna' think he…"

Connor shrugged, setting his cup down. "I'm in his way."

"Of what?"

Hell, why couldn't he stop smiling at her like some besotted fool? How could she be so clever when it came to her enemies and still so innocent about her effect on men? "Of ye."

She smiled at him like he was the one missing something. "I agree that he might care fer me, but I doubt he would try to kill ye over it."

Beside her, his mother waited for the servers, who had just arrived to place the first course in front of them, to finish and leave before she spoke. "There's no telling what a man would do to gain what he desires, sweeting."

"I will do a bit of checking on him," his father said, looking over his wife's shoulder at the Oxfords' table. "I don't like him anyway."

"I'll help," Drummond offered.

Mairi sighed, dipping her spoon into her soup. "Truly, I believe he is utterly harmless, lacking a bit of spine, especially when it comes to his sister, but harmless, nonetheless."

"There's Sedley and Edward."

Before Connor could stop him, Drummond beckoned the other men over. He hated the thoughts eating away at him that one of his oldest friends might be behind the attack on him. He would have to inform his men of his suspicions regarding Sedley soon. He didn't know why he hadn't done so already. He wasn't certain if he was correct in his suspicions, and, worse, it pained him that a friend would betray him. But if there was a chance that Sedley conspired against the king, his men needed to know.

He understood now why James did not move against Prince William without proof that he should. It also gave him another reason to wish he were back in Glencoe. Loyalties did not exist in the courts of kings, save for self-gain.

No one here can be trusted.

"You're looking rather English tonight," Sedley said, sizing Connor up with one of his famously urbane grins while he slipped into the chair previously occupied by Oxford.

"Don't insult me on my first night back."

Drummond snickered beside him and clapped him on the back. Connor winked at Edward as the young cornet sat. Edward was English and Connor's playful barb was not aimed toward him.

"Captain Sedley?" Mairi's dulcet voice across the table drew his attention back to her. She met his gaze and held it for a moment before she slipped it, along with her smile, back to Sedley. "Where is it ye call home?"

"Kent," the captain told her, eyeing the pretty server setting a plate in front of him. "My father is the Baronet of Aylesford."

The slight arch of her raven brow revealed more to Connor than idle curiosity. She was one of only three at the table who knew Connor doubted him. What was she up to?

"What does yer father think of yer libertine lifestyle?" she asked as softly as a kitten purring for its milk.

Sedley laughed and three passing ladies stopped to admire him. "Libertines are completely devoid of morals, Miss MacGregor. Surely," he said, plucking a mote of lint from his military coat, "you don't believe me so depraved."

Mairi quirked her lip at him from behind her cup. "Depravity is often distorted by the depraved, Captain

Sedley. But since I know nothing of ye save fer what I was told by Captain Grant and a handmaiden or two, I am unable to form any fair judgments about ye."

"His reputation is well deserved," said Drummond, digging into his food.

"Most reputations usually are," Mairi pointed out with a brief glance at Connor.

Sedley's grin widened. "Ah, but we are all enslaved to the service of sin."

"Aye," Mairi said, returning a rather resplendent smile of her own to the rake. "And only some are chosen by God to receive His mercy. Or so the doctrine of Calvin asserts, does it not?"

Sedley shifted subtly in his seat and glanced at the men around him before he opened his mouth to speak.

Mairi stopped him before he did. "I am not certain I understand yer faith completely, Captain, so please do fergive my ignorance, but is it not true that Calvinists believe that man is not saved through faith or virtue, but by God's mercy alone? "

"I wouldn't know, dear lady," Nick told her, his tone a bit less amicable now. "I am not a Calvinist."

"Och, my err then." Mairi softened her smile, rendering Connor, at least, immobile by her delicate feminine beauty. "I would think though that such a belief would serve a devilish rake as yerself."

"Oh?"

She nodded, taking another sip from her cup. "Ye could live the life ye chose, be as debased as ye like, knowing that if ye are one of God's elect, He will simply change ye."

"He'd have much to change in this one," Drummond said as he chewed his food.

"I am not so terrible," Sedley corrected dryly. "I have not turned my depraved charms on you, lady." He ignored Connor's warning stare and forged onward. "Not that I would try to steal you from my good friend here. Captain Grant has already warned me that you are his and whatever I believe about God, I do not yet wish to meet Him in the afterlife."

"I never claimed that she was mine, Sedley." Connor laughed, trying desperately to salvage whatever dignity he had left when it came to Mairi MacGregor.

"In truth, Captain Grant," interjected Edward, who had, until that moment, remained blissfully quiet, "you did. It was right after you told Captain Sedley not to concern himself with the color of her eyes. He asked you if she was yours and you said—"

"Edward," Connor silenced him in his best I'm-going-to-kill-ye-later voice. "Miss MacGregor already believes me an ogre who cannot take a step without falling over my knuckles, let's not try to convince her of it further, aye?"

He turned to offer Mairi a jaunty grin he hoped would convince her of the triviality of the topic. At least it was to him. But she looked right through him from across the table and she saw the way his heart beat for her. Her eyes on him softened and her lips curled slightly at the corners. It was enough to still his breath and fire his blood. She *was* his. And he would kill any man who thought to take her from him. He wanted her back, back in his arms. Back in his life. If she wanted him to fight for her, he would do that, and more.

Seeming to have concluded her subtle interrogation on Nicholas Sedley, Mairi turned the topic of conversation to one the rest at the table, including Claire, preferred.

Their battles and the wounds they suffered through them. Their laughter was loud and their banter intimate. Connor's friends listened in stunned silence while his parents recounted their encounter with General George Lambert when they rescued Claire's brother from his clutches. They were equally astonished though a bit more doubtful when Claire boasted of Mairi's skill with the sword.

"Four of the scars I bear," Connor told them, "were inflicted by Miss MacGregor's blade." He pulled at the bows around his neck, spread his collar, and unlaced his waistcoat beneath. "She struck me here in practice." Yanking at his shirt, he revealed a small scar on his collarbone. "She was angry with me about something."

"Ye told me that ye would prefer me with sewing needles in my hands rather than daggers," Mairi reminded him.

He still did, but he wasn't about to tell her that again. He was trying to win her, after all, not find one of her hidden knives at his throat.

"Pardon the intrusion."

Connor looked up and thought about smashing Henry de Vere's face into the nearest wall for the hundredth time. When he saw Lady Elizabeth linked to her brother's arm he expelled a sigh of annoyance, but managed a brief smile. She beamed back.

"Captain Grant." It was her brother who spoke. "I would like to offer you my sister's hand for the first dance."

"They are getting ready to clear the tables," Lady Elizabeth informed him eagerly.

"In return"—Oxford smiled down at Mairi and reached for her hand, bringing Connor to his feet—"I would like to be the first to escort Miss MacGregor to the dance floor."

"Mayhap another time." Connor's thick voice sliced the air and halted Oxford's movement. "Lady Elizabeth"—he turned to her with a more polite smile—"I'm afraid my steps are still too slow fer dancing. And Miss MacGregor"—he returned his hard gaze to Oxford—"is not a slice of mutton to be haggled over."

He wasn't sure which of the siblings grew redder. Henry or Elizabeth. He suspected Henry was the more dangerous of the two when he remained behind to offer them all a tight, gracious smile before he followed his sister back to their table.

"The tables are being cleared." Connor remained on his feet and reached across the table for Mairi's hand. "We're going fer a walk."

"In this rain?"

Connor tipped his head to wink at Edward as Mairi fit her hand into his. "Ye call this rain, lad? In the Highlands, we call it a trickle. Aye, Mairi?"

She nodded and smiled at him as he led her out of the Banqueting Hall.

Chapter Twenty-five

*M*airi tried hard to concentrate on a dozen differ- ent things as she followed Connor out of the palace. The glorious scent of the night air, fresh and crisp from the spring rain. The conversations with his men at the table. But her thoughts were scattered by the feel of Connor's warm hand closed around hers. It was an inti- mate, possessive touch, almost as thrilling as his kisses; a startlingly familiar one that brought her back to their childhood when he used to come for her to take her riding with him. Only now his hand was bigger, his palm rougher with calluses from all his years of wielding a sword. She looked up at his handsome profile as they entered the Pebble Court and stepped beneath one of the upper gal- leries shielding them from the rain. He'd told Sedley that she was his. She believed it thanks to Edward Willing- ham's validation and his guileless expression while he reminded Connor of his own words. It was an arrogant statement for Connor to have made, especially when he had had no idea at the time that she did not truly hate him, but it did not anger her. Aye, he was a bit primitive in his ways of thinking, but she liked it. It proved England had not changed him all that much. It proved he still cared for her, he still wanted her. But how much? Would he leave England for her this time?

"Captain Sedley is a Calvinist," she said in a hopeless attempt to redirect her thoughts away from his mouth. "He may deny it, but he follows Prince William's faith and likely wants James off the throne."

"I know," he said quietly.

She heard the regret in his voice and squeezed his hand, wanting to comfort him. "Have ye known him long then?"

"Aye, we arrived at Whitehall at about the same time. We fought Charles's enemies together, and proved our skill on the field. He rose in rank with me, without envy that I had been promoted before him. We remained friends, despite his being a Protestant. It tears at me to think he does William's bidding, even to the point of seeing me dead."

"But ye dinna' know if he was behind the attack fer certain, Connor. Or why William would even want ye dead. Besides," she added, desperate to ease his troubled thoughts, "he seems more interested in the effect his military garb has on women than on his possible enemies."

Unlike Connor, who had not bothered to tie his bows back in place. Did he know how magnificent he looked in his courtly garb? How tall and elegant he was in his stately justacorps and polished boots, or how his opened collar and discarded bows revealed a less tamed gentleman beneath? He did not seem to care all that much, which made him even more alluring. She moved a bit closer and inhaled his clean scent, slightly tinged with the fragrance of sandalwood.

"D'ye smell it?" She broke away from his hold, desperate for a moment to think clearly. She was so afraid to love him like this and lose him again. She could not survive it a second time. Could she leave Scotland for him?

She walked to the edge of the broad walk above her and looked out into the torrent a few inches from her face. She closed her eyes and inhaled deeply. "D'ye smell the grass? The wind? I vow I can almost smell the heather."

He came up behind her; so close she could feel the heat from his body, the soft exhalation of breath after he inhaled. "It smells like home." His deep, languid voice fell across her nape and made her heart crash against her chest. *Home.*

She smiled and turned to look up into his eyes. His breath appeared to stall as he reached to wipe a raindrop from the tip of her nose.

"Ye smell good," she told him before she could stop herself.

"Thank ye." His smile was as slow and sensual as his tone.

Och, to hell with trying to be coy. It was not in her nature and he knew it. "And ye look quite handsome, as well. When Lady Hollingsworth saw ye, I swear she—"

"I don't care what any other eye sees, but yers."

She smiled and looked up at the moon. It was not full, but there was enough of it to coat his tongue with silver. "Yer words are pretty, Connor, but I am no longer a child who can be swayed by them."

She moved away from him before she gave in to desire to be in his arms. She had let him back into her life, back into her heart. If they separated again, it would destroy her.

"D'ye know how I grieved fer ye?" She turned to

look at him, needing to tell him, needing him to know the truth. "Every day I worried that ye would die fighting fer a Protestant king and I would never see yer face again."

She drank in the sight of it now. Her Connor, older, a bit darker, but always her Connor. He listened silently while she told him her fears, and why she had become so cold and unforgiving toward him. He looked like he wanted to go to her, but instead let her have her say.

"Every time I saw a rider approaching Camlochlin I feared he carried a missive informing us of yer death. I waited day after day and year after year fer yer return, but ye did not come back—"

"I couldn't," he said finally, and moved a step toward her. "Not in the beginning. Ye knew that. I sent ye letters in my own hand asking ye to come to me—"

"I could not leave Scotland. Ye knew that."

"I hoped ye loved me more than Camlochlin, Mairi."

Och, God, she had loved him more. Had she been wrong about him all these years? Had he truly continued to love her even after he left? She had convinced herself that his asking her to come to him was nothing but an easy way to remove her from his life. Had she been wrong?

"Gossip traveled far, Connor. Ye had taken lovers. Yer prowess in the bedchamber became as infamous as yer faither's once was."

"'Twas ye I wanted, Mairi." When he stood over her, she trembled at the potency of his gaze. "From the moment I saw ye again I knew I would never love anyone but ye."

"But seven years, Connor..."

"Listen to me." His breath fell softly against her face, his words, quietly and earnestly against her ears. "It didn't matter how long I was gone. I never stopped thinking of ye, wanting ye. I still cannot think of my life without ye. Now quit yer arguing and kiss me."

Henry de Vere stood on the upper gallery looking down into the Pebble Court and at the couple locked in each other's arms. His heart crashed to his feet. The rain pelted down on his head, sopping his wig until he tore it off to keep the soaked curls from his eyes. He knew Grant cared for Mairi. Any fool with a pair of eyes in his head could see it. But Mairi. She'd fooled him well.

Bitch.

He hated himself for not hating her the way she deserved. Elizabeth was correct about him. He was a spineless fool, for he still cared for Mairi. He still wanted her, even knowing what she had done to his face. He wanted to forgive her. He would have, if she loved him. But there she was, kissing James's only Catholic captain, whispering with him, laughing with him. Most likely, they were laughing about him. He should have killed her the moment he knew who she was.

He turned to look behind him when he heard someone whisper his name. Lizzy. He wanted her to see and beckoned her closer, keeping his finger pressed to his mouth to urge her to be silent.

He smiled at her sharp intake of breath. It was better if she knew the truth and faced it as he himself must do. When she stormed back inside, he gave the lovers one more black look, and then followed her.

She whirled on him the instant they were alone. "I thought I told you to do something about her!"

"I tried—"

"You couldn't because you are a spineless fool, Henry! I told father as much!"

He snatched her hand as she moved to turn away. "What do you mean? What did you speak to father about?"

"That he could not depend on you without my help."

"That is untrue," he argued. "I will think of a way to get what we both want, Lizzy." He looked over his shoulder at the rain outside and thought of Mairi. He would think of something.

Chapter Twenty-six

$\mathcal{M}$airi leaned against the door frame leading to the
tiltyard and watched Connor practicing alone in
the morning rain. She wanted to go to him and pull him
in from the cold. He had just survived a grave fever. She
did not want him to fall to another. But her feet would
not move. She knew he had practiced every day before
the attack and she had avoided watching him at all cost.
Now, she could not tear her eyes away from him. His
strikes were brutal and precise. His aim was sure and
his steps light and determined. She thought of the night
before when he swore that his heart had never betrayed
her, when he kissed her and held her and made her laugh
when she what she really wanted to do was weep over all
their lost time together. He forgave her so easily for not
trusting him. It made her feel worse for not granting him
the same mercy for so long. Did she believe his words
of love? She wanted to. Och, God, how she wanted to.
Still, the thought of him with other women drove her
mad. Watching him now, his wet hair swirling around
his frosty eyes as he parried and jabbed the air with his

sword, she had trouble imagining how any woman could resist him. Soaked through, his fine, gauze shirt clung to his body, defining every nuance of muscle. His damp breeches fit like a second skin over his long, powerful legs, and against the titillating fullness between them. Was it true? Had he loved only her?

His eyes found her in the entryway and he smiled and lowered his sword. He certainly had not smiled that way at any other woman in Whitehall since he had arrived— like the sun just broke through the gloom.

She watched him sheathe his sword and cross the tiltyard on his way to her, admiring the slow, casual sway of his gait. He was sensuality incarnate. Every movement, every smile, every word was given with the leisurely confidence of a patient hunter, certain of catching his prey without any overexertion. Unless, of course, his prey gave him a fight.

"How did I do?"

She blinked and stifled the sigh fighting against her lips. "Not bad fer a man with a hole in his guts."

His dimples flashed. "The hole was sealed and is healing quite well. Feel fer yerself." He took her hand and pressed her palm to his hard belly. When his grin widened, proving that he was enjoying her sudden dis-composure, she poked him gently in his wound.

"It still has some ways to go, I would say."

He laughed and grimaced at the same time. "I vow, wench, ye'd be happy to see me in bed fer the next fortnight."

She looked away, flustered at the thought that he was not entirely incorrect. Unfortunately, he caught the very slight flush of her cheeks.

"Now that I think about it," he said, his voice rumbling low in his chest and along her nerve endings, "I'm not feeling all that well."

When she looked at him, afraid for an instant that he was falling ill again, he moistened his lips with his tongue, as if preparing them for a kiss.

"I will send for the queen's physicians right away!" she teased, and spun around to see to the task. He dragged her back and closed his arms around her.

"Ye're the only medicine I need."

He planted a series of slow, soft kisses on her mouth; enough to make her insides burn for something harder and less tamed...

He groaned from somewhere deep in his chest as he pulled away. "Ye tempt me to be uncivil and take back what I want." The something that made his eyes blaze with blue fire every time he looked at her.

She wanted to tell him to do it. Of course, she wouldn't surrender all, not without a fight. That's what he liked. Even a fool could see it, and she had been a fool.

"Then ye would force me to cut ye doun, and not with my tongue."

He curled his mouth into a slow, sensual smile, so close to hers. "I'll have ye, lass. No blade will stop me."

Did he mock her skill with a blade? Why shouldn't he? He'd never seen her fight with one. Mayhap it was time he learned who she had become.

"Are ye certain about that, Captain?" she whispered, tilting her lips to his ear, then poked him in the hip with the point of her dagger.

He looked down and laughed, then he released her and stepped back, stretching out his arms at his sides. "Do ye want to give this a go?" he challenged, his grin wide and challenging.

Did she want to give it a go? Hell, aye, she did! Claire had told her they should refrain from honing their skills while in England, lest they stir too much interest in the warriors of Skye. Mairi hadn't practiced in a fortnight. She nodded and aimed her blade at him. He laughed again, and this time she smiled with him.

"Let us discover fer certain," he drawled while pulling his sword from its sheath, "if ye fight as well as any man."

"Likely better." She followed the twirl of his long blade, impressed by the ease and fluidity with which he handled his hilt.

He swung. She blocked and her dagger fell from her hand. She produced another from somewhere within her English gown and had it pointing at him before he prepared for his next assault. She knew she was at a disadvantage with her metal being at least a foot shorter than his. She wouldn't be able to hold him off for too long. She blocked another half-dozen strikes, moving quickly on her feet. She managed to slip behind him once, but he was fast, faster than any other of the men she'd fought, and blocked her knife from going through him. When he separated her from her second weapon and yanked her forward by her wrist, she reached for the pistol in his belt.

"Then"—she breathed up into his face and then pointed his pistol at it—"I willna' stop ye with a blade."

"Hell, Mairi." He looked at her in astonishment and then laughed again and pulled her closer. "Ye're a MacGregor aright."

She smiled. The way she used to when he was the air she needed to breathe, his company and his kisses all she ever needed to be happy. He hadn't called her a lass.

"Yer mother taught me well," she said, holstering his pistol and making a mental note to thank Claire later for raising a son who appreciated the fight in a woman.

"I want to bring ye someplace," he said, staring deep

into her eyes, his arms coiled snugly around her right there in the tiltyard.

Thankfully, no one was yet awake.

"Where?"

"Come. We'll need horses."

She let him lead her to the stables, her heart beating with excitement. Where was he taking her? Was it safe for him to ride? Would they be alone? Hell, she had not done anything pleasurable since she and Colin had met with the MacKinnons last month to plan a raid on a group of Covenanters from Dumfries who were traveling to the Highlands for the games. A raid she had had to miss thanks to James's coronation.

"Are we going to the park?" she asked, hiking up her gown and pulling herself up into her saddle.

"Ye'll see soon enough." He gave her rump a gentle slap, then eyed her bare calf and looked up toward the heavens as if beseeching God to give him strength.

He winced mounting his horse, then dug his heels into the beast's flanks and rode past her with a twinkle in his eyes.

They rode for over an hour in the abating rain, following the Thames southward until they came to a lush countryside shrouded in mist. For one glorious moment Mairi imagined she was home in the Highlands.

"'Tis breathtaking," she said, reining in beside Connor.

"Aye, I knew ye would like it here."

"Where are we?"

"Not yet there."

She looked around at the wild exterior of rolling hills and vast open grasslands, startlingly green against the gray swath of sky above. In the distance, tall, ancient oaks pierced the fog.

"Look." Connor pointed to a fallow deer traipsing across the dewy meadow. "Let's follow her." He did not wait for her response but flicked his reins and took off after the deer as it disappeared into to the rising mist without a trace.

Not willing to be outrun in a chase, Mairi dug in her heels and gave her horse its head. Connor had to be in pain bouncing in his saddle, but if he was, he paid no heed to it. He turned twice to look behind him, his hair blowing across his eyes while he laughed at her attempts to pass his horse. She chased him, just as she had done before England had separated them.

He finally slowed his mount when they came to a secluded woodland enclosure. He dismounted with care and hushed her while she did the same. He brought her to a dense thicket of mulberry trees surrounded by currant bushes and crouched low, then turned and beckoned her to do the same.

Beyond the foliage, she saw a small group of red deer, a few does and their young, nibbling at the grass. Breath held, she watched as two does lifted their heads in her direction and then went back to eating.

"They are not as skittish as the deer in the Highlands," she whispered close to Connor's ear.

"There are more people here," he explained, turning to her and almost touching his nose to hers. "They are... Hell, ye're beautiful."

Win her? Och, God, he just prevailed victorious. She moved in to kiss him and frowned instead when the deer leaped away and out of sight. "I frightened them."

Connor lifted his hand to her face and cupped her cheek. He looked into her eyes like a man who had just returned home from years of battle. "I have been lost without ye, Mare."

"Fergive me," she said as his mouth covered hers.

His kiss was like a brand against her lips, scalding with checked desire. The flick of his tongue burned like a flame, consuming her until there was nothing left but him, his taste, his scent, his passion. She tunneled her fingers through his damp, silky hair and stroked her palms over his bristly jaw, opening her mouth to his.

Closing his arms around her, he deepened their kiss. She answered with equal fervor until they both tumbled off their haunches and onto the wet, leafy ground. He took most of the blow, landing on his back, but offered her a slow, scintillating smile before cupping her nape and dragging her back for more.

Mairi liked her position on top of him, though she was mindful of putting too much of her weight on his wound. She darted her tongue over his and ran her palms over the sleek muscles of his chest. She had not told him, but she had remained chaste in his absence. Why in blazes would she want another man after she had had him? When she groaned against his firm mouth, he flipped her over on her back without breaking their kiss and covered her with his body. She tried to move, still cautious of hurting him. He pressed his hand to her hip to hold her still and wedged his erection hard between her thighs, ready to take back sole ownership of her if he chose to do so. She answered by biting his lower lip in a last attempt to rein in the beast. He smiled against her teeth, pulling a groan from deep within her, and cupped her rump in his palm. He rubbed his need against her in a flagrant display of his victory—a victory that she welcomed.

"Nae," he groaned roughly, and rose back upon his haunches. "Not here." Taking her hand, he hauled her to her feet and turned her around to look beyond the grove. "Do ye see that?"

She narrowed her eyes and then she took a step forward. Was that a rooftop? A chimney?

He took her hand before she could ask him and led her and their horses through the thicket. They emerged in an open field of grass and lush carpets of bluebell and poppies. It was so beautiful that Mairi had to stop to take it all in. He urged her onward, bringing her to where the field sloped downward into a small vale.

Mairi stopped again, and this time Connor remained still at her side as she gazed at a small manor house nestled in the center of the vale, surrounded on every side by more bluebells and tall yellow flowers that swayed in the misty breeze.

"'Tis..." She caught her breath and fought the sudden sting behind her eyes.

"Aye?"

"...the bonniest place I have ever seen. Who lives there?"

"I do."

She turned to look at him, unsure if she heard him right. "Ye?" When he nodded, she shook her head. "I thought ye lived at Whitehall? How...? When...?"

He smiled. "I began building it seven years ago." He curled his fingers around hers again and picked up his steps. "It has only been finished fer two and I haven't been able to spend much time in it, but 'tis a place to come when I need a rest from society and practiced propriety."

"Ye built this seven years ago?" she asked, still stunned by the sight of it, and now by what his words meant, as well.

He'd built her a home, just as he'd promised. He had never promised where. "Is this where we were to live if I had come to ye?"

"Aye, if it pleased ye."

If it pleased her? It was absolutely perfect. Though it did not have Camlochlin's spiky turrets and solid battlements carved from the side of a mountain, it was the closest thing to her beloved Highland home that she'd ever seen. She swiped a tear from her eye and looked away from him, lest he see. How long had he searched for this location? The sloping vale, the wildflowers that scented the air, the gossamer mist that hovered above the chimney? Dear God, he had truly wanted her to come here and live with him. To be his, always, just as he'd promised.

"I was a fool," she said softly, wondering how he didn't hate her for her constant rejection. "I—"

He captured her words and her breath with a deep, needful kiss that weakened her in his arms.

"Let's begin again."

She nodded, surrendering her heart to him fully, trusting him completely. She smiled when he scooped her up and carried her to the front door, and then beyond.

Chapter Twenty-seven

$\mathcal{M}$airi didn't see the interior of the house Connor had built for her. Cradled in his arms, she saw nothing but the desire in his storm-colored eyes while he carried her up the stairs.

"I love ye, Mairi. Only ye fer the rest of my days."

He spoke true. It was all there in the way he looked down at her behind the golden wisps of his hair. He was lost, hopelessly in love with her, and helpless to do anything to stop it.

Her heart exalted. She felt as if she were dreaming. Only, her dreams had not been this wonderful. He loved her. He'd never stopped. Lord, was it true? Had God been listening to her childish prayers, and granted them now that she was a woman? Had she wasted so much time without him, hating him, angry at the world for taking him from her?

She knew where he was bringing her, and she wanted to go with him. She wasn't coy or shy about what he wanted to do with her. She had been with him before, had wished for years to be with him again.

Was he real?

She reached up to touch his face, unsure. He smiled against her fingers and then kissed them. "Tell me again."

"I love ye," he whispered, knowing what she wanted him to say. When she pulled him in for another kiss, he responded with equal fervor, opening his mouth to relish in the taste of her and give back the passion she offered as they fell onto a heavenly soft mattress.

She had no idea how he managed to undo the endless clasps of her gown with one hand, when it took an extra pair to dress her. She didn't care. His mouth covering hers distracted her from everything else. His hot, eager tongue stroked her like a flame, deep, scintillatingly slow, driving her to madness. His hands, tender yet firm, ignited her nerve endings everywhere they touched her. She felt the soft silk of her gown come away, leaving only the thin shift beneath. She didn't recoil at his seeing her scantily clad body. Nae, she knew this man. He knew her body, and she knew his.

At least, she thought she did.

When he rose up off the bed to tear at his shirt, exposing the hard, rippling sinews beneath, she caught her breath and reached for him. She'd seen him in his sickbed, not poised above her breathing heavily and ready to take her. She ran her fingertips over scars that were not there when last she lay with him. Seven years had changed him, thickening his muscles, sculpting him into something so perfect she almost couldn't believe he was hers.

He bent and swept his mouth across hers again, seeming to grow even harder as he pulled at the laces securing his breeches. He didn't undress completely, but withdrew enough to cast his hungry gaze over her.

"Ye're mine, Mairi." He vowed, kissing her again. "Ye will always be mine."

Aye, she knew it was the truth. No man in seven years came close to winning her heart. No man but Connor Grant ever would.

He swept his palms down her arms and cupped her breasts through the damp thinness of her shift. He groaned, breaking their kiss to graze his teeth over her chin, down her throat, setting fire to her nerve endings. She felt his fingers tighten on the neckline of her shift. She heard the sound of the fine linen tearing in two. Her breath stopped as her breasts spilled out into his powerful hands.

"I want ye bare, hot, and wet beneath me."

She didn't know if it was the husky pitch of his voice that made her muscles convulse beneath him or the hunger in his eyes, like a man...nae, not a man but a wolf who had just spotted its prey after weeks without food. He wanted to devour her and she wanted him to do it. She had wasted enough time rejecting him and now she wanted to give him what he desired, what was his from the day he had first touched her. Saints, but he was touching her now, everywhere, with every part of him. His tongue flicking over her sensitive nipple drove her to the edge of darkness, or mayhap it was the erotic surge of his hips, grinding all that hard male desire, still confined in his tight breeches, deeper against the heat of her inner thighs. She scored her fingernails down his back and delighted in the gentle agony of his teeth razing the soft mound of her breast, the honeyed stubble along his jaw, rough against her flesh. He was hers, and hers alone. She no longer doubted it, and she wanted more of him, every thick, throbbing inch.

She cupped his face in her trembling hands and pulled him up to kiss him again. His mouth was rough, his kiss harsh, hungry, and passionate. She pushed him off her, using her hips, clinging to his face...his lips as she turned him on his back and straddled him.

But this was not a man who would be so easily subdued, though he did enjoy the challenge. He gazed up at her, his smile dark and dangerous as he took in the full sight of her, her long black tresses falling to his hips. He tore the rest of her shift away, yanked the full length of it over her head, and then flung it aside. She did not mind being naked in front of him, on top of him. Not when the luster in his eyes revealed what he thought of her.

He told her nonetheless. "Ye're so fine, Mairi Mac-Gregor. Ye lay waste to my heart and restore my soul."

"And ye, Connor Grant, are the master of my heart." She pushed off his hips to pull his breeches down over his thighs. Dear Lord, he had grown! She smiled, despite the trepidation that coursed through her when his imposing shaft sprang forth toward the heavens. "Ye have finally succeeded in frightening me."

"I don't believe it." He laughed, beguiling her senseless with the beauty of his face. She knew every inch of it, every angle, every expression. She missed it in her life and would give up anything to have it back. Anything he asked.

He sat up to get closer to her, kicked his breeches away from his ankles, and curled his arm around her waist. "Ye've ridden me before, Mare." He wound her long hair around his fist and pulled her head back, exposing her throat to his mouth. He bit her and gave her rear a short slap, driving her up over his heavy erection.

She could have been afraid of taking such a beast,

pulsing and ready between her legs, and of the master who wielded it with such passion and dominance. But his power over her, even looking up at her, thrilled her too much to be afraid. There were no coy pretenses about her virginity. She knew what to expect and she couldn't wait to have him inside her again.

Cupping her hips against his, he laved his tongue down the valley between her breasts, kissing and sucking her nipples until she squirmed atop him. His rough palms grazed over her buttocks, squeezing and guiding her in a rhythm that matched his own.

"Look at ye." He withdrew just enough to set his simmering gaze on her. "Bare, hot, and verra wet." He moistened his lips with the tip of his tongue as though he couldn't wait to taste her.

He would have to wait a wee bit longer, for his thick shaft felt too good against her. She managed a teasing smile while she lifted her hands to scoop up her hair. "But not beneath ye." She gyrated her hips, slower, deeper.

"Ye will be," he promised, spreading her over his full length. "After I have ye from behind, then against the wall, and then on yer knees."

He bent his knees behind her, pinning her in the cradle of his hips. He swiped her backside again and moved faster beneath her, pressing her over the length of his cock. His mouth clamped down on her breast. He sucked her hard, kneading her rear in his strong hands until he pulled back his glorious head and came all over his bandaged waist.

Connor's muscles spasmed, jerking him upward, harder against her wet crux while the last of his seed spilled over his belly.

He laid back his head, gave out a lusty sigh, then smiled up at her again. "Now that we got that out of the way." He took her bottom in his hands. "Come here." He hadn't had enough. He hadn't even begun.

He was here with her...in their house, in their bed. How many years had he envisioned it? How hard had he tried to stop? She was here with him, surrendering all, finally ready to have him back. He'd asked her how long he should have waited for her. He knew now that he would have waited an eternity. This was his woman, his life mate. They'd been fortunate to meet early, when life was filled with adventure and games, fortunate to be taught what true love should feel like so they would never forget it. He never would, and he wouldn't let her forget either.

He sat up and lifted her tight rump off him. He was going to claim that too if she wasn't careful. When he shifted to the edge of the bed, his upright shaft rubbed against her and she rolled back her head, driving him wild with the need to be inside her.

He rose off the bed to his feet, taking her with him. Straddling her legs around him, he gripped his cock in one hand and her arse in the other, and glided his head over her moist entrance. She groaned and clung to him as he drove his heavy shaft inside her, halfway to the hilt. He held her tight when she cried out, waited a moment longer, then pushed against her again. He kissed away her gentle protests with exquisite care, more in control now, but still less than he wished. He didn't want to hurt her, though he was pleased to find her body so tight. Wrapped around him in nature's embrace, her silken sheath gripping him like a vise, her face, even more beautiful than she was in his dreams, worked at quickening his next release. He slowed, wanting to make love to her until the sun set and then rose again.

Taking her bottom lip between his teeth and fitting his palms beneath her buttocks, he held her up against him while he pushed himself deeper. She jerked in his arms as her pain ebbed and pleasure's talons took hold. He licked the seam of her mouth, lifting her in his hands, spreading her wide and then pushing her back down upon his full length. She cried out and he smiled, covering her mouth. Writhing in his arms, she stroked him to the precipice of madness. This time, he would shoot his bounty into her, reclaiming what belonged to him.

His ecstasy swelled, driving him into her faster, harder, until he drove her against the wall. He cradled her face in his palms and held her up with the force of his thrusts. Her nails along his arms felt like the snap of a whip across his back. She cried out again, close to her release and moving atop him now like a serpent, smooth and sinuous. He erupted watching her come and rammed her hard with each endless spurt he shot into her.

Later, they lay coiled in each other's arms, sated, for now, and basking in the relaxation their exertion had wrought.

"Tongues will be flapping by tomorrow because of our disappearance," Mairi said, tracing her finger gently over his bandaged waist.

Hell, how could the gentle stroke of her fingertips heat his blood again so soon? "They've already begun."

"Lady Oxford and Lady Hollingsworth will likely try to claw out my eyes. I dinna' blame them though. 'Tis a fine man they lost to me." She lifted her eyes to his and smiled, smiting his heart.

"Ye built a house fer me, Connor."

"I did."

"Ye pined fer me."

When his only answer this time was a dark scowl, her smile deepened and she snuggled closer to him. "Tell me about all the letters ye sent to my brother asking about me."

Hell, why did she have to look so bonnie in his arms that he was tempted to turn away before he grinned back at her like some lovesick fool. Which was exactly what he was. "Ye're a black-hearted wench, Mairi."

Her soft laughter muddled his senses, her satisfied sigh set his pathetic heart racing.

"I was thinking about Henry."

What? He pulled away from her to look at her fully. "When?"

"Well, he has been on my mind," she admitted.

Hell, he didn't want to hear this. Since the day he'd arrived, she'd spent much of her time with Oxford. Now she was thinking of the bastard while they made love? If she didn't care for him, then why? He had to know once and for all.

"What is yer interest in Henry de Vere?"

"He is a well of information. He knows everything about everyone here."

Connor stared at her in mild disbelief and horror. He knew he should feel relieved by her confession, but he had the sudden urge to throttle her.

"So ye're spinning yer web around him to gain information from him about Cameronians?"

"I told ye, I never mentioned Cameronians to him."

"Mairi, are ye mad? Do ye not realize that yer asking questions could lead to—"

She looked like she wanted to slap him, but he didn't back away. "I am not a fool, Connor."

"—one of our enemies trying to cause ye harm?"

She arched her brow at him. "*Our* enemies?"

Aye, he was going to throttle her good and then have her locked away in the Tower for her own safety. "Bloody hell, Mairi. *Our* enemies, aye. We fight fer the same cause."

"Aye, now that we have a Catholic king, we do."

"Before that, as well," he argued. "Charles may have been Protestant, but he accepted our ways of thinking and never tried to impose his laws on us. Yer own faither showed him allegiance."

She remained silent for a moment. Was it too much to hope that his spirited stubborn wench agreed with him?

"Mayhap ye are correct about asking too many questions," she admitted, bringing a sigh to his lips. "But he did bring up the Cameronians to me."

"I want ye to cease this, Mairi. I don't like that ye are involved with rebels."

She had the supreme boldness to laugh right in his face. He cupped her face in his hands and stared into her eyes. He knew she didn't like being told what to do, but that was too bloody bad. She was going to listen to him. "Hear me, woman—"

"Do not dare say it, oaf," she warned, staring right back at him. "I can take care of myself. I have done so many times before. I promise ye, my enemies never see me coming."

Oh hell, he hoped she was speaking of her subtle skills at interrogation and not something more nefarious, like her slashing her blades at men in the cover of night.

"Let me break things down fer ye, Mairi. I love ye. I have always loved ye, and I will never love anyone after ye. If ye were hurt or..." He paused, unable to speak the words, and pulled her close into his arms. "Ye would set me on a rampage that neither England nor Scotland could withstand. Do ye want that?"

She shook her head no and blinked back the moisture that made her eyes glitter like the misty mountains surrounding Camlochlin.

"But I must find out why he spoke about my enemies, Connor."

Damn her, she was stubborn. "Ye said he may have taken note of yer interest while ye were speaking to Queensberry."

She shook her head. "Nae, there is something else. I know there is, but I canna' tell ye what 'tis, fer I dinna' know myself. Something that nags at me. Something I should know. I know he cares fer me and it has created quite a dilemma that I must soon address."

"What dilemma is that?" he asked her, trying to sound unfazed now that he knew she wasn't thinking about him in a romantic way.

"I have to tell him that I dinna' feel the same way."

"I will tell him fer ye."

"Och." She gave his arm a playful slap. "Ye will leave him be."

Like hell he would.

"I will tell him myself after ye return me to the palace."

"That isn't going to be anytime soon."

"I am sore."

"I'll be gentle."

"Liar." She laughed and nestled under his arm.

Connor watched her a few moments later when her even breaths proved that she had fallen asleep. If he lived to be fifty, he would never forget her words to him last night. *I was lost without ye, Connor.* As he had been without her. They had wasted so much time. No more. He drew her in closer and kissed her head while she slept. She was his, his from the day she told him she loved him through her toothless smile and sealed his nine-year-old heart to her forever. He would never let anything separate them again.

Especially Henry de Vere.

※

Chapter Twenty-eight

*M*airi woke a short while later and looked up into Connor's tender gaze. Hell, had he been watching her while she slept? She hoped she had not been snoring and felt for any drool around her mouth. She didn't usually nap during the day. Clashing blades earlier must have drained her...along with making love to the magnificent Highlander in her arms.

"Do ye remember when we fell asleep in that cave above the braes of Sgurr Na Stri?" he asked, his thick burr purring across her ears.

How could she forget? It was two days after he had first made love to her. She stretched and then smiled when he moved over her, covering her body with his.

"Yer mother was frantic with worry because we'd been missing fer six hours."

"I thought my faither was going to kill ye when he found us locked in each other's arms."

"Aye." He laughed down at her, making her question again if he was real. "We were fortunate to be fully dressed."

She nodded, remembering. "We were even more

fortunate that ye did not leave me with a babe." A wistful sigh parted her lips and she touched her fingers to his dimples. "Although, ten and five is not too young to become a mother. I heard that Lady Hollingsworth was ten and two when her father promised her to Lord Hollingsworth."

"Aye?" He kissed her lips, her nose, her eyes with excruciating tenderness. "Do ye want to carry my bairns then?"

"Aye," she told him, unable to hide the truth from him...or from herself any longer. Her muscles tightened sharply when he rubbed the pad of his thumb over her nipple, bringing it to life. "As many as we can stand making. But..."

His kisses paused and he stared into her eyes. "What?"

She did not want to put it to him. She was too afraid of what he might say. His love did not come with a chain he would ever allow himself to be led by. He had already proven to her that he could live for many years without her. He may have wanted her, loved her during that time, but he had not allowed himself to succumb to the indignity of begging for her back. If he loved England and he wanted to remain here, he would do so, with or without her. What if he asked her to stay here with him? Could she give up Scotland, the Highlands for him? Could she live in England?

She didn't want to think on that now and smiled at him instead while he kissed her chin.

"Are ye trying to make up fer seven years in one day?"

"What am I supposed to do when ye're lying here snoring and driving me mad?" He traced the soft curve of her inner thigh with his fingers. His touch tickled and she laughed against him.

"I love yer hair," he told her, catching handfuls of it where it fell down her arms. He brought a lock to his nose and inhaled. "'Tis filled with yer scent."

"And what is my scent?" she purred beneath him.

He thought about it for a moment and then crooked one end of his mouth upward. "Like the moors after a storm and mountain air blowing through the heather.

"I love yer breasts." He lowered his head and kissed each in turn. "And how they react to my touch. How they taste in my mouth."

She gazed down at him and felt her heart swell and threaten to burst within. Only he could tame her with that tongue. He wielded it with power and dominance when she came against him, and with the beauty of his praises when she did not. She took his face in her palms to look at him. When she did, so close that she could feel his breath on her chin, she almost wept.

"I love ye, Connor."

"I know."

She waited, and then waited a little longer, before she glared at him. He laughed, obviously quite pleased with himself for teasing her. She pinched him hard with her right hand and then again with her left. She did not do it a third time though. He clasped both her wrists in one hand and pulled them over her head.

"Since ye were six if I'm not mistaken."

Arrogant scoundrel! She tried to pretend insult but she couldn't help but shine her full smile on him. "Say it!" she demanded. "Say ye were a bloody fool fer leaving me."

His right dimple twinkled. "I needed a rest from all the years I spent with ye, Mairi."

When her mouth opened to form a belligerent O,

he kissed it closed. "I was a bloody fool fer leaving ye. Ye are my stars, my sun, my world. I love ye. Are ye satisfied?"

When she nodded happily, he muttered the word "wench" and let go of her wrists to score a trail of wet, hungry kisses down the column of her neck. He paused at her pulse to feel it quicken, over the peaks of her breasts, dragging the breath from her lips. He licked the soft hollows of her belly and gave her hip a gentle bite.

She watched him move slowly, wickedly down her body with no idea of where he meant to finish.

Her hooded gaze followed him, lavishing in the sight of him rising up on his knees, taking her calf with him. He blazed a path with his mouth, from her curling toes to her inner thigh. She almost giggled at the squeak he pulled from her. Och, was he going to kiss her *there*? She groaned at the wickedness of it. Then another thought occurred to her. How did he know to kiss her there? Was this something men did often? When he dipped his head between her legs, she did not care how he knew. He flicked his tongue over her scalding bud and light exploded behind her eyes in a dozen different shades of red. She squirmed and groaned under his tender ministrations, begging him to take her and satisfy this dreadful need to be claimed by him again and again.

She almost cried out with anticipation when he moved up her body and pushed her legs apart with his knees. She looked up at him hovering above her, his muscles trembling with a hunger that had not yet been satisfied. His shaft was iron hard and aimed at the heavens, ready to take her. Och, but she was ready to be taken.

Holding her legs apart, he dipped his hips and watched his thick head penetrate her. His smile, when he set it on her, was hotter than the molten steel searing its way into her body. Saints have mercy on her, the size of him hurt! He moved slowly, gently, as he had promised, caressing and kissing her calf while his plunges grew a wee bit deeper. He was too big, but the sight of him drenched her with desire.

She arched her back, inviting him, wanting him to fill her. When he released her legs she coiled them around him and pulled him closer. He licked her mouth. She bit his lip softly in return and their joy at being together again overflowed into laughter. Soon though, they grew serious again as pleasure flowed like a deluge through their veins, quickening their dance, tightening their muscles.

"My wildcat." He took her by the hands and pulled them over her head. "Our victories approach."

She moved wildly beneath him, taking him in to the hilt and then out, almost to the tip, again and again until he grunted something sinful and held her down hard while they found their release together.

Mairi opened her eyes when she was certain by Connor's slow, even breaths that he was asleep. It would be dark soon and she wanted to look around the inside of the house, alone before the sun took its light. She had never been inside a manor house before, so she had no recollection to compare with what Connor had built.

"I'll build ye a home, Mairi, one ye'll love as much as Camlochlin."

Her eyes burned at the memory of his promise. He had kept it. Was the inside as fine as the outside?

So far, she could attest to only one thing for certain. The mattress beneath her was as soft and luxurious as hell. Even more comfortable than her bed at the palace.

She supposed the king saved his best goose down for his finer friends.

She sat up slowly, careful not to wake Connor, and looked around the bedroom. She wouldn't call the interior cavernous, though the rich wood-paneled walls likely made it feel smaller, infinitely cozy.

Swinging her legs over the side of the bed, she stepped down onto a woven carpet instead of plaited rushes. Not that the room needed either one to warm the feet, for there was no draft at all seeping through the walls. Two mullioned windows made of clear glass allowed golden light to stream in panels across the opposite wall, where stood a large bookcase of gilded wood. It was exquisite. Had Connor carved it? She went to it and her gaze perused the many titles neatly placed upon its shelves. There were books on philosophy, astronomy and navigation, as well as older volumes penned by poets and playwrights.

Something in the corner of the room caught her eye and she moved toward it next. The chessboard rested on a table made of solid walnut with carved branders, a single chair, upholstered in burgundy fabric, pushed beneath it.

She touched her fingers to the knight, carved as smooth as glass. She lifted it and smiled, recognizing it to be their uncle Robert's set. She wondered what his wife, the gentle Lady Anne, would have thought of her favored nephew if she saw him now, a proud Stuart, fighting for his kin.

Och, why hadn't she seen it this way before? The king, whatever religion he practiced, was his kin. She would have done no less for her own.

"There is a dining room and a parlor below stairs."

Mairi turned to him and smiled. "Did I wake ye?"

He nodded, coming toward her. "I heard ye sniffling."

She hastily swiped at her cheek. "Ridiculous. I dinna' sniffle." She looked away from him and down at the knight.

"I think about him at times," Connor said, reaching her and covering her hands with his.

"So do I."

"He was a good man."

"Aye," she said softly, fondly remembering her mother's late brother. "He is still missed at home."

"Tell me about it."

"Home?"

When he nodded, she took him by the hand and led him back to the bed. "Maggie is still as fiery as a hellcat on a hot day. Yer uncle Jamie still manages to love her though."

He laughed. Och, how she loved the sound of it. Rich, infectious, comforting like returning home after an absence.

She told him all he wanted to know about how the souls at Camlochlin fared. He drank in every word like a man starving for what he had lost. He had lost it because of her. He had stopped visiting because she'd asked him to do so.

"What of ye?" he asked, lying on his back and canting his arms behind his head. "When did ye start fighting Cameronians?"

"About six years past."

"Do ye fight them often?"

"Nae. It takes time to gather the information we need to find out who they are and where they will meet up next."

He remained quiet for a time, staring up at the plastered ceiling. She still couldn't believe she was confessing all to him, not because she no longer trusted him, but because she had never told anyone what she did, save for the ones who already knew.

"Do ye think ye might want to stop in the future?"

Someone rapping sharply at the front entrance halted her answer. "Hell." She leaped from the bed and reached for her gown crumpled on the carpet. "Who can that be? Do ye have neighbors?" She hoped so. She prayed it wasn't anyone from the palace. Namely, Graham or Claire Grant.

The knocking came again, this time accompanied by a voice on the other end.

Connor tossed her a grin over his shoulder as he sat up, swinging his legs over the side of the bed. "'Tis Edward."

She nodded and hurried him along, praying that the young cornet hadn't brought anyone with him.

She watched Connor lumber naked toward the door. She would have liked to watch him move about all night without the encumbrance of his clothes, but was he about to answer the bloody door that way?

"Wait!" she practically screeched at him. "Put something on!"

He looked at her, gave her an exasperated sigh, then went for his breeches. Hell, but he had nice legs, so shapely and...Edward knocked again.

Clutching the waist of his breeches in his fists, Connor pulled open the bedroom door and shouted down the stairs. "Just a bloody moment!"

He bent slightly and slipped his foot into the first hole then worked the fabric up his leg. Mairi wiped her brow. How the hell did he manage to look so sensual getting dressed? He took his time, as he did with almost everything else, and she was impressed by his ability to balance himself on one foot for so long.

"Do hurry up."

He flashed her a glare and fit the other leg through. Did he have to stare at her like that, as if he was locking away the key to her happiness, while he laced up? He turned, his breeches tied low on his waist, and she sighed at the two dimples above his backside.

Mairi followed close at his back as he pounded down the stairs. She did her best to pat her hair into some form of neatness, but she knew as he unbolted the door and swung it open that the attempt was useless.

Edward barreled into the house when the door opened. He looked quite disheveled as Mairi peered around Connor's back and was relieved to see his horse and no one else.

"Captain." The cornet swallowed, paused to acknowledge Mairi while she blushed a dozen different shades of crimson, then turned his wide eyes back on Connor. "Forgive my intrusion, Captain, but the king has returned, and he is looking for you."

Chapter Twenty-nine

The whispers of the five guests allowed audience to the king's Presence Chamber echoed off the high gilt ceiling, upon which was written the dates of historic wars that had been made.

Connor stood with his parents, slightly to the right of the cavernous hearth, resting his elbow on the high mantel. He gave his ear to his father as Graham put a dozen different questions to him, but found his gaze returning to the window where Mairi stood, conversing with her brother, who had returned with the king. He watched her smile at something Colin told her and then scowl at something he kept from her. None had been given news about what had taken place during the king's visit to Camlochlin. Instead, Colin had been given strict orders to wait for the king and queen's arrival, when all would be revealed.

They had been waiting for over a quarter of an hour, but no one appeared impatient. Indeed, Mairi looked quite content, if not slightly frustrated by her brother's silence on matters of home. Lord and Lady Huntley used the time to warn Connor of Henry de Vere's insistence on speaking with the king next.

"When I told ye to take the lass back," Graham said, a sly, knowing smile hovering about his lips, belying his careworn tone, "I didn't mean fer ye to ride off with her fer the entire day."

"I wanted to show her the house." Connor shrugged, his gaze drifting back to her. Her eyes found his and they shared an intimate smile. "And to be alone with her fer a little while."

"Things are mended between ye then?" his father asked, noting what passed between them.

"'Tis my hope."

"Oxford must be dealt with," his mother advised, trying to sound serious but barely able to conceal her joy, "He was incensed that you took her away unchaperoned for so many hours."

"I will handle Oxford," Connor promised glibly, then eyed Colin. "'Tis that one who worries me. Is that a pistol in his belt?"

A set of large doors opened and the king and his wife entered from the adjoining Private Oratory. Unlike King Charles, whom Connor had served for almost seven years, James lacked the flamboyancy, both in his attire and in his demeanor, that his brother had possessed. While he was known to sport an abundant wig of blond curls from time to time, tonight his gray regal head went bare.

On his arm, the queen granted them each a smile as delicate as her form while she and her husband waited for formal bows and curtsies to be made.

"Sit," the king invited after he and wife settled into two heavy, high-backed chairs. "We have much to discuss. I have already sent for my finest wine."

He had good news to tell them then, Connor deduced, watching Mairi take her seat beside her brother.

"The queen has advised me," James said, getting directly to the meat of the private audience, "that you all already know where I have been and why I left." He proceeded to tell them anyway. "My enemies discovered my most closely guarded secret, my firstborn daughter, Davina, whom I had spirited away to St. Christopher's Abbey when she was an infant. An attempt was made to kill her, but failed thanks to Robert MacGregor." His eyes, which had gone dark while he spoke of the attack on the abbey, brightened now on Mairi. "Your eldest brother saved her life, for which I am infinitely grateful."

Mairi smiled, swelling with pride. She looked at Connor and he winked at her.

"I must tell you, Miss MacGregor, that when I arrived at Camlochlin, I was certain it would be the last place my eyes would ever look upon. Your 'kin' do not take kindly to uninvited visitors, and if not for young Colin at my side, my men and I would very likely have been struck down with cannon or arrow before we ever reached the castle. Your father was very wise indeed to have built his fortress so strategically placed that an enemy could be seen from leagues away."

"He had need of such protection before King Charles was restored to the throne, Yer Majesty," Mairi reminded him, straightening her shoulders.

"So I was told by the chief." James offered her a smile, then continued, briefly scanning his dark blue gaze over the rest of them. "Unfortunately though, we were attacked unawares by the same men who burned the abbey."

Immediately, Graham rose to his feet. Mairi was about to do the same, when the king held up his palm. "No one from Camlochlin was injured, though I did lose thirteen of my men. We were ambushed beyond the braes of..." He looked to Colin for assistance.

"Bla Bheinn," Colin supplied magnanimously, then went back to examining a thread that had come loose from his plaid.

"Ah, yes, Bla Bheinn." The king nodded and waited while a server entered the chamber with their wine and poured each of them a drink, then left again. "Admiral Peter Gilles set his men, armed with pistol and sword, behind the hillocks and once again, tried to kill my daughter by firing at her."

"Bastard!"

Everyone turned to Claire, who returned their stares with an unrepentant one of her own. Mary of Modena smiled at her.

The king continued to tell them what had taken place after the attack and that Admiral Gilles had been killed before any could discover who had sent him.

"Then mayhap yer daughter should not be brought to Whitehall just yet," Connor told the king.

"She will not be returning at all." James set his gaze on each of them in turn. "She will remain with her new family where she will be safe."

"Pardon, Sire?" Mairi said, sounding as stunned as the rest of them looked. "Her new family?"

"Yes, I discovered, quite by accident in the midst of a bloody struggle, that your brother Robert had wed her."

Everyone's mouth, excluding the king's, his wife's, and Colin's, fell open.

"I can assure you that I was equally astounded," James went on. "But the man loves her, that I can tell you. And my daughter loves him in return."

"You gave your blessing to the union then?" Claire asked, voicing, still slack jawed, what the others wanted to ask.

"Of course. An army more ferocious than any at St. Christopher's surrounds Davina now. Besides, she was not raised among the masses. She would never find happiness at Whitehall, and I wanted to give her that, having been unable all her life to give her anything else."

Given the fact that Colin rarely smiled at anyone, Connor was equally surprised when he caught the subtle smile the sedate lad offered the king now.

"I was informed by your father and brothers, Miss MacGregor, that we are now considered your kin."

Connor watched Mairi's smile on the king go warm with newfound affection, partly because he was now, by Highland ways, her kin. But mostly because of how he spoke of his daughter, and of her clan. She would swear her fealty to James Stuart, as he had. It was a poignant moment to be certain, but Connor couldn't help but wonder how much harder she would now fight against their mutual enemies.

"He also asked that I return you home with the Lord and Lady Huntley at my convenience."

"If it pleases, Yer Majesty," Mairi said, turning her smile on Connor. "I would ask to remain here fer a wee bit longer."

"Of course," the king said, "stay as long as you like. I only wish your brother Robert felt the same way. I asked your father if I might enlist any of his sons into my army. Thankfully, one of them agreed to return. Colin will be joining us here."

Mairi's face went white against the golden light of the hearth. She blinked back what looked to Connor like tears and turned to her brother. "This is not true."

Connor wanted to go to her. He almost did when Colin looked her straight in the eye and nodded his head.

"We will speak of it later," she managed, and dipped her eyes to her hands.

Connor would speak to him about it as well. Each of the laird's sons was as much his brother as Finn was. Wars were likely coming to England, and Connor didn't want Colin fighting in them. Especially if Connor wasn't going to be at his side. Hell, he'd had enough fighting. He'd given his service for longer than he had to. He wanted to marry the love of his youth and be there to raise their bairns.

"Captain Grant."

Connor blinked his gaze away from Colin and gave his attention to the king.

"Tell me about the attack you suffered in St. James's Park."

Connor told him everything, with his father interjecting at intervals. He did not tell the king that he suspected Nicholas Sedley, or anyone else. Perhaps he'd merely been robbed for his boots and there was no plot behind it. He didn't want to see his friend hanged if he were innocent and until Connor had proof that he wasn't, he would say nothing.

"I will have the matter looked into," James promised, then offered him a more relaxed smile. "Other than that, are you recovering well?"

"Almost fully, Yer Majesty. Another day or two and I shall be back in the lists teaching yer other captains how to fight."

"Good. I'm placing Colin under your tutelage."

Mairi turned to him with an almost pleading look. She wanted him to refuse, to ask the king to send her brother home, where it was safe.

Colin didn't share his sister's concerns. For he puffed up in his chair and protested with a resounding "Nae, Yer Majesty! There's nothing he or anyone else here can teach me that I dinna' already know, I can practice on my own."

"There's always room to learn more," the king corrected him gently. "You will train under Captain Grant or you will be sent home with his father. Do you understand?"

Lesson one learned. Don't argue with the king of England—no matter how much he likes you.

Colin was every bit as stubborn as his sister was. It took much for him to nod and look away. When he did, he slipped his hooded gaze to Connor. Hell, the boy was going to come at him in the lists with everything he had. Involuntarily, Connor reached for his wound. He should be fully recovered by then.

He better be.

It was almost midnight when they finally left the Presence Chamber. Connor's parents, as well as the king and queen, left them to retire. When Colin tried to make off to his room, Connor clutched a fistful of wool from the back of his plaid and pulled him back.

"Let's walk. There are things yer sister and I would discuss with ye."

"There is nothing to discuss." Colin yanked free and walked on his own. "I have made my decision. This is where I want to be."

"How can ye leave Camlochlin?" Mairi demanded, sounding much the way she did when Connor told her he was leaving.

"There's nothing fer me there, Mairi. I am sick of fighting in the dark or over cattle. I want to be part of an army." Colin's gaze flicked to Connor's, a spark of challenge lighting their green gold depths. "A captain, mayhap."

Connor couldn't help but smile. The lad was arrogant enough to be a general. "Ye've fought small groups of men who were unprepared and unskilled. Ye don't know what 'tis like to fight an army."

"Neither did ye when ye came here," Colin reminded him as they stepped into the quiet Stone Gallery.

"But I know now. No matter how hard ye train, or how much ye know, 'tis hard, Colin. 'Tis hard on a man's heart."

"Not all men were born to battle."

Connor turned to look at him. He was correct. Connor had seen it too many times on the field; men expelling their breakfasts at the sight of limbs and even heads littering the grass. Some men could take it because they had to. It was their duty. While a rare few truly loved the weight of a blade in their hands, the thrill of looking death in the face and coming out alive. "If ye're that determined to do it," he relented, knowing Colin was one of those rare few and nothing Connor said was going to change his mind, "I'll stay here with ye and prepare ye fer what's no doubt coming."

Beside him, Mairi went stiff. When Connor turned to look at her, she avoided his gaze and spoke to her brother.

"Colin, please dinna' stay here. Ye canna' truly mean to leave home."

Connor heard the same desperate plea in her voice that he'd heard when he left her to serve the king. She didn't want to lose someone else she loved to England. She would never want to remain here . . . and how could he return home when a war was likely coming?

"Camlochlin will always be first in my heart, Mairi, but my skill can be better used here." Colin planted a kiss on his sister's face. "Dinna' fret over me. Ye know I will fare well."

"Colin." Connor called out to him as he strode away. "I'll expect ye in the lists at first light. Don't be tardy. If ye truly mean to remain here, ye'll be well prepared fer whatever comes."

When Mairi's brother looked over his shoulder, his smile was gone, replaced by his usual impassive expression. "I am heading there now, Captain. By dawn, 'twill be ye who is tardy."

"Hell." Connor shook his head watching Colin's departure. "I almost feel sorry fer the Dutch."

Mairi didn't smile. In fact, she looked so miserable Connor wanted to take her in his arms and vow that he would keep Colin safe, but that would mean his staying in the king's service, perhaps having to let her go again when she refused to remain here with him. He wasn't ready to hear her rejection yet again, and said nothing when she bid him good night.

Chapter Thirty

*C*onnor stepped into the tiltyard a little before dawn the next morning and shook his head at Colin already there, sprinting around the enormous perimeter. The lad was going to be a menace to someone. Hopefully, not to him.

Leaning against the short wall, he waited for Mairi's brother to reach him. He looked about the grounds, hoping to see her. He didn't like how they'd departed last eve after a day of making love to her. He wanted to speak with her about their future. But he wasn't sure what he wanted to tell her. He had a duty to his cousin, the king, but he wanted to begin his life with her. She liked the manor house, but it wasn't the Highlands and he knew her heart belonged at Camlochlin. Hell, she'd given him up for it once before. And what if she did agree to stay with him until James's seat on the throne was secure? What of her fighting? Would she give that up for him, as well, or continue here, where enemies were as easy to find as birds in the air?

And what about her brother? Connor thought, watching as Colin came around the last curve. He wasn't surprised that the lad of two and twelve he had left at Camlochlin had grown into a confident, stubborn warrior. Colin was his father's son. Still, whether he was a MacGregor or not, the true test of a man's mettle came from real battle. How would Colin fare against a horde of men coming at him with swords, thick with someone else's blood?

"Are ye certain ye're staying?" he asked as the lad slowed.

"Aye." Colin nodded, stopping and catching his breath.

"Then"—Connor pushed off the wall and stepped forward—"from this moment on ye're a member of the king's Royal Army, and I am yer captain. My duty is to prepare and lead my men into battle. I prefer to bring them all home alive with me when the battle is over and to do that they must obey me in all things."

"I will obey ye," Colin conceded, "but I can bring myself home."

Connor smiled, unsheathing his giant claymore. "Show me."

He barely had a chance to ready himself before Colin started swinging. If Connor didn't know any better, he would vow Mairi's youngest brother was trying to kill him. He smiled, despite the dull ache from his wound. He hadn't had a decent round of training in too long. His men were skilled fighters, to be sure, but training with any one of Callum MacGregor's sons was a different exercise altogether. And, as Connor quickly discovered, Colin had learned his lessons well. His sword arm was strong and quick, almost catching Connor twice on the hip with the flat end of his blade. His aim was precise and his feet light as he parried and jabbed, keeping up with Connor's more experienced expertise. He struck with brutal determination and even used his elbows to push Connor off when their blades met and sparked above their heads. By the time they neared the end of their session, a small crowd had gathered around the lists to watch, and Connor had worked up his first full sweat in two years. He needed a break. His wound ached and his arms felt heavy. With one final arc of his claymore, which flashed in the now midmorning sun, he delivered a savage blow that nearly set Colin on his knees. Without a moment to spare before the lad repositioned himself, Connor seized his wrist, twisted Colin's arm behind his back, and held the sharp edge of his sword to the lad's throat. "Ye're dead."

"Shyt!" Colin swore through gritted teeth as Connor let him go.

"Ye did well, but ye're a wee bit too eager and reckless. We'll work on that."

Colin didn't look happy, but he said nothing as he slammed his sword back into its sheath and nodded. At least he still possessed that much humility. When he walked away, Connor let out a deep exhalation of breath. He spotted Mairi among the onlookers. She wore a somewhat pained smile.

She went to the wall, waiting for him, and then proceeded to scold him quietly for fighting with her brother when his wound was not yet healed.

"I won, did I not?"

"Still, ye were foolish in yer completion. Rendering Colin completely helpless was an err I am certain he will make ye pay fer next time. He will train even harder."

"That is what I want him to do," he told her, tracing his finger over her lips and aching to kiss them, "He'll be victorious over all who come against him."

She smiled and nodded and he thought he might have seen a sparkle in the deep blue of her eyes.

"Captain Grant!" Elizabeth de Vere's voice shattered the moment Connor thought might be the right one to speak to Mairi about things on his mind.

"You were marvelous!" Elizabeth made no attempt to conceal either her worshipful admiration of him, or her aversion toward Mairi. "I daresay watching you man-handle that barbarian was the pinnacle of my day."

"Barbarian?"

Connor caught Mairi in midair an instant before she got her hands on Elizabeth's throat. Elizabeth merely side-stepped and smiled, almost as arrogantly as her brother often smirked at Connor.

"I do hope," she said as delicately as bells tinkling in a soft breeze, "you will not be so brutal toward *my* brother if ever you met him in the lists."

Connor caught the inference and Mairi's arm along with it when she swung at the earl's daughter. "I'm certain I will not have to be." He offered Elizabeth a tight smile, as eager to be away from her as he was to get Mairi out of arm's reach of her pretty face. "Excuse us, please." He didn't wait for a reply, or a tantrum—if the purple hue of Elizabeth's face gave clue to what was about to come—but pushed Mairi away and followed closely behind her.

"She suggests yer ferocity with Colin has something unfavorable to do with me!" She turned and slapped his hand away from her back.

"I know."

"I despise that witch!"

"I know that as well." He grinned at her when she glared at him and then around his shoulder at Lady Elizabeth. "What I don't know," he continued, this time, offering his hand to her, "is why ye let her rile ye up?"

He enjoyed watching her shine her victorious smile on Oxford's sister when she accepted his hand and let him lead her back toward the Banqueting Hall. One had to truly know the savage in order to tame her.

"I will have my day with her."

"Why?" Connor looked down at her while they walked. "She is no worse than the other ladies here are. I know she looks down her nose at ye, but so do the others. Ye don't care what any of them think of ye. What makes her different?"

He watched her bite down on her lower lip, weighing her words carefully.

"'Tis ye," she finally said, looking back over her shoulder rather than at him. "There is something about her that is annoyingly confident that ye will be hers."

He fit his index finger under her chin and pulled her gaze to his. "I won't be."

"I know."

"Then don't think about it further. Here I am about to topple over from the pain in my stomach and all ye can do is think of—"

She tugged him to a halt and reached for his waist as they came to the stairs. "Och, Connor. Did ye overdo? How bad is it?"

"Now that I think on it"—he closed his arms around her and grinned down into her bonnie face—"it doesn't pain me all that much."

He bent his head next and kissed her mouth that had fallen open. He wanted to carry her to his bed, disrobe her fine body, and take her hard and fast in his bed.

He might have done it too if someone hadn't called his name. He looked up to find Drummond and young Edward approaching.

"We've been training all morning," said his lieutenant. "We're off to the tavern. Join us, Captain?"

"Go." Mairi gave him a gentle push and a generous smile. "Drink with yer friends. I will see ye later tonight."

Tonight? No way in hell was he going to wait all day to see her. Oxford would likely hunt her down the instant Connor was away from her. "Mairi." His hand on her wrist stopped her and she turned back to him. "Come with us. The men won't object to yer company."

She looked at the others smiling back at her.

"Mayhap"—Drummond offered her a reverential nod—"ye will share with us the ways in which yer blade made contact with the captain's flesh on four different occasions."

Connor laughed and slung his arm around Mairi's shoulder. "'Twas the color of her eyes, Lieutenant. The boldness of her tongue. She beguiled me—"

"When he swings in an upward motion, he has a tendency to lean to the left," Mairi told them, proving that it was more than an enchantment she had set upon him. "If ye wait just an instant to strike, ye might be able to find yer target."

"Ah." Richard beamed at her. "Tell us more."

They left the grounds with Connor second-guessing his invitation...until she looked up at him and smiled.

✥

Chapter Thirty-one

*M*airi didn't usually drink, but today she could use the tallest tankard of ale her stomach could bear. She'd endured a restless night awake in her bed, partly because of her brother's news, but Connor's kisses haunted her as well. The way he'd held her, whispered that he loved her, and then showed her. Dear Lord, the man had stamina! Yesterday had been cast from the stuff of her dreams. The house he'd built was extraordinarily beautiful. That he had built it for her made her heart ache and her eyes burn, even this morning. Would she have come to him all those years ago if she had known about it? Would she stay with him now if he asked her? Aye, there were enough Catholics' enemies here to keep her busy for three lifetimes; but now that enemies surrounded her on almost every side, she found she didn't much care for all the danger. Mayhap, it was because her brother would now be living in the center of it all.

Colin was staying. Och, but she could have clubbed him over the head with a stick when she'd learned of his intentions. How could her father let him stay? How could

Rob have wed the king's daughter? Her head still spun from it all. She'd left her bed feeling worse than when she fell into it last night. Her brother, the one she favored above the others, was staying in England. He was going to fight whatever enemies came against the king—and hell, there were many. What if he were killed?

She looked at Connor as they entered the tavern and silently thanked him for doing what he could to aid Colin in coming out of England alive. But that meant he was staying, as well. He hadn't mentioned anything about returning home to Camlochlin. He likely never would now that he had his own home to live in—and if he meant to keep Colin safe. Could she leave the Highlands for him? She'd asked herself that question a hundred times already. She didn't want to think about the possibility of his not asking her to stay.

She followed the men inside The Troubadour and looked around. She had never been in a tavern before. There were none in the Highlands, at least, not in the mountains. Men brewed their own whisky to keep warm in the cold months. She took in the sights and sounds around her, sensing the danger that was usually associated with too many drunken men crammed into one place. She understood why Connor came here often. It was more like Camlochlin's Great Hall than anywhere in the palace. What would Connor do if there was a fight? How many noses had he already broken in places like this? There would likely have been a brawl if the men that Lieutenant Drummond had just shooed away from a corner table were not a group of cornets from Connor's own company.

They sat, each man settling comfortably into his chair, each falling directly into his role in what Mairi imagined happened whenever they came here. Drummond called for drinks. Edward did not sit for long but darted from his chair to pop over to another table to greet some friends of his.

She was happy that Connor had asked her to come along. She needed a reprieve from the thoughts that plagued her. She liked men. She liked them better than she liked women. The women at Camlochlin were hardier than the powder puffs inside the palace, but even they did not share her interests in politics or in the certain tilt of the wrist that made a blade sing.

"Good evening, Captain. What's your pleasure tonight?"

Mairi looked up at pretty blonde serving wench standing over Connor and wearing a suggestive grin on her plump lips.

"Three whiskeys, Vicky," Connor told her, then cleared his throat. "And a cup of yer good ale fer Mairi."

Vicky looked her over with surprise, as if she suddenly recognized her, or had heard of her before. "Pleased to meet you, Mairi," she said, wearing a strained smile.

Had Connor told this gel about her? Mairi cut her gaze to him. Was Vicky one of his lovers? How many more were there? She didn't want to think on it.

"Four whiskeys, please, Vicky."

She ignored Connor when he shifted slightly in his seat, obviously uneasy about the two meeting each other.

"Why ye three?" she asked them, refusing to think about him naked with someone else. "Ye are together often. How did a captain, a lieutenant, and a cornet become such close friends?"

"I've known Richard since I arrived here. He saved my life in Cornwall two years ago," Connor told her. "We let Edward come along because he does what we tell him." He tossed his cornet a grin and then winked at her.

"What about the two of ye?" Lieutenant Drummond asked her as Vicky returned with their drinks.

Mairi sipped hers. The whiskey was sour and watery. Shivering at the taste of it gave her something else to do besides blanch at the question and the thought of answering it.

"What about us?"

"We see ye together often," the lieutenant said with a smirk, letting her know that being deliberately evasive was not going to work. "How did a Stuart captain and a wee Highland lass become friends?"

She smiled, offering Connor to take this one. He declined by ignoring her and covering his mouth with his cup. Damn it. Hell, she did not want to talk about falling in love with him. The last thing Connor needed was more confidence. Look at him sitting there with a curious smile on his face, waiting for her spill her guts on the table.

"Lord and Lady Huntley live in my faither's castle. Connor...Captain Grant was born there."

The lieutenant nodded, along with Edward, waiting for more.

Mairi twisted one of the ribbons in her gown around her finger. "He grew close to my brother." She shrugged, hoping it was enough. It wasn't.

"He's told us about Tristan," Edward told her, swinging his chair around to straddle it and give her his full attention. "How did he become friends with you?"

"She followed us everywhere." Connor finally took pity on her and finished for her. When he continued, she wished she had kept talking. "She was no more than this high"—he held his palm to the top of the table—"a stubborn wee lass who never did what she was told. If we tried to climb the side of a mountain, she had to try too. I cannot tell ye lads how many times she spoiled a stealthy attack on the sheep because we didn't know she was behind us."

"Proving that I was more stealthy than either of ye."

The men laughed and Connor tipped his head, giving her the win.

"I knew she loved me," he continued on mercilessly, his grin widening at her tightening lips. "I think ye were six when ye first told me, aye, Mairi?"

She wondered what his men would do if she flung her cup at him. "I had to be quite young to be so foolish."

He laughed, then pouted, pretending insult. "What she didn't know was that I returned her love. I was quite young and foolish also." His smile on her softened and made her flesh tingle. "It didn't take her long to slip under my skin and behind my back when the three of us found ourselves in trouble. She never cried but her eyes would fill up with tears and shimmer like the mist draping Sgurr Na Stri. Her cheeks were always red from the cold…her lips, as well."

The men around the table grew quiet at Connor's very telling tale.

Then, "Captain?"

Mairi blinked and remembered to breathe as Connor's tender gaze moved from her to his lieutenant.

"Do you know that man?"

Connor turned, along with everyone else, to a peasant standing off by himself, a cup held to his bearded jaw. He was partially blocked by shadow but Mairi noted his height and the breadth of his shoulders. He turned away toward the door when he saw them looking at him.

"I've never seen him before, why do ye ask?" Connor said, turning back to his lieutenant.

Richard Drummond put his cup down and dropped his hand to the hilt at his side. "Because he's wearing yer boots."

Connor was out of his chair and on his feet before the man reached the door, but Richard Drummond got to him first. Connor did not pause in his gait while his lieutenant, who was almost as tall as the thief, gripped him by the back of the collar and practically kicked him out the door.

Mairi was right behind Connor when they left the tavern, her hands tugging up her confining English skirts so that she could get a hold of one of her daggers.

"Ye look afraid, stranger," Connor said, reaching the man still clutched within his lieutenant's beefy fingers. "Do ye think ye're looking at a ghost?"

Mairi studied the assailant and was certain that he was, in fact, the brute who had stabbed Connor. Those were indeed Connor's boots on his feet and true terror widening his eyes.

"Ye tried to kill me." Connor moved closer to pin him with his level gaze. "Why?"

"Silver," the thief admitted, gathering up some of the courage that had abandoned him a few moments earlier. "Twenty pieces."

Hell, then it was true, the man had tried to kill Connor for more than just his boots. Mairi edged closer and twirled her dagger in her fingers. "Let us kill him after he tells us who paid him and then toss his body into the day's waste."

"In a moment," Connor said, then gave the man's bristly cheek a mild smack to keep his eyes on him and off Mairi. "What are ye called?"

"Harry Thatcher."

"Who paid ye, Harry?"

"Don't know." He shrugged and turned away from Connor's watchful gaze. He doubled over an instant later from the powerful blow Connor inflicted to his guts.

"Mister Thatcher." Connor's voice remained as silky smooth as when he told Mairi he loved her. "Ye're going to hang. I can put in a word fer ye to the king if ye tell me the truth. Mayhap, he will be more lenient on ye." He waited patiently while Richard yanked him straight. "Who paid ye?"

"I don't know," Harry repeated. This time it was Connor's lieutenant who struck him in the mouth.

"He gave the coin to my sister." Harry swiped the blood from his lips. "I never saw him and Linnet didn't tell me his name. We were supposed to kill you that night...the night you left the tavern with her after the first rain."

Mairi turned slowly to Connor. He'd left the tavern with a woman? Did Harry Thatcher speak of the night Connor had danced with her? The night he'd told her she had meant everything to him? Och, the bastard! She could forgive him for Vicky, since she had no way of knowing how long ago Connor had slept with her. But the night he came to Mairi in the rain? Where had he taken the trollop? To his manor house? She stared at him while her blood began to boil. Och, but she was a fool to believe his words of love...to believe anything he ever told her! Her throat burned and her eyes stung, but she would not weep! She remained silent while Harry tried to answer more questions. She didn't hear any of them. Linnet. Och, but she sounded like an English trollop. Pity the woman had not killed Connor while he made love to her.

"Take us to yer sister then and we will let ye go."

Mairi scoffed at yet another falsehood falling so easily

from Connor's tongue. But, aye, take her to this Linnet so she could run the both of them through and be done with him once and for all.

"She's gone," Harry told them. "She left London with the coin in her purse."

"And ye with my boots."

And quite possibly with Connor's bairn in her womb. Mairi looked away when his gaze met hers. She tucked her dagger back into its hiding place beneath her skirts and walked away. He was not even worth killing. She would return to the palace and bolt the door to her room until it was safe to return home. Until that time, she would avoid Connor Grant the same way she had when she first arrived.

She did not stop when Connor called her. Nor did she slow her pace back to Whitehall when he reached her side and asked her what troubled her. He did not even have the decency to feign remorse. She rethought her decision not to stab him in the heart.

"Go to hell."

"What?" He stopped and grabbed for her arm, stopping her with him.

"Hell, Connor!" She pulled herself free of his hold and flashed him her most hateful glare. "The place ye sentenced me to seven years ago!"

"Are we back to that again?" he called at her back with the audacity to sound angry.

She was too furious...too hurt to turn around and give him the cutting retort he deserved. She hastened her march, relieved to see the gate in sight.

Without breaking stride, she raised her palm to him when he caught up with her. "Never speak to me again."

"Why?" he asked, following her through the gate.

"What has come over ye?" He brought her retreat to another grinding halt, tempting her to do all sorts of violent things to him. "Are ye angry that I didn't let ye kill Mister Thatcher? I—"

"I am angry that he didna' kill *ye!*"

He let her go with his blackest look yet. He remained silent and utterly still while his men hauled his attacker past them, pausing momentarily in their steps to hear what she and Connor were arguing about. After a warning glare that set the men on their way again, Connor returned his attention to her. When he spoke, his voice was rapier sharp, his eyes as dark and as menacing as the thick clouds forming again above their heads.

"If I hadn't just caught my confessed attacker, I might think 'twas yer hand behind that dagger."

"If I had any sense, it would have been!" She whirled on her heel to leave him for the last time. Instead, she found herself spun back in his direction then hauled over his shoulder.

She was too stunned to speak. She wanted to scream, but she refused to give him the satisfaction. Besides, why call more attention to her humiliation? "Let me go," she warned, and pounded her fists into his back.

He smacked her hard on the rump in response. She gasped and reached around for her skirts. Unfortunately he knew what she was going for and yanked her hem over her knees. He plucked the first dagger away from her left calf, and then the other from the right. The two she had strapped to her thighs came next, accompanied by a muttered oath from his lips.

"Give me back my blades, ye lying pig!"

"Be silent." He smacked her bottom again.

Fortunately, the sky opened up and a peal of thunder

absorbed most of the curses she shouted at him. The rain, though, chose not to fall quickly enough. For when they entered the courtyard there were enough people still about to get a good look at her. One of them was Lord Oxford.

"Captain Grant, I insist that you release her this instant!"

Huzzah, Henry! Huzzah! Mairi cheered silently, dangling over Connor's back end. When he walked past Henry without pause, she looked up and offered the earl's son a helpless look. If Henry saved her from this she might just kiss his face. Mayhap, she would even do it while Connor watched.

"Grant!" her champion called out gallantly. "Put her down or suffer the consequences."

Ah, finally Connor stopped. He turned slowly, blocking her view of Oxford. "What consequences would those be, Oxford?"

Och, this was about to go sour. Henry should not have threatened him. Connor had not risen up in rank so quickly because the king showed favor to his family. Gossip had not spread about his bedroom victories alone. He had earned respect on the battlefield and proved his worth to the Royal Army. Mairi knew firsthand how deadly his blade was, for she had watched him practice with his father. She prayed Henry had the good sense to know when to retreat. She could not see him to urge him to use caution.

"I will see you in the lists and trounce you properly."

Mairi closed her eyes and pounded Connor's lower back softly. Fool! However, she reasoned suddenly, she was in his one hand, and four of her daggers were in his other. Connor would have to put her down if he meant to fight. This could still work in her favor. Och, but poor Henry.

Her eyes shot open when Connor's rough palm dragged over her buttocks then patted her at the end of the trail.

"I'll meet ye there after I remind this wench of a few things."

Mairi struggled to wrench herself around and slapped Connor in the back of the head. He turned to give her a dark look that promised retribution. She wanted to slap him again but he swung back around, taking her with him.

"If ye want to try to stop me," he drawled, turning back to Henry with a lethal little smirk, "give it a go."

Mairi did not breathe in the dead silence that followed. Henry was not so foolish, after all. He possessed no more courage than she did against the knuckle-dragging oaf waiting patiently for Henry's next move. When nothing came, Connor chuckled and turned away.

He walked straight into Captain Nicholas Sedley.

"Grant, who do you have there?" Mairi heard him and turned a deeper shade of crimson. "Where did you find him?"

"Who?" Connor asked, turning around in his spot to see whom Sedley spoke of.

"That peasant being escorted by your lieutenant."

Mairi tried desperately to wrench around and get a look at Captain Sedley. He sounded nervous, a wee bit desperate—like a man who was guilty and about to get caught.

For a moment she forgot her anger and prayed Connor heard it too.

"Mister Thatcher is the man who stabbed me in St. James's Park."

Mairi closed her eyes and poked Connor in the hip for saying so much.

"He claims to have things to tell me after I've seen him fed. Drummond," Connor called out. "Take our guest to the lodgings the MacGregors occupied while they were here and get him something to eat. I will speak to him later."

"What does he wish to tell you?" Sedley asked, doing his best to mask his nerves.

"We shall soon find out."

Mairi heard the grin in Connor's voice. What the hell was he about? She didn't ask him as he toted her away but leaned up over his back and glared at William of Orange's captain. Harry Thatcher didn't need to know the name of the man who paid his sister. Mairi already knew it.

Chapter Thirty-two

"Connor, fer heaven's sake, put me doun! We need to discuss this!" Mairi said, having calmed down a bit.

Aye, Connor thought, stopping and setting her on her feet just before they reached the stairs. "We need to discuss many things like—"

"Did ye take note of Captain Sedley's reaction to Harry Thatcher?"

He looked down into her sparkling eyes and realized what he'd just done and why. He'd walked away from his attacker and the man behind it to deal with her first because she meant more to him than his own life. He smiled at her, thankful that she put his life before her anger over whatever the hell he had done.

"He knows who Thatcher is and what he did."

She nodded, then looked around her to make certain no one could hear. "Did Thatcher recognize him?" She returned a brief scathing gaze to him. "I couldna' see fer myself."

He wanted to kiss her and to hell with anyone watching. He really needed to remain focused. "He didn't seem to know him at all. He likely never saw Sedley before this day."

"He didna' need to," she said. "Sedley would not have paid a woman to do what a man needed to do without seeing her brother first."

Did he hear her right? "What a man needed to do?"

She rolled her eyes at him. "Well, ye are a big brute, Connor. Although I dinna' know why she simply didna' kill ye in her bed... or in yers."

He shook his head and laughed. "Who's bed?"

"Linnet's. But never mind that fer now. What do ye intend to do about yer friend Captain Sedley?"

His friend. All at once the bare truth hit Connor like a wave. He hadn't wanted to believe it, but Nick had tried to have him killed.

"Right after he leaves no further doubt that he is guilty, and before I bring him to the king, I intend to ask him why."

Silence clung between them for a moment before she finally spoke, her voice soft and filled with compassion. "I am sorry, Connor. Betrayal is painful."

"Mairi." He lifted his hand and traced his knuckles over her flawless cheek. "I didna' betray ye. What do I have to do to prove that to ye?"

"Ye could have told me about Linnet and how ye made love to her the same night ye told me that I had meant everything to ye."

So, that was the reason for her anger. Hell, didn't she know by now that she was the only woman who truly made him feel like a man? "Aye, I left the tavern with her. 'Twas after ye defended Oxford. I wanted to get ye out of my thoughts, but I didn't make love to her."

"Why not?"

Hell.

He could have told her that he had changed his mind because he wanted it to be her bonnie face beneath him, but she had enough trouble believing a word he said. He would be honest with her and let the stones fall where they may. "Because Colin punched me in the mouth when I stepped outside."

She smiled, delighting him to his soul. "Fortunately fer ye, I have a much more understanding nature than Colin does. Since this took place while we still hated each other, I canna' be angry with ye."

"We didn't hate each other." He smiled taking her hands in his and pulling her to him. "Admit that ye loved me while ye were being spun on yer toes by Oxford."

"I wanted to fling my daggers at ye each time ye opened yer mouth."

He moved in closer, bending his mouth to hers. "How about now?"

Her mouth was soft, yielding for the briefest of moments before surrendering to him fully. Gathering her up in his arms, he crushed her to him, spreading his tongue over hers, his hands over her back.

"There he..."

Henry de Vere's voice trailed off into stunned silence before the queen cleared her throat.

"Captain Grant?" she asked as he released Mairi and turned to her. He looked at his mother standing next to her, then away from the slight smile she wore at the sight of Mairi in his arms.

"Yer Majesty."

"Captain," she said while he bowed to her. "Lord Oxford is quite distressed over your manhandling Miss MacGregor."

Connor flicked his gaze to the dotard and vowed to punch out his teeth later.

"Have you spoken to Miss MacGregor's father about courting her?"

"When I was two and ten, Yer Majesty. And then again at five and ten, and once more two years after that. He gave his blessing."

Mary of Modena smiled at him so sweetly he felt the urge to bow to her again. "I saw no manhandling." She spread her gentle gaze over Mairi. "Did he treat you poorly?"

"He didna', Yer Majesty," Mairi told her.

Her answer seemed to take the wind out of Oxford. In fact, the man looked like all his organs had just fallen at his feet and a slight wind would knock him over.

"I was mistaken then," he announced, albeit a bit weakly. He cared for Mairi, truly. Connor felt a twinge of pity for him as Oxford turned without another word and left.

"In the future, Captain Grant," the queen said, pulling his attention back to her, "court her with a bit more discretion. Miss MacGregor, have you eaten?"

Mairi shook her head and smiled at Connor over her shoulder when the king's wife scooted her away toward the Banqueting Hall.

"Come, Lady Huntley," she called in her lightest Italian-accented voice when Connor's mother remained behind to kiss Connor on the cheek.

"Marry her and make us all happy already, will you?"

"Lady Huntley?"

"Just behind you."

Connor watched them go, then looked up the stairs to the lodgings above. He intended to take Mairi as his wife, but first there was something he needed to do.

It was time to find out if the man he'd called friend for the past seven years had truly betrayed him. He climbed the stairs and walked the long hall like a man on his way to a hanging. If his suspicions were correct, Sedley would come to the vacant MacGregor lodgings to quiet Thatcher before he had a chance to speak with Connor. Sedley had no way of knowing for certain if Thatcher could identify him, but a guilty man wouldn't risk it. But even if he were mistaken and Sedley didn't come, Connor knew he'd had enough of England's halls, filled to the brim with deceptive tongues.

In that, it didn't matter if Sedley was guilty or not. Connor wanted to go to a place where no suspicion of a brother or friend existed. He wanted to go home.

He came to the chambers and opened the door. Thatcher sat on a small stool wiping his brow with shaky fingers. A few inches away, Drummond leaned against the window cleaning his fingernails with the tip of his knife, with Connor's boots placed neatly on the floor beside him. Both men looked up when he entered.

"Where's Edward?"

"Getting him his last meal," his lieutenant told him, glancing at their prisoner. "I say, let him die on an empty stomach."

"He has likely suffered many days without food already," Connor said, crossing the room. "Men who kill fer coin are not usually wealthy."

"He had twenty silver. I'd say he's been eating well."

Connor shook his head, coming to stand in front of the stool. "His sister left England with the coin." He squatted and set his level gaze on Thatcher's. "Isn't that correct?"

"Aye." Harry nodded. "She might have gone to France."

Drummond grunted. "He still insists he does not know who paid her."

"Perhaps"—Connor stood and turned to his lieutenant—"he'll remember better on a full belly." He'd done wretched things in the service of his king. He was done with that, as well. Let others say what they would. Highlanders were not barbarians, and he would not send a starving man to the gallows. "I said I would see him fed, and fed he will be. But not yet. Go find Edward and tell him the food can wait until after Thatcher has seen the king."

Drummond left without question and Connor made a mental note to put to the king a request for Richard's promotion. His men would need a new captain when he left, and someone who would be hard on Colin.

He waited until Richard was gone and then took his place against the window. "Turn yer stool around to face me, Thatcher."

He watched blandly as his prisoner did as commanded. "Will I be hanged?"

"Ye stabbed me and then dumped me in refuse."

"Aye." Thatcher swallowed and wiped his brow again. "I should be hanged. I've done sinful things."

Connor looked at him. He didn't want to be speaking or be distracted when Sedley arrived. "Ye'll have time to confess to a priest. Fer now ye will be silent. Soon, another soul will enter this room. When he does, ye are not to turn around. Do ye understand?"

Thatcher nodded but did not speak again. They had to wait only a quarter of an hour before the latch on the door rose from its hinge. Connor pushed off the window, holding his finger to his lips. He hurried to stand behind the door when it began to open.

Connor watched with anger and sorrow vying for preeminence within while Nick Sedley peeked his head inside.

Seeing Thatcher alone, he entered the room and produced a dagger from his pocket. Connor shut the door and leaped for him at the same time. Sedley didn't have a chance to turn around before Connor looped his arm around his neck from behind and wrenched the dagger from his hand.

"Why, Nick?" he growled against his friend's ear while he held the dagger to Sedley's throat. "Why did ye want me dead."

"Grant!" Nick choked back his stunned disbelief. "What are you saying, old man? I only came to—"

"Save it." Connor pushed the sharp edge of the blade closer. "Tell me why? Did William order it?"

"I don't know what you're talking about."

"She said he was Dutch."

Connor looked over Nick's shoulder at Thatcher staring at both of them.

"My sister…she said the man who paid her was Dutch."

"He may as well be," Connor said, drawing blood. "Now"—he yanked Sedley closer, twisting the captain's arm up behind his back—"ye'll tell me why ye were willing to see me dead. How ye managed to sit at my table and laugh with me after ye had paid twenty pieces of silver to have me killed."

"Gilles." Sedley choked against Connor's arm crushing his windpipe. "Ye were asking questions about him."

"Questions the prince didn't want answered."

"I didn't say that."

"Ye didn't have to." Connor whirled himself and Sedley around to face the door. "I should kill ye right here, but ye're going to tell the king everything. Thatcher, get the door!"

Harry leaped from his stool and hurried to open the door. He collapsed to the ground before he drew his next breath, a knife protruding from his neck. Connor stood just as lifeless with Sedley secured in front of him while a figure appeared again from the shadows in the hall and flung a second dagger. There was no time to move before the blade met its target deep in Sedley's chest.

Kicking the door shut, Connor carefully lowered Sedley to the floor. The assassin had to be caught, but someone else would have to do it.

"Nick." He held his friend in his arms and looked desperately at the hilt rising and falling with Nick's shallow breaths. The wound was fatal. There was nothing he could do.

"Forgive me, old friend." Nick managed to clutch Connor's coat as he whispered his last words. "We are... both of us... at the mercy of our masters."

Chapter Thirty-three

Mairi stood at the far western wall, her eyes fastened on the dancers circling the center of the Banqueting Hall. Particularly on Connor, his palm aloft and pressed against his mother's. Hell, but he was handsome and polished in his military garb. She couldn't wait to see him in a plaid. Every lady in the hall had spared him at least one glance tonight already. Mairi tossed them all haughty smiles. He was hers, and let them hate her for *that*.

She had behaved like a child when she'd heard about Linnet. Even if he had slept with the trollop, it was before they reunited. She had put him through hell and she was sorry for it. Never again would she mistrust him. He had done everything to prove that he loved her. He continued to forgive her when she doubted him. He put up with her stubborn, oftimes sour tongue. He told her everyday how bonnie she was to him.

He'd built her a house.

The past two days had been difficult for him, poor man. A dear friend had betrayed him and then died in his arms. The king had been sympathetic but had refused to give Captain Sedley a soldier's burial. The Baronet of Aylesford, Sedley's father, was asked to leave Whitehall with his family. James listened to what Connor had told him. Sedley had not acted on his own. Connor was to be killed because he was asking questions about Admiral Gilles. The order came from above—from Sedley's master.

But still the king had refused to act against his nephew, his daughter's husband. The proof did not exist, thanks to the men who could have provided it being stabbed directly in front of Connor. And to Connor not seeing who had flung those knives.

A heavy blow that had been for him. But Mairi was unsure if it was the king's inaction or his subtle rebuke about his captain's inability to protect his prisoners that had formed the creases above Connor's brow for the last pair of days.

He caught her eye and smiled, laying waste to her heart as if it were the first time she ever looked upon him. If he was wounded, she would heal him. She no longer cared if he asked her to stay here in England with him or not. She wasn't going anywhere, save wherever he was.

"Nobles." The king appeared at her side, breaking away from his previous conversation with the Baron of Sedgwick. "They are stuffy, dim-witted beings, the lot of them."

Mairi smiled up at him. She hoped he would be a strong king, for he had not only political battles ahead, but religious ones, as well. "Ye are not only courageous, but ye are also wise, Yer Majesty."

He chuckled. "You have a spark to you, Miss Mac-Gregor. I like that. The queen is fond of you also."

"As I am of her."

"I was tempted to knight you when you had William squirming the night I left for Camlochlin."

"I would insist on ye making me a high admiral or nothing at all."

The king laughed, spreading his gaze out over the crowded hall. "And him?"

Looking to where the king motioned with his cup, Mairi spotted Colin cutting through the crowd, his sharp hazel eyes beneath his hooded mantle were fastened on them both. It was the same mantle each member of the militia wore. He must have picked it up at home and brought it back with him. She didn't worry that any nobles in attendance would recognize him from one of their raids. The militia never left anyone alive.

Her brother wore his cloak well, drifting in and out of the crowd like a shadow, without notice. She loved him very much and she didn't want him to join the king's army, but she knew his sharp mind and supreme skill would serve a greater purpose here than in Camlochlin. "In a year or two, he will be more devastating than the plague."

King James eyed Colin with interest and then nodded to him when her brother reached them and offered the king a slight bow.

"Ye have interesting guests, Majesty."

"Oh?" the king inquired as the dance ended and Connor returned.

"Aye." Colin's lips curled around a covert smirk while he angled his head in the direction from whence he just came. Mairi followed his gaze and found Lord Hollingsworth engaged in quiet talks with the Earl of Derby. "According to some," he continued, "the Duke of Monmouth intends to return to England in the near future."

"We've heard rumors of this," the king said.

"Ye may now count it as fact. I didna' hear the name, but someone's son is to meet the duke when he arrives. Ye have traitors in yer midst, Yer Majesty."

King James blinked at him, then passed a hard look to the two English lords. "Did they say where the duke would be landing? How many ships he brings with him? Do they support or oppose Monmouth's return?"

" 'Tis hard to say"—Colin shrugged—"but give me a few days. It shouldna' be difficult to find out."

The king studied him for a moment, as if trying to come to some sort of conclusion about him. Finally, he gave Colin's upper arm a solid whack and set him to the task.

"He's ambitious," James said, turning back to them. "In one evening he discovered more news about my enemies than my generals have gathered in a month."

Aye, her brother was good at such things, Mairi mused watching him go. When they were children, she'd often found him listening to one of Graham Grant's tales of when he had infiltrated the Campbell holding and befriended each and every soldier while gathering information for Callum MacGregor's infamous raid on Kildun Castle.

"I like him," the king said. "You should have seen him fight against Gilles's men at Camlochlin. I thought he meant to take them all on alone."

"He likely would have done just that."

The king set his gaze on Connor and held it there, the lines of his strong features taut with anger. "Captain, they come to take my crown."

"They will fail, Sire."

"Yes, they will, for I will blot them out, beginning with Parliament."

Mairi noted Connor's seemingly sudden permanent creases deepen. If the king was speaking of Protestants in general, why should that cause him to frown? She would ask him about it later, when they were alone. Which wasn't about to be anytime soon.

She could do nothing but nod her head when King James announced to Connor that he wanted to share a word with him in private.

She watched them walk together along the wall until they reached the entrance and disappeared from her sight. With nothing else to do, she headed back to her kin's table. She looked around for Graham or Claire and found them chatting with the Duke of Edinburgh and his wife.

She sat and reached for her cup when someone gained the seat beside her.

Och, no, it was Henry. She hadn't seen him since the afternoon when he saw her kissing Connor. Poor Henry had stayed away, likely in his room, his heart broken because of her.

"These last few days have been difficult for me, Mairi."

"I know, Henry, and I should have told ye sooner that—"

"I risked my life for you when I tried to stop him from carrying you off."

Damnation, she felt terrible. "Nae," she lied to comfort him. "I am certain Captain Grant would never harm you."

"Wouldn't he?" His wig rose over his forehead when he arched his brow at her. "He has despised me since the day he returned. He waits for an opportunity to strike me. I can see it in his eyes."

Hell, she couldn't argue that. Connor *was* ridiculously expressive.

"I understand how his fairness of face may have enchanted you, made you react without thinking, but I could offer you so much more than he." He reached for her hand and rubbed the pad of his thumb over her knuckles.

Mairi pulled away gently and set her hand in her lap under the table. "My lord, let me put this to you as tenderly as possible. I am in love with Captain Grant. I have been since my sixth summer. Likely 'twas earlier than that, but that is when I first told him." Dear Lord, it felt good to finally tell him the truth. "Fergive me, I beg ye, if I made ye believe that my heart could be yers or anyone else's. It canna' be."

"Apologies," he said softly, and sat back in his chair. "I meant no offense." Other than looking mildly ill, he took it better than she had expected. She was grateful for that.

Her brother's sudden landing in the chair opposite Henry's nearly startled the earl's son into her lap.

"Good Lord, Colin." She glared at him while he studied Henry's reaction and the paleness of his face. "I do hope ye learn how to place yerself properly into a chair while ye are here. And mayhap quit appearing without a sound, startling others out of their skin," she added when he did not look repentant at all.

"We haven't been formally introduced," Oxford said when Colin swung around in his seat and contemplated him with a narrowed gaze. "I am Henry de Vere, son of the Earl of Oxford."

"Aye, my sister has told me of ye."

"All good things I hope."

"If they had not been good," Colin told him, pushing back his hood and lifting a discarded cup of wine to his nose, "ye would not be sitting there smiling." He guzzled what was left in the cup, swiped his hand across his mouth, then stared at Henry some more.

Mairi's lips ached to curl at her brother's less than subtle approach at forcing Henry to say something. She had told him yesterday—or was it day before—about Henry's ploy to take her from Connor's bedside by giving her information on the Cameronians. She didn't know what he knew and she told her brother that it pricked her like an irksome nettle. If anyone knew how to strip a man of his secrets, it was Colin. Most times, if not for him, the militia never would have known who to fight.

"I met your brother Tristan at this very table a few weeks ago."

"Ye have my deepest sympathy fer that," Colin said blandly.

"I will take it."

"Tristan pushed Lord Oxford's chair out from under him when he bent to sit," Mairi explained, and was rewarded with an irrepressible smile.

"My good Lord Oxford," Colin said, leaning back in his chair, his smile shining brightly now, though his eyes remained as sharp as twin blades. "Tell me about yerself."

Henry patted his long wig and cut a very brief glance to the dance floor and beyond, to the exit. "What would you like to know?"

"Yer family was loyal to Charles, nae?"

"As we are to his brother."

"Of course." Colin nodded. "'Twas yer uncle who retained the Royal Horse Guard to protect our late king."

"The Oxford Blues," Henry said with a measure of pride straightening his shoulders.

"Aye, the Blues. They are Parliamentarians, are they not? They fight who Parliament tells them to fight."

"That's correct," Oxford agreed. "And the new Parliament will no doubt support James, since it is he who is handpicking most of them."

"True enough," Colin said, smiling at him and then turning to Mairi. "Clever, is he not?"

"Aye," Mairi agreed, but she wasn't certain which man Colin spoke of, the king or Henry.

✦|✦

Chapter Thirty-four

*C*onnor walked back and forth between pairs of over a hundred men, his boots crushing the soft earth beneath them. The rains from the night before had ended and the sun had returned to blaze down upon his troupe. The men looked weary and they had only been at it for an hour. He raked his gaze over George and Geoffrey, then passed them to the next two, expecting their best. They were out of form from going weeks without practicing, and with things as they were, Connor intended to drill them until they dropped for as long as he remained here.

It would also distract his thoughts away from killing Henry de Vere. The bastard had gone to the king with complaints against him involving Mairi and last night, on his private walk with James, Connor had been forced to listen to each of them. The list was quite long, too. Beginning with his forcibly keeping Oxford away from her, to carting her, as well as his sister Elizabeth, over his shoulder like sacks of flour. The king wasn't certain he believed Oxford's claims since he hadn't himself seen Connor hauling any women about. Thanks, Connor was sure, to Queen Mary, the king seemed quite pleased that his captain courted the chief MacGregor of Skye's daughter. But James had made it clear that Oxford was interested in courting Mairi, as well.

What Connor wouldn't give to simply beat Henry de Vere senseless.

His gaze settled on the small area reserved for the king and his party—more precisely, on Mairi. Standing between the queen and his mother, she watched the training with the same glint in her eye that some of his men possessed. He wanted to take her home, away from the dangers she would surely get herself into here at White-hall, away from men who sought to take her from him and tempt him to kill them. He wanted her in his bed, in his arms, away from the proprieties of court, where he could make love to her and tell her he loved her until she grew sick of hearing it. Hell, he had barely had the chance to kiss her since they left his manor house.

When she turned to him, seeming to feel his eyes on her, he smiled and then scowled and looked away. He didn't want her here, distracting him with the gloss of her curls dripping down her milky cleavage.

He eyed the other half of his company waiting outside the wall for their turn to practice. The two hundred men would practice in shifts, as the size of the tiltyard would allow—or if one on the field fell to his knees and was removed to make room for someone better prepared to meet his opponent.

"Hammond, watch yer swing!" he shouted to a soldier on the other side of the lists, then poked his blade into the man closest to him. The soldier whirled around in time to block another blow to his shoulder. Connor patted his back, then shoved him into his opponent's advance.

He found Colin among the men and was glad the lad was joining in their training. Colin might someday lead them. Connor paid close attention to his movements, looking for a flaw but finding none. He scanned the men to his left and watched his father bring Andrew Seymour and his twin brother, Alex, to their knees. Hell, if James had Graham Grant fighting among his men, victory would be swift and bloody.

He made his way across the dirt to where his father readied for his next opponent. Connor rolled his wrist, making his sword dance as he reached him. The longtime commander of the clan MacGregor of Skye smiled at him. Here was what Connor missed, a blow that drove the air from his lungs, an arm more deadly than any plague England had to offer. This was how a Highland warrior fought. One man with the strength and skill of ten. He blocked a stinging blow with the far end of his claymore and repositioned to defend himself against the next swing. His father showed him no mercy. Connor would have been insulted if he did. Still, he had to quit defending and start swinging. He brought a chopping blow down over Graham's head, then sprang out of the way of a deadly slice across the torso.

"Ye've grown soft, son." His father flashed a dimple, much like his own at him.

"Do ye think so?" Connor tossed him a challenging grin and arced his blade in a wide circle before him, then up again, hard against Graham's sword. He stepped to the side, avoiding the glint of metal close to his face and clashed his weapon into the other. After a series of parries and lethal jabs, he began advancing. Finally, he drove his father back with short, heavy blows, left, right, to the knees, the neck. He hadn't been sitting around England doing nothing all this time.

When the session was over, he sent the first group off to rest and called the second inside. He looked toward Mairi while the shift changed, then called to his lieutenant and yanked off his gloves. "Take this one. Work them hard, Drummond, especially Colin."

He was about to leave the enclosure when the point of a blade poked his belly. He looked up into Oxford's misshapen face, slapped the blade away, and freed his own. Ah, here is what he'd been waiting for. If the fool wanted to have a go at him here in the lists, Connor would not deny him.

"Let's do this," he growled, and tipped his blade to Oxford's as the lists filled with men around them.

The fool swung quickly. Connor clipped the blow away with ease. He returned the favor with a ravaging strike that nearly sent his opponent's sword flying. Oxford's arm shook and he looked about to be ill all over Connor's boots. He lowered his sword and took a step closer.

"Do to me what you will, Captain Grant, but I *will* have her. She will be mine and I will mount her on my pedestal. I will win, and then I will fu—"

His words came to a cracking halt as Connor's hilt, gripped tightly in his fist crushed the bone beneath it. He went down on one knee clutching his face in both hands.

"Ye will not have her," Connor said, standing over him, mindless of the blood seeping through Oxford's fingers. "And if ye go near her again, I will put an end to ye once and fer all."

Connor didn't wait around to hear Oxford's gurgled reply, but stepped out of the lists and into Mairi's arms.

"I'm afraid there's going to be trouble later," he told her, and pulled her away from the yard. "Come on."

"Why is there going to be trouble? What happened?"

It occurred to Connor that Mairi, packed within the crowd of his resting men, couldn't see whom he'd hit.

Good. She'd likely be angry if she knew. He smiled, leading her toward the palace. "I'll see to it later. Right now, I'm hungry." He was hungry for her. He wasn't about to spend another day not being able to touch her, kiss her.

He pulled her up the stairs with her smiling behind him once she realized they had passed the kitchens.

"Where are ye taking me?"

He looked over his shoulder at her and offered her a suggestive quirk of his mouth. "Somewhere we can be alone."

He had to tug her along when she paused, hesitant against his wicked smile. They passed the Banqueting Hall, but Connor didn't stop there. He hurried them along the long, painted halls and galleries, until they came to his room.

Turning to pull her against him, he pushed the door open with his back. "No one will disturb us in here."

Her eyes opened wide. "But 'tis the middle of the day! People will hear!"

"Then ye had best not make too much noise."

He leaned down to kiss her as they entered the sunlit room, closing the door behind him. He pushed open her mouth with his tongue and slid it over hers. She tasted of anticipation and excitement and fear. It drove him mad with desire.

"Wait." She broke away, scattering her long tresses around her face and reminding him of a mare that refused to be broken. "What happened in the lists?" she demanded breathlessly, her eyes shining with the thrill she took in challenging him. "Tell me, or I will spend the rest of the day with Lord Oxford."

"Nae, ye won't."

"And why won't I?" She fisted her hands on her hips and tilted her chin up at him. His muscles twitched with the need to take her until she cried out her surrender.

"Because I think I just knocked out a few of his teeth in the lists."

He smiled slowly when she took a step away from him, shaking her head. "Ye brute. Why?"

"It matters not. Now quit thinking about him." He moved quickly and caught her up in his arms. She fought against him for a moment, but then her kisses grew as urgent as his own. They clawed at each other's clothes, he yanking up her skirts, and she frantically untying the laces of his breeches. When they were both free, he whirled her around and flattened her chest against the door.

Ah, God, he was harder than steel. His cock pained him as he took it in his hand and guided it slowly into her from behind.

She cried out and he dipped his mouth to her ear. "Fergive me, my love, ye drive me wild with the need to be inside ye."

He felt her drench him and plunged deeper, pushing her hard up along the door. She groaned like some wild hellcat and pushed back until he had to withdraw and give his cock a hard slap to stop himself from expelling too quickly. He intended to enjoy this thoroughly, and watch her enjoy it too.

Pulling her skirts high over her hips, he watched her take him to the hilt and then retreat to the sensitive rim beneath his head. He cupped her round, succulent buttocks and slowed her undulations, guiding her over every swollen, aching inch of him. Then he gave her a short little smack and thrust deep into her, driving her feet off the floor. He pressed his body to hers, crushing her to the door. He scooped a handful of her hair away from her nape and kissed her there.

"I love ye, Mairi. I never want to be parted from ye again." He bit her earlobe softly and then scored his teeth down the back of her neck. When she writhed against him, smiling in ecstasy against the cool wood, he curled his arm around her front and found her hard little bud with his fingers. She dripped around his shaft, her sheath tight and engorged as he stroked her. Her legs spread open wider as pleasure overtook her. He thrust into her faster, deeper, burying his face in her hair as he spurt his seed into her over and over again. She came in his hand, hot, soaking, spent.

"Ye excite me, woman," he told her, turning her in his arms.

"Ye have nae heart, ye beast." She rasped, throwing her head back against the door.

"That's because I gave it to ye."

She coiled her arms around his neck and smiled against his mouth when he bent forward to her. "So, ye want me to stay with ye, d'ye?"

"Aye, ferever." He kissed her lips, so close, so soft and fine. He wanted nothing more in his life than to be her husband, her bairns' father. Perhaps he would take up farming. He smiled. The future was spread out before him in glorious array, with any path he chose, open to him. To them. "I'm taking ye home."

"Home?" She stared up at him, her glorious blue eyes wide and glimmering with hope. "To Scotland?"

"To the Highlands, where we belong."

She looked deep into his eyes, as if seeing what he saw, and smiled with him. He wanted to build their home with his own hands, high in the mountains where mist saturated her hair like a gossamer veil, and the crisp heather-scented air colored her cheeks.

"We shall leave England and the next war to the merciless men who claim to fight in God's name."

"Ye mean the Protestants."

"Nae, love." He stepped away from her and laced up his breeches before moving to a small table beside his unused bed. He poured a cup of water and handed it to her. "I mean the Catholics if James succeeds in keeping William from the throne."

When she opened her mouth to protest, he stopped her. "No one wants a Catholic king, Mare. James is in fer a long religious battle. One he will never surrender to. He is fair, but 'tis only a matter of time before he realizes what must be done to quiet those who don't support him. I fear he already knows what he will do. Ye heard him last night when he vowed to blot out his enemies, beginning with Parliament. His brother tried to do it during the field executions. I fear 'twill happen again and this time I will not take part in it."

She left the door and went to him. "What is so terrible about wanting to keep what we believe alive?"

"Nothing, but then the same can be said fer those who believe differently. The men we killed during the executions were not warriors, Mairi. They were farmers, forced to fight the king's elite in order to protect their way of thinking. I served a Protestant king. I learned as much about his religion as my own until I no longer knew which was the right one. Nor did I care. I am tired of fighting either one. Let God decide. I want to go home and if the Protestants win the war and they try to force new laws on the people of the mountains, then I will lead an army of my Highland brothers against them."

"And I will be at yer side."

A knock at the door saved Connor from a knife in his belly when he would have told her like hell she would. The only place he never wanted to see Mairi was on a battlefield.

He opened the door and found his father standing on the other side.

"Connor," he said gravely, "the king wants to see ye right away."

Chapter Thirty-five

Connor stood alone in the king's Presence Chamber waiting for James to arrive. He suspected his being summoned had something to do with Oxford. He knew he shouldn't have struck the bastard as hard as he did, but, hell, it'd felt good. Oxford was fortunate that Connor hadn't killed him for speaking so crudely about mounting Mairi. He knew he hadn't done any permanent damage, so whatever reprimand was about to come wouldn't be too severe. He tapped his boot on the floor, eager to speak to the king, now that he'd made up his mind about returning home. James would likely be angry with him for leaving his service, but Connor was no longer duty bound. He only hoped his cousin would not demand that he stay.

The door opened and the queen entered looking solemn and worried. Connor bowed but she gave him no greeting as her husband entered next.

"Sit down, Captain," the king offered, averting his gaze from Connor's.

When they were all seated, Connor noted the silent look that passed between husband and wife. When neither said a word, he shifted uneasily in his chair. Their grave expressions didn't bode well for him. Had Oxford died? Hell, Connor hadn't hit him *that* hard. Had he fallen on someone's sword? Connor hadn't stayed around long enough to find out.

"What happened this morn with the Earl of Oxford's son?" the king finally asked settling his gaze on him.

"He spoke improperly about Miss MacGregor."

"So you struck him with the hilt of your sword?"

"I was holding the hilt when I struck him with my fist." Hell, here was another reason he longed for home. He was tired of the false civility among men who ran to the king over something as minor as a broken bone, but who would ram a dagger into another's back when no one was looking.

"What did he say?" The queen sat forward in her chair, a hopeful look passing over her eyes.

"Nothing that is fit fer yer ears, Yer Majesty."

She turned to her husband but he held up his palm to silence her.

"And for speaking ill of Miss MacGregor," the king addressed him again, "you broke his nose and tore two teeth from his mouth?"

What could he say but the truth? "Aye, Sire. I did."

The queen fell back against her chair. Connor watched her with growing unease.

"I have spent the last hour with the earl," the king went on. "He is furious that one of my men would attack his son so viciously. He demands recompense."

"In what form?" Connor felt like the chair he was sitting in was closing in around him. Indeed, the enormous Presence Chamber seemed smaller, suffocating. If the king told him that Oxford had demanded Mairi's hand, he would go find him and cut his throat and to hell with the damned consequences.

"Cousin," the king implored, further stilling Connor's heart by his gentle use of their familial relation, "you must understand my position. I have too many enemies at present to create new ones. Charles de Vere has an army of over..."

Connor reeled in his seat, and then rose from it, unable to listen to anymore. He would not let Oxford take her as he'd promised. "Sire," he said, careful not to approach too quickly. "Surely Oxford had this all thought out in advance." Of course he had, the bastard! Why else would he be foolish enough to lift his blade to Connor? Oxford had wanted Connor to strike him, to hurt him, so that he could demand compensation. "Ye cannot allow Miss MacGregor to wed him." His eyes fell to the queen. Surely she would stand at his side in this. "He—"

"The earl does not seek a marriage between his son and a MacGregor."

Connor expelled a great breath of relief. His muscles suddenly ached and felt as if they were not strong enough, along with his bones, to hold him up. Too much practicing, though he hadn't suffered the effects of it until now.

"Captain..."

Connor looked at the king ready for anything as long as he didn't lose Mairi. Throw him in prison for a month or two, demote his rank, or demand some monetary compensation. *That*, he could live with.

"...it is you the earl wants."

"Me?"

The king nodded and sighed turning to his wife. Mary of Modena looked away, avoiding both their gazes.

"I don't understand, Sire."

"He wants you to marry his daughter, Lady Elizabeth."

"Nae," Connor said softly, falling back into his chair. Nae, he was going to wed Mairi. This couldn't be happening.

"I'm afraid you must, cousin. I know your heart belongs to another, but in time..."

In time? In time he would forget Mairi? In time he would come to love Elizabeth? He laughed, but the sound of it was so fraught with misery, it propelled the queen out of her chair and then out of the chamber. Connor was barely aware of her departure. In seven years he hadn't forgotten his only love, hadn't stopped dreaming of her, missing her. Seven years without giving his heart to any woman, knowing he would never love anyone but the lass from Camlochlin. In time? There weren't enough years in his life.

"Ye would sentence me to a long, torturous death fer breaking a man's nose?"

"The wrong man, Captain. I will need his father as an ally in the days to come."

Connor shook his head. No! "Ye have yer Royal Army of over five thousand men. Oxford's Horse Guards will not turn against ye. My uncle brings with him over five hundred more from France. Ye do not need—"

"In the event that William of Orange brings his forces against me," the king cut him off, "I will need everyone. I know your service to your king has been served, but I ask you to do this one last thing. This very important thing. I cannot lose the Horse Guard...or the throne."

His service. Connor scored his fingers through his hair and tried to maintain his even breathing. "I am..." He stopped, wondering how everything had just changed in an instant. "I am leaving my service."

"You may leave it, cousin...after you wed Elizabeth de Vere."

Could he throw away seven years of honorable duty by refusing the king? Would he be responsible if James lost England to William? Why him, he raged? Why did Elizabeth want him? He remembered Mairi's warning to him about the earl's daughter's being overly confident that he would be hers—the same confidence Henry spoke with today. Satan's balls, they had planned this together! He was a fool to fall straight into it. But why? Surely Elizabeth didn't love him. He barely spared her a look when she was about. Why did she want him so desperately?

"You yourself believe that William was behind the attempted murder of my daughter," the king continued. "Behind your attack, as well, because you asked questions about Admiral Gilles. You are likely correct in your accusations, but whether he is guilty or not—"

"He is guilty," Connor broke in boldly, too stunned and angry to care about impudence.

James nodded. "As I was saying, I still have Argyll and Monmouth coming toward me from different directions, and who knows who else? I cannot risk losing Oxford's allegiance. I already promised him a seat in the new Parliament. He is prominent enough among the nobles to turn them against me."

And there it was. The reason behind the demand for marriage. Connor was a Stuart, the king's cousin. What better way to secure a seat in Parliament than by having a Stuart in the family? He was a pawn. Nick Sedley's words came back to him, haunting, prophetic, and so very true. *We are...both of us...at the mercy of our masters.*

"I am sorry, Connor. I know your heart, for my wife has made certain that I understand fully what I am asking of you. But I ask it anyway. No, I command it...for England, for our line."

Connor felt as if a cold sword had just been driven through his chest and then yanked out again, wrenching his heart out with it. He had spoken true when he'd told Mairi that he no longer cared about who ruled England, but he didn't want to be responsible for the outcome. If he wed Elizabeth, he could use her father and Parliament to the king's advantage, rather than having them use him. No, he couldn't spend the rest of his life with anyone but Mairi. He couldn't lose her forever. He wouldn't. God in all His mercy, what was he to do?

"I wish there was something more to be done."

Connor clenched his fists at his sides. There was. He was a warrior and he wasn't about to surrender so easily.

Connor stepped out of the chamber and into his mother huddled by the door. His father, damp from his day in the lists, stood off to the side, his green gaze as grim as Connor's.

When she saw him, tears spilled down Claire's cheeks, an occurrence Connor had seen only one time before when the Fergussons killed his uncle Robert.

"Connor"—she threw her arms around him—"I am so sorry."

He kissed the top of her head, then stepped out of her embrace. "Where is Mairi?"

"In her room, dressing fer supper."

"Say nothing to her," he told them both. "I will find a way out of this."

"The way is simple," his father said quietly, seeming to read his thoughts when Connor reached him. "We can go home and never look back."

"Nae, I cannot run. Remember that James knows where Camlochlin is."

From behind him, he heard his mother utter a strangled oath not fit for English court.

"I must find Colin. Is he still in the lists?"

"I think so, aye," his father said, following him to the stairs. "The king favors him, but I don't think he will have any influence—"

"I need him to woo Lady Elizabeth fer me."

Graham stopped in his tracks and looked at him like he'd just sprouted another head. "Colin? Woo?"

"Whatever for?" His mother tugged on Connor's sleeve.

He turned to look at her, then at his father. "To discover if there is anything about the de Veres the king should know. James is afraid of losing the Earl of Oxford's support. But they are Protestants, and he likely never had it. If there is anything, anything at all they have done that the king would find unfavorable...Hell, there must be something. I cannot marry her."

"What can we do to help?" his father asked.

"Find out everything ye can about them. Any of them, including Henry and Elizabeth."

"What are you going to tell Mairi?" his mother asked, wiping her eyes.

"I don't know what to tell her yet. I don't want her sneaking off into the earl's lodgings looking for information to help us."

"Aye, she'll surely want to do that." Claire agreed.

"I'll figure something out."

He commissioned them to use caution. He would ask the same of Colin. He needed proof against the de Veres.

He needed a miracle.

Chapter Thirty-six

$\mathcal{M}$airi checked the pins in her hair one last time before heading out the door. She strolled along the balcony, swirling her skirts and closing her eyes, preparing herself for the night to come. She still did not like England, but she no longer minded being here. She hurried to cross the long trek that would lead her to the Banqueting Hall. To him. Ah, but how does one prepare to be swept off her feet by a dashing smile, a set of flashing dimples, and melodies in her beloved's words? Connor. She hoped he hadn't gotten into too much of a bind with the king for what he'd done to Henry. She hadn't had the chance to ask Connor why he had struck him. She shrugged. She would find out later.

Right now, she couldn't help but think of how wonderful her life would be with Connor when they returned home. Och, he wanted to go home. It had been too much to hope for. Would he build her another lovely manor house in Camlochlin? Mayhap they would live at Ravenglade in Perth. The castle had been his uncle Connor Stuart's but with no sons of his own, Claire's twin brother had given Ravenglade to his nephew. She understood it to be quite large and in need of repair, but Connor could make it the perfect home for them. They would marry and she would give him many bairns. She wanted four boys with hair like his and three wee girls, to whom she would teach sewing and swordplay. She would watch her husband work under the sun, his skin gleaming, his muscles sleek with sweat. She would cook his meals and take him to bed each night. She sighed with the glee of it and walked straight into someone.

"Judith!" she said, opening her eyes and recognizing the queen's handmaiden. "Fergive me. I didna' see ye."

"Nae, it is my fault, m'lady."

Mairi liked Judith. Of course, tonight she also liked Lady Hollingsworth. "Where are ye heading?"

"To the Banqueting Hall."

"So am I. Let us walk together." It occurred to Mairi that she missed talking with her mother, her aunt Maggie, and even Claire. They talked all the time at home. Surrounded on all sides by men, a lass needed other lasses to share her secrets with. She would need their advice and training in the art of cooking and other womanly duties. Now, though, all she had was Judith and she was bursting at the seams.

"Judith—"

"M'lady, I was hoping to run into you for the last few days. I wish to speak to you about something… someone."

"Of course," Mairi said. "Who is it ye wish to speak about?"

"Your brother, m'lady. Colin, I believe he is called."

Och, hell, not Colin.

"I cannot seem to get him out of my head. He is the most striking man I have ever laid eyes on. When I watch him in the tiltyard, he makes my stomach feel..." She paused to come up with the right words. "...all warm and out of sorts. It took me a few days, but I finally spoke to him today. He barely even looked at me."

"Judith." Mairi touched her shoulder to comfort her when the handmaiden looked down at her hands and sniffed. "Colin is determined to be the next general of King James's army. I am afraid the only way he would notice ye is if ye were a sword. What about Edward Willingham? He is verra handsome and about yer age."

Judith looked at her, her pretty green eyes round and teary. "I don't want Edward Willingham."

Lord, Colin would kill her for doing this but tonight Mairi could not ignore love. "All right then, when next ye see my brother, compliment him on his skill. That might work. Keep yer conversation along the lines of war and battle. Be forthright. Colin can sense a falsehood the way a deer senses the coming storm. He doesna' like people who speak them and willna' give ye a second chance if he catches ye at one."

The handmaiden nodded and her smile widened into a bright grin. Mairi had done everything she could to help her win Colin. The rest was up to Judith.

"Judith," she said, unable to contain herself a moment longer, "do ye recall that speech ye and I had about Captain Grant?"

"Yes, m'lady. You said he was a devil."

"I was mistaken"—she gleamed, still lost in her fancies—"I am going to be his wife."

Judith smiled at her for a moment, then frowned as if she didn't understand. "Captain Grant, m'lady?"

"Mairi, please, and aye. Captain Grant. Tall, golden hair, dimples?"

"Yes, I know him, Mairi. But I heard that he was to wed Lady Elizabeth."

Mairi's smile remained intact. For a moment. "Pardon? Ye must have misheard."

Judith shook her head. "No, she said those two names."

"She? Ah," Mairi scoffed. "So 'twas Lady Elizabeth who told ye?"

And then it all fell to pieces.

"No, m'lady. It was the queen."

Mairi did not know if Judith said anything after that. As they neared the hall, she saw Connor standing outside, alone in the twilight, wringing his hands while he waited for her approach. No, it was not true. It was another one of the queen's schemes to see them together. Connor was hers. He'd told her he was. He swore it to her. They were going home to begin dreaming again.

His skin looked a little pale and his eyes appeared more startlingly blue as the slight breeze stirred his golden hair around his face. It wasn't true. He would never give her up again.

"Judith," she said, breaking off from her as the handmaiden turned for the doors. "Go inside without me." She never took her eyes off Connor as she moved toward him, her heart racing hard in her breast. Why was he not smiling? He always smiled when he saw her, like it had not been only an hour or two since they were last together, but years.

"What are ye doing out here?" It took effort to speak, but more not to.

"I wanted to take a walk with ye." He bent his head and dropped his gaze to his boots.

She could not. He had something to tell her and she

did not want to hear it. It could not be what Judith had just told her. God, please, it could not be that.

When she stood frozen in her spot, he looked up from under his brow and passed her something she guessed could be a smile. It looked more like pain on a dying man's face. "Walk with me, Mairi."

She took a step forward and fit her hand into the one he offered then let him lead her toward the Privy Garden. They walked in silence, watching the lamplighter move from one lantern to the next, lighting their path. She wanted to coil her arm through Connor's and snuggle close against him while the sun made its descent. She did not want to know why his hand was so cold, or why he kept clenching his jaw, as if trying to keep himself silent. But she had to know.

"How bad was the trouble, Connor?" She managed to keep her voice soft and serene. Until he answered her.

" 'Twas bad."

She closed her eyes, willing herself not to throw her hands to her ears and run. "Tell me, please."

He remained quiet for so long that she opened her eyes again and looked up at him. She stopped beside a row of dogwood trees and waited while he looked at everything but her. "Connor, tell me."

And then he did. His words blurred into each other, jumbled about in her mind, refusing to fit together. It had to be a terrible jest of the queen's. But even as she told herself what she needed to believe, her heart crumbled at her feet.

Again.

She listened, numb, mute, while he told her about the Horse Guard, the Blues Henry and Colin were speaking of last night, and how the king feared losing Oxford's support. But she could only absorb one thing.

"So, are ye going to wed her?"

She knew losing him again would hurt worse than the first time, but she had let herself fall anyway. Her dreadful gaze fell to his lips, waiting...waiting for his reply.

"I must go along with this. Just fer now, Mairi."

Nae, he couldn't be breaking her heart this way again.

"I've no inten—"

She silenced him with the fingers of one hand pressed to his mouth, and the hilt of a dagger clutched in the other. The tip held to his neck.

"Dinna' follow me. There is nothing more I want to hear ye say."

She stared into his eyes for a moment, letting the crushing truth of it settle over her, then withdrew her blade and walked away. Out of his life for good.

He was wise and did not go after her. And it made the last bit of her heart shatter to pieces.

Connor felt the separation like a blow to his guts. The kind that brings a man to his knees. He was doing this for her good, he told himself, watching Mairi leave. He wasn't going to marry Elizabeth, but he needed some time to figure out a way to break the betrothal without deserting the king. It was best if she stayed out of it. He was sorry he had to break her heart to keep her safe. He understood the betrayal he saw in her eyes and it frightened him to think she would not forgive him for it this time.

He touched the drop of blood on his neck and felt the rest of it boil within him. How could he love another when his heart belonged to a passionate hellcat whose only adornments were her mane of unruly black curls and the small arsenal hidden beneath her skirts? He loved her more than life or death, more than king or country. But he didn't go after her. Let her stay as far away from this as possible. If the de Veres went to such lengths to force the king's hand into a union with his kin, who the hell knew what they would do if they knew Mairi stood in the way of it? More, if he told her his plans to discover anything foul about the earl, she might reattach herself to Henry to find out what he knew. She would likely get herself thrown into prison for killing Elizabeth.

He didn't go after her. But he wanted to.

It was better if he focused on Elizabeth for now. The sooner he found something out, the faster he could take Mairi home. He could pretend fondness for Elizabeth for a few days without Mairi in his sight. If he couldn't persuade the wench to tell him what he wanted, perhaps Colin could. Mairi had told him that her brother needed little speech to strip souls of their secrets. He hated involving Colin. This never should have taken place, and he had no one to blame but himself for falling into the de Veres' trap.

He didn't return to the palace. His investigating could wait one night. He had no stomach for it. Not after what he'd just done to Mairi. He left the grounds through the West Gate and walked the narrow streets alone until he came to The Troubadour. His men weren't there. He was glad. He didn't want any company. He wanted to get good and drunk by himself.

He was well on his way to accomplishing that goal when the door to the tavern opened and a hooded woman stepped inside.

For an instant, he thought it might be Linnet come to finish what she'd been paid to do. Then she swept her hood off her head and he saw the glimmer of golden curls dangling over her ears, instead of chestnut ones. Elizabeth.

Hell, he was a fool to think he could pretend fondness for her. What he wanted to do, thanks to his drink, or perhaps not, was close his hands around her throat until she confessed to her father's treason.

"What do ye want?"

"I already got what I wanted," Elizabeth said, pulling out the chair opposite him. "Now I want you to return to the palace where you belong. A captain should not—"

"Ye better leave," he cut her off coolly, "before ye discover what 'tis exactly ye've won."

She smiled watching him lean back and stretch out his long legs before him. "My mettle is quite strong, Captain Grant. May I call you Connor now that we are betrothed?"

He had never wanted to strike a woman before... "Ye can call me whatever ye like, wench, as long as 'tis not husband." So much for wooing her.

"But you will be just that. My father—"

"Clearly doesn't love ye as much as ye think if he would bind ye to me." Now it was Connor's turn to smile when she gave him an irritated look. "I will make ye unhappy. Ye have my word on that." He called for another drink and winked at Vicky when she hurried over with more ale.

"Do you intend to be unfaithful then?" Elizabeth asked through tightly clenched teeth.

"Aye, I do," he replied, lifting his cup to her. "Often."

She shrugged and reached for his cup when he put it down. "I can live with that as long as it's me you come home to. Speaking of home, where shall we live? I understand from my father that you have lands in Perth."

"We will live right here," he told her, snatching his cup out of her hand. "At Whitehall, where I will have my seat in Parliament beside yer father, and where I can better serve my king." Hell, this wasn't going the way he'd planned. He didn't want her to know yet how much he despised her and her role in this farce. He was a warrior and not cut out for being charming to gain information, as Mairi was. Presently, he was too deep into his cups to give a rat's arse. He wanted Elizabeth to know how utterly miserable she would be if she married him. He wanted her to run for her life, to go to her father and beg him to find her a different victim.

"Ye will convert to Catholicism, of course, fer I will not wed a Protestant." He didn't think he would ever take joy in anything again for at least another se'nnight, but watching Elizabeth's skin crawl was quite satisfying—in a cold, cruel sort of way. "I don't want any bairns with ye, but ye won't mind not sharing my bed. I tend to like it rough." He swigged his ale and shouted for more. "What else?" He thought about it for a moment, trying to clear his muddled head. "Ah, yes, ye will end all contact with yer brother, lest I see his face and am tempted to hack what remains of it off."

That got her mettle faltering. He smiled, but felt mildly ill at making plans with her for their life together.

"You will not tell me what to do!" she screeched at him.

"I will, and ye will obey. Ye're a spoiled bratling used to getting what ye want. But that's about to change." When she sprang to her feet, he snatched her back by the wrist and pulled her down so that her face was close to his. "Ye forced my hand one time. Ye never will again."

She yanked her hand and he released her and smiled when she stormed out the door.

⋇✦⋇

Chapter Thirty-seven

*M*airi did not leave her room for the remainder of the night. She refused to unbolt the door when Claire and the queen, and even Colin, tried to speak to her through it. There was nothing they could say to ease her torment.

Connor was going to wed Elizabeth. Dear God, she still could not believe it. Once again, he had chosen England over her. She had tried, between her fits of sobbing, to tell herself what losing the Horse Guard could mean for the kingdom. The possible, ultimate end of the Stuart line. Even if they were wrong about William of Orange wanting the throne, the Duke of Monmouth or the Earl of Argyll were no better. Both were Protestants and would quickly try to extinguish all Catholic beliefs. Argyll was a Campbell, and unlike his cousin Robert before him, he held no affection for the MacGregors. If *that* one claimed the throne, his first order of business would be to come after and destroy his clan's long time enemies, beginning with Mairi's kin.

She knew the consequences of Connor's refusal to

marry the Earl of Oxford's daughter, but none of it mattered compared to losing him. She wanted to go home. She wanted to forget her days...and nights with Connor. But she knew she never would. She cursed him for it, and the king...and God help Elizabeth de Vere if Mairi saw her before she left this wretched place. She was getting the hell out of here as soon as she could, alone if she had to. She would find the road to Scotland. She knew how to fight if she came against any ruffians on the way. She certainly wasn't going to wait around for Claire and Graham to bring her home after their son's wedding. They would want to be here for that. Och, God, she couldn't watch Connor pledge his life to someone else. She couldn't.

She would leave just as soon as she stopped weeping. She hated weeping, but there seemed to be no end to the tears flowing out of her like a damned river. She felt as empty inside as her borrowed English gown strewn across the chair.

How could he do it? How could he marry that contemptible creature? He would be miserable listening to her screech demands at him every day. She almost felt pity for him. Almost. She loved him too much not to feel anything but her own anguish. Och, why had he struck Henry? How could they have lost so much in one day, one instant? How would she live without him?

A harsh rap on her door startled her. "Go away," she cried out, burying her head in her pillow.

"Mairi, 'Tis Connor. Open the door."

No! She didn't want to see him. She was afraid one look and her heart would cease to beat without another, and then another.

"Go away, Connor." His name hurt on the way out. "Leave me alone." *Please.*

He pounded again. "Ye and I need to have words. Open the door."

His speech sounded the tiniest bit slurred. Was he drunk? She'd seen him sharing cups with his friends, but never without his composure intact. The perfect English soldier with the Highlands in the edge of his confident smile.

"Mairi?" he called from beyond the door, then silence before he set his fist set the wood. "Open the damned door!"

"Nae!" she shouted back. "I told ye to go away. Now go do so!"

"I'll kick it down!"

"Ye'll break yer leg, fool. But dinna' let me stop ye from trying!"

He didn't. She felt the vibration of his powerful kick and then heard him bounce back off and hit the ground. The door remained shut.

She rolled her eyes heavenward then grew a little concerned at the prevailing silence.

"I know ye're angry with me," he finally said on the other side. "But there is no need to be. Let me inside to explain what ye did not let me finish the first time."

"Go away!" she shouted again, this time reaching for the painted pottery bowl at her bedside and flinging it at the door.

"Ye're a stubborn wench! Did ye know that?" He gave the impenetrable door another smack. "Fine, I'll tell ye from out here. Is that what ye want? Ye want everyone to hear me tell ye that I love ye? Verra well, I love Mairi MacGregor! And I'm not at the mercy of any damned master!"

His voice echoed down the halls.

Lord, he must indeed be drunk. Mairi left her bed and hurried to the door. "Connor, ye bloody fool," she warned, pressing her mouth to the crack in the door. She still didn't trust herself not to weep all over him and beg him not to wed Elizabeth if she opened it. Och, how could she ask him to refuse the king? This wasn't Charles. She didn't want King James to fall. She liked him. He was Catholic. He was her kin. With him on the throne, the MacGregors would always find favor rather than malice. The queen had become her friend. What would become of her if one of their enemies took over the throne? Dear God, why did the fate of the kingdom have to fall on Connor's shoulders? She didn't want to lose him. Damnation, he'd had no choice in this. He was doing the only thing he could. She didn't hate him for it. She couldn't. "Dinna' shout treasonous words."

"Mairi," he said more softly, closer to the door. "I have loved ye all my life. I see yer face at the dawning of each new sunrise and in the fiery stars at night. I hear yer laughter in the tinkling of cups, the crack of yer tongue in the thunder. I have thought of ye in battle and it kept me alive, determined to be with ye again. And now that I am, I am haunted by yer tears."

Mairi fell against the door, cursing the barrier between them but needing it. "I canna' bear the thought of ye marrying her, Connor. Not even for the kingdom. I am no longer a child. I understand yer duty."

"To hell with my duty. I don't intend to, Mairi. I never did."

He never did? She straightened and stared at the door. "What d'ye mean, ye never did?"

"I'll probably feel more insulted later that ye didn't trust my love fer ye yet again. 'Tis getting rather irritating..."

He closed his mouth when she pulled open the door and stared at him. He was drunk, all right. He looked terrible. His normally crisp uniform was wrinkled. The collar of his coat, along with the shirt beneath, hung open around his neck. His jaw was dark and rough with a day's worth of whiskers, but it was his gaze that revealed just how truly tormented he was. His sapphire eyes had lost their luster, his dimples—even a shadow of them—were nowhere to be seen.

"Ye're so beautiful."

Mairi's heart fluttered against her ribs as they stared at each other across the threshold. It was not because she hadn't heard Connor compliment her every day since his return to Whitehall, or that he found her bonnie, even in her plain shift. Tonight, his melancholy added something more profound to his praise, as if he loved her more than the air he breathed. His eyes proved her correct as they basked in the vision before him, their vibrant color returning. And then he stepped across the threshold like an emperor coming to claim his spoils and hauled her into his arms.

"Fergive me," he whispered along her cheekbone, his lips kissing her swollen eyelids. "I thought not telling ye would keep ye safe, but I couldn't stand the thought of hurting ye again."

Locked in his beloved embrace, Mairi was tempted not to breathe, let alone think clearly, lest doing either would break this magical spell she'd fallen under yet again.

And then she remembered the hellish night she'd just endured.

Pushing him off her, she looked up into his handsome face, and then slapped him across it. "Ye let me believe ye were going to wed that little—"

He pulled her back, ignoring the sting of her fingers. "I thought it best. Ye risk yer life to gain information about Cameronians. How much more would ye do fer me?"

"Anything. I would do anything fer ye. But what in blazes are ye talking about? What does my gaining information for the militia have to do with any of this?"

He told her his plans, his hopes to discover something about the de Veres, the Blues, Parliament... anything that might change the king's mind about needing—or even *having*—the earl's support.

"And if there is nothing, Connor? I have spent many hours with Henry and he has expressed nothing but allegiance to James."

"It doesn't matter," he told her, "I will not wed Elizabeth. If I have to take ye to France to escape this, I will."

"Could ye do that?" she asked him quietly, lifting her fingers to his jaw. Dear God, she thought she had lost him again. Lost all the dreams he stirred back to life in her. Dying slowly with a dozen enemy arrows in her chest would not have been as painful. But she hadn't lost him, just as she had never lost him seven years ago. He would defy his king and shame his name for her. She loved him even more, if that were possible, but she couldn't let him do it.

"I want to help ye."

"Nae. I want ye away from here." He dipped his head and kissed her with exquisite care until she went soft against him. "I want to bring ye to the manor house fer a few days. If anything happened to ye—"

"Nothing will happen to me, Connor. Let me aid ye..."

He shook his head even before she finished what she wanted to say. Hell, but he was stubborn. And so strong when he lifted her in his arms, kicked the door shut behind them, and carried her to her bed.

Connor couldn't speak. What does one say to a goddess, a siren come to lure him away from everything that ever had meaning in his life?

Mairi *was* his life.

He would rather be shot in the back as a traitor than live his life with anyone but her. Her safety came before all else, but he'd had too much to drink at The Troubadour and not enough to distract him from the memory of her walking away from him in the garden. She had done it before, walked away, cut him out of her life without looking back. He couldn't let it happen again. He wouldn't. He'd left the tavern, knowing he had to tell her the truth. He wouldn't lose her to the de Veres and as sure as hell not to her stubborn resistance.

She answered the desire in his eyes now with a provocative smile and pulled her shift over her head.

Connor didn't rush to have her the way his body wanted to. He simply stared at her, thinking that every moment he'd spent waiting for her, wanting only her, was worth it. Her breasts, so round and firm, heaved beneath the silky curtain of her tresses, her nipples peaking through and waiting for his mouth. He moistened his lips, taking in the rest of her while he fumbled with his coat. His gaze slid over the creamy satin of her belly, the tantalizing curve of her hips, and then settled on the scintillating ebony thicket between her legs.

His cock pushed against the tightening fabric of his breeches.

She pulled him down to meet her in an eager, hungry kiss. Her fingers tugged at the shirt clinging to his tight muscles. He couldn't get enough of her mouth, the seductive wantonness of her swirling tongue, the alluring yield of her lips. He thought he might burst if he didn't have her soon.

He smiled, groaning with the pain of his desire and the pleasure of her boldness when she pushed him onto his back and straddled him. She liked being dominant, untamed by any master, and Connor liked it too.

He closed his eyes when she ran her hands down his chest, feeling him, enjoying every muscle that grew harder at her touch. When her small hands began to untie the laces of his breeches, he opened his eyes, curious and aflame at the thought of her touching him. But she had more in mind than doing just that. He watched her, as he had in his most lurid dreams, while she set his cock free.

She startled at the urgency of its ascension, then bit the edge of her bottom lip, perusing him with a hooded, lusty gaze that made him stiffer, straighter, before her eyes.

"My, but ye look good enough to eat." Her husky appraisal made him ache deep down in his shaft. When she moved down his hips, pulling at his breeches as she went, he thought of the ways he wanted to have her. She would submit to all by the time he was through.

He doubted his own conviction a moment later when she crawled between his bare thighs and took his shaft in her hand. She dipped her head. Connor bit his lip and nearly came in her mouth when her lips caressed his thick head. He made himself think of a hundred different things to relax his body, like how she knew to do such a thing. He didn't care. This, he could have her do all night. She took him a bit deeper, her teeth gently scoring his flesh. The muscles in the backs of his thighs spasmed and he pulled her toward him before he expelled too quickly.

He laid her back against the soft mattress and kicked off his boots and the breeches crumpled around his ankles. "I want to be inside ye."

Nestled against her heat, he looked down into her eyes, loving her more than he thought possible. He was sick with it, would perish without it. "Ah, Mairi Mac-Gregor, what ye've done to my poor, pitiful heart."

"And ye to mine, Connor Grant." She spread her thighs beneath him, offering him everything he wanted.

He kissed her parted lips, delving slowly, deeply into the furthest recesses of her mouth. She answered by laving her tongue over his and sucking gently when he withdrew.

They stared into each other's eyes while he pushed his arousal against her opening. He pressed several more slow kisses along her chin and neck as his head broke through.

Having lived among his troupes for years, he knew he was big by other men's measurements. He never cared before, but there was something about watching her take all of him that fired his blood to scalding.

"I love ye," he whispered at her ear, sinking into her. She cried out, still unable to take him fully without pain. It proved that sucking his cock was an innate skill, not a practiced one. She was a woman, no matter how much she despised being one. "Only ye. Always ye."

She coiled her legs around his waist and bucked under him. She tossed back her head, caught up in their dance, rubbing her hungry little bud over his hard shaft. He rode her like a tumultuous wave, holding her close, looking into her eyes.

She smiled at him, her languid gaze begging him for more. He obliged by slipping his hand beneath her, cupping her buttocks. He rose to his knees and pushed her up to meet his forceful thrusts. He watched her climax begin and lifted the rest of her off the bed and into his arms. She threw back her head, spilling her long hair to the mattress and drenching him in a sea of sweet nectar. Driving into her harder, he drowned her in an ocean of his own.

Later, they spoke of love, and of children...and of her knowledge of cooking—or rather, her lack of it.

Mairi almost sighed with pure delight. It was what she had always wanted. She would leave the militia and devote her life to her husband and their bairns.

But not tonight.

And, if she was being truthful, she likely wouldn't give up practicing with her blades every day...in the event of some king barging in on her happy, peaceful life.

But she might never have that life if someone didn't discover something soon. Connor said they needed proof that the king may have already lost the de Veres' support. She couldn't imagine it being so. Unless Henry was so well skilled in the art of deception that he had fooled her. Nae, he loved her. That was all she had ever seen in his eyes. But...she remembered, she had never figured out her whole Cameronian dilemma with him.

Well, there was only one way to find out information. Getting close to your enemies.

She waited until Connor began to snore, then slipped out of the bed. She didn't make a sound, learning long ago how to move about a room without disturbance. She didn't want to wake him, but she didn't care if she did. She wasn't going to sit idly by while her future was given to another. It was sweet of Connor to want to protect her...but a little insulting too. She couldn't fault him entirely for fearing for her safety though, since he didn't know how many times she had done this before.

She dressed quickly, choosing her Highland skirts for easier reach to her daggers, should she need them, and pinning up her hair with the rapier-thin knife Hamish MacLeod made for her three summers ago when he taught her to pick locks. She would have to make certain that the Earl of Oxford was still enjoying the gaiety of the Banqueting Hall and not already in his lodgings.

She slipped out of her room, shut the door behind her, and looked up into Henry's horrifying face.

Chapter Thirty-eight

*G*ood Lord, what had Connor done to him? The flesh around Henry's eyes was purple and yellow, his nose swollen to over half its size. When he opened his mouth to speak to her, she noted two of his teeth missing.

"Miss MacGregor," he said stiffly when she recoiled. "Are you leaving?"

"I am on my way to the Banqueting Hall for something to—"

"You are wearing your Highland attire," he cut her off politely, then flicked his gaze over her back, to the door. "Are you leaving Whitehall?"

"In a few days, aye." She moved away from her room, hoping he would follow her. She didn't want Connor waking up and spoiling her plans. Having Henry here was bad enough.

"You will not be attending the wedding then?"

"Nae." She cast him a hard look over her shoulder and continued walking.

"Nor am I." He hurried to reach her. "How can I

celebrate my sister being bound to the animal who did this to me."

Mairi looked him over. He appeared terribly serious. Hell, she wouldn't want Connor for her brother-in-law if she were Henry.

"How could ye indeed?"

She hadn't considered that he would disapprove of the union. How far would he be willing to go to stop it? Mayhap she wouldn't have to sneak into the earl's lodgings at all. "Pity there is nothing ye can do to put an end to this."

"Put an end to it?" he asked. "But how?"

"I dinna' know. That is why I said there is nothing ye can do." She sighed and looped her arm through his.

He paused momentarily while he looked to be mulling over something he could, in fact, do. "Perhaps a second blade would accomplish what the first could not."

Mairi blinked at him as he picked up his steps, taking her with him. "Ye mean kill him?" Hell, she didn't think he would go that far.

"I can think of no other way to stop my sister from marrying him."

"Nae, ye canna' kill him." Heart pounding, she softened her voice, choosing her words carefully. "Consider what the king's new Parliament would do to yer faither if 'twas ever discovered that ye had James Stuart's nephew killed."

"But how would they discover it if the only soul who knew was you?"

Mairi stared at him impassively, though it took great effort. Hell, but she had underestimated him. Tender gaze intact, he smiled as the veiled threat left his lips. "Would you tell them because you love him, Mairi?"

She could challenge him, but that would be foolish.

He hated Connor and he would hate her as well if she defended his rival. She wanted information from him, and admitting that she would go to the king if he harmed Connor, or that she would do so after she spilled his intestines on Whitehall's marble floors, would gain her nothing.

She smiled up at him from beneath the rings of her lashes trying hard to ignore the many colors between his eyes. "Have I misled ye to believe me a fool, Henry? Who would ever believe the word of a Catholic Highlander over the son of a prominent earl? Besides, I dinna' approve of what Captain Grant did to ye."

He patted her hand and laughed softly. "You don't need to resort to violence, do you, Mairi. Your womanly wiles are your true best weapon. As far as the king's new Parliament," he continued while she stared up at him wondering if he had seen through her this easily from the beginning, "I dare say they would do nothing if they weren't the king's, after all."

Her heart froze. There it was! Exactly what Connor had hoped for! A de Vere's confession that James did not have their support!

But it was too easy. Why would Henry even suggest such a...

She stopped thinking when something soft covered her mouth and an acrid scent stung her nostrils. She wanted to reach for one of her daggers, but she couldn't move. She felt herself falling and someone catching her, but everything went black after that.

Connor sat bolt upright, awakened from his dreams by a pound to his arm, and ready to send the striker to his end.

"What are ye doing in my sister's bed?" Colin demanded

when Connor released his plaid and pushed him away. "And where the hell is she?"

Connor looked at the other side of the bed, then at the small archway leading to the private privy. "Mairi?" he called. When no response came, he swung his legs over the side of the bed and snapped off his covering a moment after Colin turned away and cursed him again.

"Is the hour late?"

"Aye, 'tis," Colin told him while he pulled on his breeches. "And she is not with yer mother."

"How do ye know?"

Colin turned to him. "Lady Huntley retired earlier."

Hell. Connor felt a wave of panic course through him as he sat again to shove his feet into his boots. He knew he shouldn't have told her anything. She was likely in the Earl of Oxford's lodgings at this very moment! Thick-headed wench!

"Come!" Connor commanded, springing to his feet. "We have to stop her before she gets herself thrown into prison."

"Stop her from what?" Colin followed him around to the other side of the bed, where Connor snatched his shirt from the floor.

"From prowling about in Charles de Vere's rooms in search of—"

Colin stopped him with a hand to his arm. "Oxford?" He grew pale and for the first time Connor saw fear in the young Highlander's eyes. "Och, hell, Connor. 'Tis what I came to speak to her about. I was thinking about last night, when I sat at Mairi's table. It hadna' occurred to me at the time why Henry nearly fell out of his chair when he saw me. 'Twas my hood." He spoke quickly when Connor shook his head, not understanding. "'Tis the mantle

I wear when I..." He paused for just an instant, likely not wanting to admit to Connor what he already knew. "...when I go on raids with the militia"

"So? Colin, fer hell's sake, let's go. Tell me on the way."

Connor was the first out the door. He made his way for the promenade on the west wing with Colin at his side.

"Connor, the sight of me scared the shyt out of him. It hit me tonight why? He recognized that mantle. I didna' think 'twas possible, but I canna' deny his reaction."

"But how could he recognize it unless he..." Connor's words trailed off and his boots slowed. The drumming of his heartbeat in his ears nearly drowned out Colin's voice as he finished for him.

"Unless he was where he shouldna' have been."

"'Tis proof that he, and therefore, most likely, his father, work against James with the Cameronians." Connor would have grinned at such brilliant news if Mairi weren't off somewhere alone and in possible danger.

"Aye, 'tis proof. But there is more."

More? Connor thought picking up his swift pace again. This was exactly what he needed to bring before James. The only thing better than this was a confession. Had Colin managed to get one? "Tell me?"

"We all wear the mantles, Connor."

This time, Connor stopped dead and turned to see the same terrible, suffocating fear on Colin's face that he wore on his own. "Are ye telling me he might recognize Mairi, as well?"

"We took precautions," Colin said hastily, keeping pace when Connor began to run. "There was one night... in Glen Garry when she swung her blade at our enemy in the dark. I didna' check to make certain he was dead."

Hell. Oxford's scar! Had Mairi's blade given it to him? Oxford had to know, or suspect it. That was why he knew to speak to Mairi about the Cameronians. He hadn't heard her while she spoke to Queensberry. He knew who her enemies were. He'd known exactly how to lure her away. But if he meant to harm her, why hadn't he tried already? "He loves her." He didn't realize he'd spoken aloud until Colin asked whom he meant.

"Henry. He's in love with yer sister." For the first time, Connor was thankful for it. He had to get to the earl's rooms. Or should he go to Henry's? No, Mairi would not have gone to Henry's private chambers. He had to find her and get her the hell out of Whitehall. He leaned over the walkway when he heard men's laughter from below. He was grateful when he saw Andrew Seymour and his twin brother, Alex, leaving the Privy Garden with two of the king's female guests.

He called to them. Their shoulders straightened when they looked up, ready to do their captain's bidding.

"Alex, go to Henry de Vere's lodgings and make certain he is alone. If he is with Miss MacGregor, bring her to me. Let nothing stop ye. Andrew, wake Lieutenant Drummond and then my father. Tell them to meet me at the Earl of Oxford's door. Go now!" he shouted. "Make haste!"

He didn't wait to see the frown the two ladies sent him but continued quickly on his way with Colin hot on his heels.

Questions nagged him while he turned left down the long walkway to his destination. If Oxford knew it was Mairi who cut him, what plans did he have for her? Nothing pleasant, Connor thought, remembering Henry's crude words about her in the tiltyard. Hell, how could no one know that the de Veres were involved with Richard Cameron's followers? What did it mean for the king? How could they bring this proof before James without admitting that Mairi and Colin were Highland assassins?

Satan's balls, he would think on it later. First, he had to find Mairi.

When they reached the earl's door, Connor tried the handle. Locked. Mairi couldn't be inside unless the earl had discovered her and locked her in.

"Let me." Colin pushed him aside and produced a thin blade from the folds in his plaid. He worked the lock for a moment or two while Connor watched, remembering how easily Mairi had stolen into Queensberry's rooms and sickened that she was as skilled at opening doors she wasn't meant to enter as her brother was.

The locked clicked open and Colin entered the room without haste. He made no sound as he searched the dark rooms and finally stood over the earl's bed.

Mairi wasn't here. But the earl was, sound asleep with a serving wench snoring across his chest.

Connor's heart faltered. Could she be with Henry? Was he overreacting? Had she simply gone to get something to eat? They left the rooms and stepped back into the hall to see Alex Seymour hurrying toward them.

"Lord Oxford was not in his room, Captain."

Connor felt the blood drain from his face. Both Oxford and Mairi away from their beds at this ungodly hour? It was more than just coincidence. They were together. But where? They weren't in the garden. Alex and Andrew had come from outdoors only moments ago. They would have mentioned seeing Oxford. Had Mairi gone with him willingly? Hell, he feared she might go to him for the answers Connor needed. Surely though, she would not wander off with him alone when more than half the palace was asleep? He was about to run for the Banqueting Hall when he spotted a glimmer of golden curls before they disappeared around the bend of another corridor.

Elizabeth!

"Alex, wait here fer the others. Tell them Miss MacGregor is with Lord Oxford and must be found."

"Where are ye going?" Colin raced to keep up with him when he took off after Elizabeth.

"The better question is where is *she* going?" Connor pointed to the back of Elizabeth's gown as she hurried down the stairs a few yards away.

Chapter Thirty-nine

*M*airi awoke to the kind of terror she had never felt before. She was bound. Her wrists, above her head...her mouth...her ankles. Suspended from rope, shrouded in darkness. Panic engulfed her making her dizzy. God, she couldn't pass out again. She fought to breathe, to calm herself. She couldn't let fear overpower her. It was something every warrior was taught, and Claire had been fearless indeed.

What had befallen her? She couldn't remember how she came to be here. She had been with Connor...

Something—or someone—moved past her, unseen in the absence of light, making her hair rise off her body. Her resolve faltered and she struggled heedlessly against her bindings.

A sudden flash of light before her face stilled her efforts. Her vision took a moment to adjust to what stood before her. Or rather who. His face, a grotesque mask of lumps and bruises. Henry. She had been walking with him...

He placed his candle down on some sort of perch

beside her and lit another, and then another, until her surroundings shimmered in the golden light.

Where the hell was she? She looked around at nothing but stone walls and a dirt floor.

"Did you know that Whitehall was once called York House?" Henry turned to her and removed his wig. "It was once inhabited by the archbishops of York and became the seat of Cardinal Wolsey. He, as you may or may not know, was a man of rather savage inclinations and had these passageways built beneath the wine cellars for his personal pleasure."

She was still inside Whitehall. But what good did it do her? She doubted anyone even knew about this place, save for Henry.

He moved toward her. Mairi stiffened. She could hold on to the rope above her and lift both her feet to send him sprawling into the nearest wall. But she would remain bound until he recovered—and then.... She had to think, but she couldn't when his fingers touched her face.

"I am going to remove the cloth from your mouth, but if you scream I will cover it again." He looked up at the low stone ceiling. "I don't think anyone would hear you anyway, but I am no longer a risky man."

He pulled the gag to her chin. She didn't scream. No one would hear her. No one would find her.

Nae! She took hold of her wits and made herself concentrate on getting out, not staying in. What had they been speaking about? How had he managed to knock her out cold without laying a fist to her?

"What is the purpose of this, Henry?"

"You were kind to me, Mairi." He moved his fingertip down her eye, her cheek, her chin. "If not for that, I would have killed you sooner."

"Why?" she demanded, pulling away from him. "If ye are going to kill me now, then be man enough to tell me why? Is it fer yer sister? Do ye do her bidding?"

He laughed and let his wig fall to the floor. "Mine is a more personal motive." While he spoke, he moved closer still, until his chest touched hers. His hand touched her next. He roved it up the slit in her skirts, over her bare thigh. She remained still, promising to cut him down the middle if she got out of this.

It was over before it became too much to bear. Impotent sot. His hand reappeared before her face, along with the gleam of her dagger.

"I could have forgiven you," he said softly, running the tip of her blade down her face with the tenderest of care. "If you hadn't chosen him."

God in heaven, she was about to be killed by a madman. "Forgiven me fer what? I never told ye I loved ye, Henry. In fact, I—"

"Glen Garry, Mairi." His words silenced her. "You and your friends raided the home of Archibald Frazier and then stopped a coach trying to flee the carnage. Do you remember killing the coachman and then my glove hard across your cheek?"

Mairi stared at him, unable, mayhap unwilling, to believe what had just fallen from his lips. He couldn't be that man. She remembered. She hadn't killed as many as she'd boasted to Connor. But she had killed that one.

Hadn't she?

But as the truth settled over her, so did another. If he was that man, then he had been attending a meeting with the Cameronians. That was how he knew what to tell her to lure her away from Connor's sickbed. All this time he knew who she was. He couldn't go to the king with charges without having to explain how he found himself in attendance at a secret meeting of the king's enemies.

None of it mattered presently. Her blade had done that to his face, changed him into the solitary man he had become. He was going to kill her for certain.

She closed her eyes, praying silently for God to get her out of this somehow and she would be content to be nothing but a lass for the remainder of her days.

Something occurred to her and she opened her eyes and frowned at him. He'd deceived her this entire time? Impossible. Hell.

"Excellent work, my lord," she conceded gracefully. After all, the charade was over. "Ye had me perfectly fooled. I truly believed ye were sincere in yer kindness to me."

"I was," he grew serious instantly. "I fell in love with you. After I learned who you were, I loved you still."

"Then ye're not going to kill me?"

"I didn't say that." He turned on his heel and disappeared into the shadows.

"Henry?" Hell. Mairi twisted her fingers around the rope, trying desperately to work out the thick knot. She had to free herself. It was her only hope. She remembered the thin knife in her hair. Pulling herself up, she curled her fingers around the small hilt.

"I would have liked a life with you for a time. But then, your attraction to my brother-in-law would begin to make me hate you. Ultimately, I would kill you. I am saving myself the trouble."

"How did ye know I would never have fallen in love with ye?" It was something. A fragile, pathetic tether, but if it made him doubt his intentions, then let it be so. "Are ye so certain in yer failure at everything that ye do, that ye dinna' even bother to try?"

He came out of the shadows wearing what Mairi prayed was a hopeful look.

Another voice in the darkness, shrill and irritating as hell, halted his advance.

"Are you not finished with her yet?" Elizabeth de Vere stomped her way into the light. "They are looking for her above stairs! Can you not do anything right?"

The colors painting Henry's face faded to ghostly white. "Why have you come down here? Someone could have followed you!" He pushed her out of the way and held one of his candles outward.

"No one followed me, Henry. I am not the bumbling idiot you are."

Och, but Mairi hated this beast of a woman. There was no way in hell she was going to die and let her have Connor.

She worked the knife around in her fingers until the sharp edge cut across the rope. Hope filled her soul. She worked harder, until the fibers began to tear.

"Did you tell her who you are?" Elizabeth asked her brother when he reappeared. "Then," she said after he nodded his head, "you must kill her. Mustn't you."

Her brother nodded again.

Mairi continued her frantic work on the rope until finally, she managed to free one hand.

"You don't want to disappoint Father again, do you? You know it is too soon to lose the king's favor. If you leave her alive and the king hears of your activities..."

"It speaks much about ye, Elizabeth," Mairi said, drawing both sets of eyes to her, "that ye know the only way to beat me is to kill me."

"Beat you?" Henry's sister laughed. "I am not a savage Highlander. And besides, there is nothing I need to beat you at."

"Ye would never have Connor while I lived—or after I die. His heart is mine."

Elizabeth's lips tightened and her ringlets trembled as she moved toward Mairi. "Henry, give me your knife. I will kill this bitch myself."

Mairi's blade flashed in the candlelight as it swooped down on Elizabeth's cheek, slicing it clean open.

Elizabeth de Vere screamed, mayhap loud enough for anyone high above to hear.

Henry rushed forward and then went down with such force, the passageway echoed with the sound of bones crunching against the floor.

Someone was on top of his back. It was Connor. Connor!

And Colin! She saw an instant later when he appeared so naturally out of the shadows and took hold of Elizabeth while she continued to scream.

Mairi used her knife to cut her other hand loose, and then her ankles, while Connor hauled Henry to his feet. He drew back his fist and punched Henry hard in the guts, and then once more just behind his back. Henry went down again, this time more quietly.

Mairi practically leaped into his arms when Connor reached her. She held on to him, her arms coiled around his neck, never wanting to let go. He'd found her. She thanked God, remembering the promise she'd made with Him.

"Are ye hurt, Mairi?"

"Nae." She breathed against him, then tilted her face up to kiss him.

"Mayhap that can wait until after we have brought these two to the king?" Colin suggested with a motion to Henry rising to his knees.

Connor winked at her before he turned to take up Henry. Mairi's heart fluttered about in her chest. How was it possible that she could love one man so much?

"Henry, say nothing...!"

"Lizzy," Henry said softly, seeing her full on for the first time since Mairi struck her. "Your face."

Elizabeth began to cry, and then shriek and wail. Mairi almost felt pity for her, that is, until Henry caught her eye. What did she see in his gaze? Not anger. Not hatred, but something more like satisfaction. Mayhap now, the score would be a bit more evenly matched between him and his sister. Whatever it was disappeared when he looked at Connor.

"If you release us both, my father will see to it that you don't have to wed Elizabeth."

Connor didn't reply but yanked Henry forward. Mairi followed him into the shadows with Colin and Elizabeth close behind.

"There is no reason he needs to know that Miss Mac-Gregor runs with a band of murderers."

"Henry, whatever are ye speaking about?" Mairi said, carrying a candle out before them to light their path. "The king is my kinsmen. He willna' believe yer accusations against me without proof."

"Then we will not speak of the Cameronian issue to His Majesty?" Henry asked, glancing behind him to look at his sister.

Mairi knew that if Connor hadn't arrived Henry would have killed her whether he claimed to love her or not. He had no choice after he told her who he was. She knew too much about him and his family now. She could have fought with one hand, but for how long? She shivered and moved closer to Connor.

"She won't be speaking of them," Connor told him, "but ye will."

Henry chuckled but the sound was void of any mirth. "You're mad if you think I would implicate my father in—"

"You will if ye want yer sister to live." Connor cut him off. "She will be taken to my rooms and guarded while I bring ye to James. If ye don't confess all, she will not leave my rooms alive."

Henry made a tight little sound that blended with Elizabeth's gasp. At first, Mairi thought Connor had chosen the wrong hostage, but Henry did love his sister, poor, pitiful man that he was.

Safe now, Mairi had time to consider that it was likely she who made Henry what he had become. She had liked Henry. She was sorry she had sliced his handsome face and robbed him of his self-worth.

Hell, she'd never been repentant of harming a Cameronian—or a friend of one. She felt like weeping a little. Damnation, it had to be because of all she'd endured in one day. She wasn't some soft, weak-willed lass who fell to pieces in the face of danger.

But, she thought, swiping a tear from her eye, she was a lass, and looking up at her beloved Highlander, she was thankful to be one.

Chapter Forty

Thanks to a golden curl laid upon his lap by Colin, Henry de Vere confessed everything to the king. Not only did he tell James about his father's request that he have dealings with Cameronians, but also his plans to travel to Dorset in the spring to meet with the exiled Duke of Monmouth. Under the threat of hanging for treason, Henry's father, the Earl of Oxford, later supplied the king with vital information about the duke's arrival. He was to land in Lyme Regis with three ships, four light field guns, and fifteen hundred muskets.

James arrested the earl, along with his son and fifteen other noblemen, including Lords Oddington and Hollingsworth. He then sent word to his admirals to change their course and sail for Dorset. War would be avoided, at least for now. Unfortunately, the earl knew nothing of the attack on St. Christopher's Abbey, unable to prove or disprove the duke's innocence... Or the prince's guilt.

Walking the long upper gallery with Mairi under his arm shortly after they left the king, Connor pondered James's continued reluctance to believe the worst in

William of Orange. A reluctance that could eventually cost him his kingdom.

"Sedley would not have tried to kill me if the order had been issued by anyone other than the prince."

"Aye, I know," Mairi said softly against him while he walked her to their door.

"There are so many facts staring the king in the face, yet he refuses to acknowledge any of them."

"He is no fool, Connor. He knows what is in front of him, but remember whatever action he takes, he takes against his daughter, as well."

They walked the rest of the way to her door in silence. When they reached it, she looked up at him again and lifted her hand to his jaw. "I would stay with ye any-where, Connor. If ye want to remain here I will stay with ye. I love ye more than Camlochlin."

He smiled, closing his arms around her. "I don't want to stay. The king doesn't believe William will try to depose him anytime soon and risk a war with France, and I agree. But if I told ye that we'll be sailing off to France in the morn instead of going home, ye wouldn't protest?"

"I wouldna' protest because we are not going to France." She pushed herself up on her toes, kissed him quick on the mouth, then broke away from him. "We are going home, and 'tis already the morn, so ye had best get to packing."

Aye, he wanted to make love to her in the hills, on a bed of heather and the vast blue sky above them. The sooner they left England, the quicker they could get to it.

"No traipsing off with any more men after I leave." He gave her rump a pat before he walked off. "I'll leave without ye."

"Not without a blade in yer back, ye won't."

He grinned listening to the door closing softly behind her. He could melt her body, win her staunch warrior heart, but he'd never tame that tongue.

When he came to his door, he remembered that Lady Elizabeth was still inside with his lieutenant and likely one of the queen's physicians he'd told Edward to fetch for her face. He'd looked at the wound when they had returned to the light. It was but a scratch. She would not suffer from it, but how would she take the news of her father's arrest?

He let out a gusty sigh, happy that this would be the end of traitors and betrayal and the courtly life for him.

He opened the door then moved aside.

"Ye're free to go, Lady Elizabeth."

She leaped from the chair she'd been sitting in, one curl springing across her bandaged cheek. "My father? Henry? What of them?"

She wasn't happy with the news, nor was he in giving it. When she left in tears, he knew hers were only the first to be shed by England's daughters. William might not be coming soon, but he was coming. Wars made widows out of wives. But Mairi would not be one of them.

James had lost much support and an entire regiment tonight. But he'd insisted that Connor go home. There would be no war with Monmouth or Argyll once James caught them and had them both hanged. Connor had served the throne long enough and his cousin wouldn't have him waste away his days here when he wasn't needed. Besides, the king had sat back in his chair and pointed at Colin. That one could likely fight three battles on his own and win.

Connor pulled off his shirt and tossed it over a chair. He stripped out of his breeches and military boots next, bidding them farewell for the last time. He was going home.

Finally.

"Are you certain you will not change your mind and wed your beloved here?" The queen took Mairi's hand and walked with her to where Graham and Claire waited with their horses in the early morning light. "I would so love to see the ceremony. I feel as if I am partly responsible for it, you know." She graced Mairi with her most tender smile. "I knew Captain Grant loved you from the moment I saw him feast his eyes on you. You were both just too stubborn to do anything about it."

"Without yer aid."

The queen giggled behind her small hand. Mairi would always like her.

"I wish to wed Connor in the presence of my kin, in the place of my birth. But I too wish that ye and the king would travel to Camlochlin fer the ceremony. Ye could meet his daughter. I am told she is nothing like Mary or Anne."

"Alas, we cannot. It is too dangerous at present. If we are followed..." She let the rest of her words trail off.

Mairi nodded, knowing she was correct. "Then I will tell Davina what a wonderful and gracious stepmother she has."

"That is kind of you, Mairi. Tell her also..." And at this, the queen's luminous inky eyes sparkled from within. "...that I am trying diligently to give the king a son. Hopefully, it will not be too long before she is not the king's only Catholic heir."

Mairi wished her God's blessings in her endeavors and thanked her for her part in convincing the king to let

Connor leave his service. Aye, there were more battles to be fought in the future, but those would be fought without Connor. She was not *that* generous.

She looked across the yard to where her brother stood talking with Judith. In truth, Judith was doing most of the talking. Colin looked a tad bit bored. Mairi would thank him before she left for showing his attention to the queen's sweet handmaiden, even for one day. Judith would discover on her own that Colin was not right for her. Likely, he was not right for anyone or anything but battle... either on the field or off it. Mairi preferred him off it, since there were too many pistols and muskets in England. That was why she had gone out of her way to point out to the king how clever and devious her brother was, how perfectly capable he was of *stopping* battles before they were fought.

He caught her eye and winked at her and she hoped with all her heart that he would forgive her.

The queen tapped her on the arm, pulling her attention away from Colin, and motioned for her to look toward the palace doors. Mairi's heart stalled at the sight of Connor coming toward her.

It wasn't the way his eyes shone on hers, like clear blue oceans swelling with love and adoration that made her heart rejoice and ache at the same time. Nor was it the vitality in his smile, always confident, a wee bit arrogant, and at times so warm she wanted to lose herself in it and forget the rest of the battle-hardened world. Nae, her knees nearly gave out beneath her at the sight of his Highland plaid draped about his broad shoulder, swinging about his shapely legs. When he reached her, he pushed his bonnet up over his forehead and leaned down to kiss her.

"Walk with me." He took her hand and said something to the queen that made her blush. Mairi was not sure what it was. She only saw the flash of his white smile, the flicker of his deep, irresistible dimples. Hell, he was the finest-looking man in all of Scotland and England combined, and he was hers. Nothing else mattered but that.

"Do ye remember the summer of my twelfth year," he asked her, gazing into her eyes, "when I returned with Tristan from our summer at Campbell Keep?"

"Aye, 'twas the year I had the fever and could not go with you."

He nodded, touching his finger to her face. "My aunt Anne gave me something that summer. Something I wanted to give to ye."

"What was it?"

"My grandmother's ring. I hid it in our cave, beneath a silver rock with the symbol of a heart...well, I tried to make it look like a heart, but it looks more like a circle."

She laughed softly and planted a kiss on his mouth. "Ye hid yer grandmother's ring in a cave?"

"Aye, 'twas where I wanted to ask ye to be my wife."

Dear God, how she loved this terribly romantic man, how she had always loved him.

"Then ask me there, in our cave, and I will say aye and make love to ye while the wind cuts through the braes."

"I've always loved that sound," he told her, pulling her closer into his treasured embrace.

"Aye, my one and only love," she said as he lowered his mouth to hers. "So have I."

Epilogue

*M*airi did not care much for sewing, but her embroidery *was* improving. Counting stitches also kept her mind off food, and the scent of peat moss and burning candle wax, things she normally loved— when she was not early with child. It was her third, and she had hoped that this time she might escape spending her mornings with her head in a basin.

She examined her work and what was supposed to resemble a thistle but looked more like a thorny twig. Close enough. Her eyes settled on the heavy ring encircling her index finger. They had retrieved it together from the place under the rock with a circle carved into it. Connor had bent to one knee and promised her the moon and the stars and every summer spent at Camlochlin until they grew old together, and then they made love for the last time in their private, secret place.

She sighed, feeling ridiculously happy and a bit weepy. She looked up at the women sharing the new day with her. Claire lifted her robin-blue gaze from her stitching and smiled at her. Maggie paused behind Davina's chair to have a look at her work, nodded her approval, and then continued to rock Rob and Davina's baby daughter, Abigail, in her arms.

"Well," she said, checking Mairi's work next, "at least ye've learned how to cook."

Mairi caught Isobel's brief look to heaven, and then the two exchanged a covert smile. Dear Lord, who would have ever thought she and Isobel Fergusson would become such good friends? When she had first returned home and discovered that Tristan had wed the daughter of her clan's worst enemy, she did not speak to her brother for two days. But Isobel soon won her over when she told Mairi that she did not give a rat's arse if she liked her or not—and then offered to teach her how to cook.

Mairi looked down at Isobel's swollen belly and felt a pang of envy that her sister-in-law suffered no ill effects from her present babe, or her son before it.

Her mother's soft voice reading aloud from one of her cherished books drew Mairi's eyes to her next, and to the minky-haired babe in her lap trying to claw at the pages. Her daughter Caitrina was still too young to understand her grandmother's tales of love and honor, all of Kate's grandchildren were, but that did not stop her from telling them.

Hell, but she loved being home, surrounded by the people she loved most in the world. She loved Ravenglade with its high turrets and towers and sprawling green fields. It was her home. Wherever Connor was, was home. But Camlochlin.... She wiped a blasted tear from her eye and sniffed just as the solar door opened and the men entering threatened to purge her of every drop of water in her body.

Her father brought the scent of heather with him, clean, misty, fresh, and familiar. He caught her eye while bending to kiss the top of his wife's head, and winked at her. Rob entered right behind him, arguing a point with Tristan, who hefted his son in one arm and Rob's eldest in the other. He smirked at the rest of them, proving that he did not care a whit who was right. He just enjoyed getting Rob riled up.

Colin appeared next, back from England for a se'nnight's visit with his kin. Mairi smiled at him, deciding that even his justacorps and droopy bow beneath his chin could not hide that he was born and bred in the Highlands.

Stepping through the doorway after them, taking his own leisure, as usual, came the two who near caused Mairi to weep all over her embroidery. Her watery eyes took in her husband's shapely legs, the great plaid belted at his waist, and their two-year-old son squirming to be off his shoulders.

Connor smiled at her tears, knowing well enough by now that they sprang from her deepest emotions. The oaf liked that she had no control over them in her condition. He still irritated the hell out of her at times, but she suspected he did it because he liked fighting with her.

He set their son down and watched when Malcolm ran to her.

"Momma, I'm going to help faither build ye a house! He said I could!"

She brushed her needles aside and gathered her eldest son into her lap. "Are ye now? And where might this new house be?"

Mairi followed his gaze to Connor pushing off the door to come to her. "I thought just below the braes of Bla Bheinn would be nice."

Here? In Camlochlin? Where he'd first told her he loved her?

Finally, the surging well burst.

Damn it.

On a secret mission
for the king of England,
Colin MacGregor never
expected a "traitor" like this:
lovely, gentle—a damsel in
genuine distress.

Please turn this page for
a preview of

Conquered by a Highlander

the stunning conclusion to
Paula Quinn's series

Chapter One

*C*olin MacGregor reined in his horse along the rocky cliff side behind Dartmouth Castle and looked around for a flat place to sit. Dismounting, he pushed back the hood of his mantle and he untied the sack dangling from his saddle. He pulled a small pouch from inside and took a seat beside the pounding surf. He was about to change his identity, including his religion, his moral code, and his entire past.

Hell, he thought, opening the pouch to eat, the cheese looked a bit moldy. He sighed, rubbed his belly, and tossed the cheese back from whence it came.

Leaning back on the rocks, he gazed up at the sheer fortress wall. Dartmouth was more of a fort than an actual castle, built in the fourteenth century to guard the mouth of the Dart estuary. Isolated and deep within Protestant territory, 'twas a good enough place to land an army of ships if a certain Dutch prince wished to invade England.

Colin scanned the gun tower and surrounding gun platforms added later by Henry VIII. Pity, there were no fearsome looking soldiers guarding the walls. He ached for a good fight when the time finally came.

When he'd left his home on Skye to join the king's Royal Army three years ago, he had no idea that his battles would be silent, purely political ones. Back home, he had fought in the rebel militia for a cause that had more to do with protecting Highland rights than with a religion. 'Twas what he continued to fight for in England. That, and the fact that her monarch was not only Catholic but Colin's kin by marriage, as well. For that, James had his loyalty in whatever kinds of battles needed to be fought. Mostly, those battles required the sharp edge of Colin's mind, rather than his blade. He honed both with the same relentless diligence, despite his glorious war having become dull and rather tarnished. Worse, his king, his friend, had become a tyrant. And he, the king's snake.

Reaching for his bag of water, Colin wondered if England would not be better off without James. It pained him to think on it. He'd once respected the king's sacrifice for his beliefs, even giving up his firstborn daughter. But James no longer had the good of the people first on his mind. His passion for absolute power had created many enemies. And now, with his wife, the lovely Queen Mary, pregnant with a possible male Catholic heir, those enemies were about to take action.

Wetting his tongue, Colin raised his gaze to the square battlemented tower and the high lookout turret rising from it. He wouldn't let his nerves get the better of him. He never did. This wasn't the first time he would be living as Colin Campbell of Breadalbane, cousin to the Campbells of Glen Orchy. A spy. A snake, living among nobles who already knew him as a Protestant Campbell.

The information he had gathered at various tables from France to Scotland about secret correspondences between England and Holland had all led back to Geoffrey Dearly, Earl of Devon. This was it, Colin was sure of it, the last time he would have to sit in the company of his enemies and speak like them, laugh with them. He would learn their secrets and then return in battle to butcher them.

Hell, 'twas about time.

A movement high atop the turret caught his eye, and as he focused on what it was, his thoughts of victory scattered to the four winds. Slowly, he corked his water bag and let it drop to the rocks.

'Twas a lass, her long flaxen tresses and flowing white gown snapping against the bracing wind as she stepped up onto the edge of the crenellated wall. Was she a woman about to leap over the edge to her death, or an angel readying to take flight? He waited, his heart beating more wildly in his chest than it had in years, to see the answer. If she was a woman, he could do nothing to save her if she fell. He had seen death, had caused much with his own blade, but he had never been witness to someone taking her own life. Why would she? What in hell was so terrible in her life that smashing her body against jagged cliffs and rocks was a better alternative?

When she bent her knees, his heart stalled in his chest.

He couldn't catch her. Damned fool.

But she didn't jump. Instead, she nestled herself into the groove of a merlon. He watched her, unnoticed while she wrapped her arms around her knees and set her chin toward the estuary. She reminded him of a painting he'd seen in King Louis's court, of a woman looking out toward the sea, waiting for her beloved to return to her. Something about this lass above him stirred his soul. Was she waiting for someone? Mayhap a guardsman from Dearly's garrison? She looked small and utterly alone surrounded by stone, water, and the vast sky behind her. Who was she?

A better question he put to himself next was what the hell did he care who she was. He didn't. 'Twas the most vital part of this duty he was born to carry out, what made him better at it than anyone else. He attached himself to no one. Mercy could get him or, worse, the king killed. He had no issues about befriending no one, since the men he'd been sitting with over the past three years had been traitors to the throne and could never be trusted.

Pulling his hood back over his head, he looked at the lass one last time. She dipped her head, catching his movement. When she scrambled to her feet, he clenched his jaw to keep himself from calling out, have a care! She would not hear. Thankfully, she stepped back down off the wall and disappeared.

Left with nothing but the passing memory of her, Colin returned his thoughts to the duty at hand: find a place at Lord Devon's table: infiltrate his garrison, learn their secrets and their weaknesses, and get out alive. 'Twould be simple enough, he thought, returning his pouch and himself to his horse. If he was correct about Devon's alliance with the would-be usurper—and Colin was certain he was correct—the earl would need every available sword for hire he could find. Fortunate for him, the deadliest mercenary ever to wield a blade or fire a pistol was about to land on his doorstep.

Colin smiled to himself as his horse cantered through the yard of St. Petroc's Church, sited before the castle, where a dozen or so of Devon's men were loitering, looking bored until they saw him.

Dismounting, he pushed back his hood and held up his hands as the men raced toward him.

"Stranger." One stepped out from among the rest and gave him a thorough looking over. He was tall and broad shouldered in his stained military coat. His dark, oily hair fell over gray, bloodshot eyes. "What brings you to Dartmouth?"

Colin watched while the man eyed the swords dangling from both sides of his hips beneath his wind-tossed mantle, then at the pistol tucked into his belt. "I seek an audience with the earl."

The man's gaze settled on the flash of a dagger hidden within the folds of Colin's open vest. "You carry many weapons." He dipped his wary gaze to Colin's leather boots next, where more daggers peaked out at him.

"The roads are dangerous," Colin explained with a slight a crook of his lips, still keeping his hands up.

"So is straying into a place you don't belong," the speaker countered, reaching around his belly to the hilt of his sheathed sword. "Who are you and what business do you have here?"

"I am Colin Campbell of Breadalbane and I've come to offer my blade to Lord Devon."

"Well, Colin Campbell of Breadalbane," the soldier said, puffing up his chest, "I am Gilbert de Atre, Lieutenant of Dartmouth, and I'll be the judge on whether or not you're fit to fight by my side."

Colin lowered his hands slowly but kept them where de Atre could see them. He knew hundreds of men just like this one. He'd seen that same challenging smirk dozens of times before. He wasn't sure what it was about him that made some men want to test him. Mayhap 'twas his weapons and the way he carried them, or the cool, composed indifference of his expression. He feared little and it intimidated less formidable men. Usually, he ignored such bravado, especially when his task was to make nice and fit in. This time though, he had to fit into an army, not at a noble's table. He would need to earn their respect before they trusted him. Colin did not mind having to fight to prove himself. In fact, he looked forward to it. A test of his skill would provide an excellent opportunity to learn what he was up against, and also to show these men that he would be an asset to their company. He would go easy on them all, of course. No reason to reveal too soon what they were up against.

"Remove all those daggers and pistols you have hidden on you," de Atre demanded. "I don't trust any Scot with two hands."

Stripping himself of his extra weapons, Colin promised himself that de Atre would be among the first to feel his blade when he returned with his army. Especially after the lieutenant attacked while he was removing a dagger from his boot.

Colin fell back on his haunches, then rolled away in time to avoid the blow. He came back up on his feet instantly and slid his sword from its scabbard.

De Atre's smile widened into a yellow grin. "Come, stray, let us see what you've got. But be warned, I've sent all your brothers back to their mothers castrated and broken."

Colin's lip curled as he readied his blade. "Not my brothers, you haven't."

His metal flashed as it came up, blocking de Atre's next strike above his head. He parried another hit, and then another, scraping the edge of his blade down de Atre's. Pushing off, he stepped back, loosened his shoulders, and rolled his wrist. The blade danced with fluid grace beneath the sun, casting a flicker of doubt in de Atre's eyes.

Not yet.

He tightened his stance, as if suffering from a bout of nerves at what he was facing. De Atre advanced and swung wide. Colin avoided the slice to his belly with a step to his left. He ducked at a swipe to his neck and parried a number of rather tedious strikes to his knees. After a few moments, it became clear that he could fight the lieutenant while he was half asleep. He suppressed the urge to yawn, thinking about what kinds of beds were given to the garrison soldiers. Hay would be a welcome respite from the hard, cold ground he'd been sleeping on for the past se'nnight.

He blinked when de Atre's blade struck his, raining sparks down on their faces. After a quarter of an hour, Colin did his best to look suitably worn down from such a worthy opponent.

A spot of bright military blue-and-white lace crossed his vision and he followed it. The captain of the garrison caught his gaze across the crowded courtyard and held it curiously while Colin parried and blocked another blow.

'Twas time to lose.

Colin hated to do it, but 'twas for the good of England and Scotland. He held up his blade and feigned a swipe. De Atre struck his sword and Colin let it fall to the ground. Defeated, he raised his palms once again. "Perhaps after I've filled my belly, we could give it another go?"

De Atre sized him up with a snarl. "You have balls to ask for food after you just showed yourself wanting. Filling your belly won't help you."

Humility and reverence. No man could resist having each displayed at his feet. "I am hungry and eating may not help with fighting against you, but if you feed me I'll swear my blade, as unworthy as it is, to your lord."

"You have potential, Campbell. That's why I let you live. You will—"

"You there. Come forward."

Colin flicked his gaze to the man who spoke, taking in polished black boots, crisp breeches, and a clean military coat adorned in lace. He was older than the lieutenant, mayhap in his fortieth year, clean-shaven and lithe of build.

"I am Captain Gates," he said when Colin reached him.

"Captain." Colin met his level gaze. If his father or brothers were standing in his place, they would have dwarfed the Englishman, but Colin was not built purely for brawn, but for speed and agility, as well.

"Your name?" the captain asked, scrutinizing him with narrowed blue eyes the same way his lieutenant had, but with interest rather than challenge.

"Colin Campbell of Breadalbane."

"What do you want here, besides our food?"

"I wish to offer my services to your lord."

"And what kind of services might those be?"

"Sewing, most likely," someone jeered to Colin's left. Good. Let them believe him no threat.

"I could use some training, I know." He caught the captain's slow smile when he turned to offer de Atre his brief acknowledgment. "I am a quick learner. I wish to offer my sword to the earl."

Gates arched his brow at him. "Why?"

"Because my cousin, the future Earl of Argyll, assured me that Lord Devon would soon be needing more men to guard his castle."

"Did he?" the captain asked with skepticism narrowing his eyes. "What else did he tell you?"

Everything. With France occupied in campaigns by Germany and Italy, Prince William of Orange had begun to assemble an expeditionary force against the king. He would not attack though without penned invitations from England's most eminent noblemen inviting him to invade. According to Argyll, Colin's cousin on his mother's side, Dartmouth was to be the host of the invading Dutch army, and Lord Devon, the man arranging it all. Colin's task was to discover when the prince meant to invade, how many men he would bring with him, and who among King James's vassals signed their names to the invitations.

Colin smiled slightly, just enough to prove to the captain that he spoke true. "He told me why."

The captain's subtle reaction was exactly what Colin expected. A hint of surprise that a mercenary knew a prince's intentions, and then a nod of acceptance because the only way he could was if a prominent ally such as Duncan Campbell had told him.

"Very well," the captain said, "I will take you to the earl. If you wish to fight for him, let him decide if you are worthy."

"My thanks," Colin offered. He retrieved his daggers, and followed his escort toward the castle.

At the doors, Gates stopped and turned to him. "So that we are clear on this; I did not train or choose my lieutenant. If you are here for any other purpose than the one you claim, I will personally remove your head."

He waited until Colin nodded that he understood and then led him inside.

"Gillian!" The thunderous shout reverberated through

the long halls, scattering servants every which way. "Gillian!" the voice bellowed again, followed this time by the pounding of boots down the stairs. "Answer when I call for you, bitch! Ranulf! Where are my musicians, my wine?"

Colin looked up at a tall, lanky nobleman stomping toward them. His dark, perfect ringlets bounced around the shoulders of his crisp justacorps. His complexion was pale, as if painted. His dark gray eyes darted about the hall before coming to rest on Colin.

"Who are you?"

"My Lord Devon." Captain Gates stepped forward. "This is Colin—"

"Captain Gates." The earl shifted his haughty gaze to the captain, his interest in the mercenary standing in his hall, already gone. "Where is my cousin? I've been calling for her. Your duty is to guard her. Why are you not with her and bringing her to me?"

"She was asleep when I left her, my lord."

"Well, wake her up! And her bastard with her! No reason that brat should sleep all day."

Captain Gates offered him a brisk nod, then started toward the stairs.

"There is no need to fetch me, my good Captain" came a soft voice from the top of the stairs.

Colin watched the woman descend, her pale, wheaten waves falling lightly over her white, flowing gown. 'Twas the woman from the battlements.

She didn't look at him. Her eyes, like twin blue seas, churned with a frosty glitter as she set them on the earl.

"I hope my lord will forgive me for sleeping while he bellowed for me."

Colin was tempted to smile at her. Her ability to speak

such a humbling falsehood and sound so convincing while doing it impressed him. The truth lay in her eyes if one but looked.

"I won't show you mercy next time, Gillian," he promised, gloating at her surrender. "Now make haste and bring me some wine." He lifted his manicured fingers and snapped at his captain. "Go with her, Gates, and make certain she doesn't dally or it will cost you a month's wage."

Lord Devon watched them leave the hall to their errand, and then settled his gaze on a serving girl on her way to some chore. He snatched her arm as she passed him and yanked her into his arms.

"What are you still doing here?" he demanded, lifting his mouth from her neck when he saw Colin. "Who are you?"

Verra likely yer worst enemy. Colin granted his host his most practiced bow. "I am the man who will lead your army to victory."

Davina Montgomery is
the Crown's greatest secret.
But when a powerful warrior
steals her heart,
their passion may destroy
the English throne.

Please turn this page for
a preview of

Ravished by a Highlander

Available now.

Chapter One

*H*igh atop Saint Christopher's Abbey, Davina Montgomery stood alone in the bell tower, cloaked in the silence of a world she did not know. Darkness had fallen hours ago, and below her the sisters slept peacefully in their beds, thanks to the men who had been sent here to guard them. But there was little peace for Davina. The vast indigo sky filling her vision was littered with stars that seemed close enough to touch should she reach out her hand. What would she wish for? Her haunted gaze slipped southward toward England, and then with a longing just as powerful, toward the moonlit mountain peaks of the north. Which life would she choose if the choice were hers to make? A world where she'd been forgotten, or one where no one knew her? She smiled sadly against the wind that whipped her woolen novice robes around her. What good was it to ponder when her future had already been decreed? She knew what was to come. There were no variations. That is, if she lived beyond the next year.

She looked away from the place she could never go and the person she could never be.

She heard the soft fall of footsteps behind her but did not turn. She knew who it was.

"Poor Edward. I imagine your heart must have failed you when you did not find me in my bed."

When he remained quiet, she felt sorry for teasing him about the seriousness of his duty. Captain Edward Asher had been sent here to protect her four years ago, after Captain Geoffries had taken ill and was relieved of his command. Edward had become more than her guardian. He was her dearest friend, someone she could confide in here within the thick walls that sheltered her from the schemes of her enemies. Edward knew her fears and accepted her faults.

"I knew where to find you," he finally said, his voice just above a whisper.

He always did know. Not that there were many places to look. Davina was not allowed to venture outside the Abbey gates, so she came to the bell tower often to let her thoughts roam free.

"My lady—"

She turned at his soft call, putting away her dreams and desires behind a tender smile. Those she kept to herself and did not share, even with him.

"Please, I…" he began, meeting her gaze and then stumbling through the rest as if the face he looked upon every day still struck him as hard as it had the first time he'd seen her. He was in love with her, and though he'd never spoken his heart openly, he did not conceal how he felt. Everything was there in his eyes, his deeds, his devotion—and a deep regret that Davina suspected had more to do with her than he would ever have the bold- ness to admit. Her path had been charted for another course, and she could never be his. "Lady Montgomery, come away from here, I beg you. It is not good to be alone."

He worried for her so, and she wished he wouldn't. "I'm not alone, Edward," she reassured him. If her life remained as it was now, she would find a way to be happy. She always did. "I have been given much."

"It's true," he agreed, moving closer to her and then stopping himself, knowing what she knew. "You have been taught to fear the Lord and love your king. The sisters love you, as do my men. It will always be so. We are your family. But it is not enough." He knew she would never admit it, so he said it for her.

It had to be enough. It was safer this way, cloistered away from those who would harm her if ever they discovered her after the appointed time.

That time had come.

Davina knew that Edward would do anything to save her. He told her often, each time he warned her of her peril. Diligently, he taught her to trust no one, not even those who claimed to love her. His lessons often left her feeling a bit hopeless, though she never told him that, either.

"Would that I could slay your enemies," he swore to her now, "and your fears along with them."

He meant to comfort her, but good heavens, she didn't want to discuss the future on such a breathtaking night. "Thanks to you and God," she said, leaving the wall to go to him and tossing him a playful smile, "I can slay them myself."

"I agree," he surrendered, his good mood restored by the time she reached him. "You've learned your lessons in defense well."

She rested her hand on his arm and gave it a soft pat.

"How could I disappoint you when you risked the Abbess's consternation to teach me?"

He laughed with her, both of them comfortable in their familiarity. But too soon he grew serious again.

"James is to be crowned in less than a se'nnight."

"I know." Davina nodded and turned toward England again. She refused to let her fears control her. "Mayhap," she said with a bit of defiance sparking her doleful gaze, "we should attend the coronation, Edward. Who would think to look for me at Westminster?"

"My lady..." He reached for her. "We cannot. You know—"

"I jest, dear friend." She angled her head to speak to him over her shoulder, carefully cloaking the struggle that weighed heaviest upon her heart, a struggle that had nothing to do with fear. "Really, Edward, must we speak of this?"

"Yes, I think we should," he answered earnestly, then went on swiftly, before she could argue, "I've asked the Abbess if we can move you to Courlochcraig Abbey in Ayr. I've already sent word to—"

"Absolutely not," she stopped him. "I will not leave my home. Besides, we have no reason to believe that my enemies know of me at all."

"Just for a year or two. Until we're certain—"

"No," she told him again, this time turning to face him fully. "Edward, would you have us leave the sisters here alone to face our enemies should they come seeking me? What defense would they have without the strong arms of you and your men? They will not leave St. Christopher's, nor will I."

He sighed and shook his head at her. "I cannot argue when you prove yourself more courageous than I. I pray

I do not live to regret it. Very well, then." The lines of his handsome face relaxed. "I shall do as you ask. For now, though," he added, offering her his arm, "allow me to escort you to your chamber. The hour is late, and the Reverend Mother will show you no mercy when the cock crows."

Davina rested one hand in the crook of his arm and waved away his concern with the other. "I don't mind waking with the sun."

"Why would you," he replied, his voice as light now as hers as he led her out of the belfry, "when you can just fall back to sleep in the Study Hall."

"It was only the one time that I actually slept," she defended, slapping his arm softly. "And don't you have more important things to do with your day than follow me around?"

"Three times," he corrected, ignoring the frown he knew was false. "Once, you even snored."

Her eyes, as they descended the stairs, were as wide as her mouth. "I have never snored in my life!"

"Save for that one time, then?"

She looked about to deny his charge again, but bit her curling lip instead. "And once during Sister Bernadette's piano recital. I had penance for a week. Do you remember?"

"How could I forget?" he laughed. "My men did no chores the entire time, preferring to listen at your door while you spoke aloud to God about everything but your transgression."

"God already knew why I fell asleep," she explained, smiling at his grin. "I did not wish to speak poorly of Sister Bernadette's talent, or lack of it, even in my own defense."

His laughter faded, leaving only a smile that looked

to be painful as their walk ended and they stood at her door. When he reached out to take her hand, Davina did her best not to let the surprise in her eyes dissuade him from touching her. "Forgive my boldness, but there is something I must tell you. Something I should have told you long ago."

"Of course, Edward," she said softly, keeping her hand in his. "You know you may always speak freely to me."

"First, I would have you know that you have come to mean—"

"Captain!"

Davina leaned over the stairwell to see Harry Barns, Edward's second in command, plunge through the Abbey doors. "Captain!" Harry shouted up at them, his face pale and his breath heavy from running. "They are coming!"

For one paralyzing moment, Davina doubted the good of her ears. She'd been warned of this day for four years but had always prayed it would not come. "Edward," she asked hollowly, on the verge of sheer panic, "how did they find us so soon after King Charles's death?"

He squeezed his eyes shut and shook his head back and forth as if he, too, refused to believe what he was hearing. But there was no time for doubt. Spinning on his heel, he gripped her arm and hauled her into her room. "Stay here! Lock your door!"

"What good will that do us?" She sprang for her quiver and bow and headed back to the door, and to Edward blocking it. "Please, dear friend. I do not want to cower alone in my room. I will fire from the bell tower until it is no longer safe to do so."

"Captain!" Barns raced up the stairs, taking three at a time. "We need to prepare. Now!"

"Edward"—Davina's voice pulled him back to her—"you trained me for this. We need every arm available. You will not stop me from fighting for my home."

"Orders, Captain, please!"

Davina looked back once as she raced toward the narrow steps leading back to the tower.

"Harry!" She heard Edward shout behind her. "Prepare the vats and boil the tar. I want every man alert and ready at my command. And Harry..."

"Captain?"

"Wake the sisters and tell them to pray."

In the early morning hours that passed after the massacre at St. Christopher's, Edward's men had managed to kill half of the enemy's army. But the Abbey's losses were greater. Far greater.

Alone in the bell tower, Davina stared down at the bodies strewn across the large courtyard. The stench of burning tar and seared flesh stung her nostrils and burned her eyes as she set them beyond the gates to the meadow where men on horseback still hacked away at each other as if their hatred could never be satisfied. But there was no hatred. They fought because of her, though none of them knew her. But she knew them. Her dreams had been plagued with her faceless assassins since the day Edward had first told her of them.

Tears brought on by the pungent air slipped down her cheeks, falling far below to where her friends...her family lay dead or dying. Dragging her palm across her eyes, she searched the bodies for Edward. He'd returned to her an hour after the fighting had begun and ordered her into the chapel with the sisters. When she'd refused, he'd tossed her over his shoulder like a sack of grain and brought her there himself. But she did not remain hidden. She couldn't, so she'd returned to the tower and her bow and sent more than a dozen of her enemies to meet their Maker. But there were too many—or mayhap God didn't want the rest, for they slew the men she ate with, laughed with, before her eyes.

She had feared this day for so long that it had become a part of her. She thought she had prepared. At least, for her own death. But not for the Abbess's. Not for Edward's. How could anyone prepare to lose those they loved?

Despair ravaged her, and for a moment she considered stepping over the wall. If she was dead they would stop. But she had prayed for courage too many times to let God or Edward down now. Reaching into the quiver on her back, she plucked out an arrow, cocked her bow, and closed one eye to aim.

Below her and out of her line of vision, a soldier garbed in military regalia not belonging to England crept along the chapel wall with a torch clutched in one fist and a sword in the other.

THE DISH

Where authors give you the inside scoop!

♥ ♥ ♥ ♥ ♥ ♥ ♥ ♥ ♥ ♥ ♥ ♥ ♥ ♥ ♥

From the desk of Vicky Dreiling

Dear Reader,

While writing my first novel HOW TO MARRY A DUKE, I decided my hero Tristan, the Duke of Shelbourne, needed a sidekick. That bad boy sidekick was Tristan's oldest friend Marc Darcett, the Earl of Hawkfield, and the hero of HOW TO SEDUCE A SCOUNDREL. Hawk is a rogue who loves nothing better than a lark. Truthfully, I had to rein Hawk in more than once in the first book as he tried repeatedly to upstage all the other characters.

Unlike his friend Tristan, Hawk is averse to giving up his bachelor status. He's managed to evade his female relatives' matchmaking schemes for years. According to the latest tittle-tattle, his mother and sisters went into a decline upon learning of his ill-fated one-hour engagement. Clearly, this is a man who values his freedom.

My first task was to find the perfect heroine to foil him. Who better than the one woman he absolutely must never touch? Yes, that would be his best friend's sister, Lady Julianne. After all, it's in a rake's code of conduct that friends' sisters are forbidden. Unbeknownst to Hawk, however, Julianne has been planning their nuptials for four long years. I wasn't quite sure how Julianne would manage this feat, given Hawk's fear of catching *wife-itis*.

After a great deal of pacing about, the perfect solution popped into my head. I would use the time-honored trick known as *The Call to Adventure*. When Tristan, who can not be in London for the season, proposes that Hawk act as Julianne's unofficial guardian, Hawk's bachelor days are numbered.

In addition to these plans, I wanted to add in a bit of fun with yet another Regency-era spoof of modern dating practices. I recalled an incident in which one of my younger male colleagues complained about that dratted advice book for single ladies, *The Rules*. I wasn't very sympathetic to his woes about women ruling guys. After all, reluctant bachelors have held the upper hand for centuries. Thus, I concocted *The Rules* in Regency England.

Naturally, the road to true love is fraught with heartbreak, mayhem, and, well, a decanter of wine. Matters turn bleak for poor Julianne when Hawk makes his disinterest clear after a rather steamy waltz. I knew Julianne needed help, and so I sent in a wise woman, albeit a rather eccentric one. Hawk's Aunt Hester, a plain-spoken woman, has some rather startling advice for Julianne. Left with only the shreds of her pride, Julianne decides to write a lady's guide to seducing scoundrels into the proverbial parson's mousetrap. My intrepid heroine finds herself in hot suds when all of London hunts for the anonymous author of that scandalous publication, *The Secrets of Seduction*. At all costs, Julianne must keep her identity a secret—especially from Hawk, who is determined to guard her from his fellow scoundrels. But can he guard his own heart from the one woman forbidden to him?

My heartfelt thanks to all the readers who wrote to let

me know they couldn't wait to read HOW TO SEDUCE A SCOUNDREL. I hope you will enjoy the twists and turns that finally lead to happily ever after for Hawk and Julianne.

Cheers!

[signature: Vicky Dreiling]

www.vickydreiling.com

From the desk of Jane Graves

Dear Reader,

Have you ever visited one website, seen an interesting link to another website, and clicked it? Probably. But have you ever done that about fifty times and ended up in a place you never intended to? As a writer, I'm already on a "what if" journey inside my own head, so web hopping is just one more flight of fancy that's *so* easy to get caught up in.

For instance, while researching a scene for BLACK TIES AND LULLABIES that takes place in a childbirth class, I saw a link for "hypnosis during birth." Of course I had to click that, right? Then I ended up on a site where people post their birth stories. And then . . .

Don't ask me how, but a dozen clicks later, my web-hopping adventure led me to a site about celebrities and baby names. And it immediately had me wondering: *What were these people thinking?* Check out the names these famous people have given their children that virtually guarantee they'll be tormented for the rest of their lives:

Apple	Actress Gwyneth Paltrow
Diva Muffin	Musician Frank Zappa
Moxie Crimefighter	Entertainer Penn Jillette
Petal Blossom Rainbow	Chef Jamie Oliver
Zowie	Singer David Bowie
Pilot Inspektor	Actor Jason Lee
Sage Moonblood	Actor Sylvester Stallone
Fifi Trixibell	Sir Bob Geldof*
Reignbeau	Actor Ving Rhames
Jermajesty	Singer Jermaine Jackson

*Musician/Activist

No, a trip around the Internet does *not* get my books written, but sometimes it's worth the laugh. Of course, the hero and heroine of BLACK TIES AND LULLABIES would *never* give their child a name like one of these. . . .

I hope you enjoy BLACK TIES AND LULLABIES. And look for my next book, HEARTSTRINGS AND DIAMOND RINGS, coming October 2011.

Happy Reading!

Jane Graves

www.janegraves.com

♥ ♥ ♥ ♥ ♥ ♥ ♥ ♥ ♥ ♥ ♥ ♥ ♥ ♥ ♥

From the desk of Paula Quinn

Dear Reader,

Having married my first love, I was excited to write the third installment in my Children of the Mist series, TAMED BY A HIGHLANDER. You see, Mairi Mac-Gregor and Connor Grant were childhood sweethearts. How difficult could it be to relate to a woman who had surrendered her heart at around the same age I did? Of course, my real life hero didn't pack up his Claymore and plaid and ride off to good old England to save the king. (Although my husband does own a few swords he keeps around in the event that one of our daughters brings home an unfavorable boyfriend.) My hero didn't break my young heart, or the promises he made me beneath the shadow of a majestic Highland mountain. I don't hide daggers under my skirts. Heck, I don't even wear skirts.

But I am willing to fight for what I believe in. So is Mairi, and what she believes in is Scotland. A member of a secret Highland militia, Mairi has traded in her dreams of a husband and children for sweeping Scotland free of men who would seek to change her Highland customs and religion. She knows how to fight, but she isn't prepared for the battle awaiting her when she sets her feet in England and comes face to face with the man she once loved.

Ah, Connor Grant, captain in the King's Royal Army and son of the infamous rogue Graham Grant from A

HIGHLANDER NEVER SURRENDERS. He's nothing like his father. This guy has loved the same lass his whole life, but she's grown into a woman without him and now, instead of casting him smiles, she's throwing daggers at him!

Fun! I knew when these two were reunited sparks (and knives) would fly!

But Connor isn't one to back down from a fight. In fact, he longs to tame his wild Highland mare. But does he need to protect the last Stuart king from her?

Journey back in time where plots and intrigue once ruled the courtly halls of Whitehall Palace, and two souls who were born to love only each other find their way back into each other's arms.

If Mairi doesn't kill him first.

(Did I mention, I collect medieval daggers? Just in case . . .)

Happy Reading!

Paula Quinn

www.paulaquinn.com

♥ ♥ ♥ ♥ ♥ ♥ ♥ ♥ ♥ ♥ ♥ ♥ ♥ ♥ ♥

From the desk of Kendra Leigh Castle

Dear Reader,

It all started with the History Channel.

No, really. One evening last year, while I was watching TV in the basement and hiding from whatever flesh-eating-zombie-filled gore-fest my husband was happily watching upstairs, I ran across a fascinating documentary all about a woman I never knew existed: Arsinöe, Cleopatra's youngest sister. Being a sucker for a good story, I watched, fascinated, as the tale of Arsinöe's brief and often unhappy life unfolded. And after it was all over, once her threat to Cleopatra's power had been taken care of in a very final way by the famous queen herself, I asked myself what any good writer would: what if Arsinöe hadn't really died, and become a vampire instead?

Okay, so maybe most writers wouldn't ask themselves that. I write paranormal romance for a reason, after all. But that simple, and rather odd, question was the seed that my book DARK AWAKENING grew from. Now, Arsinöe isn't the heroine. In fact, she's more of a threat hanging over the head of my hero, Ty MacGillivray, whose kind has served her dynasty of highblood vampires for centuries, bound in virtual slavery. But her arrival in my imagination sparked an entire world, in which so-called "highblood" vampires, those bearing the tattoo-like mark of bloodlines descended directly from various darker gods and goddesses, form an immortal nobility that take great

pleasure in lording it over the "lowbloods" of more mud-
died pedigree.

Lowbloods like Ty and his unusual bloodline of
cat-shifting vampires, the Cait Sith.

Now, I won't give out all the details of what happens
when Ty is sent by Arsinöe herself to find a human
woman with the ability to root out the source of a curse
that threatens to take her entire dynasty down. I will say
that Lily Quinn is a lot more than Ty bargained for, carrying
secrets that have the potential to change the entire
world of night. And I'm happy to tell you that it really
tugged at my heartstrings to write the story of a man who
has been kicked around for so long that he is afraid to
want what his heart so desperately needs. But beyond that,
all you really need to know is that DARK AWAKENING
has all of my favorite ingredients: a tortured bad boy with
a heart of gold, a heroine strong enough to take him on,
and cats.

What? I like cats. Especially when they turn into
gorgeous immortals.

Ty and Lily's story is the first in my DARK DYNASTIES
series, about the hotbed of intrigue and desire that is the
realm of the twenty-first century vampire. If you're up for
a ride into the darkness, not to mention brooding bad boys
who aren't afraid to flash a little fang, then stick with me.
I've got a silver-eyed hero you might like to meet. . . .

Enjoy!

Kendra Leigh Castle

www.kendraleighcastle.com